INDISCRETION

HANNAH FIELDING

LONDON
WALL
PUBLISHING

First published in hardback and paperback in the UK in 2015 by
London Wall Publishing Ltd (LWP)

First published in eBook edition in the UK in 2015 by
London Wall Publishing Ltd (LWP)

Family crest pvi © Shutterstock

A CIP catalogue record for this book is
available from the British Library.

PB ISBN 978-0-9926718-8-4
EB ISBN 978-0-9926718-9-1

1 3 5 7 9 10 8 6 4 2

Print and production managed by
Jellyfish Solutions Ltd

MIX
Paper from
responsible sources
FSC® C020471
www.fsc.org

London Wall Publishing Ltd (LWP)
24 Chiswell Street, London EC1Y 4YX

*To burn with desire and keep quiet about it is the greatest
punishment we can bring on ourselves.*

FEDERICO GARCÍA LORCA

En la sangre hierve España sin fuego.
In Spain, blood boils without fire.

SPANISH PROVERB

THE DE FALLA FAMILY

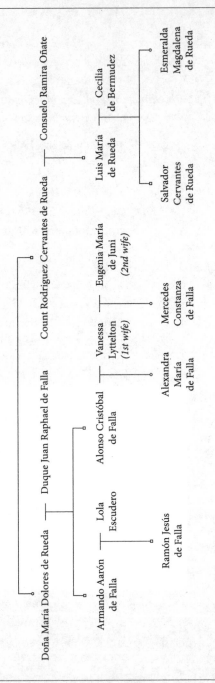

Doña María Dolores de Rueda — Duque Juan Raphael de Falla

Count Rodriguez Cervantes de Rueda — Consuelo Ramira Oñate

Armando Aarón de Falla — Lola Escudero

Alonso Cristóbal de Falla

Vanessa Lyttelton (1st wife)

Eugenia María de Juni (2nd wife)

Luis María de Rueda — Cecilia de Bermudez

Ramón Jesús de Falla

Alexandra María de Falla

Mercedes Constanza de Falla

Salvador Cervantes de Rueda

Esmeralda Magdalena de Rueda

PROLOGUE

London, 1950

The shrill summons of the doorbell echoed through Newton Place, a grand old mansion house by the river in Cheyne Walk. Alexandra de Falla glanced at the clock on her bedroom mantelpiece. It was just past eight in the morning but she had been sitting at her desk since dawn, chewing over the outline of a new story, one that had nagged her out of an already fitful sleep.

Who on earth could it be at this hour?

Putting down her pen, she closed her notebook and tucked it next to her typewriter. Outside the wide bay window, the gloomy morning hugged pavements wet with overnight rain and a chilly January wind stirred the bare branches of the tall trees lining the elegant Chelsea street, whining against the window panes like a dog left out in the cold. The only other sounds were the clink of bottles in their crates as the milkman finished his morning deliveries and the clip-clop of his horse as the cart moved off in the direction of Albert Bridge. From Alexandra's bedroom, the view of the Thames, London's glittering main street, was magnificent. It swept upstream to the trees of Battersea Park on the opposite bank and downstream past the dark mystery of warehouses and wharves. She imagined it flowing past the Tower of the capital, standing formidable against a pale sky smudged with pewter-white clouds and which, this morning, must seem especially solemn in its stark and gloomy solitude. There was still a frosty mist in the air. Alexandra loved the city but longed for the warmth and colour of spring to burst through this grey dampness. The relentless silence of the morning made her even more restless than usual.

She sighed. Today was her twenty-fifth birthday, shouldn't her life be turning a corner by now?

Sometimes Alexandra felt like she was waiting for something – *anything* – to happen. Somewhere inside she could taste it, the immense potential of her passions and dreams. Where did it come from, the feeling that she didn't quite belong? Was this burning desire to know more of the world something she had inherited from her mother? But that was a question, like so many others, she would never be able to ask her.

Once more the doorbell resonated rudely through the house. As Mrs Jeffrey, the housekeeper, had gone out, Alexandra pulled on her dressing gown and descended the stairs to the large oak-panelled hall.

'Yes, I'm coming,' she called out, drawing the brass bolts back and opening the door.

The man standing on the doorstep had his back to her, staring up at the sky. Short and dark, he was holding an enormous bunch of pink roses. He turned, looking both embarrassed and anxious.

'Hello, Alexandra, *querida.*'

For a moment she could hardly breathe. His face was so familiar to her and yet he was almost a stranger.

'*Papá? Papá* … is it really you?'

'*Sí, soy yo.* Fifteen years is a long time, I know.' Don Alonso de Falla paused and then his mouth broke into a most disarming smile. 'I'm glad you still recognize me.'

Her face frozen in shock, she didn't return his smile. 'What are you doing here, *Papá*? You didn't write to say you were coming to London, I wasn't expecting you.'

'I wanted to surprise you on your birthday. Here, these are for you. May I come in?'

'Yes, yes, of course. Thank you. They're lovely.' Alexandra took the flowers from him and placed them on the hall table.

'I see the house hasn't changed at all,' noted Don Alonso as he stepped into the hall. 'Oh, but enough of that. *Mi querida Alexandra, deja que te mire*, let me look at you,' he declared, holding his daughter at arm's length. 'You've grown into a beautiful young woman … so like your mother.' Cupping her face in his hands, he kissed her warmly on both cheeks. 'I know you must have a lot of questions, *niña*. Is there somewhere we can talk comfortably?'

Trying valiantly to regain her composure, Alexandra led him into the drawing room, to the two wing-backed chairs facing each other in front of the fire, which was already lit. Stunned, she sat down, looking across at the man she hadn't seen since she was ten years old.

The one photograph she had of him, standing with her mother, depicted him as a much younger man, the way he was in her childhood memories. Now, although still handsome, his black hair and goatee were peppered with silver and his face was narrower and slightly worn-looking.

So he was back, after fifteen years, looking at her as if he were seeing her for the first time, no longer the vulnerable ten-year-old he had left behind in the charge of her protective but rather austere English aunt.

Don Alonso settled himself in the chair and gazed at her. 'You have your mother's pearly complexion and her beautiful dark copper hair,' he told her wistfully.

Alexandra's eyes momentarily clouded with tears. She had no real recollection of her mother and the few black-and-white photographs that Aunt Geraldine possessed were faded. Still, years of suppressed anger and resentment at her father's absence made her reluctant to talk about her mother in front of him. She decided to be blunt.

'So why have you waited until my twenty-fifth birthday to come back to London, *Papá*? Are you here on business for the family estate? When are you going back to El Pavón?'

'Of course, I wanted to come back sooner.' Don Alonso raised his hands defensively at her barrage of questions. 'You know from my letters how difficult things have been. The uprising at home … then the war in Europe. And it wouldn't have been easy to leave the country these past five years either.'

Knowing that wasn't quite true, she stared at him defiantly. 'But not impossible.'

'No, not impossible.' He shifted uncomfortably in his seat. 'Thankfully, the government seems to be steering us out of isolation, which is good for business.' Noting her arched brow, he added hastily, 'and of course, it made it easier to arrange this trip to see you. I've been out of your life far too long. You know, I've always regretted not being here, leaving your Aunt Geraldine to bring you up but, as your mother was gone, I thought you needed a female substitute. A girl needs a woman to guide her.'

'They also need their fathers,' Alexandra replied softly.

'Yes, *querida*, so they do.' He smiled sadly at her now and tapped his fingers on the arm of the chair as if deliberating what to say next. She almost felt sorry for him. At least he had taken the trouble to surprise her on her birthday and he *had* remembered the date, after all. She smiled at him for the first time.

'I'm pleased to see you, *Papá*, truly I am. It's just that it's a bit of shock, seeing you after all these years with no warning at all.'

'Are you still writing?'

'Yes, *Papá*. I sent you my two novels, did you read them?'

'Ah *si, mi hija del novelista*! My daughter the novelist!' Don Alonso ignored her question but smiled at her indulgently. 'Always, your nose in a book. And even when you were small, scribbling away … all those little stories … wanting to go on adventures. So like Vanessa …' He broke off, as if lost in his own memories.

'I hope *Mamá* would have approved then, if we are so alike.'

He looked up at her. 'Mmm? *Sí, por supuesto*. Yes, of course.' She thought he was going to tell her more about her mother and suddenly wanted so very much to hear about her but Don Alonso clapped his knee and leaned forward.

'Come, I'll wait while you dress and then let me take you out to breakfast, we can talk while we eat. I haven't had an English breakfast with sausages, bacon, eggs and all the trimmings in years and, God knows why, I miss it.'

*   *   *

Don Alonso took Alexandra to Hazlitt's, the fashionable eighteenth-century hotel just down from Piccadilly Circus, a place redolent with atmosphere, with its oak-panelled walls, tall windows draped with luxurious gold velvet, and marble fireplaces. It was Alexandra's favourite because it had been the haunt of so many writers in the past. Her father led her to a table in the corner of the dining room, which hummed with the murmurings of polite conversation and the tinkling of silver. Don Alonso took great delight in ordering almost everything on the menu.

Alexandra and her father spent hours talking, making up for lost time, and he made her laugh with stories of her childhood antics. Her resentment towards him began to soften. Their conversation was so easy and he was so charming, it was almost as if she had rediscovered an old friend.

'So, *niña*, have you thought much about us over the years?' Don Alonso poured them both another cup of coffee.

She smiled. Her fascination for her roots exerted a pull she couldn't understand. 'Yes, I have. Often. My memories of the family are minimal, given I was only three when you and *Mamá* brought me over to England, but I've often wondered what my life would have been like, had we stayed in Spain.'

'Yes, life would have been different indeed. For all of us.'

'I remember you telling me stories about the family on your visits when I was a child but, of course, I've forgotten much of it now. I do remember that Grandmother very much ruled the roost – I suppose she had to after your father died. You were young when it happened, weren't you? A riding accident.' Alexandra said quietly.

Don Alonso's eyes clouded momentarily. 'Yes, I'm afraid the story of the de Falla family has often been governed by the winds of capricious fate. Your uncle Armando, myself and our cousin Luis María were only boys when my father, *Duque* Juan Raphael de Falla, died, though Luis María was a few years older than my brother and me.' Don Alonso's face brightened. 'But we were inseparable growing up, despite the difference in age. We got into some fine old scrapes. As we say in Spain, "*El que de joven corre de viejo trota*, he who runs in youth, trots in old age," and I suppose that explains why your old *Papá* has slowed down so much now.' He grinned.

'What happened to Luis María?'

'He married a real aristocratic beauty, Cecilia de Bermudez. She was a distant relative of the *Duquesa* but a young widow, and *Mamá* did not approve. Cecilia had been left with two children, Esmeralda and Salvador: a situation totally unacceptable to the *Duquesa*, of course. Luis María adopted the children, giving them his name.'

'Why did Grandmother not approve?' Alexandra shook her head, then added, coolly. 'I suppose she thought that Cecilia wasn't good enough for him because she had been married before. Knowing the *Duquesa*, she regarded her as second-hand goods.'

Don Alonso sighed. 'You have to understand my mother had single-handedly run El Pavón after my father died. One has to respect that. I know she's somewhat formidable but it's just that she has a particular vision for the family dynasty. Protecting the de Falla bloodline has always been uppermost in her mind. It wasn't only Luis: neither Armando nor I married as she would've wished.'

'Nothing excuses Grandmother's treatment of *Mamá*.' Alexandra's eyes flared with barely suppressed emotion.

Don Alonso, suddenly uncomfortable, fiddled with the napkin on his lap. 'That's as may be, but you still have to respect her for managing to steer both the family and the business through the most harrowing period in the de Fallas' history. We barely survived the Civil War.'

Alexandra burned with desire to know more about her family, despite her antipathy towards the *Duquesa*, but thoughts of her mother haunted her even more. She sipped her coffee, feeling anything but calm. 'When *Mamá* went off to the South of France, I thought she would come back for me, but then … the car accident … and then, to make matters worse, you returned to Spain. I presume you made it back into Grandmother's good books. I hope it was worth it.'

There was a moment's silence that hung between them, full of so many unspoken things. She realized now how heavy was the weight of sadness, bitterness even, that she'd carried for the past decade.

'*Mamá* would like to meet you,' Don Alonso said suddenly.

Alexandra's face shut down. She shook her head, saying, 'She's too late.' True, her grandmother, the *Duquesa*, had started to write her the odd letter when she was a teenager, asking about her life in England, but Alexandra had shoved them in a drawer and never replied.

'Your grandmother is getting old, *niña*. She doesn't want to die before seeing her granddaughter. She talks about you often. I believe she sent you a family heirloom of great value that had belonged to your great-grandmother?'

'Yes,' Alexandra conceded, 'after the success of my first book.' It was a charming medallion made of chased gold, encrusted with diamonds and rubies. The *Duquesa* herself had worn it as a young girl, she explained in the accompanying note, in which she had also expressed the strong desire to meet her granddaughter. Alexandra had accepted the gift reluctantly and had briefly thanked the old lady in a short letter, but remained deaf to further attempts at reconciliation made by the dowager.

'So, as you can see, your grandmother has always taken a great interest in you and doesn't understand your reluctance to take up her invitations to go to Spain …'

'If she is so concerned about me now after all these years, I wonder why she didn't bother taking more trouble to find out about me when I was a child. What's more, if she had made my mother's life happier when she was in Spain, rather than driving her away, perhaps *Mamá* might still be with us now.' She picked up her spoon and stirred her coffee distractedly, even though she hadn't added sugar to it. 'Besides, England is where I belong, not Spain.'

Still, as Alexandra uttered those last words, she felt the lie on her lips.

CHAPTER 1

Andalucía, a few months later

The hundred-year-old steam locomotive lurched through a parched yellow and brown countryside on worn-out tracks, winding north along Andalucía's rocky coast. The train was crowded but, amazingly, more people managed to force themselves inside at every stop, causing those who were already packed in into even closer intimacy. Spaniards, Alexandra noticed, seemed to journey with an obligatory stock of food, and that of the passengers was now roped on the luggage racks above their seats. At the last station, a huge barrel of a man had boarded the train with a basket from which protruded the head of a protesting goose.

Alexandra had been determined to experience Franco's New Spain like a native, and that meant travelling like one. After all, she was half-Spanish, even if this was her first time in the country since her early childhood. Aunt Geraldine had warned that it was madness for a woman to travel unchaperoned in such a conservative country, not to mention a place still broken and impoverished by civil war, but Alexandra had stubbornly dismissed her concerns. It would be just the kind of adventure she had always longed for, she admitted to herself; besides, she was going to see her family so she wouldn't be with strangers.

For the first time since she had left England, she wondered about her compulsion to make such a journey, asking herself why she had accepted this truce with the de Fallas after so many years of stubborn denial.

At La Linea, just outside Gibraltar, where she had arrived by passenger ship, she had found a train heading north, up the coast to Puerto de Santa María, via Cádiz. Coming face to face with the *tren mixto*, Alexandra had momentarily been tempted to switch to the more civilized and comfortable *rápido*. The carriages of the passenger and freight train had been full to bursting with baskets of clucking hens, men whistling and shouting to each other, women with luggage and paraphernalia piled high against the windows, and even the odd goat or two; but after taking a deep breath, she struggled with her cases into the hot and stuffy compartment and gamely squeezed herself into an empty seat next to an elderly woman.

The train had high-backed wooden benches, the seating arranged in cubicles on either side of a gangway. Some of the windows were broken and people climbed through them to grab a seat. A chattering, shouting medley of voices had filled the carriage – there was none of the usual reserved and dignified behaviour Alexandra had read about the Spanish in the books that she'd picked up at her local library. The exotic smells of food, sweat and livestock permeated the atmosphere.

Now, looking around at her fellow travellers, Alexandra made a mental note of their various characteristics so that she might, if she wished, use them in her writing. Some were astonishingly ugly, with screwed-up wrinkled faces and flabby mouths gaping open, but there were so many alert and twinkling eyes, animated by one lively expression after another. Knotted, pudgy or skinny hands gesticulated energetically with each conversation. Accompanying their mothers or grandmothers were a few young boys and girls with bright, dark eyes, red lips and olive skins that had been washed in some cases and not in others. Alexandra had seen such familiar scenes and characters in dozens of Spanish paintings and now it seemed these Goyaesque figures had come to life before her. She suddenly felt very English in her impeccably cut, pale-green suit.

'Where are you going, *señorita*?' The old lady next to her, crocheting a lace mantilla, had been eyeing her with open curiosity.

'Puerto de Santa María, I have family near there.' Alexandra shifted uncomfortably in her seat but managed a smile.

'On your own, are you? Where is your husband?'

Alexandra was starting to get used to cheerful Spanish bluntness and the lack of inhibition with strangers: the couple who had looked after her on the boat from Southampton had asked her dozens of questions about herself and had even given her their address in Gibraltar, should she ever need a place to stay. It was difficult to imagine any English person she knew offering the same to a complete stranger.

'I have no husband. I'm travelling alone, actually, from England.'

'Your Spanish is good but, ah, your accent! Yes, English.' The woman smiled but then added: 'Be careful, *señorita*, young women don't go about on their own here.' She stopped crocheting and nudged Alexandra with her elbow, nodding her head towards a man who had been staring at her from across the carriage. 'And a pretty, well-dressed girl like you will always attract attention,' she lowered her voice conspiratorially, '*especialmente de los picaros y gitanos*, especially from rogues and gypsies. You stay close to me, *señorita*.'

The old lady patted Alexandra's arm, rested her handiwork on the voluminous bag on her lap, which reached as high as her equally voluminous chest, and promptly dozed off, leaving Alexandra to her own thoughts.

She stared out of the window at the countryside as the train climbed up and up across Spain towards Cádiz. Fascinated, she lost herself in her new surroundings as they slipped by.

They were running over gently undulating ground, which rose and sank in larger billows. The murky Guadalquivir followed the train all the way, through a valley that sometimes widened to the Sierras, blue mountains walling the horizon, their bare, sharp peaks and rainbow-coloured spears of rock – yellow, orange and crimson – stabbing the air. In the distance, Alexandra could see towns, extremely white, beyond the wheatlands and olive orchards that divided the landscape. One such town nestled brightly at the base of a hill, topped by a Moorish castle, golden against the azure sky.

They passed wide expanses of pasture, where lordly bulls were being hoarded in anticipation of the season of *corridas* and *ferias*. From time to time they passed primitive, winding mule tracks that led up high to a village.

The wildness, the hills, the beautiful images her romantic brain made out of the barren jagged cliffs – the pure foreignness of the place – caught Alexandra by the throat. She still couldn't believe it – how in the world had Aunt Geraldine been persuaded to let her go on this 'intrepid' journey to the 'outlandish' place that had been her mother Vanessa's downfall? And yet it had happened.

At first, Aunt Geraldine was horrified by the whole idea and opposed her fiercely: 'Nothing good can come out of this escapade. You're already twenty-five, darling. Some of your friends are mothers by now. It's high time you settled down, had children and made a home for yourself in your own country, among your own people. This constant soul-searching can only lead to tears. Remember, your mother broke the rules and look how that ended.'

'I can't ignore my Spanish blood any longer. It's part of my identity.'

'Listen, my dear, Franco has brought Spain to its knees. It's completely backward in its development,' her aunt protested. 'They may have a little more freedom and tolerance now but apparently they still lack decent roads. Their telephone system is poor, non-existent in most places. Besides, their ways are totally different to ours,' she went on relentlessly. 'Believe me, they're narrow-minded and bigoted. You certainly wouldn't have the freedom to gallivant around the place the way you do here. They smothered your mother with all sorts of "dos" and "don'ts". I really think this is a bad idea, Alexandra. You'll live to regret it one day.'

But Alexandra had persevered and, like the little drop of water that made a hole in the rock, the young woman's persistent pushing had forced her aunt to acquiesce.

She planned to write a third novel on the trip. Already Alexandra María de Falla was a popular name in romantic fiction. When she'd first submitted her short stories to the editor of *Modern Ladies' Romance* magazine he'd found them colourful but unpretentious, and had been surprised by their popularity. After that, with his encouragement, she had published her first two novels. Both were selling well and now she found herself in the lucky position of being financially independent.

Certainly, she had no shortage of ideas for new books, ones that would not involve her travelling to another country to meet a family she hadn't seen since childhood. Still, she'd chosen to go ... Curiosity had certainly played its part in her decision-making but, more than anything, the growing need to find her roots had finally made up her mind.

For years, Alexandra had tried to ignore the emptiness that often haunted her, the feeling that there was a whole part of her left undiscovered. Despite the persistent sense that it was her Spanish blood calling to her, she had remained deaf to all attempts made by her grandmother, the *Duquesa*, at reconciliation. She hadn't even answered the letters the dowager sent after Don Alonso's visit to London. Then, a few weeks ago, when early intimations of spring had stirred her restless soul, and while reading Thomas Hardy's 'Heredity', she came across a verse that made her pause:

I am the family face;
Flesh perishes, I live on.

For days afterwards she had pondered Hardy's profound words. Perhaps it was time to listen to the quiet voice inside urging her on, time to acquaint herself with her own 'heredity'. The exotic allure of her homeland had always been undeniably potent. Would she discover the missing piece of herself there?

Suddenly, a flood of memories assailed her, bringing with them that sense of loss, crashing back against her heart. Alexandra was five again and Aunt Geraldine was explaining that her mother would not be coming back, that a wicked gentleman had taken her far away. She remembered crying for weeks, hiding her face in her bedclothes, trying to stifle the sobs. Her only consolation had been the countless fairy stories her aunt read her at bedtime. She'd listened avidly as beautiful princesses went on great adventures and fell in love with handsome princes, or lost children were reunited with their mothers and fathers, stories in which everyone lived happily ever after. Soon she began to make up stories of her own, escaping into the world of her vivid romantic imagination.

Later, she was told that her mother had met a flamboyant French artist and, weary of a husband who was never around and his family who had never accepted her, hadn't hesitated to exchange a life that brought her so little for a love that promised so much. But her newfound happiness had been short lived: a year after running away with her lover, Vanessa had died in a car accident while holidaying on the French Riviera.

'You mustn't hold it against her,' Aunt Geraldine had told Alexandra years later. 'I know she would've come back for you when she was settled, but things were difficult for her. Your mother suffered tremendously, you know. She didn't belong in the same world as Alonso, being neither Spanish nor Catholic born. It was almost impossible for the de Falla family to accept such a marriage. In those days, the rules of the Catholic Church were much more rigid. Even if your mother had not left, your parents would have eventually parted. Their marriage was doomed from the start.'

And it was true that while her mother was still alive and they were all together in London, her father had often been away in Spain, helping to run the family wine business.

Three years after Vanessa had died, Don Alonso had announced that he had a new wife, Eugenia, in Spain, and that Alexandra now had a baby sister, Mercedes. He wrote to tell her that she could visit El Pavón and meet them whenever she wanted, if her aunt would bring her. *He might have known Aunt Geraldine would never agree to that*, Alexandra thought bitterly.

Over the next couple of years, her father's visits to London became rarer and, by the time she was ten, he had ceased coming at all. Once Franco's military uprising had isolated Spain and war swept through Europe, there was no news of him and Aunt Geraldine now occupied her parents' double bed in the London house in Cheyne Walk.

She had tried not to miss him but it was difficult. Over time, even though after the war Don Alonso sent her extravagant presents every now and then with the briefest of notes, he had become a stranger. Her grief channelled itself into anger against his family – they had shunned her mother and then they had taken her father away.

Alexandra was jolted out of her reverie as they reached another station. Bundles were loaded and unloaded, new seats negotiated and, after another interminable halt, the whistle finally blew. She noticed that the bulky silhouette of a *Guardia Civil* had entered the train. On his arrival, the carriage had miraculously emptied, except for the lady beside her, who was asleep, and a few others, who all stopped talking. She glanced up at the man who was the cause of the sudden silence. So it was true what newspapers in Britain intimated about the Spanish Civil Guard – they really were feared. The guard remained standing, leaning affably on his rifle, looking down at the travellers for a few moments, before moving on to the next carriage.

The old woman next to her was now awake and rummaging in her large bag, an elbow scissoring up and down uncomfortably in Alexandra's side. Seeing the window seat opposite was now vacant, Alexandra moved across to face her. She had produced some large slices of bread and chorizo, and a bag of boiled eggs.

'You hungry, *señorita*?' The woman jabbed a sandwich in the young woman's direction. Alexandra smiled back, shaking her head.

'That's very kind, but no thank you.'

Now that Alexandra could see the woman more clearly, she noted a fierce and rather ruthless look; there was nothing particularly kindly in her features. Her face was sun-shrivelled, with high cheekbones and an almost male strength of jaw. She wore a black cotton dress and a kerchief covered her grey hair. The only colourful thing she had was a purple crocheted shawl draped around her bulky shoulders.

'So, you say your family live near Puerto de Santa María, *señorita*. Where exactly?' She regarded Alexandra expectantly.

Alexandra could see that this was to be the start of a typical Spanish interrogation and suppressed a sigh.

'Jerez.'

'Ah, you're travelling to Jerez. What a coincidence, my family are from Jerez. I used to work at a hacienda near there for a short time. I was a maid for one of the noblest families in Andalucía, the de Fallas.'

Alexandra's eyes widened at the mention of the family name but her curiosity about the de Fallas had now grown to such proportions that she kept quiet. Although she felt guilty about doing so, she knew that she might learn a great deal more by remaining so.

'How very fortunate to have such a position.'

'Oh yes, very fortunate indeed.' The woman bit into her sandwich and kept talking as crumbs scattered on to her shawl. 'To work at El Pavón was to have one of the best jobs in Andalucía, make no mistake. The *Duquesa*, Doña María Dolores de Falla, ruled that place with a rod of iron but a better employer you couldn't hope to find. She was good to all her workers, even through the war. That's when I was working for them, during the uprising and after. And I can tell you, other aristocratic families weren't treating their employees half as well at the time. The *Duquesa* was always respected by the locals,' she leaned forward and lowered her voice, 'even though she did put up with gypsies on her land. As far as I know, they're still there.'

'And were they a large family? Were the other members of the family as kind to you?' Alexandra enquired innocently.

'Well, of course, I was a valued member of the household,' the old woman replied proudly, not really listening to Alexandra's questions now that she had embarked on her story, 'and so I saw a lot of the comings and goings in that family. The three young men all married badly one way or another, particularly the two sons … *mujeres que eran de un origen social más baja*, the women were from a lower social background and even the cousin's aristocratic wife was a widow with children. *Muy mala, muy mala*, not good … and the *Duquesa* never approved. *Madre de Dios*, who could blame her? Take the middle one, Armando. His wife was one of those trapeze people and she'd lived her whole life in a circus when he met her. Imagine! But their son, poor Ramón, he was the one who bore the brunt of it. When the father died and the mother left, it was he who felt the edge of the *Duquesa*'s tongue.'

Alexandra pondered whether she should be telling this woman that the people she was talking about with such candour were her own family. She felt a fraud, betraying the de Fallas somehow in listening to such indiscreet gossip but, equally, she felt compelled to hear more when it was so freely given.

'And what of the others?'

'Well, the youngest, Alonso, was a widow and remarried.' The old woman finished her sandwich and started peeling an egg, warming to her story, 'to a lady from one of the richest families in Castille, Eugenia de Juni. *Dios mio! Esta es manipuladora, sin un corazón convenida, entremetido*, she is manipulative, without a heart, a real meddler.

'*Le juro a Dios*, I swear to God, that woman wanted to get her hands on the estate the minute she stepped through the door. When their only child was still in the cradle, she was planning how the girl would marry young Salvador, of course. I once heard her say as much … not that I'm the sort to listen at keyholes, you understand, may all the demons in hell swallow me up if I lie, but it was plain as day, what she was up to.'

'Her daughter?' Alexandra knew this must be Mercedes.

'Yes, the daughter … Mercedes, that's right. Moody, spoilt little thing she was, even when I knew her. She'll be a teenager now, ready for marriage, if her mother has anything to do with it. Probably already married to Salvador de Rueda.'

Alexandra suddenly remembered something her father had said at Hazlitt's: 'Young Salvador Cervantes de Rueda, the new heir to the estate, grew into an indispensable member of the family. And I must say, took on his duties with more gravitas than any of us, including the *Duquesa*, could have imagined.

In all fairness, he's earned his right to El Pavón and now couldn't be higher in her favour. Again, how fate twists itself. Though, at times, *Mamá* can be rather … indulgent of his flaws, his … entanglements. But that's all in the past.' Don Alonso had waved this comment away with a flourish of the hand and before Alexandra could ask him any more about her cousin, the waiter had arrived with coffee.

'The de Fallas sound like a complicated family,' said Alexandra pensively, as much to herself as to the old woman. She was intensely regretting the dishonest role she was playing in their conversation. The woman's indiscretion had probably been caused by Alexandra being a foreigner and, therefore, of little importance. True, curiosity to know more about her family had prompted an encouragement of the old woman's gossiping. Still, the former retainer ought not to have been quite so indiscreetly personal before strangers, even if she was no longer in the service of the family.

Her talk was not only embarrassing now, as she continued to prattle on, it was faintly alarming. The only person she had a good word for was the *Duquesa*; everyone else in the de Falla household sounded positively terrifying. Having heartily maligned the women of El Pavón, she was now attacking the men. At the top of her list was Salvador. She seemed hell-bent on destroying the young man's character.

'Weird, that's what I'd call Salvador de Rueda. Weird and sinister, in an attractive way, of course. You know, the sort that *que parece santa* looks saintly, when the man could hardly be more worldly. Keeps strange company … the likes of gypsies and other *personas extrañas*, strange individuals. You know the type I'm talking about, or maybe a nice lady like you wouldn't. There's that air of power about him … gets what he wants without bothering too much about the way he gets it … you know, the manipulative kind, especially with the *Duquesa*. And proud too. I never knew a prouder man for all his cool politeness. He was supposed to become engaged to the daughter of a friend of the family but she preferred a *Marqués* ... I think she's a widow now. Anyway, I've seen them together in town unchaperoned ... what the world is coming to, I just don't know.'

Just then, the train slowed down and the woman peered out of the window.

'Ah, Cádiz. This is my stop.' Stuffing the remains of her food together with her crocheting into her bag, the woman held on to the bench as she stood up, bracing herself against the rocking of the carriage as the train hissed into the station. '*Adios, señorita.* Enjoy your stay in Jerez. And be careful of the *gitanos*, they'll rob you as quick as look at you.' With that, she shuffled off down the gangway.

Alexandra was alone once more, looking out of the window at the hustle and bustle on the platform. She was reminded of the old woman's conversation about chaperones when she noticed a boy and a girl, obviously *novios* from the way they were gazing at each other, walking together on the platform, not arm in arm as they would in England but with a modest air of submission on the part of the girl and a manly proprietorship on his. They were followed by a rotund matron, who was keeping a close eye on them.

As the train jerked into motion once more, Alexandra pondered everything the old lady had said about the de Fallas, the family she was soon to meet. Perhaps the *Duquesa* was not so hard as she had always imagined. Still, she was slightly apprehensive at the prospect of meeting her grandmother, the matriarch, not to mention her stepmother, Doña Eugenia, or her 'spoilt' younger half-sister, if the picture the old woman had painted of them were true. Was this the reason for the growing sense of disquiet that murmured indistinctly beneath her thoughts?

What had Vanessa de Falla's life really been like among those who had made her so unhappy? 'It wasn't easy for her, I suppose, being English and trying to fit into a close-knit noble Spanish family,' her father had admitted over that same breakfast at Hazlitt's.

'Impossible, by all accounts,' Alexandra had noted bitterly.

'You mustn't believe everything your Aunt Geraldine says. She doesn't understand the ways of our family.'

The ways of our family. Their ways had made Vanessa de Falla so wretched that she had taken her only child back to London after just three years at El Pavón.

Although her mother was English, she was 'as fiery and passionate as any Spaniard' her father used to say. Perhaps that was what had first attracted Vanessa to Don Alonso de Falla, making her dream of an exotic life in Andalucía – at least that was what Alexandra had always imagined. And now, she was following her mother's footsteps into the dream of another life, not knowing where it would lead her. But one thing she did know: she was embracing a longed-for freedom, the chance to throw off the stuffy atmosphere of England, and of that she was glad.

*   *   *

The train shuddered to a halt with a great screeching of brakes. Alexandra opened the door. A breath of fresh air, overlaid with the faint tang of iodine, greeted her. She ventured hesitantly on to the platform and stood there motionless, holding a suitcase in one hand; with the other, she shielded her eyes against the blinding glare of the Spanish sun. There were no porters in sight, nor were there any trolleys. With difficulty, and a mounting sense of irritation, she carried the rest of her luggage from the carriage. *This is ridiculous*, she thought; she should have listened to Aunt

Geraldine and travelled by plane from England. Maybe coming to Andalucía alone was not such a good idea after all.

The station at the small port town of Puerto de Santa María swarmed with the oddest characters. Water sellers with huge earthenware pitchers and merchants selling wine, sweetmeats and shellfish bustled about next to the train. Brown urchins pushing barrows heaped with mountains of luscious fruit called out their offerings. '*Que vengan todas las Marías, que traigo sandias y melones dulces como el caramel!* Come all you Marías, I bring watermelons and melons sweet as caramel!' Crippled beggars squatted in corners, palms outstretched. There were peddlers hawking their cheap wares of soap, matches, lace and miniature bottles of cologne, plus gypsy knife-sellers with trays of hand-crafted *navajas*, shouting '*Afilo cuchillos y Tijeras! Vamos! Barato!* I sharpen knives and scissors! Come! It's cheap!', plus lottery ticket touts and a host of others.

Presumably, Alexandra thought, in this part of the world, the arrival of the train was the only event of the day to break the monotony of provincial life; and the railway station would be, she supposed, the obvious meeting place for everyone. Her gaze searched the crowd for a familiar face. Travellers hurried along. Newcomers and locals jostled each other as they came and went. A few spectators, leaning idly against the wall or seated on small benches in the sun, looked on as others passed by. She was surrounded by a babble of shouts, exclamations and laughter, but no one seemed to be waiting for her on the platform.

As she stood there, with the sun on her face, taking in the sights and smells that seemed strange, yet curiously familiar, Alexandra felt she had stepped out from the shadows of her old life into the dazzling light of a new world. The momentary annoyance at being left alone with her luggage suddenly vanished. England was never further away than at this moment

– a dull moth to the colourful butterfly of Spain – and she ached to unfurl her own wings and discover it all. This was the stuff of novels, and yet here she was. The thought made her stomach tense with a mix of excitement and trepidation.

It was then that a gypsy woman, dressed in bright colours and bearing fans and red roses, accosted her. '*Hermosa joven*, beautiful young lady, buy one of my roses, fresh-picked this morning. It will bring you luck.'

Alexandra met the falcon-dark orbs that were watching her slyly. The gypsy was of an uncertain age with a nest of coal-black hair hanging untidily at her shoulders, her features regular but coarse in a sun-scorched and wind-beaten oval face. Alexandra shook her head and tried to smile politely. 'Thank you, not today.'

The *gitana* grabbed her arm, clasping it tightly in long bony fingers. 'Give me your palm. I can read the heavens and I will tell you the secrets the stars hold for you in the future.'

But that was the last thing Alexandra needed or wanted, remembering the woman on the train and her warning. She knew there was only one way she would rid herself of the old witch. 'Here …' She took a few pesetas from her pocket, 'I'll buy one of your beautiful roses.'

At this, the penetrating jet-black eyes lit up greedily. The gypsy took the money and handed Alexandra the crimson flower. '*Que Dios los bendiga*, God bless you, kind and generous lady. *Que los ángeles te miran*, may the angels look upon you,' she squawked before turning to cast her designs on her next victim. '*Bella dama … Apuesto caballero …*'

Somewhere a bell rang. Doors slammed. The train began to move, its ancient frame creaking. Motionless, Alexandra watched it pull out of the station. As it disappeared she could hear its piercing whistle in the distance, one moment raucous, the next strident, and then there was nothing: a kind of stillness she would have found oppressive had the sun not been shining.

She glanced quickly around her in the hope of finding a porter. Most probably she would be met outside the station. Like actors after the curtain has fallen, travellers and tradespeople had vanished to leave a deserted stage. The platform was empty, the waiting room dark and damp-looking. Alexandra moved briskly towards the exit in search of help.

'*Buenas tardes, señorita,*' beamed the man behind the ticket office window. 'What can I do for you today?'

'*Buenas tardes,*' she said, smiling back at him, continuing in impeccable Spanish, 'can you tell me where I can find a porter. I've left quite a bit of luggage on the platform.'

'I'll come and help you. Manuel, our porter, is usually here but his mother-in-law died and he had to go to the funeral.'

'Oh dear, poor man.' She paused, not wishing to seem unsympathetic. 'Can you please tell me where to go for the bus to Jerez? My guidebook says it leaves from this station.'

'You've just missed it, I'm afraid. The two o'clock bus left ten minutes ago. You'll have to wait until tomorrow morning.'

'But there's supposed to be three a day, and I have to be in Jerez by this evening,' Alexandra exclaimed. 'Is there no other way to get there before dark?'

The man eyed her quizzically. 'You're not from these parts, that's for sure,' he muttered, shaking his head. 'You could always try this evening. There's usually a bus that leaves after seven but there have been works on those roads. Access is sometimes difficult, especially after dark, as most of the main roads have no lights. It can be dangerous, so on some days the evening bus is cancelled. Of course, there's no way of knowing in advance ...' He caught sight of Alexandra's impatient look. '*Muy inconveniente, estoy de acuerdo,* very inconvenient, I agree.' He shrugged his shoulders helplessly.

Alexandra was puzzled. Her father had assured her that she would be met at the station, but it looked like she was stranded here for the moment.

'Do you have a telephone I can use?'

The stationmaster shook his head again. '*Lo siento!* I'm sorry! The lines are down in Puerto de Santa María due to the storm we had two days ago. You'd do better to visit our town,' he went on in his slurred Andalucían brogue. 'Puerto de Santa María is the most beautiful port in Andalucía,' he proudly announced. Then, as Alexandra hesitated, he surveyed her Titian waves of shoulder-length hair, her long legs and lithe slenderness shown off by her elegant suit. With a mixture of curiosity and logic so typically Spanish, he added: 'Anyway, what's a nice young lady like you doing on the roads alone, and what do you want in Jerez when you're already in our excellent town? If you ask me, there's nothing worth seeing there except its *bodegas*.' He grinned enthusiastically. 'Though if you want to sample a little of our Andalucían wine, *señorita*, it's a fine place to start.'

But Alexandra wasn't listening. Maybe she should hire a car and drive to Jerez, asking the way to her family's hacienda, El Pavón, when she got there, or she could take a taxi. Still, she did not relish travelling any further on her own; after all, she had no idea what the roads were like. For the time being, the only reasonable course of action was to wait patiently; someone was bound to turn up.

'Is there a *parador* close by where I could spend the night?' she asked.

'There is one just down the road. Why don't you take a look around and I'll look after your baggage?'

Alexandra was tempted. It was a glorious afternoon. If, by next morning, nobody had come for her, she could take the early bus to Jerez. It was rather annoying that the telephone lines were down. Still, in the meantime, she was determined not to let the present circumstances spoil such a lovely day.

'*Muchas Gracias*,' she said when he had helped her with the cases. '*Voy a seguir tu consejo y visitar el Puerto*, I think I'll follow your advice and visit the port.'

She set out, pensively turning into one of the winding narrow streets that led down to the harbour.

Like most young women growing up during the war, Alexandra had not travelled much outside England. Although she had been slightly perturbed that things had not gone according to plan at the station, now a sense of excitement suddenly took hold of her. She began to thrill to the unpredictability of her new adventure and had the strange sense of being a fictional character in a novel, one of those heroines she knew so well.

Again, thoughts of the past infiltrated her mind as she picked her way through the cobbled streets lined with tall, whitewashed houses with their protruding casement windows. Bright purple bougainvillea cascaded down walls and honey-scented jasmine spilled out of windowboxes, their aroma mingling with the distinctive salty tang of the sea, invading Alexandra's senses. They took her back to a half-forgotten childhood full of sun, earthy smells and music; memories imprinted on her mind and body like a persistent dream.

She found herself following the bank of the peaceful Guadalete. Gangs of naked brown children ran about, laughing and splashing in the shallow, murky waters of the slow-moving, wide river. On the flat swampy bank, flocks of pink flamingos rested languidly in the sun. She walked a long time through the old quarter – the *barrio* of fishermen and gypsies – lined with wine and tobacco shops, some with whitewashed walls, others painted in bright colours. The sun was scorching and, although hungry, she was reluctant to buy food or refreshments from any of the streetsellers.

Soon she came to the harbour. It teemed with a picturesque populace, so very foreign to her but so very intriguing. Men in wide-brimmed hats strolled with women in brightly coloured dresses and mantillas, while old men played draughts at quayside café tables. The clamour of fishermen and fishmongers was everywhere. Sea air mingled with the acrid smell of tar and the reek of fishing nets.

In front of her, the ocean disappeared into infinity. Lines of huts, their mouldy wood gracefully draped with white nets drying in the sun, stretched as far as the eye could see on the shore's expanse of golden sand. In the far-off backdrop of hills loomed the sombre green shadow of pinewoods and, on the opposite side of the harbour, Cádiz, the bright pearl of the Costa de la Luz, lay shining under a scorching sun.

To the north, she could see the vast terrace of a public beach, framed by palm trees, and the parasols and tables of cafés. Out in the turbulent bay, multi-coloured fishing boats and pleasurecraft, sailing boats, small tugs and an enormous liner swayed and bobbed on the phosphorescent waves of the Atlantic Ocean like tipsy dancers in a carnival.

Alexandra joined the bustle on the jetty where the trawlers were moored. She made her way through the unsavoury, eager crowd gathered there to watch the unloading of the big fishing boats. Never before had she seen so many fish. They were of all sorts and all sizes; some grey and silvery, others blue and pink; big fish with thick scales, others thinner and daintier, wriggling and jumping about like quicksilver; crabs, prawns, lobsters, shrimps … all spread out in a slippery, crawling mass of pincers, shells and scales.

Men in shirtsleeves, out of breath and sweating, were piling this abundance into big, flat baskets; then, bent double under their heavy burdens, they loaded them into carts for delivery to the various markets. Fishermen close to the shore were bringing in their nets. Alexandra watched them carry out this endless task, seemingly ill-rewarded, for their catch appeared meagre. It was hard to say how long she spent daydreaming, admiring the strange landscape of light and colour, but she was brought back to earth by the chimes of the town clock. Six o'clock already, it was time to return.

She crossed the road, then turned to get a last glimpse of the flaming sunset. The sea was turning gold, the sky streaked with rose and orange and angry red; a canvas where the supreme artist used colours unknown to any earthly palette. Wanting to imprint this painting on her soul to use it as the opening of the first chapter to her new book, Alexandra stood there breathless and, lifting her face to the sky, she stepped back, inadvertently bumping into someone. Jerked out of her contemplation, she turned apologetically.

'*Lo siento...*' she breathed as she looked straight into the striking grey-blue eyes of a man, a man very different to those she had glimpsed since she had arrived in Spain.

Tall, slim and well built, he was gazing at her intently, the greyness of his wintry eyes emphasized by a tanned complexion.

Alexandra felt the rush of heat burn her cheeks and gave him an embarrassed smile. 'I was admiring your dazzling sunset, I've never seen such amazing colours.'

'One can just as much be dazzled by a lovely sunset as by the unexpected encounter of a stunningly beautiful woman,' the stranger murmured almost imperceptibly.

Alexandra knew that these words, spoken by a Spaniard, were just an ordinary compliment that one should not take seriously, a compulsory courtesy that was part of the Latin charm. Besides, as he pronounced them, the stranger's face had kept its inscrutability and she had seen nothing she could easily interpret in his pale eyes. So why did she feel a secret stirring inside her?

She had no time to answer him. The dark *hidalgo* had taken Alexandra's hand and, bringing it to his lips, brushed it with the whisper of a kiss.

'*Adios, señorita*,' she heard him say softly. Turning, he disappeared into the crowd still milling about on the pavement, leaving the young woman in a daze.

Alexandra began to walk and then almost immediately stopped to ask the way. Going back through the same crowded streets did not seem a pleasant option and she was relieved to learn there was a shortcut to the station.

Turning into the Calle de la Iglesia, she was immediately struck by the contrast between the quarter she had just walked through and this one. Here, the street was immersed in the shade of giant flame trees and life suddenly slowed to a more leisurely pace. She passed white houses tucked away between clumps of pomegranate trees; orchards hemmed in by dry stone walls; hedges of aloe; secret, leafy patios, the domain of women and their families, where the warbling of birds and the smothered laughter of young girls mingled with the soft murmur of fountains.

She had almost reached the end of the street when bells began ringing the Angelus, calling worshippers to Evensong. To her right was a small chapel. It seemed so welcoming, the garden planted out with roses and mimosas, front doors open, inviting passersby to enter.

On impulse, she went in. Inside, it was dark, quiet and cool. The organ was playing softly and the scent of orange blossom and roses filled the place. Alexandra was overcome by a feeling of great serenity and slowly moved towards the altar.

Her eyes took a few minutes to grow accustomed to the relative gloom. On each side of the main aisle, ten or so rows of oak benches stood in perfect orderly fashion. There were flowers everywhere: in garlands, in dainty crystal vases on the altar, in bunches of various sizes, placed as offerings at the feet of the statues of saints that filled the church. Several candles burned in thanks for prayers that had been answered; all were witness to the faith and gratitude of the devout worshipers who had carefully placed them there.

At first, Alexandra thought she was alone but she soon noticed a man, a few paces away, kneeling on a prayer stool at the foot of Saint Mary of Mercy's statue. His broad shoulders were hunched beneath a shock of jet-black hair, his face hidden in slender, suntanned hands. It was dark, so why she should think that this was the stranger she had already encountered on the seafront and why her heart was beating so hard against her ribs, she couldn't say, but she had no doubt at all that it was the same man.

Footsteps and whispering made her turn around. A man began to speak in a nasal singsong voice that echoed strangely from the walls of the little church, disturbing the peace and tranquillity: 'This is the Church of Santa María. As in most of our Spanish towns, Our Lady of Mercy is its all-powerful and well-loved patron saint, a friend who protects all, be they lords or paupers.' It was a tour guide who had appeared in the doorway, ushering his party of tourists into the church.

'Our land is rich in legends about the Virgin Mary. The most moving is the one about the young Jewish girl who fell in love with a Christian knight. Despairing of ever attracting his attention, the beautiful maiden turned to our Virgin here, on whom everyone called. Humbly, she gave all she possessed: a pin decorated with a tiny glass bead. The miracle happened: the knight passed by at that very moment, saw her, and his heart was forever linked to hers by the pin she had given as an offering.'

The group of sightseers passed Alexandra and disappeared through a low door at the back of the church leading to the crypt. Peace returned.

All the while, the man on the prayer stool had not moved. Alexandra went up to the statue of Our Lady of Mercy to light a candle but a priest had just gone by to clear up the melted wax from the previous batch of devotees' offerings, and she neither had matches nor a lighter handy. A faint *tch* of annoyance escaped her lips.

'*Permita me señorita.*'

Alexandra had scarcely time to register the quiet words spoken unexpectedly, close to her ear, before the stranger's brown hand had flicked a gold lighter in front of her, bringing to life a tiny blue flame and at the same time brushing against her arm.

The spark that went through her at the Spaniard's touch made Alexandra shudder and, emitting a slight gasp, she instinctively drew back in the first instance. But then, as she realized he was only trying to be helpful, she raised her face, smiling as readily and uninhibitedly as she always did.

'*Gracias, muchas gracias.*'

There was utter silence in the church. The man did not smile but merely inclined his head, leaving Alexandra, as he had earlier on, with the impression that inbred courtesy had prompted him to lend his assistance, rather than the more usual reasons men found for helping her. Still, her green gaze met his. She was struck by the expression of sadness reflected in his arresting grey irises and the sternness of his hard, regular features.

An almost visible current leapt between them. For a split second, the determined line of his jaw stiffened, his well-defined lips parted and she thought he might speak. Her heart missed a beat, but someone was coming. The interlude was over; the spell had been broken.

A beautiful young woman with a mane of flame-red hair cascading down her back was making her way towards him, holding two large candles.

With a tightening in her heart that she couldn't explain Alexandra nodded her thanks again and withdrew to take a seat in one of the pews at the back of the church.

The Spanish lady smiled at the stranger as she came up to him, lit her candles from the ones that Alexandra had just placed in front of the altar and, taking the man's arm in a proprietorial way, walked with him out of the church.

While his companion had been lighting her candles, Alexandra had had plenty of time to scrutinize the man. He wasn't particularly young – in his early to mid-thirties, she guessed – but he had an aggressively male attractiveness to him. He was tall – very tall by Spanish standards, definitely over six foot, she judged – with a powerful, broad-shouldered frame, honed to hard-muscled perfection. This, together with his copper-brown face, suggested someone who was used to an active outdoor life, although the immaculate white shirt he wore, the well-cut dark suit that moulded itself to his form, and the gold watch that she had noticed he sported on his wrist all made it clear that he was a man of standing.

Speculating on his relationship with the stunning redhead was difficult, for Alexandra hadn't noticed any rings on either of his hands, and yet the way they had walked out of the church suggested an intimate involvement.

Having ended their visit, the small party of tourists now returned to the nave and moved towards the exit. Alexandra's gaze followed them. She hung back a few more minutes in the chapel, prey to a curious inner turmoil. There was an unknown danger about the stranger that she felt keenly, yet could not define. Who was he, and why had she been troubled so by their brief exchange? Alexandra glanced at her watch: the bus would soon be leaving. How had she lost track of the time so easily?

Already the evening congregation was crowding into the church. The garden, earlier deserted, was now brought to life by clusters of people, talking and laughing. Suddenly, Alexandra noticed the stranger's tall, distinguished figure among the chattering groups. He was standing beside the gate, still in the company of the beautiful woman. In the daylight, Alexandra noticed that she wore a pale-green frilled muslin dress, a velvet cape of a deeper green, and white kid gloves. The woman laughed noisily, tossing back her graceful tresses of flame-coloured hair, on which was placed the most exquisite black lace mantilla.

The stranger turned his head and directed his steely gaze through the crowd towards Alexandra. For an instant she was transfixed. A sudden surge of inexplicable panic rose inside her. She lowered her glance, squeezed her way through the gathering and hurried towards the gate.

Arriving level with the young man, his intense scrutiny hit her again like lightning and a swift wave of colour invaded her face. He whispered something she could not hear and his companion's voluptuous laughter erupted once more, filling the space about her.

As though pursued by a pack of hounds, Alexandra darted through the gate and began to run towards the station. She had to get away, catch the bus and leave town as quickly as she could. But she arrived at the station in time to witness the seven o'clock bus leaving. Her blouse was half-hanging out of her suit, her hair coming down, cheeks burning, and she was quite out of breath. She clenched her fists furiously, and then, with her hands planted on her hips like a fishwife, she watched the bus drive off in the direction of Jerez.

CHAPTER 2

Now she was stranded. Exasperated, Alexandra was on the point of making her way back to the ticket office when a young man came up to her, smiling.

'Alexandra?' he asked, eyeing her quizzically. She raised her eyebrows in surprise. He bowed and introduced himself, 'Your cousin, Ramón de Falla, at your service.'

Scarcely recovered from her surprise, Alexandra regarded the newcomer. He was not much taller than she and wore white belted slacks and a crimson open-neck shirt with the sleeves rolled up, highlighting his suntanned skin. His looks were similar to those of a gypsy, she imagined, with a wiry body and the thick black curling hair of the people of his country, worn loose, although it wasn't in the oily ringlets that, according to the paintings she had seen, the gypsies sometimes affected. Under this unruly mop of dark curls was one of those lively angular faces; all points – ears, nose, chin – and the most sparkling eyes. In build, he was a curious mixture of strength and almost feminine gracefulness, which Alexandra put down to the genetic influence of his trapeze artist mother. His entire healthy being smacked of the warm South and his open expression put her immediately at ease.

'Very pleased to meet you, Ramón.' She smiled and extended a friendly hand. 'I was just about to book in at a hotel but I'm so glad that I'll be able to sleep at El Pavón tonight after all.'

Suddenly aware of the unladylike sight she must be offering, Alexandra's hands went to her hair. She pushed away the rebellious tendrils that had gone astray and tucked her blouse into her skirt. The lovely suit she had bought at great expense at Harrods was now stained with dust and torn at the hem. They looked at each other and burst out laughing.

With his hazel eyes Ramón regarded her warmly and a good-natured smile lit up his face. 'I'm sorry I missed your train this afternoon. My car broke down and I had to walk miles to find a mechanic. Your father had to leave Jerez for the day and, as he won't return until this evening, I was only too pleased to meet your train and be the first to welcome you. Though, as you can see, I've bungled it and I'm sorry about that,' he ended somewhat sheepishly.

Alexandra warmed to her cousin at once. There was nothing underhand about him; on the contrary, he seemed reassuringly straightforward.

'Please don't apologize, these things happen. In fact, I've spent an enjoyable afternoon exploring the port.' The encounter with the stranger in the church had been an unnerving end to it, she thought, but now that Ramón was here, she began to feel more relaxed.

Together they went through the barrier and up to the counter to collect Alexandra's luggage. The station master was still there.

'Ah, there you are,' he said as they approached. 'I wondered where you were. You've missed the bus again, but don't worry. My uncle's going to deliver some wine to one of the big estates in Jerez tomorrow morning, so you may prefer to …' he stopped, noticing Ramón. 'Oh, I see you've found your party,' he remarked, grinning broadly. '*Así que todo está bien*, so, all is well. Here, don't forget your luggage,' he added as he brought round the suitcases on a rusted luggage trolley. 'Shall I help you take them to your car?'

Ramón took hold of the trolley and pressed a tip into the station master's palm. 'No thank you, *amigo*,' he said cheerfully. 'I can manage.' Alexandra thanked the man for his help and followed her cousin out of the station.

Ramón settled her in his old Fiat, tucked the suitcases in the boot and returned the trolley to the station.

'You must be tired as well as hungry,' he said as he slid into the car beside her and paused, tapping his fingers on the dashboard. 'Where shall I take you for supper?' Ramón said, thinking aloud. 'Ah, I know where …' he announced. 'There's an excellent *taberna* that serves delicious Basque cooking. It's not far from here.'

Alexandra looked at her watch. Her brows knitted together anxiously. 'What will they say at the house?'

'Grandmother will be cross with me, no doubt. Meals are the only times when all the family can get together so she holds them as sacrosanct.' He gave a mock frown. 'Punctuality is inviolable. Whoever doesn't keep to her daily schedule has no place at the dining table … with the exception of Salvador, of course.' He laughed stiffly and pulled out into the wide cobbled street flanked by lines of bicycles and scooters.

'That's our cousin Salvador, I take it?'

He grimaced. 'Yes, Salvador. My very irritating, can-do-no-wrong "cousin". He's not actually a blood relative, of course. He and Esmeralda were adopted by our father's cousin, Luis.' There was an awkward pause, during which Alexandra wondered if this was perhaps the wrong time to ask more about the intriguingly controversial Salvador, and then Ramón changed the subject. 'Anyway, as we're not going to make dinner at El Pavón, I suggest we have a meal before setting out. The hacienda is only a few miles away, on the outskirts of Jerez.'

Alexandra had not eaten properly since the night before. Her breakfast on the train that morning had consisted of watery coffee and a stale chorizo sandwich bought at the station before leaving La Linea. Ramón's plan sounded appealing and she was relieved that she wouldn't have to steel herself to face her Spanish family that night. After a good night's rest and a warm bath, she would be in a much fitter state to meet them.

'It sounds an excellent idea,' she said enthusiastically. 'I must admit, I didn't get much of a chance to eat on the way here.'

'So, how was your train journey?'

Alexandra laughed. 'It was interesting, that's for sure. I feel a little black and blue but I survived.'

He grinned at her. 'Ah, yes, our trains are probably less civilized than those you're used to, though I'm afraid that's partly the legacy of Franco's war. Spain's damaged train system has never recovered and is rather antiquated, to say the least.'

Ramón turned into a large, elegant plaza lined with palm trees and ornate buildings fronted by Moorish arches.

'We're nearly there. The views over the ocean at this restaurant are stunning. Tonight there's such a beautiful moon, it would be a pity not to take advantage of it. Besides, you'll have plenty of time to have stilted meals with "the herd". I promise we'll reach the hacienda before midnight.'

Alexandra glanced briefly at him. 'You don't seem to think much of family gatherings,' she observed.

He raked his fingers through his black curls. 'I sometimes find all their restrictions tedious,' he admitted. 'But you'll see for yourself soon enough.'

Ramón parked the Fiat in the public car park. It was difficult to take a vehicle into some of the narrower streets, he told her. The restaurant was not too far and, besides, it was a pleasant, balmy evening.

They walked, turning into one of the flagged lanes that converged on the harbour. It had no pavement and was lined with shops selling nets, bait and fishing equipment, which alternated with bars and public houses without shopfronts or signs.

'We've arrived,' declared Ramón at last, stopping outside an unmarked building and guiding her down a badly lit flight of steps. 'Pedro Gomez, the owner, is a friend and his *taberna*'s very popular on the coast. It's patronized by a small, select crowd because he serves the best *chipirones* and the most exquisite *kokotxas*.'

Alexandra laughed. 'But what are "*chipirones*" and "*kokotxas*"? Forgive my ignorance but it's my first visit to Spain. I may be half-Spanish but, believe it or not, I haven't yet sampled the cuisine. My aunt isn't a huge fan of Spanish food,' she added, seeing his surprised look.

'Well, let me enlighten you, my poor deprived *chica Inglés*,' he laughed. '*Chipirones in su tinta* is ink-fish cooked in its own ink, a Basque speciality that Don Pedro, originally from San Sebastían, is very proud of. As for *kokotxas*, they're small pieces of dried cod cooked in garlic, the favourite dish of the fishermen. During their long journeys, they cook huge saucepans of it then eat the ragout while sitting in a circle, sharing the one dish and dunking their bread in the thick, sticky sauce … But enough talk of food, let's eat. You're looking pale, Cousin.'

Alexandra did feel quite weak. She wasn't used to skipping meals and was light-headed and weary as a consequence. Relieved, she let him steer her towards a table.

Señor Pedro came in person to take their order, beaming, his arms outstretched towards Ramón. In his sixties, he was round-faced and tubby, with bulging, dark, sparkling eyes, a big bushy moustache and greying side-whiskers. The two men exchanged a few words in the incomprehensible Basque dialect and then he turned to Alexandra. To her surprise, he addressed her in English.

'So, *señorita*, you have come a long way to visit Spain, eh? Splendid!' He chuckled. 'I am the humble Pedro Gomez, *Pépé* to my friends, a solitary exile from San Sebastían, the most cosmopolitan of Spanish towns, the heart of the Basque culture and mother of its cuisine. What a brilliant idea *Señor* Ramón has had, to bring you to my restaurant. In my *taberna*, and only here, you will sample authentic Basque cuisine without having to go all the way to San Sebastían,' he told her proudly. He nodded his head, in mock earnest. 'I bring refinement and culture to these poor, simple inhabitants of the South.'

Alexandra giggled uncontrollably at the comic buffoonery of the odd man. 'Bravo!' she applauded. '*Señor* Pedro, if your talent for cooking is as great as your eloquence, I've no doubt that your *taberna* is the most sought after, not only on the south coast, but in the whole of Spain.'

The small dining area was on a terrace outside, under a vine-covered pergola. As promised, the views overlooking the harbour were fabulous and dinner was a delight. Alexandra felt at ease in the company of her cousin and was surprised at how quickly a relationship of camaraderie and trust established itself between them. Her only regret was not having known Ramón earlier. *He would have made a good brother*, she thought wistfully. Watching him during their conversation, she noticed that there was also more to him, perhaps, than met the eye. His frank smile, showing brilliant, regular teeth, punctuated his conversation but, in repose, Alexandra noted, his face was lined and somewhat bitter for a man of his age and she wondered why. He could only be a few years older than she was and no more than thirty, if that.

'So, Alexandra, tell me about life in London,' said Ramón, tearing into a chunk of bread. 'It must be so much more *divertido e interesante* than life in a provincial Spanish town like this.'

'Well, Ramón, as I've only just arrived, I've yet to be the judge of that,' she laughed. 'But I suppose you could say it's superficially exciting in the sense that there are plenty of West End jazz clubs, dinner parties and trips down to Brighton for the weekend, that sort of thing.' Although these social engagements moved her in an endless spin of glamour and sophistication, they were hollow pleasures and she had tired of the same old set of faces and conversations. Excitement and freedom was what she craved.

Ramón nodded in exaggerated seriousness. 'Yes, *mi primita*, my little cousin. I see why you would want to flee such torture and come to our backward country to meet your warm and easygoing family.' His eyes flashed with amusement.

'Right, so I'm not exactly making it sound awful but in its own way, it's stifling and you're not the only one who understands what it's like to live under restrictions. But I have my writing and that's my one escape. My sanctuary, if you like.' She angled her chin up instinctively, almost defensively. 'It's what I've chosen to do.'

'Ah, yes, my cousin is a writer, as the *Duquesa* has often told us. You've published some books, she says.'

Alexandra raised an eyebrow at the mention of her grandmother's interest. She must be proud of her, she conceded, if she often referred to her writing. 'Indeed, romantic novels. As a matter of fact, I'm using my visit here partly as an opportunity to research my next one, which is to be set in Spain.'

'In that case, you must allow me to assist in whatever way I can to acquaint you with our ways. And, here, your first lesson has arrived.' At that point, Pedro appeared and deposited plates of steaming paella and delicious-smelling *kokotxas* before turning on his heel, quickly for such a rotund man, and disappearing back into the kitchen.

'I've never seen yellow rice before,' admitted Alexandra, glancing at the colourful dish in front of her.

'It's the saffron, an aromatic spice from the crocus flower,' Ramón added, seeing her blank look. 'Ah, so much to learn,

Cousin. We use it a lot in Spanish cooking. *Buen probecho*, let's eat,' he encouraged with a wave of his hand and they both tucked into the food with gusto.

After a few moments, Ramón looked up at Alexandra mischievously. 'So, *mi primita*. If you're an expert on romance, is there a *novio* waiting for you in England?'

For a moment, the eyes of the stranger she had met at the port that afternoon swam before her and she remembered the spark of awareness between them.

'No, Ramón. Ironic it may be, but I'm far too busy with my writing for that sort of thing. Though my Aunt Geraldine would have had me married off by now if she'd had her way.' Alexandra didn't add that she had always felt out of step with her peers. Many of them were beginning to marry and have babies but, while she herself was never short of admirers, the truth was that the men she came across, often young suitors paraded in front of her by her aunt and well-meaning friends, all seemed so dull and buttoned up. Besides, she had her dear childhood friend, Ashley, who had grown up with her in London and was a devoted companion, though he had always wanted to be more. She thought of his proposal of marriage, a month ago, that she had turned down, gently but firmly. It still flooded her with guilt and embarrassment.

Ramón nodded again and said through a mouthful of bread: 'Yes, Uncle Alonso has mentioned your aunt. The daunting Englishwoman, terrifying all who cross her path.'

Alexandra laughed. 'Well, maybe that's how she used to be when I was a child. Aunt Geraldine has mellowed an awful lot since then. Except she can be rather set in her ways when it comes to marriage, I suppose.'

'Rules and principles, eh?' He shrugged. '*La adicción de la edad*, the addiction of the old.'

Alexandra grinned. 'Perhaps. I know that she grew up in a different time but she doesn't seem to realize that the world has changed since the war. Yes, there's still food and petrol rationing in England and even clothes were only taken off the list last year because the black market made it so impossible to enforce.'

'The war has taken its toll on us all,' mused Ramón. He lowered his voice. 'Though here we've been devastated by our own civil war, too.' He fidgeted in his chair, keeping his voice down. 'I shouldn't be saying it but this self-sufficiency Franco is obsessed by is madness, it'll never work. We're an impoverished country that needs investment, raw materials, food even. Young people are feeling desperate and hopeless, they're leaving Spain in droves.' He lit a thin cigar and shrugged. 'But at least it looks like relations with America are improving. Hopefully Spain won't be a global outcast for long. But I didn't know you were still going through such hard times in England.'

Alexandra nodded thoughtfully before taking a sip of wine. 'People are still feeling the pinch of poverty everywhere. I think in a funny sort of way, though, my aunt misses the war. She was the first to join the volunteers ripping the railings down in London streets. There was a phrase we used during the war in England: "Make do and mend". That was always Aunt Geraldine. And, of course, her husband, my Uncle Howard, was there during the war too. Life hasn't been easy for her since he died a couple of years ago.'

'But your life in London is comfortable? You like it there?' Ramón sat back in his chair and studied her with curiosity.

'Yes, of course … well, I mean, I'm one of the lucky ones. My Uncle Howard set up a trust fund for me, so I'm privileged enough to have money, and I have the royalties from my two books … But it's rather suffocating at times. I can't explain, it sounds so ungrateful. Then there's always Aunt Geraldine's expectations that I'll give up my writing and settle down for the sake of security. I know she only wants what's best for me but it's different for women now.' Alexandra looked up at her cousin, her face alight with hope. 'I want more, Ramón.' She surprised herself at how comfortable she already felt with him, so much so that she was able to voice those desires she would have hesitated to reveal to her London friends. 'There are places I long to see. I don't want to be dragged down some preordained path just because I'm twenty-five, a woman and unmarried. I need to follow where my writing takes me, that's why I'm here.'

They talked briefly about the family. Alexandra sensed a reticence in her cousin, as though he did not consider himself one of the 'clan'. He spoke of travelling and of emigrating to the United States, where he would start his own plantation.

'Are you so desperate to leave Spain? You're lucky to be part of a noble Spanish dynasty and a flourishing business,' she pointed out.

'Believe me, Cousin, being part of an aristocratic family in Spain is not necessarily a passport to an easy life,' explained Ramón. 'Under Franco a family's mere survival can invoke suspicion and envy among surviving dissenters. The iron grip of *El Generalissimo* still prevails, and we de Fallas have always practised caution as a religion. It's the one thing I admire our grandmother for: she's never embraced Franco's politics, even though our status as Spanish nobility and landowners should, by rights, have made us partisan with the nationalist cause. She trod a fine line and it paid off.'

Alexandra shook her head. 'Back home, reports of Spain's troubles were overshadowed by the war in Europe, I suppose. We don't know about the Civil War and life in Spain from an insider's perspective,' she said softly.

'We're a nation of spies and victims,' Ramón muttered, and drained his glass.

'And that's why you want to leave?'

'Partly, yes.'

'Would you not miss the family?' After all that he had told her, Alexandra was still surprised that Ramón would cast himself adrift in the world.

'Once you've acquainted yourself with them and have lived some time at El Pavón, you'll understand my need to get away,' was his reply.

Alexandra's curiosity was sparked. She wondered if Ramón's outsider status within the family, something she had sensed, was part of the reason why she felt so at ease with him. An outsider herself, she had always been fearful of the family, of the secret power the de Fallas seemed to hold over her soul. Although Ramón's comments added to the uneasy sense of foreboding she could not shake off, her desire to get him to reveal more about the family was stronger.

'I know that the family must be very strict and conventional. After all, they made my mother feel so unwelcome she had to come back to England,' Alexandra persisted. 'But you're a de Falla by blood, why should you not feel comfortable here?'

Ramón hesitated before pouring himself a glass of wine. He lit another cigar, inhaled deeply and, leaning back, said: 'Our grandmother rules the hacienda like a general over her troops: her word is law. Because of that, anyone who doesn't see eye to eye with her risks her wrath and rejection, though I suppose it's not difficult to see why she's become that way.

'She's a formidable woman who's led a formidable life ... and that's made her tough and determined. El Pavón was built up as a wine-making and horse-rearing business by Count Rodriguez Cervantes de Rueda, the *Duquesa's* brother, whom she worshipped. First Rodriguez died and then her husband, Juan Raphael. Just imagine, as a young widow she was left to manage El Pavón until Luis María came of age, and he took over the control and management of the estate. And then he died too, of course.'

Ramón flicked the ash off his cigar. 'Do you want me to go on?' he asked with a faint smile.

Alexandra was fascinated, not least because the conversation with the old woman on the train had made her want to hear more. 'Oh, yes,' she said. 'Our family history has all the ingredients of a Greek tragedy. It's so dramatic.'

'It seems that drama is a de Falla speciality, *mi primita*. When Luis María died, El Pavón passed back to our grandmother and she rebuilt her empire. From then on, she's been determined to exert complete control over the de Fallas and fit us all into her plans and schemes ... whatever the consequences.' Ramón raised an eyebrow. 'As you know, when both her sons thwarted her designs by marrying our mothers and tainting the de Falla name, she succeeded in driving them both away.'

'Yes, I've always wondered what it must have been like for *Mamá*, an outcast in my father's family.'

The prospect of meeting the formidable *Duquesa* was once again making Alexandra feel apprehensive; perhaps the old lady would judge her granddaughter also unworthy of the de Falla name. And yet she had sought Alexandra out ...

'I can understand how the loss of so many people close to her must have strengthened the *Duquesa*'s sense of family,' she suggested.

'Perhaps you're right, *mi primita*.' Ramón gave an ironic smile as he gulped down the last of his wine. 'Though, knowing our grandmother, the loss of El Pavón to Luis María, for those few years, would have been a bigger blow.'

'And what about you, Ramón?' Alexandra asked. 'Did you grow up at El Pavón?'

'Yes, but when I was a teenager my father died. My mother couldn't face remaining among the de Fallas without him and decided to go back to her family in Granada. I could have gone with her but she wanted me to make something of myself here.'

As if feeling the need to break the serious tone of the conversation, Ramón looked up at Alexandra and grinned. He picked an orange from the fruit bowl on the table, rolling it up his forearm to flick it high into the air, catching it with the other hand. 'After all, who can blame her? You must have heard the shameful truth about my origins, Cousin.'

'And what would that be?' Alexandra mouth twitched in amusement. She was warming to him more and more.

Ramón stared at her in mock horror as he plucked another orange and began juggling them in one hand. 'I'm half de Falla and half Circus.'

Alexandra giggled. 'I'm shocked, of course.'

'So you should be, a nice girl like you. But as you're half-English and therefore technically an outcast too, I forgive your unkindness. The irony is that the circus would have suited me better than El Pavón, I think.' He arched an eyebrow playfully and brought the spinning oranges to a stop. His fingers, which she did not doubt were strong, looked as delicate as those of a girl.

'You mean clowns and that sort of thing?'

He fixed her with a mock-offended look again. 'I prefer the term "bohemian", *mi primita*. Anyhow, I'm certainly much more like my mother than I am my uptight, aristocratic father's family.'

'And what became of your mother?'

'She remarried and has a good life back in Granada. I see her from time to time.'

'So you must have grown up with our other cousins, Luis María's children?' She gazed at him quizzically, recalling what she had heard both from her father and the gossiping woman on the train, particularly about Salvador. Ramón suddenly looked restless.

'It's getting late. I think I'll pay Pépé's slate and tell you more on the way back.'

After protracted goodbyes to the ebullient *Señor* Pedro, they were on their way in Ramón's old Fiat, leaving the town behind as the roads twisted uphill through the starry night. There was so much that Alexandra wanted to know that they hadn't yet touched upon, particularly about her sister, Mercedes, the intriguing Salvador and her other cousin, Esmeralda, but perhaps she had asked Ramón too many questions already. There were some things she would simply have to discover for herself. For now, as they drove past dark clumps of trees studding the hillsides and the warm earthy fragrances of Andalucía surrounded her, she contented herself with listening to him continue his account of the family's history.

What was left of Ramón's tale was not much different from what he had already told her, and the bits and pieces she remembered her father recounting. Once more, tragedy had struck the de Falla family and sent fate on a new course. Luis María and his young wife Cecilia had died in a dreadful typhoid epidemic, leaving behind the adopted children, Esmeralda and Salvador, then aged five and eleven. After Luis María was gone and Alonso was widowed, the de Fallas were reunited at El Pavón. The *Duquesa* then reigned over the family with an iron fist.

'Only one person has been able to weasel himself into the old dragon's affections, and is safe from her demands and fits of rage: Salvador. And *qué broma!* what a joke, he doesn't even have a drop of de Falla blood. In her eyes, her beloved heir can do no wrong, though that is as far from the truth as chickens are from angels, I can tell you. But that's another story where, for now perhaps, *la mejor palabra siempre es la que queda por decir*, the best word is the one left unsaid.'

'Our cousin sounds … complicated.'

Ramón glanced at her before continuing: 'To say the least. Salvador is a mixture of the coldness and intransigence he learned from the *Duquesa*, the recklessness and impulsiveness of his adopted father, and the sensitivity and pride of his mother. A peculiar combination that inevitably brings tragedy in its wake.'

'Wasn't Salvador to be married?' Alexandra had no idea why the question had suddenly popped into her head. Perhaps she pitied the woman who had found herself mixed up with this man.

Ramón shook his head slightly as he slowed the car in front of a pair of huge iron gates. 'Yes, he was engaged once but even that was doomed from the start.'

Once again, the uneasiness that had gripped her earlier crept back. She wondered what Ramón had meant. Hadn't the old woman on the train mentioned something about it? No matter. She was reluctant to hear more about Salvador at that moment. It was plain that Ramón was not overly fond of his so-called cousin but she must not let herself be influenced by prejudice at this stage.

'You don't like him much,' she remarked.

'No, not much,' he sighed. 'He's too moody, too self-centred … you'll see …'

*   *   *

El Pavón loomed darkly through the willow trees as they drove along the gravel drive and pulled up outside the main entrance to the hacienda. The soft glow from a pair of carriage lamps mounted on the front of the house gave just enough light to illuminate the few steps to the imposing wooden front door. So this was the place of her Spanish ancestors. Perhaps it was just the silence, the lack of moonlight and her fatigue but, to Alexandra, it seemed, in the blackness, like a giant, shadowy tomb, holding dangerous secrets to be discovered by those who dared penetrate its intimidating walls. For a moment, she wanted to run away, back to England, back to her comfortable life and forget this foreign venture altogether.

Everybody at the hacienda had gone to bed, except for José, the ageing but strong and wiry-looking manservant. No, Don Alonso had not yet returned, he explained. Yes, Doña Alexandra's room was ready and there was plenty of hot water. Sarita, the maid, would bring a warm drink up to the *señorita's* room in a few minutes and would help her prepare for bed, he announced.

Ramón accompanied Alexandra upstairs to check that everything was in order and she had all she needed, before bidding her goodnight.

Once alone, Alexandra looked round the huge room with its two tall windows opening on to a balcony. The impression of space was emphasized by the height of the ceiling and the whitewashed walls, bare of ornament except for a tapestry representing a pastoral scene, which hung over the canopied bed, a wooden crucifix on one wall and a magnificent mirror mounted above the dark oak dressing table.

Her gaze wandered from the delicate sparkling crystal chandelier hanging from the ceiling, with its shining candle lights, to the heavy curtains of thick silk. Alexandra loved everything: the elegant winged chair in the left-hand corner of the room, the carved cabinet that lay between the window and the Louis XVI writing desk; the antique bronze lamp and leatherbound books on the bedside table.

She walked across the room to admire the vase of spring blossoms that formed a colourful display on a chest of drawers between the windows. This room was furnished with exquisite simplicity and impeccable taste. Someone had taken a good deal of care to create a welcoming atmosphere. Overwhelmed with gratitude, her previous doubts and foreboding melted away.

There was a knock at the door as Sarita, the young maid, came in carrying a cup of steaming hot tea. She then moved to the adjoining bathroom and started to run Alexandra's bath in the cast-iron pedestal tub before rejoining her to ask if she would like her to unpack the cases. Alexandra was thankful for the offer, suddenly overcome by a wave of weariness to which she had refused to submit throughout her long and eventful journey.

Half an hour later, she slipped between the silky sheets of a bed that must have dated from the last century. As Alexandra stared into the darkness, her mind wandered back to the church and the stranger who had so disturbed her. She found herself imagining what he might have said, had they not been interrupted.

An unfamiliar heat crept through her body as she recalled his arresting gaze, which had struck an unusual chord in the depths of her heart. She lifted her hand to her throat, startled by the memory: so powerful that she could feel his eyes on her again. What was this curious, incredible sensation that inflamed her so she felt as though he had actually touched her? It made her aware of herself, her body, her womanhood, in a way she had never known before. In the last moments before exhaustion took over, she ruefully wished their paths might cross again but that was the stuff of fairytales, she thought, and sank into a deep sleep.

Alexandra dreamt of piercing eyes that reminded her of England's grey wintry skies; steel eyes, cold as the waters of the North Sea; sad, desperate eyes that seemed to be following her. She knew she had seen them before.

Abruptly the scene changed. She found herself inside a marvellous cathedral. She was seven years old … it was her first communion. The organ was playing and someone was singing a hymn to the Virgin Mary. She was standing at the altar, dressed in white. Beside her stood a beautiful young woman, who also wore white. Alexandra looked up at her to recognize her mother. She reached out for her mother's hand but already she was moving away.

The child tried to follow her but then a man suddenly appeared out of nowhere. At first he had no face, then his features seemed to take shape. She stared wide-eyed, trying to identify him, but the image was blurred, almost illusory. Then the scene changed once more, and now she was no longer a child; it was her wedding day. The man at her side was smiling; he had Ramón's features. But when she looked again, it was no longer Ramón: it was the man on the prayer stool and the smile had disappeared.

*   *   *

Alexandra slept fitfully until early morning. She woke feeling less tired, but restless. As she drew back the heavy curtains, the room filled instantly with light. The brilliant sun heralded a magnificent day. Stretching lazily, she raised her head to let the warm rays wander over her face. Through the window she could see small groves of pink-blossomed trees, the ground sprinkled with clumps of bluebells. These shady areas were framed by paths leading off on either side to a colourful patchwork of smaller gardens that, she guessed, extended round to the front of the house. She was just about to leave her vantage point when she noticed two people at the edge of one of the groves that cut through the gardens.

The woman was tall and slender, with ash-blonde hair falling loosely to her waist. *That must be Esmeralda*, thought Alexandra. Her father had spoken about Salvador's very beautiful sister. He had described her as cold and distant, always daydreaming, and compared her to a lovely yet lifeless statue. However, this apparently passionless ornament was now locked in the embrace of a young man in a faded blue shirt and was returning his kisses with an ardour that appeared to match his. Suddenly, breaking away reluctantly from her partner's arms, she ran off towards the house.

Alexandra, feeling slightly embarrassed at having watched the passionate, and obviously private, scene, looked at the clock on her bedside table. It was still early, not even seven-thirty. There was plenty of time to explore the grounds before breakfast.

She ran herself a bath. The water was rather lukewarm but she did not mind it: after all, the temperature was several degrees higher than she had been used to at Grantley Hall, where the boiler always had a mind of its own. From the age of twelve, Alexandra had spent all her holidays at the huge and rambling country house in Kent, after Aunt Geraldine had married Lord Howard Grantley. Looking round the bathroom here, with its exotic blue-and-orange mosaic tiling and dark, carved oak mirrors, she was reminded of how far away she was from Grantley Hall and everything English.

She washed rapidly and went to the wardrobe to choose an outfit. Sarita must have come in while she was asleep: her beautifully pressed dresses, blouses, skirts and trousers were all hanging up and her underwear had been neatly folded and tidied away in the chest of drawers. She selected a fresh-looking, full-skirted dress in white lace and cotton. The wide red patent-leather belt, bought on a trip to Italy with Aunt Geraldine, encircled her tiny waist and showed off to advantage her graceful and shapely form. To protect her face from the sun, she wore a straw hat with a wide brim embellished with a couple of pink roses. In twenty minutes she was on her way to the garden.

Alexandra had no difficulty in finding her way through the house. Walking along an oak parquet corridor, she passed a series of *cuarterones*, heavy panelled doors inspired, she noted, by ancient carved Moorish screens, some with deeply panelled squares and others with a variety of geometric shapes. She guessed that behind them must be other bedrooms, dressing rooms and guest accommodation. The wide marble staircase swept down to a vaulted entrance hall that, on either side, led to huge ceremonial rooms lined with oriental rugs and embroidered hangings.

The chimes of the great wooden Catalan clock standing grandly in the hall resonated noisily through the sleeping household, startling her; it was now eight o'clock.

Once outside, Alexandra stood and looked at the front of the house. It had been too dark to see anything much when she'd arrived the night before, and she was curious to get a view of the hacienda in daylight.

El Pavón was a large, rectangular edifice with three quite distinct storeys, its whitewashed walls splashed here and there with patches of brilliantly coloured purple bougainvillea that crept up to brush the rounded brown tiles of its roof. Its style was neo-classical, the proportions pure: an austere structure.

An imposing seventeenth-century portal, which she later discovered was originally from a convent in Toledo, flanked by double Tuscan columns at the top of three widely fanning steps led into the vaulted hall. Placed at equal distances from the main entrance, at each end of the long façade were two identical narrow doors, richly decorated with carvings and marquetry. They opened on to separate wings, the private apartments of members of the family. Together they enclosed an inner shady courtyard. The ground-floor rooms at the front of the house each had French doors that opened on to an uncovered terrace running the length of the building, punctuated by fragrant miniature orange trees in large terracotta pots. Fronting the house was a wide gravel carriage circle that enclosed a huge round lawn, spread out like an emerald carpet beyond the foot of the main steps. Balconies with wrought-iron consoles and uprights lined the upper two storeys.

Flanking the great house were great expanses of manicured lawns and landscaped gardens curving round to the back of the hacienda. Beyond these, on the west side, stretched protective groves of oleander trees where statues and fountains joined in an interplay of cascading water and iridescent spray. The de Fallas, of which the present generation was the fourth to have lived at the house, had built up a sizeable business in wine production and horse breeding on the estate; and to the east of the hacienda, beyond the lawns, lay the stables and pastureland, neighboured by stretches of flourishing vineyards.

The house and its grounds, set in the wild and arid Andalucían countryside, seemed like a flashing jewel thrown on a sandy beach by a giant hand. With its green lawns, colourful shrubs, myriad flowers and tall trees, the hacienda had all the grandeur and panache of the peacock, *el pavón*, after which it had been named.

Alexandra relished the prospect of discovering every part of this spectacular place, realizing that it would take more than one morning to discover all its secrets. Now she turned towards the flowery grove where she had seen her cousin earlier. Soon she reached a path at the end of the garden where centuries-old sycamores and cypresses spread their dense shade. On either side, orchards of carefully tended lemon, pomegranate and orange trees exhaled their intoxicating scent. She paused momentarily, not wanting to become lost before she could make it back to the house in time for breakfast, but an impulse to explore further got the better of her. All at once, at a bend in the avenue of trees, she came to a clearing where the shade was less dense, a sort of elevated plateau overlooking the surrounding countryside from where several narrow paths ran in different directions.

Alexandra stopped to take in the impressive view that stretched boundlessly to the horizon. Scattered in the distant, windswept hills were modest whitewashed buildings, olive groves, fig trees, and herdsmen on horseback with their long lances, tending the horses and bulls. She breathed in the air, listening for the slightest sound.

England seemed so far away: the house in Chelsea ... Aunt Geraldine ... Alexandra's attention returned to the landscape and she leaned against the trunk of a cypress tree, closing her eyes. The air was balmy, dense, charged with a multitude of different sounds and intermingling scents. There was the soft rustling of leaves and the continuous buzzing of insects, the noisy chirping of birds and the muffled murmur of a nearby stream, punctuated by the strident creaking of *norias*, ancient water wheels that still dotted the countryside, the buckets attached to them used to raise water and transfer it to various irrigation channels. Suddenly, she was startled by a voice calling from behind her: 'Doña Alexandra, I presume.'

She turned sharply. Lounging against the trunk of a lemon tree, in the orchard beside the track on which she was standing, his arms folded, a man was looking at her with a mocking smile. She watched as he approached. He was tall and fair, with a weather-beaten complexion that emphasized the colour of his corn-yellow hair, which seemed to Alexandra a trifle too long. His countenance looked, to her mind, somewhat vulgar, although doubtless many women would find him seductive. She instantly felt a visceral dislike for him.

He gave a slight bow. 'Fernando Lopez, steward and trusted servant of His Grace the Count of Rueda, at your service,' he announced smiling and, without waiting for her reply, he went on: 'Isn't it a glorious morning?'

'Indeed,' she agreed. 'I couldn't resist your dazzling sun. I'm afraid I've managed to get lost,' she added, eager to escape from the man as quickly as possible. 'Perhaps you would be good enough to direct me back to the house.'

'It will be a pleasure to escort you there, dear *señorita*,' the steward replied in an oily voice.

'I can make my own way, thanks. What time is it?'

'Twenty past nine, you'd better make haste.'

She disliked his proprietory tone. 'And why is that?'

'Because breakfast is served at half-past nine,' he shrugged. 'It's common knowledge that her Grace the *Duquesa* has rather eccentric views about punctuality at mealtimes, and I don't think it would be wise to run foul of the old girl when you've only just arrived.'

Alexandra raised her eyebrows in surprise at the evident lack of respect that Fernando Lopez had just shown towards her grandmother. She surveyed him coolly. 'I don't think my grandmother's requirement that her family join her at mealtimes is the slightest bit eccentric,' she said curtly. 'On the contrary, it shows a sense of family and is completely justified, since she's the head of it. I'd be grateful if, in the future, you restrain yourself from criticizing any member of the family in my presence.' Her green eyes flashed angrily. She was taken aback by her own vehemence on behalf of the *Duquesa*, towards whom she herself had felt such antagonism for so many years. Still, through some impulse of instinctive loyalty, she felt compelled to set aside her mixed feelings in the face of such impertinence.

Clearly aware of his tactlessness, the man bit his lip. They returned in silence, an intangible feeling of animosity establishing itself between them. Alexandra sensed that her rebuke had already made an enemy of him.

Don Alonso de Falla was waiting for his daughter on a stone bench on the lawn at the front of the house. A broad smile lit up his face as she appeared and he rose, folding the newspaper he had been reading as he did so. Alexandra hurried towards him, thankful to put some distance between herself and the steward. Even though it had been only a few months since father and daughter had last spent time together in London, she was happy to see him again and was looking forward to getting to know him on his own turf. Hopefully, he would become an ally: someone who would help her acquaint herself not only with this newly found family but with a land that seemed so different to everything she had known until now.

'My dear Alexandra, you're here at last,' Don Alonso declared, kissing his daughter warmly on each cheek. 'You're more beautiful than ever. Our Spanish sun agrees with you already, I can tell. Ah, good morning, Fernando,' he said, addressing the steward who had come up behind Alexandra. 'I see you have met my daughter.'

Fernando Lopez nodded.

'Have you shown her around the stables yet?' Don Alonso asked and then beamed at Alexandra. 'Are you still riding? Perhaps we can go out after breakfast.' Without waiting for his daughter's response, he nodded to the steward: 'Would you ask Miguelto saddle up two horses? Prince for me, and Chiron for Doña Alexandra.'

'Very well,' replied Lopez, and he strolled off unhurriedly towards the stables.

Don Alonso turned to his daughter and placed an affectionate hand on her hair. 'As you walked up the drive just now, I thought I was seeing your mother again … the same large green eyes, you are like her in so many ways, *querida*.'

Alexandra hugged her father. She could not help but smile at his obvious emotion on seeing her again. Riding would not have been her first choice of how to spend her first morning with him but she told herself she would find a way to get out of it later. 'And now you are finally here at El Pavón …' Don Alonso sat her down on the bench beside him. 'I can't tell you how happy it makes me to see you with the family at last.'

'Yes, *Papá*. And now that I'm here I'm also hoping to capture the whole flavour of Spain for my new book. Perhaps we could spend some time together and you could help me with my notes on Spanish culture?'

'*Sí, sí*, I remember you told me in London you were writing about your homeland. That pleases me too, *querida*. What is it that Lord Byron said? "Oh, lovely Spain! renown'd, romantic land!" An Englishman, but impeccable taste nonetheless.'

Don Alonso grinned and took his daughter's hand, patting it affectionately as they sat side by side, looking out across the lawn and colour-drenched gardens.

Since he hadn't answered her question directly, Alexandra gently persevered. 'There's much I'm sure you could show me in the local area that I couldn't discover on my own.'

'Mmm?' Don Alonso turned to look at her and, as if carried off on some other thought, he smiled wistfully. 'You know, I do wonder what it would have been like if your mother had remained in Andalucía and you had grown up here.'

As Alexandra had often observed with her father during his stay in London, their conversation was going to be like trying to catch butterflies and so she quickly changed the subject.

'How is your family?' she asked tentatively. 'Mercedes must be nearly eighteen now. I can't wait to meet her.'

'They're your family too, my dear,' Don Alonso replied. 'I have told her so much about you and I'm sure she's just as eager as you are.'

'Has she asked about me much then? She must be curious.'

'Of course, of course.' He smiled and waved his hand nonchalantly. 'Our dear Mercedes is curious about everything and everyone. Such spirit! It's difficult to keep up with her half the time. The two of you will get on *espléndidmente*.'

Alexandra had learned a little of Mercedes from her father's letters but had never even seen a photograph of her Spanish half-sister. She would have loved to have had a sibling for company when she was growing up, instead of rattling around on her own for hours in the house in Chelsea or at her aunt and uncle's country seat in Kent, though she wondered what kind of welcome she would receive from the child who had been used to her parents' undivided attention. She still hoped that they could form some kind of sisterly bond, given time.

'Does she look like me?'

Don Alonso looked surprised. 'Do you know, I've never even thought about it. You have the beauty of your mother, particularly your eyes. Mercedes is a pretty girl, there's no doubt about it, but she's more like Eugenia and the apple of her mother's eye, of course. She has no shortage of admirers already but, between you and me, Eugenia and I have high hopes that she and Salvador will make a good match when she's a little older. He's a fine young man and it would strengthen the family to have such a marriage.'

Don Alonso had just started to enquire about her journey, apologizing for not having been there to greet her, when a girl in her late teens strode across the lawn towards them. Alexandra took in every last detail of the girl, who, she guessed, must be Mercedes. Petite and well proportioned, she had two bunches of black corkscrew curls held up with blue ribbons that swung gracefully at each side of her heart-shaped face. Her overly elaborate blue-and-white organza dress seemed somewhat out of place in the country and at this time of day. Like the woman she had seen at the little Santa María church the day before, Mercedes seemed to evoke another era. Alexandra was reminded again that the modern world had not yet reached this quaint and wild country, which seemed to have been frozen in time.

'Good morning, *Papá*,' the young girl said, giving Don Alonso a peck on the cheek while casting a sidelong glance at Alexandra through long lashes.

'Ah, Mercedes, there you are,' he exclaimed in a tone that forced cheerfulness. Alexandra could sense that he wasn't entirely comfortable. After taking a breath, he added, 'This is your sister, Alexandra. I'm sure you'll get on very well. You'll have plenty to talk about.'

Mercedes pouted but did not answer; her almond-shaped black eyes surveyed the newcomer without a hint of warmth. Looping an arm through her father's, she cast a wan smile towards Alexandra, who was disappointed though not entirely surprised by the cool reception.

During the awkward silence that followed, Alexandra inspected her younger sibling. So this was the adored child of her father's second marriage to Doña Eugenia de Juni. Everything about her was small and dainty, like a china doll.

'Shall we go into breakfast? I'm famished,' suggested Don Alonso with feigned enthusiasm. 'Mother is expecting us and you know how she hates to be kept waiting.'

CHAPTER 3

A lexandra followed her father and Mercedes into the dining room through the French doors that led from the terrace. She found it even grander than she'd expected. Research for her book had involved hours spent looking at photographs of Spanish architecture and furniture within the pages of collectors' magazines such as *Connaissance des Arts* and *Apollo*, but the articles she'd read did not do justice to the distinctive style of the real thing. Impressive though the interior was, and beautiful in its own way, Alexandra did not warm to it and felt like she'd stepped into a daunting theatre set.

It was a huge, high-ceilinged room, situated on the west side of the house, with an open arch to the right that led to other living rooms. The oak furniture was dark and austere. Hangings in the typical Spanish 'repostero' style, decorated with coats of arms, lent warmth to the white walls, while an exquisite Afghan carpet covered part of the floor, its rich hues scarcely dimmed by age.

On the left, two chairs with ornate backs stood on either side of a heavily carved sideboard. To the right of it was a handsome what-not in rustic style, dating from the seventeenth century, surmounted by a hexagonal mirror with a richly decorated frame. At the far end of the room, between two large doors of Moorish inspiration, constructed with carved ornamental slats like jalousies, was a small dais upon which stood a copper brazier with a pointed cover. In the centre, surrounded by upright chairs, the dining table was massive yet still dwarfed by the vast dimensions of the room. Only its legs were carved, the upper surface having the simplicity of a board. Around it, the de Falla family was already assembled, talking in quiet tones as congregations do before the start of a church service.

Doña María Dolores sat at the head of the long table, upright in her chair. She was smaller than Alexandra expected, and surprisingly youthful-looking for her age. Her shock of perfectly groomed white hair crowned a handsome face, with proud, high cheekbones and a mouth that was not given to easy smiles. Two women were seated further down the table, the youngest of whom Alexandra recognized as Esmeralda.

'*Mamá*, may I introduce Alexandra,' said Don Alonso as he came into the room.

As though by common accord, all conversation ceased. Stiffly, like a choreographed corps de ballet, all three heads turned towards the newcomer. A deathlike silence followed, making the distance Alexandra had to cover between the doors and where her grandmother sat seem endless.

She didn't speak as she crossed the room, taking in the figure who'd been the focus of her mixed emotions for so many years, and who appeared every bit the intimidating matriarch she had expected. Finally she found her voice, though it was not as assertive as she would have liked. 'Good morning, Grandmother.' She kissed the old lady lightly on the cheek as their eyes met. Those of the *Duquesa* were jet black and, for a moment, her penetrating gaze held Alexandra's searchingly.

'Good morning, my child,' said the dowager at length. 'Sit here, beside me. José, draw up a chair for Doña Alexandra, to my right,' she ordered imperiously.

Someone let out a faint, stifled gasp at this invitation. The signal was clear: the newcomer was being given the most important position in the room. Like mechanical tin soldiers that had been wound up again, the family once more began to move.

As Alexandra sat down next to her grandmother, Don Alonso moved round the table to stand awkwardly behind the chair of the horsey-looking woman diagonally opposite. He cleared his throat.

'Alexandra, this is your stepmother, Doña Eugenia,' he said, gesturing towards his wife with an anxious smile.

Eugenia María de Juni was of indeterminate age and, although her appearance was meticulous down to the smallest detail, there was nothing particularly charming about her features – in fact, nothing that stood out at all. Above all, she lacked warmth. She had clearly married Don Alonso rather late in life, producing their only daughter, Mercedes. Whatever youth she had hurried through had long since dried up to be replaced by a seemingly permanent sour expression. She gave something that passed for a smile to Mercedes as her daughter took up the seat next to her before staring icily across at Alexandra.

'And this is your cousin, Esmeralda,' Don Alonso said. The young woman next to Alexandra turned to look at her with grey-blue eyes that were distant and yet oddly familiar. Where had she seen those eyes before? Esmeralda's beauty was undeniable, with hair the colour of champagne falling in tendrils across a delicate face, but those steel-blue eyes held no vitality.

'*Bienvenidos a El Pavón, querida Prima*, welcome to El Pavón, dear Cousin. We're glad you've come.' Her smile was stilted, the words spoken rhetorically as though her mind were elsewhere.

How strange, thought Alexandra. *The warmest welcome so far, if you could call it that, has been from my grandmother.* She had expected the *Duquesa* to be the standoffish one but it was the others who had given her a chilly reception.

Breakfast resumed in almost complete silence. The only sounds to be heard were José's muffled tread as he served and the clinking of silver against the china.

'I trust you slept well?' The *Duquesa* glanced across at Alexandra as her coffee cup was filled.

'Yes, thank you,' Alexandra replied. She was not about to admit to restless dreams about the stranger in the church, whose eyes had followed her everywhere through those night-time visions. 'I woke early and went for a walk to explore El Pavón.'

Doña Eugenia's narrow gaze had never left Alexandra's face. 'So I see you've already sized up the estate before the rest of us had even set foot out of bed. I applaud your diligence, my dear.'

Unsure of her step in the face of this openly barbed remark, Alexandra paused. 'It's such a lovely morning, I was merely enjoying the grounds. They're so beautiful,' she replied pleasantly.

Don Alonso shifted an uncomfortable gaze away from Eugenia to smile fondly at his eldest daughter. 'Do you have any memories of the gardens from when you were here as a child? You took your first steps on the front lawn, you know.' He might have continued with this reminiscence but at that point caught his wife's eye and pursed lips, and seemed to remember himself.

'I recall flashes of colour and the wonderful light here. Nothing of the house, though.'

There was an audible sniff from Doña Eugenia. 'Yes, our Spanish sun cannot be compared to the grey, soulless climate of your country. Strange your mother couldn't wait to return to it. Especially as, like the rest of the English, she must have suffered a sallow complexion as a result.'

Alexandra felt her temper flare, but before she could react, the dining-room door creaked: it was Ramón. Too absorbed by her own thoughts, she had not noticed the young man's absence from the breakfast table. He had exchanged his casual clothes of the previous day for a more suitable outfit with a jacket.

'Good morning, Grandmother,' he said as he sat down at the other end of the table.

The *Duquesa* looked up, her expression hard. 'You are late, Ramón,' she said curtly. 'Your mother may have been brought up in a circus but that is no excuse for you to behave as though you're living among the gypsies.'

Alexandra glanced at Ramón sympathetically and he returned the look with an 'I told you so' arch of his eyebrows. The quiet click-clack of knives and forks continued.

'You were up early this morning, Esmeralda. I saw you from my window. Where had you been?' asked Doña Eugenia. Her question hung unanswered for a long moment. It was plain to Alexandra that mealtimes would, most likely, be dominated by toxic political machinations on the part of her stepmother. She had no doubt that the woman meant to make trouble.

Esmeralda was caught off-guard. At first, Alexandra thought she would panic but she was wrong. Not a muscle moved in that beautiful oval face, not the bat of an eyelash betrayed any inner turmoil. She simply grew a little paler and her large wintry eyes became a shade darker.

'I was coming back from the lodge,' she said flatly. 'Salvador came to see me at dawn. He asked me to visit Marujita. It seems the child had another fit and a bad night.'

Was she lying? Alexandra knew, at least, that one part of Esmeralda's morning activities were unaccounted for: her tryst with the somewhat shabbily dressed young man, but the young woman gave nothing away and, though Doña Eugenia might have had her doubts, she was forced to take her at her word and drop the subject.

'Where's Salvador?' asked Mercedes suddenly, as she helped herself to a second pastry. 'It's not like him to be late for breakfast. I thought I saw him this morning. And why isn't he here?'

'Salvador's been called into town urgently,' her father explained. 'There are difficulties with the two stallions we sold last month to Don Miguel. He'll probably have to go to Seville and might be away for a few days.'

'But what about the masked ball?' The girl was unable to hide her disappointment. 'He promised me the first dance.'

Alexandra pricked up her ears. The romance of a masked ball appealed to her greatly but she smothered her questions, feeling disinclined to draw attention to herself and invite further snipes from Doña Eugenia.

Don Alonso smiled and said in an overly bright tone, 'Don't worry, my dear. I'm sure he'll be back for it. You will not only have your first dance with him but a few others as well, I should think.' He gave a satisfied chuckle. 'Salvador's temper seems much improved lately and I think I can guess why.' He gave a knowing smirk towards his wife, who returned a warning glance. Doña María Dolores stiffened. 'And I think, Alonso,' she said coldly, 'that Salvador has far too many responsibilities to concern himself with such trivial matters. Perhaps if he could count on one of you to take on some of his duties he would have more time to spend on frivolities. Unfortunately, he is surrounded by dilettantes and daydreamers.'

With this, she rose briskly and ordered Alexandra to follow her. As the door closed behind them, Alexandra heard someone give a snort of derision and then Ramón's voice: 'Her dear angel, Salvador, has fallen to earth with a crash due to one certain frivolity, I'd say.' If he was expecting laugher at his jibe he didn't get it.

The *Duquesa* turned to Alexandra with a softer look. '*Venir conmigo, mi hija*, come with me, my child, we must get to know each other.'

As she followed the old lady through the dark corridors of the house, Alexandra couldn't help but feel dismayed at the family she had finally encountered. Her thoughts flitted from her disdainful stepmother, Eugenia, and the capricious Mercedes, who she now saw was likely to be no end of trouble rather than the sisterly ally she had hoped for, to Esmeralda, whose melancholy and nervousness made her unreachable. And when would the mysterious Salvador himself put in an appearance … this cousin who had stirred up such strong reactions in more than one member of the family?

Although it was clear that her grandmother was determined to draw Alexandra into the fold and had shown her a modicum of warmth, she was still an impossibly dictatorial old matriarch. Alexandra could see why Ramón was impatient to leave. How tiring it must be to live under a roof where you were constantly spied upon and where every gesture, word and action was discussed, judged and criticized in public. She could never imagine living permanently at El Pavón.

More than one intrigue was no doubt being plotted in the gloomy corridors of the big house and she wanted no part of it. Except for Doña Eugenia, taken individually, the members of her family seemed tolerable enough, but together they made a most unpleasant group. Even her father had seemed a different person. Where was the lively and affectionate man she'd got to know in London? Today he'd seemed artificial and diminished somehow; almost a stranger.

When Alexandra had finally made up her mind to make the journey, her father had insinuated a hope that she would consider El Pavón her permanent home. And although she couldn't really imagine that it ever might be so, that she could leave her family and friends behind and suffer the strictures of her dominant grandmother, still she had hoped that the Spanish aristocratic life would be a change, and possibly even fun, at least for a short time. But less than twenty-four hours had gone by and already she was aware that more than a few weeks at a time in such a stifling atmosphere would be insufferable.

Her grandmother's apartments were on the ground floor at the back of the house. Doña María Dolores showed Alexandra into a room of Moorish design. In one corner, a part of it was raised, with low furniture and brightly coloured cushions on the platform, harking back to the days when Arabs ruled much of Spain. The de Falla matriarch was as much part of the interior as this throne-like dais, and yet the space was more relaxed elsewhere in a way that surprised Alexandra. Carved tables and a carpet with patterns reminiscent of Arabic ceramics were placed in the lower part of the room, in front of a European sofa and comfortable armchairs. French doors opened out on to a courtyard with a wide-slatted, semi-open ceiling that allowed sunlight and shade to mingle as twines of bougainvillea trailed across its beams. There were palms, climbing jasmine and clumps of oleander, and dwarf orange trees grew in tubs around the edges; the warbling of birds mingled happily with the sound of small singing fountains. The effect was peaceful, intimate and utterly charming.

The dowager watched Alexandra's face brighten with delight and there was a smile in the old lady's eyes. She led the way out on to the patio. 'We will be more comfortable here,' she explained, as she seated herself in one of the two bamboo chairs with wide circular backs, placed in a cosy corner of the courtyard in front of a matching round table.

'Talk to me about your novels. My son tells me you are busy writing a third, set in our beautiful Spain. A very good choice, my dear. Our country is so rich in colour and passion.'

'Yes, Grandmother, I have always thought so.' Alexandra found herself answering the dowager nervously. After all, this was the woman whom she had resented for so long and perhaps even feared slightly. There had been so many things she had wanted to say; questions she wanted answering. Now she was tongue-tied and reticent.

The *Duquesa* smiled, her face transforming from her customary dignified mask into something softer. 'You have thought much about Spain while you were growing up in England, I imagine ...'

'Of course, I had much to think about ... I believe knowing one's roots is important.'

'Indeed, my child, and I'm certain that Spain has always been in you. One can tell by the way you write. Your passion is your strength. *Está en su sangre*, it's in your blood and that's what brought you here at last.'

Alexandra was startled at such a direct and unexpected comment. She felt as if the *Duquesa* had read her like a book.

'So you're familiar with my work?'

'*Por supuesto*, of course, my child. I made it my business to get to know something of you through your writing, even if I couldn't know you in person.'

Unlike my father ... The bitter thought flashed across Alexandra's mind unbidden. *He clearly couldn't be bothered to read my books, to get to know me better even that way.* Venturing to look more closely at her grandmother now, feeling a new spark of curiosity, she saw a tinge of regret behind her eyes. 'And what did you discover about me?' The bold question came out before she had time to think.

The *Duquesa* laughed throatily. 'You're no shrinking violet, for one. It is the truth of things that pulls you, and one's roots are one's own truth. Yours are here, as you have always realized, I'm sure.' Doña María Dolores fixed her with a knowing look. 'Even if you were not ready to see it ...'

They talked for some time and Alexandra found herself more comfortable in the *Duquesa*'s company than she had anticipated. She was amazed to discover her grandmother had not only read her novels but she appeared to recollect everything about them, down to the smallest detail.

They touched on many topics. The *Duquesa* was interesting, thoughtful and even witty. She talked and argued, but surprisingly also knew how to listen. The condescending tone she adopted with most members of her family was now scarcely noticeable and Alexandra, who'd been on her guard, began to relax and even warm to her grandmother.

'Wait here,' said the old woman, standing up unexpectedly, 'I'll be back in a moment.'

She disappeared into the house and returned, carrying a small wooden box inlaid with mother-of-pearl. 'The contents of this box,' she explained, 'are of Moorish origin. They belonged to Gulinar, an Eastern princess in the sixteenth century. They were given to my great-grandmother by the wife of an emir in gratitude for her hospitality when they came to El Pavón to buy horses.'

Doña María Dolores opened the box, uncovering the most superb parure, set in white gold. It consisted of a tiara, a matching necklace, a bracelet and a pair of earrings, intricately and delicately carved, embedded with tiny precious stones and pearls.

'I want you to wear these at our masked ball,' she said as she handed the box over to Alexandra.

Overwhelmed by a host of conflicting emotions, Alexandra hesitated for a moment, not knowing whether to accept the magnificent present. The Alexandra she had left behind in London would have scowled at this gesture, even suspected it as a piece of bribery for her affections.

The *Duquesa* studied her granddaughter's face and smiled. 'So many wild things are going on in your mind, my dear child.' She laughed and her face looked almost young. 'Your eyes betray your thoughts. I must teach you the art of hiding your feelings if you want to survive in this household.'

'*Gracias*,' Alexandra whispered as she felt the blood rush to her cheeks. She kissed her grandmother and spontaneously leaned forward to give her a hug.

'It is my pleasure.' The *Duquesa* looked momentarily taken aback by this obvious demonstration of affection, then patted her granddaughter's hand. 'Now that we have settled that business, tell me what costume you have in mind for our ball.'

'You've taken me by surprise. I haven't had time yet to think about it.'

'Well, there's not much time. It's at the end of the week, but I'm sure it will not be too difficult to sort out. Perhaps Ramón could take you into town later today,' Doña María Dolores suggested. 'You should be able to find all you need at *Mascaradas*. Were Salvador here, he would have taken you himself. He's a friend of old Jaime, the owner.' She paused, and then added, as an afterthought, 'I'm sorry Salvador has had to go away for a few days. He'll be back for the ball, though. I'm quite certain you'll like each other.'

For some reason, and to her slight embarrassment, Alexandra felt a blush creep on to her cheeks. There was something there in her grandmother's tone, underlying her words.

If the *Duquesa* had noticed, she didn't show it but continued, 'The poor man has been very ill. He was thrown from his horse, which almost left him a cripple, you know. He bravely endured two years of pain and luckily now he's able to resume a normal life.' Sadness clouded her eyes. 'Life has not been kind to him. First his parents, then …' she added in a faint voice, as though talking to herself.

Someone had walked on to the terrace and her sentence remained unfinished. It was Ramón, come to offer his services.

'For once you're here when you're needed, young man,' noted his grandmother dryly. 'Alexandra requires a costume for Saturday's ball. Could you take her into town.' She didn't frame it as a question. 'I have no doubt old Jaime will find her a disguise that matches her beauty.'

With his usual good humour, Ramón ignored his grandmother's barbed salutation. 'I shall be delighted to accompany my charming cousin into town.' He beamed at Alexandra.

'If you leave immediately after lunch, you should be back in time for dinner. Take the new car, that way you'll have no excuse to be late.' She arched an eyebrow, pulling her shawl around her shoulders.

Ramón nodded obediently and, bidding his grandmother goodbye, he took Alexandra's arm. They left Doña María Dolores on the patio, her jet-black eyes following her newly found granddaughter thoughtfully. At the door, Alexandra turned and smiled at her. She had not forgotten her grandmother's reputation, and wondered what lay behind the raised brow, but she realized now that something had shifted in her opinion of the old lady.

At that moment, a proud-looking Spanish woman in a maid's outfit appeared from the other side of the patio with a glass of water and a pill for Doña María Dolores. 'Ah, thank you, Agustina, I always forget,' said the dowager.

Once in the corridor, Ramón turned to his cousin and wagged a threatening finger at her, his eyes twinkling mischievously. 'I see you're in the old dragon's good books. Try to remain there, *mi parita*, and do watch your step.'

Alexandra had great difficulty in keeping a straight face. 'Our grandmother is an admirable woman, Ramón,' she replied reprovingly. 'You're wrong to treat her with such disrespect.' He gave her a sidelong glance and they both laughed.

'She's a great schemer, that's what she is. Don't be fooled.'

*   *   *

It was about four o'clock in the afternoon when they drove into the bright town of Jerez, with its palm trees, *bodegas* and beautiful old churches. The cobbled café-lined backstreets led on to wider boulevards and plazas populated by statues and fountains.

'Will you be all right if I leave you on your own for a while? I've some errands to run,' Ramón announced, turning the elegant Fiat sedan into a large plaza dominated by a dramatic statue of a sweeping matador and his bull. 'I suggest I drop you off in the main square here, outside *Mascaradas*. You may want to browse around the other shops before choosing your costume. I'll join you in an hour at old Jaime's. Or, if you'd prefer, you can brighten the dullness of my chores with your sparkling company,' he glanced sideways, with a courteous, flourishing wave, 'and then we can choose your costume together.'

'Tempting though the offer is, I think I'll shop alone, thanks, Ramón. That way, if I choose my own costume, I can remain incognito at the ball,' Alexandra proposed cheerfully.

Ramón grinned. 'Dear Cousin, I would recognize you under any disguise.' He reached over and gave her an affectionate pinch on the cheek.

He dropped her off outside *Mascaradas*. 'I'll see you here in an hour.' He winked. 'Have fun.'

'Thank you. Good luck with your errands.'

The sun was shining; Alexandra felt light-hearted and jolly. It was good to be away from El Pavón and to breathe again. She strolled around the square, lined with magnificent rows of jacaranda trees, and bought a few Spanish knick-knacks to take back to England. The vibrant shopfronts and pretty awnings were an open invitation to browse the various objects in the windows, from the mouth-watering offerings of the *pastisseria*, *bomboneria* and *xocolateria* to shops selling clothes, hats, guitars, scent and fans.

'*Que vendo las tartas, los bollos rellenos de vainilla a tres pesetas, y las merengues!* Come, pretty *señorita*, I sell cakes, buns filled with vanilla for three pesetas, and meringues!' The *ducero* at his pavement stall waved Alexandra over, winking.

'*No Gracias, señor, parecen muy apetitosos pero arruinan mi figura*, no thank you, *señor*, they look delicious but you'll spoil my figure,' she laughed, and the man raised his arms in playful mock-disbelief as she walked on.

She was relaxed and felt part of the scenery, almost like a native enjoying the afternoon. Alexandra's father had spoken Spanish to her when he was at home and she was pleased she'd continued with her Spanish lessons. Being fluent in the language was making it so much easier for her to understand the culture in this country, which she now saw she had a right to by birth.

Fascinated by the many crafts practised on the pavement, she stopped occasionally to watch men repairing carpets, old crones making lace and cobblers with their round spectacles, reminding her of fairy-tale characters from her childhood. But the chimes of the clock in the square jogged her back to reality. Once more she had forgotten the time; she realized that she didn't have long before Ramón would return and so she hurried towards *Mascaradas*.

She arrived out of breath. *Mascaradas* was an old-looking shop with a once elegant antique green front, panelled wood and glass façade, and faded gold signage. She pushed the red wooden door; it opened with a creak, loud enough to announce her arrival. Her eyes took a few seconds to get used to the dimness inside and then she made out tall mahogany cabinets with open drawers that coughed out ribbon and lace, illuminated shelves of mannequin heads adorned with feathery hats and masks, shimmering garments hanging from walls, draped over chairs and spilling out of trunks. A fusty odour of damp clung to the place and Alexandra felt like she had walked into some kind of dusty, exotic cavern. Emerging from the depths of the shop, a scraggy man with a shiny bald head, hooked nose and ragged goatee came to stand behind the counter, peering at her beadily through round spectacles. This was undoubtedly old Jaime. *Another fairy-tale character*, thought Alexandra.

'*Señorita*, can I help you?'

Alexandra smiled engagingly. 'I've been invited to a masked ball and I'm looking for a costume. Do you have any suggestions?'

'The masked ball at El Pavón presumably?' asked the man.

'Yes, that's right.'

'You're rather late, *señorita*. I have very little left. You can take a look in there,' he said, pointing at two large, faded-leather trunks, resembling pirate chests from the last century, tucked beneath an ornately carved hatstand. She glanced at them apprehensively.

'I haven't much time, I'm afraid. My cousin is coming back for me shortly and I don't want to make him wait.'

'Are you *la Señorita* Alexandra de Falla?'

'Yes, I am,' she said, surprised that he should know her name.

'*Señor* Ramón came by earlier to inform you that his errands have taken longer than he thought and he'll be late.'

Alexandra heaved a sigh of relief. 'Oh, good. I'll be able to take more time to make my choice in that case.'

Old Jaime scurried round the side of the counter and pushed open one of the trunk's lids. 'Here, I'll help you look. I haven't been through these for a while and I'm not sure there'll be anything of use but *la diligencia es la madre de la buena ventura*, diligence is the mother of good fortune, as they say.'

Together they went through the contents of the two chests, untangling and sorting a mass of trimmings of all types and colours. When they had finished, Alexandra was still without a costume.

Disappointed, she wearily turned to the shopkeeper. 'Haven't you anything else to show me, *señor*?'

The man reflected for a few seconds, scratching his scraggly beard. 'I do have something … it's a genuine Moorish costume,

which belonged to an Arabian princess ... A real museum piece
... *magnifico*, entirely embroidered in silver thread and set with
tiny pearls and precious stones.' He hesitated and looked at
the young woman over the rim of his spectacles. 'Unfortunately,
this costume is not for hire, only for sale. The price might seem
somewhat extravagant for a garment you'd wear for just one
evening, though.'

'Let me be the judge of that,' Alexandra retorted, hardly able
to contain her excitement. If her grandmother had made her
the present of such a sumptuous set of Eastern royal jewels to
wear with her costume, a princess from Arabia was exactly the
part she needed to play.

'Of course, *señorita*, of course,' old Jaime replied hastily.
'I'll fetch it for you *immediatamente*.'

He disappeared behind a heavy curtain into the back of
the shop and Alexandra fancied she could hear murmurings
from within. *Old Jaime was certainly an eccentric*, she thought, as
her eyes travelled round the room. They fell on two mannequins,
looking as if they were engaged in silent close conversation
and dressed entirely as samurai warriors except for their bowler
hats. The man emerged a few moments later carrying a large
cardboard box, which he opened ceremoniously to reveal a
garment carefully wrapped in several layers of tissue paper. After a
lot of huffing and puffing, the costume was laid out.

Alexandra gasped at its richness and dazzling beauty. She
didn't need any further encouragement: when Jaime produced a
pair of silvery sandals, delicately carved, her mind was already
made up. The costume would be perfectly suited to the beautiful,
priceless heirloom her grandmother had given her that morning.

'I'll have it,' she said impulsively. 'How much does it cost?'

Again, the shopkeeper eyed her craftily over his round
spectacles. 'I forgot to add, *señorita*, that I can't sell the sultana's
costume without selling the sultan's one as well,' he announced.

Alexandra's brows drew together in surprise. 'I don't understand,' she said.

The man's eyes darted back to the heavy closed curtain behind him. 'These costumes were sold to me about ten years ago by the descendant of a Moorish nobleman,' he told her, earnestly. Lowering his voice a little, he added, 'According to legend, the wearers of these costumes are destined to fall in love. It would be unlucky to sell the costumes separately.'

'What nonsense,' Alexandra exclaimed indignantly, dismissing his comment as the sales talk of a shrewd businessman. 'I'm not superstitious.'

'But *I* am,' he retorted.

'Jaime, *muéstrame los vestidos*, show me those costumes,' ordered a man's voice suddenly, from the back of the shop.

'Right away, *señor*,' old Jaime replied. Quick as a flash, before Alexandra could protest, he picked up box, costume and tissue paper, and disappeared once more behind the curtain separating the two rooms, leaving her fuming. Who was this man, presuming he could commandeer the shopkeeper, and her costume, at the drop of a hat?

She was tempted to leave but then she would be without a costume. Gritting her teeth, she called out impatiently: 'Well, shall I go then?'

'*Un momento, señorita*.' The shopkeeper poked his head through the curtain. He seemed very excited and returned a few seconds later to the front of the shop. 'His Grace the Count has bought both costumes.'

Alexandra almost lost her temper. She was on the verge of giving the man a piece of her mind, when he handed her over an envelope, adding hurriedly: '*Su Gracia El Conde* asked me to give you this, *señorita*, together with the costume of the sultana and his compliments.'

Alexandra took the envelope and opened it. Her eyebrows rose slightly as she scanned the note, wondering whether she should be amused or offended. The writing on the card was bold and vigorous and read: '*In homage to your beauty, until Saturday evening!*' It was left unsigned.

The writer in her couldn't fail to be intrigued by such a romantic gesture but she was not about to let on to either the shopkeeper, now staring back at her anxiously, or the arrogant author of the note, who was no doubt still within earshot. Alexandra shook back her auburn mane and shot the shopkeeper a baleful look.

'I really can't understand all this mystery,' she declared crossly. 'Why didn't he give it to me himself? And just who is this mysterious *Conde*? He didn't even have the courtesy to sign his message.'

She was about to insist old Jaime should reveal the identity of the stranger when Ramón burst into the shop.

'Sorry, Cousin. My watch must have stopped and now it's late,' he said, running a hand through his hair. 'We'd better leave right away or we won't make it back in time for dinner, and then we'll be in trouble. Let's not make the next de Falla mealtime any more painful than it needs to be.'

Alexandra had no other alternative but to take the costume and follow her cousin.

*   *   *

Seated that evening at her dressing table, preparing for dinner, Alexandra found herself musing over her mysterious benefactor.

For no palpable reason, she hadn't mentioned the incident at *Mascaradas* to Ramón and had refused to show him her costume, merely hinting that it was stunning and she was very happy with her choice of outfit for the ball.

She took the envelope from her handbag and examined the note, looking for some clue as to the author's identity. Disappointingly, the curious message revealed nothing, save that 'His Grace the Count' was possessed of an arrogance that she found not entirely displeasing. However, it was rather presumptuous of him to assume she would be willing to go along with his frivolous game.

No matter. She shrugged and let her mind wander a while, recalling the warm deep voice that had summoned old Jaime in such a firm tone, and attempted to give it a face. It was a sensual voice but the voice of a man who was in the habit of being in charge. He had only said a few words but something in his tone … Her pulse quickened slightly and she closed her eyes for a moment, a strange emotion welling up inside her. Unbidden, the face of the stranger at the church in Puerto de Santa María floated in front of her eyes. A handsome face … a warm deep voice … already the attributes of a romantic hero for the new novel were beginning to form in her mind. A man with winter storms in his eyes, secrets in his heart and fire in his soul. Spain was perfect for her story; she had chosen it for its people, whose traditions were deep and mysterious and whose blood burned with passion and music and desire. Everything she had conjured in her imagination before, every hero, every emotion, now seemed bland and wanting in comparison.

Alexandra smiled to herself and went to the wardrobe where she had hung the sultana's costume. She thought about trying it on straight away instead of waiting until after dinner, but they had only just made it back to the house with a few minutes to spare and there was no time. She opened a drawer and took out the jewellery box her grandmother had given her that morning. Taking it to the dressing table, she lifted the lid gently, revealing the magnificent gems. Her heart leapt with excitement. *What a strange coincidence to have come across the costume of a Moorish sultana after having been given these by Grandmother,* she thought, staring at the Eastern princess's gleaming jewels.

There was a peremptory knock at the door and it swung open. Mercedes sauntered in.

'Good evening, dear sister.' A mocking smile hovered on her lips. 'Ramón tells me you've bought a marvellous disguise which you're being rather secretive about. I imagine …'

Dumbfounded, she stopped short, staring at the open jewellery box sitting on the dressing table in front of Alexandra. She moved swiftly to it and snatched up the tiara, frowning. Her jet-black eyes smouldered with heat as she glared at her sibling.

'Where did you get this?' she demanded.

'Grandmother gave it to me this morning.'

'I don't believe it, the jewels of Princess Gulinar!' Mercedes looked suddenly on the verge of tears. 'You've only been here a day and already you've got your hands on the best thing in *Abuela*'s collection. Everyone knows it's her favourite.' She looked bitterly at Alexandra, attempting to keep her composure, but her words were charged with resentment.

'She's always refused to lend it, let alone give it to anyone. Salvador himself was unable to part her from it when he was engaged to Doña Isabel, even Esmeralda has never been allowed to wear it. *Mamá* was right, *eres una vibora*, you *are* a real viper in the nest!'

Alexandra, almost shaking with shock, was about to say something but her younger sister beat her to it. 'Congratulations, your scheming's paid off. I hope you enjoy the ball.' Having delivered this venomous speech, she turned on her heel and flounced out of the room.

For a while, after Mercedes had left, Alexandra remained still, too dismayed to move. It was clear that the sweet little sister she had hoped for would remain a figment of her imagination but the malevolent accusations had stung her to the core, making her tremble with a mix of hurt and anger. Should she return the heirloom to her grandmother to avoid any further ill feeling among the family, or remain silent? Perhaps it would be wisest to do nothing: making a drama of it would only aggravate matters.

The matter was soon taken out of her hands. Doña María Dolores had sent word that she wouldn't be attending the evening meal and although the atmosphere at the table had suddenly relaxed without the presence of the *Duquesa*, it was not for the better.

As Alexandra entered the dining room, Mercedes was taking up a seat next to her mother, her doll-like face pinched into an expression of silent fury. Don Alonso was playing with his napkin, looking uncomfortable, while Ramón was murmuring to Esmeralda.

'I tell you, it's just not fair, *Mamá*. Why can't you do something about it?' Mercedes hissed under her breath.

'There you are,' Doña Eugenia announced, glaring at Alexandra as she took the seat next to Esmeralda, while Ramón shot her a quizzical look. José was already circling the table, pouring wine into small crystal glasses. 'Apparently, you've done such a good job ingratiating yourself with the *Duquesa* that you've already managed to wheedle a nice little trophy out of her. *Madre de Dios*, you English girls are quite something.'

'Eugenia, my dear, I don't think ...' Don Alonso began, but Alexandra interrupted.

'It's all right, *Papá*.' Alexandra schooled her features as she turned to her stepmother. 'If it's the jewels that Grandmother gave me as a present today that you're referring to—'

'Present, is it?' Doña Eugenia's eyes narrowed. If Alonso's wife had been simply cold before, now she made little attempt to disguise her dislike of her stepdaughter, whom she clearly felt had arrived for no other purpose but to usurp the favoured place that should have been Mercedes'. 'And what would the *Duquesa* be doing giving the Gulinar jewels, her most prized family heirloom, to someone who's only been here five minutes and is barely a de Falla?'

The insult struck at Alexandra's sensitivities. Still, she wanted to avoid a row, even though she could feel her temper simmering. Suddenly she felt sorry for her father. What could possibly have attracted him to such a woman? She was also rather disappointed in him. How could he sit there at the table, clearly wishing himself elsewhere, making no real attempt to silence his wife, not even for the sake of his own daughter?

'It seems to me, Doña Eugenia, that I am no less a de Falla than yourself,' she answered. 'I didn't marry into the family, after all, and half my blood comes from my father.' She glanced at Don Alonso for a sign of some reaction.

He took a weary breath. 'Indeed it does, *niña*. Now, try the paella. I'm sure you won't have had this back at home,' he said with forced enthusiasm as José stood there, holding an appetizing dish of the saffron rice with all its delicious trimmings, waiting for Alexandra to help herself.

But Eugenia ignored her husband's attempt to change the subject, continuing to eye Alexandra contemptuously. 'As we say in Spain, *al árbol por el fruto es conocido*, the tree is known by its fruit. Like mother, like daughter, I say.'

Alexandra set her chin and looked her stepmother directly. 'I take that as a compliment. Like me, my mother also found it difficult to tolerate discourtesy.' She turned away to spoon some rice on to her plate. 'Another failing of the English, perhaps.' At this statement, she noticed Esmeralda gazing fixedly at her. The young woman seemed to be taking notice of Alexandra for the first time. The expression on her cousin's beautiful pale face was one of surprise and a hint of admiration flickered in her eyes.

Eugenia's mouth narrowed to a thin slit and she was about to say something when Ramón chipped in.

'We Spanish can be somewhat direct. You'll find no shortage of it while you are at El Pavón.'

Aware that her demeanour had become icy, Alexandra tried to relax and nodded at Ramón with a smile. She was not about to give her stepmother the satisfaction of seeing that she had got under her skin.

'I think Alexandra will become used to our ways in time,' offered Esmeralda. 'And besides, she's no caged bird. Luckily for her, she's free to fly the nest whenever she pleases if we're not to her liking.' She turned smoky, sad eyes to Alexandra, searching her face with some curiosity as she spoke.

Eugenia put down her fork and looked up sharply. 'Anyone would think you were not satisfied with your own lot here, Esmeralda, the way you're always disappearing off these days.'

'Then I shall be careful to rattle my cage more loudly in future to make my presence known.'

'Mind your step, Esmeralda.'

'All I ever do *is* mind my step, *Tía*. Isn't that what we all do here?' She suddenly looked exasperated, as if something had momentarily broken through the remoteness she wore like a cloak.

At that point Mercedes gave up her petulant silence, determined that her mission would not be ignored. 'Oh, Esmeralda, don't be so dramatic. Anyhow, we're getting off the point. What about the Gulinar heirloom? Those jewels were to be mine, when I marry, weren't they, *Mamá*?'

'*Si, querida*,' Eugenia answered her daughter, her gaze steady on Alexandra as she did so. 'By rights, they should go to Mercedes and remain in the family, here on Spanish soil, to be passed down to generations of pure Spanish nobility, not carted back to England to be lost among whatever inferior baubles and trinkets you might possess.'

Disconcerted, Alexandra bit down an angry response. Mercedes had made no mention that the jewels were promised to her during the angry tirade upstairs.

Ramón gave a sugar-sweet smile. 'Mercedes, surely you don't need the Gulinar jewels to confirm that you're a little princess. We all know that already.'

'*Very* funny, Ramón,' snapped Mercedes. 'And I suppose you're on *her* side, boasting about her secret costume for the ball, making it sound as if she's going to be the best dressed there.' Her voice became increasingly shrill, her cheeks reddening in frustration, making her appear even more like a painted figurine.

'You exaggerate, as usual, Mercedes.' Ramón took a piece of bread and broke it in two.

'If Salvador were here, he'd be on my side.'

'If Salvador were here, then the *Duquesa* would be too, most likely, and you wouldn't be squeaking your complaint so loudly then,' Ramón retorted. 'Besides, what makes you so sure that you were to have the Gulinar jewels? How strange that our grandmother has never made that public knowledge.'

'Not everything is public knowledge in this house,' said Eugenia coldly.

Ramón cocked an eyebrow. 'How very true, *Tía*.'

Alexandra felt Esmeralda shift uneasily in her chair.

'The *Duquesa* and I have an understanding,' Doña Eugenia continued. 'I do not expect you to understand, Ramón. You don't have the ear of the *Duquesa*, far from it. And you, my dear,' she said, turning her hard, black eyes on Alexandra, 'if you think you can waltz in here like an upstart and pull the wool over your grandmother's eyes …'

'That's enough. Leave her alone, *Tía*,' Ramón shot Eugenia a challenging look. 'Alexandra's come all the way from England to meet us, her family. What kind of a welcome is this? Can't we, for once, at least give the illusion that we *are* a family?'

'I'm under no illusions, my boy. But when have you ever wanted to be part of this family? You spend more time outside the hacienda than in it. Lord knows what you do or where you go. All I know is you're never around when you're needed.'

'What am I needed for, *Tía*? To make this house even more miserable than it already is?' His voice was quiet but his eyes loudly proclaimed his bitterness.

'What's this? First Esmeralda, and now you. Neither of you would have piped up with such talk before your cousin came to stay. *El ruin pajarillo, descubra su nidillo*, the wretched bird fouls its own nest.'

Alexandra looked over at her father, bemused, wondering why he wasn't putting an end to this stream of relentless spite. Don Alonso caught her eye and, as if guilt had stirred him out of his apathetic silence, turned to his wife.

'Please my dear. Is all this unpleasantness really necessary? Ramón is right, we're hardly behaving like a family.'

'And what kind of family would you have us be, Alonso? Like an English one?' Doña Eugenia's expression changed from one of haughty distain to something nastier. 'Perhaps you'd prefer it if I were like your English wife? At least a Spanish wife stays to raise her child herself and doesn't make a fool of her husband—'

'Eugenia!' Alonso, finally jolted out of his lethargy, roared at his wife.

What Don Alonso may or may not have said at this point was not to be heard, however, as everyone became suddenly aware of the *Duquesa*, who stood glowering in the doorway.

Doña Eugenia's eyes rounded and alarm flashed across her face. '*Mamá*, we did not expect you for dinner. We thought you were staying in your room tonight,' she uttered, half rising from her chair.

'Sit down, Eugenia, and tell me how I could possibly be expected to stay in my room with all this commotion going on under my roof. What is the meaning of this unearthly noise? I could hear you halfway down the corridor.'

'Sorry you've been disturbed, *Mamá*,' said Don Alonso, regaining his composure. 'There was just a little ... misunderstanding ...' He gave an apologetic wave of his hand.

'*Misunderstanding*?' The *Duquesa* lifted an enquiring eyebrow, her slate-grey eyes fixed upon her son with a freezing stare.

'Grandmother, had I realized my acceptance of your gift would cause such trouble, I would have insisted you kept it,' interjected Alexandra, looking anxiously at the matriarch who stood there motionless, like the statue of wrath.

'And I would have tolerated no such thing,' the *Duquesa* said in a low voice, but her tone was fierce.

'But if they were intended for Mercedes ...'

Doña Eugenia looked uncomfortable. 'I was only explaining that there may have been a misunderstanding about the Gulinar jewels. You might have lent them to Alexandra for this special occasion ...'

The *Duquesa*'s gaze now fell frostily on her daughter-in-law. 'No explanations are needed, Eugenia. There is no misunderstanding. The Princess Gulinar jewels are mine to give to whomever I please.'

'But, *Mamá*, Mercedes ...' Doña Eugenia began to object.

'Mercedes has nothing to do with it. I will not have my decision questioned on this matter and that is all I have to say.' The *Duquesa*'s stare swept over her small audience before she sailed out.

The atmosphere pulsed in the room for several moments after Doña María Dolores had gone. Dinner was now served in complete silence. Doña Eugenia pursed her lips and Mercedes, though wide-eyed with indignation, knew better than to speak.

Instead, she went into a pouting sulk and was motioned by her mother to finish up her paella before it became cold.

'Well, that seems to have settled things,' said Ramón sardonically, ignoring Doña Eugenia's glare. 'Perhaps we can continue to eat now. All this excitement has made me ravenous.' He sent Alexandra a reassuring wink as he passed the bread but her appetite had vanished.

So this is the family I have been curious about for so long, Alexandra thought gloomily. She could swallow neither another mouthful of food nor her desperate disappointment. How different was the reality compared to her wistful imaginings. She realized now how deep-seated her longing for a family had been: the father she could have relied upon, the companionship of a sister she might have confided in, even a stepmother who might have come to love her as her own. The reality of this woman's contempt, and the other girl's antipathy towards her, felt utterly horrendous.

She thought back to the *Duquesa*'s disparaging remark at breakfast that morning about Lola, Ramón's mother. Having seen first-hand the autocratic way her grandmother treated her family, she could now understand why her mother had felt so oppressed. She could imagine exactly how her grandmother must have been cold to Vanessa, regardless of the *Duquesa*'s current warmth towards her granddaughter. Undercurrents of animosity that rippled through the family were undeniable. Aunt Geraldine may have been right after all: it was pure folly to have come to Spain.

Alexandra retreated into her own world for a while, grateful to be ignored, even though Ramón sporadically tried to engage her in conversation.

For the rest of dinner, no further mention was made of Princess Gulinar's jewels. The conversation presently moved on to a new subject. Apparently, the condition of Marujita's sick child was worsening by the day. That name again. It had cropped up that morning at breakfast. Alexandra wondered who Marujita was and why everyone was so concerned about the young woman and her offspring. *She must be some close friend of the family*, she guessed.

As she had barely spoken a word since the *Duquesa* left, nobody paid much attention to Alexandra. Even Ramón seemed to forget she was there, not bothering to fill her in on the background to this new piece of gossip, though he too said little, perhaps reluctant to stumble into another altercation with his aunt. For her part, Alexandra was only half listening to the conversation, too preoccupied by the unsavoury argument at the start of dinner.

She foresaw that her stay at El Pavón would probably not be without similar incident, and wondered if it would be preferable to return to London before any further unpleasantness occurred. The old woman on the train had sown a seed of doubt about the family and now one certainty had taken root: Mercedes and Eugenia, each in her own way, would be difficult, to say the least. Still, she was not one to give up at the first obstacle; quite the reverse, she had always been up for a challenge. She had never hesitated to fight for her beliefs, or for whatever she needed. Had the issue taken place in the morning, before she had made better acquaintance with her grandmother, she would have had no hesitation: she would not have chosen to put up with such a suffocating and confrontational atmosphere. Except, the very 'dragon' that everybody feared had charmed her, and then stood up for her. An unfamiliar feeling was growing in her heart: a mixture of warmth and tenderness towards her grandmother, unknown to her until then.

Alexandra was distracted by the sound of chairs being drawn back. Dinner was over. On her way to the door, Doña Eugenia continued her monologue for anyone who might care to listen.

'*Mamá* ought to have been firmer right from the start and not let the situation reach this point. There's nothing to prove that the girl is telling the truth and, even if she were, she wouldn't be the first to find herself in such a position. This sort of thing is quite common among those people. Of course, she is very young. Still, if it had been up to me, the problem of this indiscretion would have been solved without all this fuss. A few gold coins slipped in the right direction and matters would've been settled. Salvador's too soft.'

Salvador's name jerked Alexandra out of the haze of her own thoughts. What were they talking about now? And what did Salvador have to do with it? Whoever the girl was, another piece of intrigue seemed to be at work at El Pavón. A now familiar wave of uneasiness gripped Alexandra as she went pensively up to her room.

CHAPTER 4

Alexandra glimpsed Marujita for the first time on the day of the masked ball. It had been nearly a week since she'd arrived at the hacienda and she had taken to having a daily walk through the grounds. It was a relief to get away from the oppressive mood of the place when the family were around and often she went out with her notebook to scribble down ideas for her novel.

Following her usual route along the avenue of sycamores, she reached the clearing where she'd stopped a couple of days before to admire the landscape. From the clearing, by chance, she turned into one of the narrow tracks, alongside the lemon orchard, that ran on from the shaded walk. Further on, the sunken path opened out into a secluded private garden.

There, hidden away amidst a tumbling golden cascade of mimosa, was a single-storey cottage of white stone with turquoise shutters. The doorway was ajar and a birdcage hung outside the open window. To the left, some distance away, surrounded by pomegranate and lemon trees, was a fountain, its steady warbling the only sound to disturb the tranquillity of this enchanting retreat.

Alexandra was peering at the cottage from behind a bushy shrub and did not see the girl immediately. She was sitting beside a basin, leaning over the edge, looking at her reflection in the mirrored surface. One of her hands was playing dreamily with the translucent water, letting it filter between her long, graceful fingers while with the other she stroked the big purring black cat that lay at her feet.

'Marujita! Marujita! Where are you?' called a voice from inside the house. A stout woman appeared at the door. 'Ah, there you are! *Siempre soñando*, always daydreaming. Come and help me hang out the washing.'

The girl turned. She drew herself up languidly, and reluctantly followed the matronly woman into the house, holding a bunch of Spanish jasmine under her nose as she did so. The black cat wagged its bushy tail and trailed after the young *gitana*, the girl carrying herself with a sensuality allied somehow with a fragile, almost adolescent grace. Alexandra had no doubt that for most men those looks, while unconventional, would be both bewitching and unforgettable. Marujita possessed a fiery beauty: long ebony hair, dusky, golden, satiny skin, a slightly aquiline nose and high cheekbones. Her jet-black, velvet eyes, beneath the smooth arc of perfect eyebrows, reflected a haughty arrogance matched by the provocative fullness of her lips.

A vague, troubled feeling crept over Alexandra once more, almost a dark presentiment, which had been her frequent companion since she arrived in Spain. So this was the infamous Marujita. Something about the girl made Alexandra sense danger. What had she just stumbled on? Slowly, apprehensively, she went back the way she'd come.

As she turned into the avenue of sycamores, the faint sound of voices made her stop in her tracks. This time, she heard a man in anger and the subdued, imploring tones of a youth. A shrill cry split the air. Without hesitation, Alexandra hurried towards the orchard on the other side of the pomegranate trees, from where the cry had come.

She soon spotted them, at the base of one of the trees.

'I think you filthy *gitanos* must enjoy being beaten. Do you think I don't know what you're always up to?'

Fernando Lopez, the blond-headed steward Alexandra had disliked from the moment she had seen him on that first morning at El Pavón, was holding his victim by the ear, his face twisted in a cruel sneer. He was on the verge of striking the boy again with his fist when he saw Alexandra. Immediately he let go of the boy, who could not have been older than fourteen. Gritting her teeth, Alexandra approached the pair, making a determined effort to keep her temper. She bent down and placed a protective arm around the lad.

'What do you think you're doing?' she hissed, finding it difficult to contain the outrage in her voice. 'Aren't you ashamed of yourself?'

The steward's eyes darkened. He attempted a smile but only managed a grimace.

'You don't understand, *señorita*,' he said sharply. 'These gypsies, they're a cursed people, they bring bad luck and this one will only learn from a beating. I'd shop him to the authorities but unfortunately the Count and the *Duquesa* choose to protect this lot. It's not the first time I've caught the dirty little *ratero* stealing and I—'

'Even if he did steal,' Alexandra cut in, her eyes flashing, 'no offence gives you the right to carry on so contemptibly. I don't know what rules govern this estate but in England you'd be dismissed for far less.'

The youth was huddling by a tree, his swollen and bleeding face rendered almost unrecognizable by the blows. Looking more closely, she saw that he was one of the stable boys she'd noticed working with old Miguel, the head gardener and stableman.

'Go and fetch help,' she ordered curtly. 'We'll take him to the house.'

Again, the smile from Lopez did not reach his eyes. '*No te preocupes*, don't worry yourself. Let me deal with this. I'll take him to his family. They live on this land, not far from here. Besides, as I said before, Pablo is a bad lad and it's not the first time he's been in trouble.'

'Very well, I'll accompany you then.'

'That won't be necessary, Doña Alexandra,' Lopez replied, and made as if to start hauling the boy to his feet. 'I wouldn't want to put you to any more trouble.'

'But I insist,' she said dryly, glancing at Pablo, who was still cowering on the ground.

The estate manager paused, narrowing his eyes, and gave a grudging nod. 'Just as you wish, *señorita*.'

Alexandra motioned to indicate that he should carry the boy. Reluctantly, Lopez bent down and picked up the lad, who groaned painfully.

They left the shade of the lemon trees, following the avenue of sycamores, and turned into the sunken lane, retracing Alexandra's footsteps. Finally, they stopped in front of the picturesque white cottage capped with mimosa.

'Consuelo! Marujita!' Fernando Lopez called out in a surly voice.

The older of the two women appeared at the doorway, hands on hips.

'Hey, not so loud,' she exclaimed, 'you'll wake the baby.' Suddenly aware that the estate manager was carrying her son, she rushed to the boy, her hands to her mouth, muffling the cry that died on her lips.

'Pablo, Pablo, *mi hijo*, my child! Santa María, how did he get into such a state?' she wailed.

Standing unnoticed, well behind Lopez, Alexandra couldn't make out the man's answer. Marujita ran up now, alarmed by her mother's cries. The trio and their burden disappeared inside the house and, for a moment, she wondered if she should wait to check that the steward made no further trouble for the boy but decided, given her intervention, that was unlikely. He wouldn't dare risk her anger again. For the second time that morning, Alexandra started back to El Pavón, her thoughts disturbed by what she'd seen.

Her relations with Fernando Lopez had already got off to a shaky start. She had no doubt this incident would damage them further. Lopez was clearly a cruel and dangerous man. He had seemed to enjoy hurting the boy; Alexandra had sensed that he was almost enacting some sick fantasy; she shivered. People like that ought to be locked up. She must have a word with her father.

*   *   *

As the afternoon slipped into early evening, Alexandra sat in her wide pedestal bath, immersed in the comforting warmth of the hot water, freshly run by Sarita and scented with homemade flower oils. She played absent-mindedly with the soapy foam on her sponge. The time of the ball was growing closer and, with every minute, a strange excitement built up inside her. Only a few hours away from discovering the identity of the mysterious stranger, this so-called *Conde*, she had to admit she was intrigued. She closed her eyes. The recollection of the deep tone of his voice sent a pleasant sensation rippling down her spine. Her writer's fantasy was conjuring up all sorts of situations for their imminent meeting.

Then something more than romantic fancy unsettled her, and the stranger from the church once more intruded into her thoughts. She could feel his soft grey gaze on her again, melancholy yet probing in a way that had stirred her inexplicably, and the prickling sensation in her spine intensified, moving lower, making her muscles clench deeper inside.

After wiping the wet sponge over her face, she opened her eyes. It was a shocking realization that no sooner had she set foot on Spanish soil than two men were occupying her fantasies. She had inherited her looks from her mother; perhaps she had inherited some wayward streak from her too, she wondered. Had she been so deprived of romance back in England that the attentions of both these strangers had made her lose control? After all, Latin men were famous for their effusive, flamboyantly romantic ways. *Silly girl*, she chided herself, *you're acting like an unsophisticated teenager.*

A knock on the door startled her. She rose, dripping, from her bath, wrapped herself hastily in a large pink towel and went to answer it. Standing in the doorway was Agustina, her grandmother's chambermaid.

'Her Grace the *Duquesa* has sent me to help you with your costume.'

'How kind of Grandmother,' said Alexandra. 'You've come at the right time, I couldn't possibly have managed my hair by myself,' she smiled.

The maid laughed. 'I should think not! Agustina will handle it.'

Alexandra had seen Agustina on the first day when the housekeeper had given Doña María Dolores her medicine, and often after that in the dark corridors of the house, but she had never paid much attention to her. She was a matronly woman in her fifties, handsome, with the golden-brown skin and large dark eyes so typical of the women of her country. Agustina had undoubtedly been a great beauty in her youth. Her hair, black and shiny like a raven's wing, was strewn with a scattering of silver threads and was drawn back into a large chignon, held at the nape of her neck by a net and a wide tortoiseshell comb. Her black frock was of heavy silk that rustled when she moved; a stiff white collar and a starched apron trimmed with lace brightened up the rather austere outfit. She smiled frequently, as she was doing now, showing off two rows of perfectly straight white teeth. There was an intelligence in that face and Alexandra could well understand why her grandmother had appointed Agustina as her personal servant. She followed her to the dressing table and sat down.

'I'm going to give your hair Agustina's special treatment,' the *duenna* said, picking up the brush and running her fingers through Alexandra's copper mane. 'It will leave it so *sedoso*, silky and shiny, that all the women at the ball will be envious.'

Alexandra smiled and gave a docile nod, instantly warming to the older woman. 'I'm in your hands, Agustina. I've never been to a masked ball,' she admitted. 'It's very exciting. What a marvellous idea of my grandmother's.'

'The masked ball has been a tradition at El Pavón since the days of Her Grace's late brother, the Count. She was still a young girl then,' explained Agustina, brushing Alexandra's hair energetically.

'Is it held for any particular reason?' asked Alexandra, glancing up at the *duenna* in the mirror.

'I was a child but my mother, who was in service here at the time, told me about it. In the old days, it was open house to all the European *nobleza*. The festivities lasted a whole week and ended with the masked ball at the house. At the back of the hacienda, at the other end of the garden where the gypsy camp is now, the servants had their own celebrations. It was a sort of *feria* to honour spring and mark the end of the late orange harvest. Nowadays, only the great Spanish families are invited, along with artists and writers, and all sorts of distinguished types.' Agustina put down the brush. 'As for the domestic staff, their festivities now take place later in the year, at the end of the grape season.'

'When is that?' asked Alexandra. She moved over to the bed where the sumptuous costume of the sultana was laid out.

'In the autumn, on the banks of the Guadalete. Ah, just to hear the guitars and castanets! You'd love it, I'm sure. Everyone takes part: women, children, masters and servants, even gypsies. Nobody sleeps much, as most of the night is spent singing and dancing. The gypsies fall on all the free food and drink given out for the occasion. The crafty ones hold their own fiestas during this season: weddings, christenings and the like. In my opinion, they're usually an excuse to cause chaos.'

'If they are so troublesome, why does Grandmother allow them to camp on her property?'

'They've been here for generations,' explained Agustina. 'They were here before this house was built by your ancestors, though their camp used to be near where the horses are now kept. The *gitanos* always help out with the orange harvest. It's good money for them, and they know which side their bread is buttered.'

'I've read a little about the gypsies in Spain and suppose it must be difficult for their kind in this country. It can't be easy being treated like second-class citizens and it must be hard to find work.'

Agustina shrugged. 'The Franco government sees their people as undesirables. They're not the only ones. Freemasons, homosexuals, socialists, Marxists, Jews … they all get a hard time but they seem to survive somehow. The gypsies are a wily bunch, you see. If they're not tricking people out of their money, they're stealing it from them outright. Just look at Andalucía's *bandoleros* in the old days: gypsies, murderers and thieves, the lot of them. As they say, *Dime con quien andas y te diré quién eres*, tell me who you go with, and I will tell you who you are. Mark my words, bad company seeks out bad company. El Tragabuches, that famous *bandolero*, he was a gypsy. And they say his father ate a newborn donkey.' She shook her head and muttered an oath.

Alexandra laughed, delighted by the *duenna*'s description. 'Agustina, how can you possibly believe such things? Nothing but old wives' tales and colourful legends.'

Agustina lowered herself into a chair and began tidying the brush. 'Anyhow, it's always better to have these people on your side. We have a saying in Spain: *Deja el jabalí dormir, es solo un gran cerdo, molestalo y estas muerto*, let the boar sleep and he's just a large pig, upset him and you're dead. It's the same with the *gitanos*. Leave them alone and the damage is small: a bit of poaching and petty thieving. Attack them, try to pick a quarrel, and you open the gates to a flood of troubles.'

'You seem afraid of them,' Alexandra remarked as she did up the cuff buttons of her blouse.

'*Los gitanos trae mala suerte*, gypsies bring bad luck,' muttered Agustina under her breath, shaking her head with disdain. '*Desgraciado*.'

Only that morning, Fernando Lopez had used the same words to describe young Pablo. The day before, old Jaime the shopkeeper in Jerez had also mentioned bad luck. This was a land riddled with superstition and prejudice. Lost in her thoughts, Alexandra remained silent until she had finished dressing and Agustina had done her hair.

At last she was ready. It had taken a while to don her outfit: the magnificent sultana's costume was made up of several distinct parts. First, there was a transparent jerkin that moulded to her body perfectly and was worn under a bodice with loose-fitting sleeves. The bodice itself was made of fine ivory-coloured silk that revealed the delicate curve of her breasts. Over the bodice came a short bolero jacket, entirely embroidered with silver thread, seed pearls and precious stones. Loose-fitting trousers, also in ivory silk, clothed her legs in graceful folds; they were bound at the ankles with a bias band and held in at the waist by a wide belt, similarly embroidered with pearls and stones.

Agustina had skilfully plaited the lustrous hair on either side of Alexandra's head and brought it up into a braided chignon. The veil resting on the crown of her head was fastened in place by the tiara her grandmother had given her. Dangling at the centre was a pear-shaped pearl, resting on her forehead like an iridescent tear, while the matching pair of drop earrings swung gently from her ears.

Alexandra studied the willowy image gazing back at her from the mirror, excitement lending her pearly complexion a glowing hue. Her large eyes, rimmed with thick brown lashes, seemed a deeper green now, seen through the narrow slits of the black velvet mask drawn across her face. She ran her fingers lovingly over the fabulous necklace encircling her swanlike neck and lifted her head proudly, smiling back at her reflection. Her image really did call to mind the mysterious characters from the tales of *One Thousand and One Nights*. *The anonymous Conde would not be disappointed*, she thought with satisfaction. She turned round, aware Agustina was watching her silently.

'Agustina, you're a fairy godmother.' Alexandra rushed to her and planted two big kisses on the *duenna*'s blushing cheeks. 'I would never have managed such a complicated hairstyle without you. It suits my disguise so well, I'm really grateful.'

Agustina beamed. 'You are too kind, *señorita*. I simply let nature do its work.' She hesitated and her eyes clouded, suddenly grave. '*Tener cuidado*, be careful, my child. If you don't mind my saying so, you're a very beautiful young lady. Tonight many people will be jealous of you and *los celos son la madre de la malicia*, jealousy is the mother of malice.'

*   *   *

For the week leading up to the masked ball, confusion had reigned on the ground floor at El Pavón. Servants had shifted out furniture, rolled up carpets, prepared tables for the buffet in the dining room, and chandeliers, wall sconces, columns and cornices had been decorated with garlands of bright roses interspersed with jasmine and orange blossom from the garden. As the evening began, and the sweeping strings of ballroom music filled the hacienda, El Pavón seemed transformed into a magical palace.

Although the ball was in full swing as dusk gave way to night, cars were still arriving. They stopped at the foot of the stairs with a rasp of gravel and young drivers in dark-grey suits and caps leapt out to open the doors.

In the garden, an array of colourful lanterns hung from arbours, dangled between fruit trees, encircling the fountains and pools, twinkling with light. While in the great ballroom, overlooking the east-facing gardens, Doña María Dolores' guests, attired in all sorts of disguises, drank, joked and glided happily on the polished oak dancefloor.

The ballroom was long and rectangular, taking up the entire length of the house. At each end, French doors opened out on to terraces stocked with exotic plants. Down one side, more windows led to the wide green lawn at the side of the hacienda. High mirrors hung between the windows, framed with gilded beading. Supported on marble columns was a gallery with a wrought-iron balustrade where musicians in evening dress were playing romantic dance melodies from tangos to Viennese waltzes.

Alexandra paused on the threshold of the vast room, a trifle overwhelmed by the grand spectacle. All the guests wore masks of velvet, satin or lace, giving them a mysterious air. She watched for a moment as Ondine, Goddess of the Northern Seas, leant against a column, lost in a dream, her head slightly tilted to one side. In her long tunic of turquoise silk sprinkled with iridescent sequins, she appeared to have just risen from the depths of the ocean, her beautiful golden hair draped gracefully about her bare shoulders. A *torero* in black silk breeches, drawn in at the hips, with a waistcoat brocaded with silk, knee-length stockings and shiny flat shoes, gazed at her. Just as he had decided to approach, another gallant figure, Oreste, bearing his father's sword in his belt, swooped in first and, bowing deeply before her, drew her on to the dancefloor. They passed a maharani wearing a magnificent sari of dark gold brocade, who was walking towards the veranda arm-in-arm with a American Indian in a headdress of multi-coloured feathers and a jacket of brown suede.

A hand tapped Alexandra's shoulder. Startled, she turned, almost bumping into a couple of waiters carrying trays laden with appetizing tapas and small glasses of fino sherry. The intruder was a musketeer in a wide soft hat, loose breeches and a leather doublet. A black mask hid his twinkling eyes but she recognized the beaming smile.

'Well, Cousin,' he said cheerfully, 'I didn't have to search very long to find the most beautiful girl at the ball. I told you I could spot you under any disguise.'

She smiled at Ramón, happy to find a friend in this sea of masked strangers, but it was difficult to concentrate on what he was saying. Her eyes were scouring the dancefloor, eagerly scrutinizing the whirling couples from behind her velvet mask. What, or more precisely who, was she looking for, exactly? After all, she knew nothing of the mysterious *Conde*, except that he had a deep and seductive voice. Recalling it made her pulse run faster and her knees slightly weak. Could the peculiar episode at *Mascaradas* have been merely a foolish jest designed to mystify her? Surely Old Jaime would not have taken part in a practical joke? She started with indignation at the idea she might be the victim of some prank. Yet, the more she thought about it, the more that seemed improbable. It would be an expensive joke to play, after all. No, the sheer cost of her beautiful costume had to be proof of the generosity and admiration of her romantic stranger.

Ramón's voice broke into her thoughts once more. '*Madre de Dios!* Doña Isabel has just walked in. I didn't know she'd been invited. After the way she behaved two years ago, I'm amazed to find her here this evening. I wonder if Salvador had anything to do with it.' Ramón peered over the heads of the guests, as if talking to himself. 'He certainly seems keen to move on from all that business, and doesn't exactly shun her company. Far from it … *Dios Mio*, this really will set the cat among the pigeons, as you English say. Both *Abuela* and Eugenia will be furious, though for different reasons. I don't think Mercedes will be getting many dances with Salvador now,' he chuckled, then shrugged his shoulders and took Alexandra's hand. 'Anyway, what do I care about all that? Come, let's dance.' He forced a passage through the couples and squeezed himself on to the crowded dancefloor.

Alexandra's curiosity was aroused. 'Tell me more about Doña Isabel.'

'She's the daughter of the owner of the second biggest *bodega* in Jerez, the one who almost married Salvador. Doña Isabel ditched him, definitely a bad move. He is, after all, one of the most prosperous wine growers and stud owners in the region. Anyway, she married a *Marqués* forty years older than herself, who died shortly after that of a heart attack. Today, she's titled and enormously rich, very much the cheerful widow.'

Doña Isabel. Alexandra knew she'd heard that name before: maybe in the prattled gossip of the woman on the train. She studied her curiously. A mask of white satin and lace concealed the young woman's face so well that it was impossible to distinguish her features. However, something in the way she carried herself, throwing her head back every time she laughed, reminded Alexandra of something, which at that moment escaped her. She could not explain her sense of déjà-vu and dismissed it as ridiculous. There was nowhere she could have met the *Marquesa* before this evening.

Doña Isabel Herrera was wearing the costume of a noblewoman of the sixteenth-century Spanish court. The full crinoline dress in topaz blue, drawn in at the waist, emphasized her slim figure, while her slender neck was set off by a stiff ruff in pleated lawn. She wore her flame-red hair coiled on the top of her head and held in place by a crown encrusted with precious stones. Two magnificent peacock feathers were set into the top, sweeping above her white satiny-lace mask, which put the finishing touch to her splendidly regal disguise.

The young man accompanying her was also dressed in the fashion of that haughty and stately court, with knitted silk stockings, short cape and long sword. He was tall and fair-haired, like the Spaniards from the North, and wore a mask of blood-red velvet.

'Don Felipe, the elder brother of Doña Isabel. A good match for any woman, no doubt, as far as most are concerned,' Ramón offered wryly as he noticed Alexandra's interest in the newcomer, who was surveying the room silently. 'Though he's as handsome as a Greek god and as rich as Croesus himself, he's also a crafty fox. He has a sixth sense for the kind of bait young ladies and their mothers set for him. He has more than one trick up his sleeve when it comes to avoiding the hook, and can boast many a broken heart.'

Alexandra laughed wholeheartedly – her cousin's good humour was catching. 'Ramón, you're incorrigible. I don't know of a man more fond of tittle-tattle than you. You're never short of scandal to entertain me.'

'The things I do to bring a smile to your pretty lips,' he replied, winked at her affectionately and then paused, looking at her askance. 'I suppose you'd like to meet him?'

'Maybe it would be nice later in the evening, but not now.'

'Good, can't say I'm disappointed, *mi primita*. Come, in that case, I'd like to introduce you to a good friend of mine, Sergio

Valentini. He's an Italian artist who specializes in portraits. He saw you with me in Jerez the other day and is dying to meet you.' Ramón began to steer her back through the crowds, away from the dancefloor, towards the dining room. 'Don't be surprised if he speaks to you in French, by the way. His French accent is quite abominable but he seems to think it makes him sound more sophisticated.'

Alexandra spent the next half hour being charmed by Valentini, a pedantic little man with a corkscrew moustache who constantly referred to her profile as '*quello di una dea*, that of a goddess'. She was mildly amused by the pantomime of his good-natured flirtation and entered into the spirit of the game, though always slightly distracted. As they talked, other people joined them for a while, entertained by their lively conversation. Ramón introduced them to her, but Alexandra's eyes frequently moved away, skimming over the crowds impatiently, not knowing how or when the *Conde* would make himself known to her. She became aware of Valentini waiting for a response from her and hastily switched her attention back to the diminutive artist, who was smiling at her expectantly.

'I'm sorry? Yes, yes, of course. I'd be delighted for you to paint my portrait, Monsieur Valentini.'

'*Mais c'est merveilleux!*' he exclaimed. 'When do we start?'

She laughed, and arched her brow. 'Not so quickly, Monsieur.' At the request of Aunt Geraldine she'd already sat for her portrait once before and was in no great hurry to repeat the experience.

'*Mon ami*,' said Valentini, turning to Ramón with feigned vehemence. 'You've heard? She accepts and then when I ask her for a rendezvous, she backs down. Ah, cruel Titania, I can see you're going to break my heart.'

'Well, let her break it over dinner, *amigo*. They're just announcing it now and I, for one, could eat a horse,' said Ramón jovially, slapping his friend on the back and offering his arm to

Alexandra, who was gazing absent-mindedly in the other direction. 'Come, oh preoccupied Titania,' he grinned, moving her into the tide of other guests heading off the dancefloor.

Dinner was held in the vast, austere dining room. For the event, it had been brightened up with ten or so small dining tables, spread with white tablecloths and decorated with carnations and coloured candles. Tall silver candelabra also lit up the room, their flickering light throwing gigantic shadows on the high, bare walls.

Four long sideboards, arranged along one wall, were set with delicate and delicious dishes: Iberian cured ham and chorizos, huge terrines of *gazpacho* decorated with cherry tomatoes, *calamares* and smoked fish, overflowing plates of wild mushrooms and peppers, *jamon croqetas* with *manchego* cheese, and mouthwatering paellas.

Sergio Valentini turned out to be a brilliant storyteller, the lively raconteur *par excellence*. They sat down at one of the tables and were soon joined by the fabled French milkmaid Pérette in her skirt of white-and-green striped cotton and a white bonnet edged with lace. A ravishing brunette joined them too, wearing the national costume of the women of Montehermoso, with its ten richly coloured petticoats that she raised every time she sat down.

The Italian painter revelled in the opportunity to entertain three glamorous ladies and Alexandra was still laughing when she returned to the ballroom.

As the evening progressed and there was still no sign of the mysterious *Conde*, Alexandra was forced to admit that she must have been the victim of a practical joke. It was gone eleven o'clock, surely he would have shown up by now if he was going to? Putting aside her disappointment, she told herself it had all been merely a captivating puzzle, one that had fired her romantic imagination and aroused her yearning for adventure, nothing more. At least she had some ideas for her new hero, she reminded herself, and decided to enter fully into the festive spirit, now that she had given up on her elusive stranger.

She didn't notice the oriental prince, wearing a costume similar in style and colour to her own, observing her quizzically from a far-off corner of the room.

A pierrot in a black-and-white silk suit with a collar of pleated tulle and a bonnet decorated with black pompons asked Alexandra for a dance. She allowed him to move her around the dancefloor, with only half an ear on the eager conversation he was making as she took in the sea of colourful guests. It was almost midnight. Don Felipe was paying court to a shepherdess in a crinoline gown. Further along the room Mercedes, disguised as a bluebell, wearing a crown of tiny blue flowers and a dress with a bodice of green velvet and an organdie skirt, with petals of periwinkle blue, was squabbling with Electra, who was sulking in a corner. Isis and Osiris were discussing something with a pretty redhead in Savoy costume.

Ondine, Goddess of the Northern Seas, was there again. Her elegant back and pale golden mane were just visible as she stood alone, looking out of the French doors as if searching for something. She turned her head. Despite the emerald mask covering her face, that graceful movement and champagne-coloured hair was unmistakeable: it was Esmeralda. Her cousin seemed to gaze at her for a moment before looking away and then disappearing quickly into the garden.

Alexandra was once again aware of the pierrot, who drew her closer to him. 'Soon it will be midnight,' he whispered into her ear, 'and the lights will go out—'

'Excuse me *señor*, I've come to collect my wife,' interrupted a deep, warm voice. Alexandra smothered a gasp. Her heart gave such a jolt she thought it might leap out of her mouth.

The first notes of a Strauss waltz began. Before she could recover, the stranger swung Alexandra into his arms, holding her so tightly to him she was unable to lift her head to see his face. The blood pounded in her veins. She was conscious of his strong, sinuous length against her and the turmoil of her own body as his warmth soaked into her, adding to the heat welling up inside her like a furnace. Her temple brushed against his jaw; his skin was smooth. He smelled of soap, mint and tobacco, indefinably masculine. As they twirled around the dancefloor, Alexandra was carried away by an overpowering tide that left her light-headed, almost breathless. It was as though she were under a spell, a bewitching charm of the mind and senses that had no place in the dictionary of her experience.

Eventually, the giddy whirlwind ended and they found themselves on the terrace. In contrast to the brightly lit ballroom they had left, it was bathed in an almost unreal, diaphanous light from the moon and the glowing lanterns in the trees. They waltzed in silence for a few more minutes, taking in the melancholy softness of the night.

'I owe you an apology for stepping in just now but I could see no other way of tearing you away from the arms of your too-forward partner,' he said, in those same ardent, deep tones that had so haunted Alexandra over the past few days.

She caught her breath, unable to reply immediately and all the while hoping he wasn't aware of the urgent beating of her heart. He still held on to her firmly and she could only look up at him with a smile. The moon disappeared behind a cloud, shadowing his features.

The stranger was almost a head taller than Alexandra. Under his light cloak she could see that his costume was very much like hers. It was in a similar cloth of pure, ivory-coloured silk, yet less decorated. His head was clad in a plain turban, which entirely concealed his hair. In the wide *faja*, the silk band that clasped his waist, he had placed a *navaja*, much like the ones Alexandra had noticed at the station in Puerto de Santa María on the day of her arrival, the difference being his was set with genuine precious stones. His shoulders were broad; his embrace firm and close.

As a shaft of moonlight fell briefly on his face, Alexandra's heart missed a beat. In spite of the half-shadow and the narrow mask shielding his tanned features, she recognized the stranger she had seen on the seafront and then in the Church of Santa María: the man on the prayer stool who had so deeply disturbed her. So it was the same man after all. One man who now made something inside her thrill deliciously at his nearness.

Somewhere far off, a clock struck midnight. An owl hooted, as if in response. The air was fragrant with the sweet smell of jasmine and orange blossom. Masks fell and shouts of joy burst from all sides under a shower of confetti.

The oriental prince leaned his head forward towards his sultana.

'Will you allow me, *señorita*?' he whispered, his lean fingers with infinite gentleness removing her velvet mask. His gaze delved deeply into her large, glowing green irises, reading the emotion in her upturned face as her body yielded helplessly to his touch. A rush of blood coursed wildly through Alexandra's veins as his hand once more slipped about her waist, pausing before pulling her against him.

Softly, his mouth barely brushed her lips, hesitant and yet longing, parting them tenderly and taking in her sweet breath; his hands on her felt so warm, so male. Alexandra closed her eyes, waiting for something more, though she knew she should not. The smiling moon sailed out from behind a tree and lit up their faces, caught in that lingering anticipation of a kiss. The night was perfectly still. They remained thus, locked in each other's arms, bathed in silvery moonlight on the deserted terrace. Time was immaterial; there was neither past nor future. Nothing mattered, only the present and the fire that had broken out between them.

Alexandra was the first to come back to earth, slightly dazed. She drew away from him reluctantly, trembling inwardly, and her face was flushed. A strange emotion overwhelmed her. Never in her life had a single touch enflamed her so; only the slightest gesture ... the feathery brushing of her lips ... but she knew in an instant that the sweetness and euphoria that filled her as she had been held in this stranger's arms would never be equalled by another.

They were now leaning against the marble balustrade that ran along the vast paved terrace. He had not yet removed the velvet mask covering his brow and his stunning grey eyes surveyed her enigmatically with slight amusement.

Her heart pounded rapidly; her thoughts swirled haphazardly in a hazy mind. His nearness was still drugging her senses. The outrageous romance of it all had seduced her. She should not be alone with this man ... this 'Count' who had so arrogantly assumed that she would play along with his charade ... that in hiding behind a mask he could take advantage of being alone with her and confuse her in this way.

She gazed up into his face, her head slightly thrown back, almost defiantly.

'Aren't you going to take off your mask?' she asked, fighting hopelessly against the mischievous urge to pull it off.

'My identity, Doña Alexandra, will be revealed to you all too soon.' There was an edge to his voice but then he laughed softly and moved his mouth closer to murmur in her ear. 'Tonight, let's forget who we are and simply be a prince and a princess from a faraway time, brought back to life for a fleeting moment by mischievous *djinns*.' He looked up and gestured with his head. 'Listen, and you will hear them dancing to the devilish rhythm of an imaginary tune.'

'How do you know my name?' Alexandra asked, her curiosity growing.

The stranger's mouth quirked. 'What an impatient girl you are,' he said, this time laughing outright, deep in his throat. 'Why does it matter what our names are now? I promise that sooner or later you will have the answer to all the questions milling around in your pretty head.'

Alexandra's spine stiffened. She was having none of it. Being at a disadvantage was not to her liking and the stranger's patronizing tone annoyed her. 'You must have heard me talking to the shopkeeper at *Masquarades*,' she persisted.

The stranger smiled faintly. 'If I tell you that I've been dreaming of this evening since the moment I first laid eyes on you, would you believe me?' he asked earnestly, his steely irises peering at her through the narrow slits of his black mask.

'But how could you know that day at the Church of Santa María that I would be at the ball?'

'Perhaps I saw you in my dreams well before I saw you there. Perhaps the Fairy Queen granted me one wish and I asked her to lend me these few hours to live a fairytale. Do you believe in fairytales, Alexandra?' he asked softly, the bright pewter of his eyes suddenly softening and changing, becoming deep blue pools anxiously searching her face for a secret answer she did not hold.

Common sense told Alexandra not to leave herself defenceless against the steady gaze of those sensuous smoky-indigo irises that reflected such wondrous unspoken promises, but she felt her resistance weaken. Desire burned in his eyes, struggling with some other feeling or thought that she longed to discover. She lifted her face to him, her mind in turmoil, emotions confused; the whole of her being exposed and vulnerable. His gaze never left her face as a lengthy silence enveloped them. Then he drew her slowly towards him.

She knew she had to move away, say something that would break the spell, but all reason was thrown to the wind. She stood there helpless, hypnotized by the intensity of the caressing, deep sapphire-grey scrutiny so near her own. All she wanted at that moment was to get closer to him, to have his powerful arms imprison her in their strong embrace, his fiery mouth to claim hers. The intoxication of being alone with this man, succumbing to the strange new emotions he had awoken in her, was overwhelming. Already she had allowed too much. Who was the man behind this mask? What dangerous game was she getting herself into?

His response to her mute request was to cup her chin in one hand and lift her mesmerized face up to his. As he started to bring his mouth down towards hers, a rustle of leaves behind them, followed by a swish, startled them. A black cat leapt out of nowhere on to the balustrade, making them break apart. Alexandra recognized it as Marujita's. The creature stood still for a moment, considering the couple with its elongated eyes that shone like neon lights in the dark. It yawned, stretched itself, mewed and jumped off the railing into the garden. The stranger flinched and Alexandra felt him shudder almost imperceptibly.

She was both relieved and frustrated at the interruption. However much she wanted to remain in her handsome stranger's arms, she knew perfectly well she was playing with fire and now she must control the rush of unruly hormones that had assailed her in a most unexpected and unfamiliar way. She walked a few steps along the terrace. The stranger followed her. For a while they remained silent, lost in their own thoughts, savouring the sweetness of the moment and of the night.

'Thank you for allowing me to wear such a magnificent costume this evening,' Alexandra said after a time, forcing her tone to become detached. 'I'm afraid I can't accept such a costly present from a stranger. How can I return it to you?'

'Keep it as a token of my admiration for your beauty.' He lifted a finger, trailed it gently down her cheek, and sighed. Those eyes fixed on her again. 'Pity, my innocent dove, that it's too late for us.' His voice was barely audible, and then his mood once more seemed to change. He shot her a taunting smile. 'The jewels you're wearing are uncommonly beautiful and also immensely valuable. Her Grace the *Duquesa* must think highly of you to have entrusted them to you. Try not to lose them, they're very dear to her.'

Alexandra was cut to the quick. 'What do you know about my grandmother's jewels?' This strange man was decidedly not lacking in audacity. 'You yourself are wearing a *navaja*, which seems to me just as valuable,' she retorted. 'Just slipped into your waistband like that, it seems to be running a greater risk of getting lost than my jewellery, which is perfectly well secured.' She stopped, suddenly aware of how pompous she sounded.

'You're right,' he said, taking the dagger in his strong, powerful hands, which moments earlier had been around her waist, drawing her passionately to him. He turned it over and then held it out to her. 'It belonged to my grandfather and it means a lot to me,' he said slowly. 'I would be deeply sad to lose it.'

Alexandra took it, looking at it admiringly; it was inlaid with a number of precious stones of different shapes and colours.

'It's absolutely beautiful.' She returned it to him.

'According to ancient superstition,' he continued, 'diamonds give protection against your enemies, emeralds bring wealth, rubies ensure peace of mind, sapphires secure happiness and amethysts guarantee a good digestion. A rich man would wear a belt set with fifty or so precious stones in the hope of safeguarding all these things: happiness, security, honour and health.'

She gave a teasing smile. 'In that case, I presume you're a fulfilled and contented man with nothing left to wish for in life.'

In the half shadow, Alexandra could only make out his profile, but all of a sudden he was remote and haughty. She felt him stiffen and guessed that under the black mask his eyes had assumed their steely look again.

'It's time I went,' he said abruptly, turning to face her. A bitter smile twisted his beautifully moulded lips. 'It was selfish of me to monopolize you. You must be impatient to return to your admirers, please forgive my rudeness.' He paused, and Alexandra saw his jaw tighten as he suddenly looked around him, listening for something. 'I should not be here … *Señorita, por favor*, take this piece of advice: leave this house. There's nothing but unhappiness here. Leave El Pavón and leave Spain before it's too late.'

Thereupon, he moved close to her and brushed her cheek lightly again with the tip of his forefinger, gazing intently into her eyes through the slits of his mask. Then, without warning, and before she had time to stop him, he leapt over the balustrade, wrapped himself in his black cloak and disappeared into the warm night.

Bewildered, Alexandra remained motionless for a while. Somewhere out in the darkness a toad croaked harshly, tearing through the silence. The violins had stopped playing and the light-hearted chatter of guests came to her as if through a mist, punctuated from time to time by bursts of pealing laughter, which she found vaguely familiar but was unable to determine why.

Slowly, she made her way back to the brightly lit room, still reeling from the intensity of the encounter with her masked stranger and the unexpectedly dramatic and cryptic warning with which he chose to end it. Deeply absorbed in her thoughts, she did not notice the man who'd been hidden all the while by the bushy foliage of an exotic plant adorning one corner of the terrace. He emerged behind her from the shadows and watched her go, his lips parted in a sardonic smile.

The ballroom was nearly empty. A few couples remained, finding it hard to leave after such a magical evening.

'*Ah! Vous voilà enfin!*' called Sergio Valentini as Alexandra came in from the terrace. 'I've been seeking you everywhere, cruel Titania. You mustn't abandon me like that,' he added, lifting his arms to heaven in a melodramatic gesture. 'But you're quite pale. What is the matter?' he enquired with a frown.

'I'm feeling a little faint,' she replied, truthfully. 'You must have poured me too much champagne, I'm not used to such treats. I think I shall retire. I'll be better in the morning.' Without waiting for his reply, she turned to go, leaving him speechless.

She had barely reached the big marble staircase that led to the upper floors when Ramón appeared on the bottom step next to her. 'Alexandra, where have you been?' He looked at her reproachfully. 'You promised to keep the midnight dance for me.'

Embarrassed, she evaded his eyes and continued to climb the stairs. There was too much confused emotion in her face that she was still struggling to subdue and she didn't want him to witness it. 'I went into the garden for some air, I wasn't feeling too well.'

He leapt up behind her and caught her arm. 'Come into the drawing room. Everyone is anxious to know the identity of the ravishing and mysterious sultana.'

'Ramón, I really do have a horrible headache. I'm sorry, but I don't feel up to facing them.'

Gently, she pulled away but he waved a hand dismissively. 'Oh, you've probably had too much of José's punch. It's very potent, you know. I'll fetch you one of Agustina's herbal brews, you'll be better in no time.' He smiled disarmingly. 'First of all, I insist you come with me,' he said, taking her elbow. 'We can't keep everyone waiting. Besides, *Abuela* has asked to see you.'

Too tired to resist now, and aware that she hadn't thanked her grandmother for the effort she had put into organizing the evening, she let herself be led by her cousin into the drawing room.

Doña María Dolores was seated regally in an enormous armchair upholstered in maroon brocade. In her dress of beautiful black lace, adorned by three rows of large baroque pearls and a diamond brooch, she fitted her grand surroundings perfectly. Her queenly bearing and the imperious flash of her eyes attested to the fact that she was sovereign of the house and, at this moment, she was most definitely holding court. A small crowd of men and women, bereft now of their masks, make-up a little smudged, outfits slightly ruffled by an evening of games, dancing and other pleasures, were gathered around her.

The old lady's face broke into a broad smile. 'Come, Alexandra, my child, let me introduce you to our friends, who are all eager to meet you. This is your cousin, Salvador,' she said, turning to the figure standing behind her chair, half hidden in the shadow, 'I don't think you've met.'

The young man moved out into the light and gave a slight bow. 'At your service, dear Cousin.'

Somehow Alexandra heard his voice before she took in his appearance. Her breath caught in her throat, her heart leapt uncontrollably and she gripped the side of her grandmother's chair in case her legs, which had suddenly turned to jelly, should give way. The world narrowed, the others in the room might as well not have been present. She met the penetrating grey eyes and held their stare. On the terrace they had been partially hidden from her by his mask; now they watched her steadily, twinkling with a mixture of amusement and curiosity.

Salvador had exchanged his sultan's costume for that of a Basque peasant, which was perfectly moulded to his muscular form, setting off his broad shoulders that tapered to a narrow waist and lean hips. Once again, Alexandra was painfully aware of his uncompromising good looks. Her mouth went dry. Under his piercing gaze she felt herself tremble as her mind went back to the kiss they had nearly shared earlier. She stammered something incomprehensible and moved away, letting Ramón guide her around the circle of guests as though in a dream, smiling feebly at some, shaking hands with others, and trying desperately to exchange small talk. Her mind was numb but her head ached violently; the pulse in her temples beat desperately, eradicating any possibility of intelligible conversation.

After half an hour Alexandra simply could not bear it any more. She could sense Salvador's eyes following her the whole time, though he never tried to speak to her again. Taking leave of her grandmother, she hurried out and back to her room. Fully dressed, she threw herself on to the great bed and, away from prying eyes, buried her head in her pillow and wept like an adolescent after her first disappointment in love. She felt like a fool, played with and rejected. Finally, thoroughly exhausted, she fell into a deep sleep as the small hours crept towards dawn.

*   *   *

Alexandra didn't see Salvador again until the next evening. After a day spent walking alone in the orchards with her book, she had ended up in the drawing room, where they had been introduced the night before, and sat down at the grand piano. She began to play one of her favourite pieces, Beethoven's 'Moonlight Sonata', allowing herself to be carried away by the music.

From a tender age she had shown an aptitude for music. She'd been delighted when her father had given her a piano. One year in Cheyne Walk, much to everyone's astonishment, the brand new Steinway had been delivered to the house with a note from Don Alonso. Aunt Geraldine, who herself played the violin well, had been glad that the girl's father had at least remembered his daughter's musicality and, in turn, she had ensured her niece nurtured her talent. From then on, when Alexandra was not reading a book or writing her stories, she began to teach herself to play, finding some release for her pent-up emotions. Without being a virtuoso, she had mastered her favourite instrument. Over the years she had derived enormous pleasure from it and had gladly entertained friends at musical evenings, a regular pastime in her circle made up of artists, intellectuals and musicians. Writing was her passion but playing the piano provided a different kind of escape and relaxation. More often than not it was at the keyboard that she found inspiration for her novels and that evening she felt growing within her that very special impulse.

Standing in the doorway, Salvador watched her lost in her music. Her copper hair was still scooped up in the complicated braid she'd worn the night before, leaving exposed the nape of her graceful neck. All the French doors were open to the garden and the drawing room was bathed in evening light.

He moved and the floor creaked under him, causing her to turn. How long had he been standing there, she wondered, as her heart leaped into her mouth and her gaze met his. Again, Salvador's look held so many different things but tonight there was tension and a restless quality to it.

'Good evening, little cousin,' he said as he ambled towards the piano and leaned against it. 'I didn't know you had a talent for music as well as a gift for writing. What else do you hide behind those mysterious eyes?'

She bridled under his latent mockery, holding back a biting reply, and merely glared at him. Her green eyes deepened to dark emerald, glinting resentfully.

'I haven't seen you today, Salvador. I trust you've had a good day.' She deliberately remained aloof, determined not to succumb to her irritation.

'I've been riding.'

'All day?'

'Yes, Balthazar, my favourite horse, needs a good deal of exercise.' Salvador watched her face and she tried to steady herself under the intense gaze of those eyes. 'He's a fiery stallion, a handful to ride, a vigorous horse. But he's got a good heart and a sure footing in these rocky hills.'

'So, do you exercise him every day?'

'No, most of the time Fernando takes him out … But I find there's no better way to release tension than to ride recklessly on a wild horse.' The grey-blue eyes twinkled with mischief as he added, 'Presumably when you are tense you exercise your passions on the piano?'

How did he know the way she felt? The way she'd been feeling since she had been in his arms the night before. She didn't like it one bit that he could read her so well.

Picking up her music, Alexandra made no reply and began to leave the room but he caught her swiftly by the wrist and pulled her towards him.

'You know, your eyes are even more hypnotic than your photo.' He stared at her, the fingers of his hand softening their grip, and she was acutely aware that he was only a step away now.

'What photo?'

'The one in your grandmother's study, she showed it to me not so long ago. It was how I recognized you at the harbour.'

She gritted her teeth at the thought of his deliberate subterfuge.

'Alexandra, are you still angry with me for last night?' He was serious now and his gaze bore deep into her stormy green eyes.

But she had no time to answer, for someone had just come into the room, disturbing their tête-à-tête. Alexandra pulled her hand from Salvador's clasp and stepped away.

'The door was open so I came in without knocking,' explained the beautiful redhead. She walked over to the piano, an enigmatic smile floating on her lips, which became more fixed as her eyes moved from Salvador to Alexandra and back again. Her extravagant lilac satin dress had dozens of flounces of tulle. She wore no hat but carried a white lace parasol and a fan. Even though she looked as though she had stepped out of a nineteenth-century romantic novel, she was elegant and undeniably attractive.

Alexandra was hit by the same feeling of déjà vu that had swept over her at the ball. In a flash, she remembered the scene she had witnessed at the Church of Santa María. This was the young woman with pealing laughter who had lit a candle, with whom her cousin had been talking at the gate that day.

'Salvador,' continued the redhead in honeyed tones, 'you must introduce me to your charming companion.'

Salvador tensed. His steel eyes narrowed imperceptibly. 'Doña Alexandra de Falla, my cousin, *Marquesa* Isabel de Aguila.'

'Ah yes, I see,' went on the newcomer in caustic tones, though still smiling. 'The little cousin in exile who's come to ingratiate herself with her Grace the *Duquesa*.' She took off her white kid glove to display a tiny hand, which she held out haughtily to Alexandra.

The insult hit Alexandra like a whip; her cheeks turned a burning red.

'I'm sorry, but the art of ingratiation seems to have suddenly deserted me.' Ignoring the outstretched hand, she turned abruptly and walked out of the room, desperately trying to hide the tears of humiliation threatening to scald her eyes.

'Isabel,' she heard her cousin growl indignantly as she reached the hall, 'you could have spared your malicious comments. That was cheap and unworthy of you.'

'Come, Salvador,' replied the *Marquesa* in wheedling tones, mixed with an undercurrent of reproachment, 'I was only teasing. Don't get so worked up. What does this girl mean to you that you take her feelings so much to heart? You don't seem to ...'

Alexandra was already too far away to hear the remainder of the phrase, or Salvador's reply. Out of sight now, she ran up the wide staircase. Once in her room, she gave full vent to her feelings. For the second time in less than twenty-four hours she felt ridiculed and humiliated. She could not fathom why Salvador had gone to such lengths to orchestrate his absurd masquerade at the masked ball. Surely he realized she would soon discover his true identity? Equally, she saw no justification for the other woman's outright hostility, which she had made no attempt to conceal.

Alexandra went to the window and leaned her head against the cool pane of glass. She caught sight of Salvador and Doña Isabel climbing into a smart 1920s Hispano-Suiza open-topped car. A pang of jealousy wrenched her heart as she noticed the delicate gloved hand rest possessively on her cousin's arm, and the smile he gave her as he helped her into the vehicle. Alexandra bit her lower lip sharply, shaken by the turmoil of her own emotions. How dare he play with her like a toy, while encouraging the attentions of another woman. What had she done to merit such treatment, such a lack of respect? The Spanish man was described as an *hidalgo*, a gentleman, was he not? In that regard, Salvador's attitude was more than a little disappointing. She sighed. *This is ridiculous*, she thought. Her composure was deserting her again. Where was the poised young woman she usually tried to be? She must get a grip on herself before it was too late.

She went out on to the balcony. At this hour, just before the onset of night, the garden vibrated, bathed in a dazzling soft light. The whole of nature quivered and seemed to be making one last desperate attempt to hang on to the day. Everything was beauty and colour. A gentle breeze shook each flower, each leaf. The warbling of birds and the buzzing of insects neared their climax before nightfall; the sound was almost unbearably loud. And then, gradually, out of the west, night came stealing on leaden feet.

In the twilight, Alexandra made out a figure running along the pathway that led back from the stables. Long blonde hair streamed behind her like an ashen cape and her sequinned silk tunic billowed out behind her. Esmeralda. Although Alexandra couldn't see her features distinctly, something in the way she ran betrayed a state of great distress.

The convulsive sobs that shook her were clearly audible as the young woman finally reached the steps of the front door and disappeared inside the house. Alexandra heard her on the upstairs landing and wondered if she should go to her cousin's aid. She had no doubt that a variety of intrigues and dramas were plotted in the secret corners of the ancestral house and, until now, had preferred to keep out of them. And yet something about Esmeralda, her sadness, the sense that she was pinned and encased like a beautiful butterfly, aroused her sympathy as well as her curiosity.

Alexandra stole into the corridor and made her way to Esmeralda's door, which was slightly ajar. She listened carefully; the young woman was still crying.

Alexandra knocked first before gently pushing open the door. Esmeralda sat at her dressing table, her head resting on her arms, shoulders shaking as she wept. At the sound of the door opening, she lifted her head sharply, her pale face streaked with tears and her beautiful grey-blue eyes rimmed with red.

'What are you doing here?' she gasped between sobs.

'I'm sorry, I don't want to intrude but I saw you run in from the garden …' Alexandra moved tentatively into the room.

'I … I … It's nothing, Alexandra.'

'Esmeralda, it doesn't look like nothing. Something has obviously upset you.'

'Please, Cousin, there's nothing you can do. I just need to be left alone.' She wiped her eyes with delicate, tapered fingers.

Alexandra paused. 'Has it to do with that young man I saw you with in the garden a few days ago?'

Esmeralda looked at Alexandra with alarm and her cheeks flushed. 'When did you see us? What do you know about him?'

'I know that you clearly have feelings for him and I suspect you don't want anyone to know that. Certainly not the family.'

'I have no idea what you're talking about,' came Esmeralda's reply. She had stopped crying and was gazing at Alexandra steadily.

'Come, Esmeralda, I wasn't born yesterday,' said Alexandra, though her look was kind. 'Besides, your secret's perfectly safe with me. In case you hadn't noticed, I'm hardly universally adored by our family.'

Esmeralda's features relaxed into a weak smile. She watched Alexandra curiously for a moment. Her voice when it came was almost a whisper. 'Yes, I have a lover … the boy you saw me with.'

'So, what's the problem?' Alexandra looked at her, so perfect, with her hair falling over her shoulders like a river of gold, and yet her eyes haunted and melancholy.

Esmeralda sighed and let her hands fall into her lap, where her fingers began to play nervously with a fold in her dress. 'The family are desperate to marry me off. They keep parading other men in front of me but of course it's no use, I've already promised myself to …' She broke off. 'We're deeply in love but the family would never approve. I'm sorry, I can't say any more.' She shook her head.

Alexandra sat down on the bed in front of her cousin, gazing at her sympathetically. 'I know how it feels to have men thrust at you, whom you feel nothing for. Before I came out here I even had to turn down a proposal of marriage from my best friend. It was a match that my aunt and his parents longed for. Anyway, it was painful for us both, but especially him.' She was struck by the fact that, apart from her conversation with Ramón, she had not once thought of her loyal and devoted friend Ashley until now. *Poor Ashley*, she thought. He had seen her off from Southampton harbour with such wounded resignation.

'Did you ever think that it might be easier just to give in? Marry him?' Esmeralda's large eyes were fixed on hers, intently.

Alexandra shook her head. 'We were thrown together from an early age. For him it became more than sibling-like affection as we grew up. Not for me, though. For some, I suppose, the respect and fondness I have for him would be a sufficient base on which to found a marriage.' She smiled sadly. 'That's not true for me.' Alexandra had always assumed she would find it easy to decline a proposal but because it was Ashley, and she loathed hurting him, it had been awkward and painful.

'I feel the same,' agreed Esmeralda. 'I refuse to marry anyone else, no matter how hard I'm pushed. And while that's the case, I'm trapped here.' Her face took on an anguished, distant look again. 'Tonight, it was difficult ... he wants me to make a decision but ...' she trailed off and shrugged her shoulders, reluctant to say more.

'What does Salvador think?'

Esmeralda frowned. 'Salvador? How can I tell Salvador?'

'But he's your brother ... aren't you close?'

'Yes, we're close. I know everything about him, more than anyone else, I imagine.' She saw Alexandra's puzzled expression. Picking up a tissue, she began to wipe away the wetness from her cheeks. '*Querida*, it's not like England here. What do you think would happen if I told my brother all this? He would be duty-bound to put an end to this relationship and make me marry someone suitable, even if he didn't want to. It's a question of honour, and Salvador is no less bound by it than any other Spanish nobleman. More so, I would say.'

Alexandra shook her head, disapprovingly. 'So he would sacrifice his sister's happiness for the sake of some outdated notion of honour? Do you think he suspects anything?'

'He knows, of course he does. But he chooses to turn a blind eye, for both our sakes. Besides, he already has his own troubles to think about.'

'So I gather.' Alexandra glanced at her, wanting to know more but wondering how much she was prepared to say herself. Perhaps Esmeralda was alluding to Salvador's preoccupation with his revived feelings for Isabel ... if they had ever been fully smothered. She swallowed painfully. Finally, she said, 'Your brother seems to be full of dramatic pronouncements. I got the impression he almost thinks this house is cursed.'

'And so it is, in a way.' Esmeralda screwed up the tissue tightly in her hand. 'The gypsies ... they've always spelled trouble.' She looked at her cousin warily. 'It's not for me to say but my poor brother has much to contend with.'

At that moment, quiet footsteps sounded in the corridor and someone stopped outside the door. Esmeralda gave a start and motioned for Alexandra to be still. Whoever it was paused, then the footsteps moved away and down the stairs.

'I heard someone outside ... didn't you?' Esmeralda whispered, her eyes wide with panic.

'Yes, but they've gone away.' An uneasy feeling stirred again in Alexandra, though she tried to look unconcerned. Esmeralda seemed jumpy enough as it was at the prospect of someone overhearing.

'I think you should go now, just in case. The walls have ears at El Pavón and things are already difficult enough for you.' Esmeralda gave the briefest of smiles, though she still looked anxious and tired. She took a shawl from the back of her chair and pulled it tightly round her shoulders, like a protective shield.

'*Gracias*, Alexandra, for coming in to check on me.'

Alexandra smiled back and moved towards the door. She made to leave and then paused on the threshold. 'I'm here if ever you need to talk, Esmeralda.'

Esmeralda nodded but said nothing.

Alexandra returned to her room to dress for dinner. There was still time before she had to endure the company of her family – and face her cousin Salvador again. The doors to the balcony were open, framing the dark blue sky. She stepped outside and inhaled the air, fragrant with the breath of night. The garden, so alive earlier on, was now veiled in darkness, which brought with it a nocturnal mystery as unfathomable the people around her, she reflected. As she stared into the vast, inky canopy, her growing sense of foreboding murmured quietly to her.

Since her arrival at El Pavón, so many things had puzzled her and her talk with Esmeralda had only gone some way towards enlightening her. It was now clear what Esmeralda was concealing from her family but the hidden agendas of the rest of the de Fallas remained obscure. Why had Salvador warned her to leave Spain? Equally, how had he come to deserve such muted disapproval from the rest of his family? And what was behind the hushed whispers whenever Marujita's name was mentioned? Strange that Esmeralda hadn't mentioned her at all, even though the girl appeared to hold quite an importance in this household where so many comments carried ambiguous meanings. Alexandra could think of more than one occasion when the conversation had stopped dead as she walked into a room. Often, during her walks, or while she read in the shade of a tree, she sensed an evil presence, as though invisible eyes were watching her.

The hostility of certain members of the family, the fact that they took her for some wily schemer come to rob them of part of their inheritance, was undeniable. Yet Alexandra had the clawing sense that these indefinable impressions of danger whenever she was alone had their roots elsewhere but, like all her other unanswered questions, the truth remained elusive.

Endowed with a fertile imagination she might be, however, she was not an alarmist. She was determined soon she would somehow have proof that her uneasy feelings were justified.

Time marched on. She couldn't tell how long she'd been on the balcony, wrapped in sombre thoughts. The evening breeze, gentle and cool, brushed her lips lightly, giving her the ephemeral illusion of a kiss. She shivered; all of a sudden she was cold. Going back inside, she shut the window and finally dressed for dinner. She made her way down to the conservatory at the back of the house where the family was assembling, as the great dining room was still being cleaned following the ball. Alexandra much preferred the informality of this charming space opening out on to the gardens, lit with softer lamps, its glass walls hung with vines.

Esmeralda didn't appear that evening. At the beginning of the meal, Doña Eugenia announced starchily that a migraine was keeping the young woman from joining them for dinner. If some had any doubt as to the veracity of this excuse, they kept it to themselves. Once more Alexandra had the notion they were acting by common accord, as though a tacit conspiracy was going on, which deliberately excluded her. Still, inwardly she allowed herself a satisfied smile, knowing they were unaware of the conversation she'd just shared with Esmeralda. For once she knew what was behind their masks.

Dinner tonight was conducted in stern silence. Even Ramón failed to make his customary quips, and Don Alonso was in his own world as usual. Doña María Dolores sat opposite Salvador, her expression more grim and severe than ever. Alexandra had tensed a little when her cousin had taken the seat next to her on the large round table, meeting his easy smile with barely suppressed irritation lighting her eyes. The young man had returned from his jaunt with Doña Isabel in his vintage car a few minutes before dinner and seemed totally unaware of either

Alexandra's or his great-aunt's mood as he tried singlehandedly to keep the conversation going.

'Alexandra, have you any engagement for tomorrow?' he asked, glancing at his cousin. 'I need to travel to Seville on business,' he went on without waiting for her reply. 'My work should take only a short time. We'd have the rest of the day to visit one of our most beautiful cities. I thought it may interest you and ...'

'Oh, Salvador,' Mercedes cut in, suddenly coming to life and throwing a dagger-like look at Alexandra. 'Can I come? I adore Seville and I could stop off in the Calle de Sierpes and ...'

'My dear child,' interrupted Doña María Dolores, 'you're forgetting that Monday is the day you read to me.'

'But *Abuela*,' she protested indignantly, 'I could read to you just as well when I come back from Seville or, if it's too late, on Tuesday.'

Alexandra wasn't sure if she was more alarmed at the prospect of Salvador's invitation or the idea of Mercedes joining them. However, she had no chance to voice her misgivings. Ignoring the objections of one granddaughter and the silence of the other, Doña María Dolores turned to Salvador and announced that Alexandra would be delighted to go with him to Seville.

'Sarita can accompany you,' she added. 'Her old mother lives nearby in Triana, she's not been very well. I'm sure Sarita would welcome the opportunity to visit her for the day.'

Alexandra bristled. She had ambiguous feelings about spending a whole day in Salvador's company. Despite her anger and confusion towards her cousin, part of her thrilled to the idea of being alone with him again but she was still somewhat taken aback by her grandmother's dictatorial tone and the fact that she'd not been consulted. But that was the *Duquesa*'s way, as she'd already learned: she was the head of this family and ruled it in accordance with her ideas and plans. It had always been so. For the time being, Alexandra thought it best not to rock the boat.

'Oh, *Abuela*, please let me go too,' whimpered Mercedes.

However, the dowager's attention had already moved on, the conversation at an end.

Alexandra stole a glance at Salvador, who was cheerfully tucking into his food, the ghost of a smile around his mouth, though he studiously avoided looking at her. Courses were cleared away and dessert appeared, which Doña María Dolores declined.

'*Tía*, did you know that Alexandra is an accomplished pianist?' Salvador remarked to the *Duquesa*, a smile flickering in his eyes as he watched for his cousin's reaction. Alexandra gave none; she wasn't going to satisfy him by showing any discomfort on his account.

'I did. You must play for me some time, *querida*,' said the *Duquesa*.

'Of course, *Abuela*,' answered Alexandra. 'I should be happy to play for you whenever you wish.'

Doña María Dolores directed a pleased nod at her grand-daughter. She looked at Alexandra for a moment and paused before turning to Salvador, her features once more austere.

'A word, *por favor*.' The *Duquesa* rose from her chair and moved away, motioning for Salvador to join her. The two of them stood in the archway leading to the living room beyond and, as Mercedes began to chatter on to her mother about having piano lessons, the *Duquesa* lowered her voice. 'We need to talk about the company you're keeping at the moment. I don't understand why you're rekindling this old flame.'

Within earshot, Alexandra purposefully kept her eyes level, concentrating on her pudding, though her stomach turned painfully at the thought of Salvador and Doña Isabel together – for who else could it be that her grandmother was referring to, she reasoned? A few seats away, Doña Eugenia pricked up her ears, giving a sour look to no one in particular when she clearly failed to earwig satisfactorily.

'Come, *Tía*, you worry too much,' said Salvador. 'You know what they say, *hacer una montaña de un grano de arena*, don't make a mountain out of a molehill.'

'Unfortunately, you often give me cause to worry, my boy,' the *Duquesa* muttered. 'We must discuss this in private, but I want to know your intentions.'

'My intentions? Oh, the list is endless, *Tía*,' he smiled charmingly at his great-aunt, deflecting her inquisition. 'Topping it is sorting out the new stock of horses. Speaking of which …' And with that, the sound of their conversation was lost as they walked into the next room and out of sight on their way to the *Duquesa*'s apartments.

Alexandra tried to shake off her mood but it wouldn't pass. At home, in England, she had more authority over her feelings; here, she felt constantly baited and vulnerable in a way she didn't care for at all. Salvador seemed determined to provoke her at every turn and she was now apprehensive as to what a whole day with him in Seville would bring, during which she had no doubt he would continue with his infuriating sport. Whatever happened, she must not betray her attraction to her beguiling cousin, an attraction that frustrated as much as it excited her.

That night, as Alexandra twisted and turned in her bed, unable to find sleep, she heard the sound of furtive footsteps in the corridor. She was certain someone was outside her room. In a few strides she was at the door, wrenching it open.

'Who's there?' she cried out, hearing the startled tone in her own voice. The ominous silence of the long, deserted corridor answered her. She remained a moment in the doorway and quickly looked about her. Summoning all her courage, she ventured a few steps down the corridor and listened intently.

Again she heard the soft footfalls, then the muffled sound of a door closing gently somewhere below, on the ground floor.

She was conscious of the rapid pounding in her chest and realized she was shaking. Slowly she shut the door and turned the key in the lock mechanically. She remained a moment, leaning against the heavy panelled wall separating her from the sinister shadows of the house, and then, turning, suddenly she let out a stifled cry of horror: it seemed as though someone was standing before her.

Her own shadowy reflection gazed back at her from the tall cheval mirror Agustina had brought up to her room before the masked ball. She gave a sigh of relief. 'No question about it,' she muttered to herself, 'you're as nervous as a kitten tonight.'

Alexandra poured herself a glass of water and sat for a few seconds on the edge of her bed. Either there had been a prowler outside her room or else her imagination had been playing tricks on her. If it had been the former, she wondered who was creeping around the corridors at such an unearthly hour and why they hadn't answered her.

That night she slept badly, dreaming that ghostly shadows were pursuing her through the hacienda and a voice she knew well was urging her to leave.

CHAPTER 5

They arrived at Seville in Salvador's Hispano-Suiza by ten o'clock. Alexandra's stomach had been beset with a host of butterflies at the thought of the day stretching ahead with him, particularly after he'd helped her into the car with a gentle hand to the small of her back, sending a tingling frisson up her spine. She glanced at Sarita, the maid, huddled in the back, and felt self-conscious. Well, she supposed that was the point of her presence, a chaperone to uphold the family's honour, but as she and Salvador would be alone all day, it seemed a bit of an empty gesture on her grandmother's part and having Sarita there did little to calm her nerves.

Surprisingly, Salvador quickly put her at her ease as they drove through the countryside. He was full of animated and amusing conversation about the surroundings, the Spanish and the delights of Seville that awaited them. Now and again he turned his head to stare at her appraisingly, making her pulse jolt. It was his open, unapologetic, Latin temperament, she told herself, though its intimacy disconcerted her.

They parted company with Sarita near the Golden Tower, the *Torre del Oro*, where the maid was to take a tram across the River Guadalquivir into Triana, the poorest quarter of Seville. After parking the car at the Plaza Hotel, Salvador took a few minutes to drop off a letter for one of his clients before offering to take Alexandra on a guided tour around town.

It was a sunny, immaculate morning, bathed in golden rays, with a velvety, azure-blue sky devoid of cloud. Already a colourful throng swarmed along the pavements lined with artisans' shops, cafés and taverns.

'Where are all these people going?' asked Alexandra, surprised at the bustle at such an early hour.

'Seville is a town for the stroller,' explained Salvador, as they walked down one of the avenues that gave on to the main shopping street, la Calle de Sierpes. 'You have to wander leisurely, with no particular aim in mind. I suggest we do just that, it's such a glorious day,' he grinned.

He was in a radiant mood and she was discovering he could be all at once cheerful, talkative and funny, a side to his character that had eluded her up until now. Whether it was pride, stubbornness, or simply the desire to savour the relaxed feeling between them, neither one had mentioned the masked ball or the unfortunate incident that had taken place in the drawing room the previous afternoon with Doña Isabel.

For the first time since her arrival in Spain, Alexandra felt truly alive as they walked side by side under the shade of palm trees, mingling with the exuberant crowd. There was no doubt about it: Seville's carefree and happy atmosphere was contagious.

That morning, she had chosen to wear a simple Yves Saint Laurent chemise dress, pale green with three-quarter sleeves, held around her slender waist by a wide striped belt. From time to time, Alexandra would look up at Salvador, the green of the silk material reflecting in her eyes, making them seem softer. She wore no make-up and, with her mass of freshly washed copper hair tumbling down her shoulders, framing the delicate oval of her face, she looked like a schoolgirl, scarcely out of adolescence. From her appearance now, it was difficult to believe that only two evenings before she had been the sophisticated sultana from a bygone era, whirling around the dancefloor, an elegant and mysterious figure in the brightly lit ballroom.

Salvador himself walked with the air of someone who'd decided to take a holiday from a usually stressed life. For once, he seemed relaxed, almost carefree. '*Que bonito es hacer nada, y leugo descansar,* how beautiful it is to do nothing and then rest afterwards, as the proverb goes. That phrase could have been coined specially for the Sevillians, I think.' He turned to her, his eyes alight with a twinkling expression she'd not seen in them before.

'It's not a sentiment you can relate to?'

'*Me?*'

He laughed and turned again to look at her. This time the steady grey pupils reflected a gravity akin to melancholy that went straight to Alexandra's heart, reminding her of the way they'd looked at the church in Santa María. 'I'm always too busy, and too restless in any case to enjoy such a leisurely pastime ...' But it didn't last. He was grinning again, she noticed, in that same lighthearted way as he surveyed the passing crowds.

Alexandra took in Salvador's physique as they strolled. She had never had the opportunity to survey her cousin in broad daylight until now. Her first impression when they had met on the night of the ball had been one of height; now this was reinforced as he strode alongside her, towering above the crowd in his impeccably tailored clothes. His handsome Grecian profile was brooding and imperious under a shock of jet-black hair. Stealing a furtive look at his tanned complexion that gave a strange luminosity to his steel-grey eyes, Alexandra realized how unusually changeable those eyes were, varying in tone according to the mood he was in. She wasn't sure whether they affected her most when they reflected the stormy skies of winter or when they mirrored the cobalt-blue depths of the Mediterranean Sea.

What should she make of his many contradictions? He exuded a mixture of strength and vulnerability, candour combined with reserve, confidence tinged with shyness. How should she take his quirky smile, which sometimes revealed a playful humour and at others a sort of gentle disenchantment? Add to this his dignified and somewhat solemn bearing and courteous manners and, without doubt, Salvador was the most seductive man she had ever met.

They finally turned into la Calle de Sierpes, a narrow cobbled Moorish-looking street where no wheels were allowed and which consisted entirely of pavement. It was lined with historic old houses that seemed to Alexandra the very setting for romance, with their colourful façades, elaborate casement windows and ornate balconies. Salvador pointed out the grandest, at the head of the street: the place where Cervantes was once held prisoner because of his debts. Now a bank, the Royal Audiencia's sixteenth-century façade was a dignified mixture of umber-coloured brick and white mouldings, making Alexandra wonder what dark and desolate tales were hidden behind its old walls.

'Why is this street named after snakes? It seems rather odd,' she observed, looking at the narrow and short layout of la Calle des Sierpes.

Salvador grinned wolfishly. 'Ah, one of the city's many legends. The story goes that, some time in the sixteenth century, the children of Seville began to disappear and no one could fathom who was abducting or murdering them. It was a prisoner from the Royal Jail, trying to escape, who dug down into the sewers beneath the prison and found the bodies. It was a twelve-metre snake that had been dragging the children into the sewers and eating them. The prisoner killed the giant serpent and they made him a hero. What do you think of that?'

'I think that in Seville crime does appear to pay on occasions.' She looked at him mischievously.

Salvador laughed, his eyes sparkling. 'Well, you know what they say: the devil's children have the devil's luck.'

'So they say.' Her eyes met his and then she looked away, slowing her pace to absorb the view of the colourful street. 'It's so full of life here, I can hardly take it all in.'

On either side, low stalls in front of intriguing shops spilled out on to the kerb. Shopkeepers sat on stools, idly chatting or smoking a pungent type of cigar. From time to time, one of them would glance slyly at Alexandra out of the corner of his eye and mutter appreciatively under his breath. As a rare foreigner in Andalucía, she inevitably attracted comments and she was aware of her companion tensing, barely perceptibly, at every remark made. His face had hardened slightly, and once or twice she caught sight of him glaring dangerously at one of these vocal admirers, instantly silencing the upstart.

'They have an air of infinite leisure,' Alexandra remarked to Salvador, trying to hide her amusement, 'as if they've been there since time began and will continue until it ends.'

Salvador's expression relaxed. 'Sevillians, like all Andalucíans, learn early the Arab maxim: life is shorter than death.'

Alexandra hadn't heard this saying before; it seemed just the sort of thing the cheerfully morbid Spaniards would use, but she kept that thought to herself.

They wandered through a labyrinth of alleys, shaded by plane trees and purple jacarandas, into a plaza full of quaint eating-places. Above one of the doorways of an old government building, Alexandra noticed a carving in the stonework.

'Salvador, look there. I've seen that sign all over the city. What does it mean?' She pointed to the carved letters 'NO8DO'. The middle figure, an eight, had been represented like a piece of yarn. They paused in front of the doorway and she felt him standing close as he folded his arms.

'That rebus appears on Seville's coat of arms and their flag. It provides the city's motto. The knot is the *madeja* … so if you read aloud "*No madeja do*", it sounds like "*No me ha dejado*", which means, "It has not abandoned me", meaning Seville. The people of Seville were awarded the coat of arms in the thirteenth century after they refused to back Sancho IV when he tried to usurp the throne from his father, Alfonso X. They remained loyal to their scholar-poet king.' Salvador glanced sideways at her. 'It's a legend based on the idea of fidelity and honour.'

'How rare to find such tenacity in a people.'

His chin lifted a fraction. 'Not where Spaniards are concerned,' he said, almost arrogantly. 'Historically, Sevillians are among the proudest and most passionate people in our country. After all, Seville is famous for its Flamenco, its bullfighting, its fiestas …' He paused. 'Everything we Andalucíans do, we do with intensity.'

His voice had taken on that deep, smooth sound with the knack of obliterating all thought, causing her head to spin. Alexandra gazed up at the carving, deliberately not looking his way, but felt him watching her.

She tried to focus. Her mind went back to Esmeralda and the secret the young woman was keeping, even from her brother. 'This sense of honour is so very particular, don't you think?' she said, still not meeting his gaze. He was standing so close that their arms were nearly touching.

'But of course, Alexandra. What is a man, Spanish or otherwise, without honour? The nobleman has his code of honour, as does the gypsy, but at its root lies the same thing: duty. A responsibility to one's family and dependants, to behave with dignity and courage in all things … and to fight for what is right.'

'It sounds positively medieval.' Alexandra smiled casually as she spoke but when she turned to look at him, his eyes were silver-bright and ardent, almost feverish. Her mouth went dry.

Salvador took her elbow and her heart leapt at the gentle but firm contact of his fingers. 'Come, Seville is also famous for its food, and we're in the perfect place.'

Stopping at a tavern, they sat outside under a bright red awning, sipping sangria and eating a few olives, shrimps and other tapas that Salvador ordered. Most of Seville appeared to have congregated there to do much the same thing or to stroll aimlessly in groups of three or four.

Salvador grinned, showing off a flash of even, white teeth. 'As you must have gathered, the favourite pastime in Seville is watching the crowds go by. There is in each Andalucían, and particularly in every Sevillian, something of the voyeur and something of the exhibitionist.'

'I find this carefree and happy atmosphere intoxicating,' Alexandra admitted, suddenly elated by the lively bustle of the café and the strange perfection of this city.

'I hope you're enjoying your stay at El Pavón ...' Salvador drained his glass of sangria and surveyed her. 'After your glittering life in London, our remote corner of the world must seem rather dull.'

Alexandra was about to comment sarcastically that, on the contrary, since her arrival she had been greatly entertained by him and various members of his family, but instead she bit her tongue. 'I find the change refreshing,' she merely replied. 'It seems as if your life at the hacienda is anything but boring.'

This seemed to catch her companion off guard. He sat just a few feet away and his metallic gaze held hers across the table. For a lightning second the brooding, taciturn man she had glimpsed a few times before reappeared but this lapse of self-control was so brief it might have been an illusory trick of the light, or perhaps Alexandra's own fertile imagination. In the momentary silence that followed, he never took his eyes off her face.

'I would like to show you the *Alcázar*,' he said, choosing not to answer her question and gesturing for the bill. 'The visitor at first may take it to be a Moorish palace. Actually, it was the Christian kings who built it on an old Moorish site, of which almost nothing remains today. It's interesting to see to what extent Christianity in Spain has been influenced by Arab culture and by Moorish habits and customs.' He stared at her intently again. 'Do you like Moorish architecture?'

'This is my first visit to Spain, so I've not experienced it first-hand, but I've read extensively about its mixed architecture and the pictures I've seen have always caught my admittedly rather romantic imagination.' She laughed somewhat shyly. 'Isn't there a legend associated with this palace?' She remembered having read that somewhere.

A smile tugged at the corner of his mouth. 'You mean the love story of Pedro the Cruel and María de Padilla?'

She frowned, convinced she had read something about this. 'I thought that Pedro the Cruel was in love with another María, the one who burned her own face.'

'You are referring to María Coronel,' he corrected.

This time she raised her eyebrows. 'Was Pedro the Cruel in love with *two* Marías?' The moment the words were out, she wished them unsaid. Her expression and the shocked tone of her voice seemed hopelessly naïve but it was too late to retract them.

'That's right.' He gratified her with a brilliant grin. 'Didn't you know that in Andalucía, love is as inconstant as it is passionate and jealous? A liking for the harem has been handed down to us through centuries of Moorish civilization.'

Alexandra heard the barely concealed relish in her cousin's voice. *I asked for that, and he's enjoying this now*, she thought. All the same, she laughed, hoping it didn't ring as hollow in Salvador's ears as it did in her own. 'I never know when to take you seriously.'

'But I'm very serious, dear little cousin.' Salvador's voice was even, an enigmatic smile touching his lips. His eyes had lost their steely edge and had deepened, as they sometimes did, into a Mediterranean blue. Gleaming, they held a hint of mischief as they scanned her face and Alexandra had no doubt that he was laughing at her. 'The legend tells of how at first Pedro the Cruel fell in love with Doña María Coronel but she was married to another. He condemned her husband to death but promised to spare him if his wife was accommodating. She refused to yield to him and her husband was executed. She sought refuge in a convent but Pedro the Cruel tracked her down. In despair, she burned her own face, thus putting an end to the accursed love that her beauty had inspired. Don Pedro then consoled himself with María de Padilla.'

Alexandra shuddered. 'What a dreadful story!'

He regarded her provocatively. 'If the preferred love is unavailable then what can you do but seek out another to soothe your soul?'

'So much for your famous Andalucían fidelity and passion. Not my idea of romance, I'm afraid.' She tried not to read into his words the whisperings of her own uneasiness: that she was perhaps merely his own diversion, a plaything because Isabel was not available to him.

Salvador, seemingly oblivious to her concerns, simply grinned. 'Legends blossom spontaneously on our fertile Spanish soil, each one more fantastic than the other. Like I said before, we Andalucíans do everything with intensity.' He laughed, taking great pleasure in tantalizing her, but Alexandra had given up. She would remain casually detached and not leave herself open to any more of her cousin's teasing banter, she had decided.

They left the café and took a leisurely stroll south through bright, tree-lined streets, eventually arriving at the *Alcázar*.

Alexandra was dazzled by this palace straight out of *One Thousand and One Nights*, with its vast rooms covered in glazed tiles. Never before had she seen so many marble columns, arabesques, arcades, galleries and cool, echoing corridors. They walked through the silent gardens covered in clouds of roses, laden with the pungent scents of myrtle hedges and the sweet balmy breath of orange blossom.

'This is the chamber of "*Las Doncellas*,"' explained Salvador as they were admitted into yet another sumptuously decorated room to the side of a magnificent courtyard.

'I presume this is the room where ladies received visitors,' she suggested.

Salvador shook his head. 'No, not exactly.'

She turned to him abruptly and met the cobalt blue eyes regarding her with cool amusement. 'What then?'

He gave her a wry glance. 'It is said that every year, as tribute to their victory, the sultans received in this room one hundred captive virgins taken prisoner in each of the Christian cities they conquered.'

Alexandra lifted a quizzical eyebrow, holding his gaze defiantly. 'Has a liking for this barbaric custom left its trace on the Spanish people as well?'

This time Salvador gave his laughter full rein, delighting in her response. 'I was in no doubt my independent and emancipated cousin would disapprove of such a custom. Did you know you can be read like a book?'

'Yes, so they say,' she replied lightly, trying to hide her annoyance at herself for still coming across as transparent and naïve when she had tried to meet him with dignified sarcasm. Once again she had waltzed straight into his trap.

By this time they had come out into one of the formal garden enclosures, constructed in such a way that the occupants could not be overlooked.

'Who says?' he prompted, imitating her curtness, 'Your admirers? You're a very lovely young woman and I'm sure you're not short of suitors.' Without missing a beat, he added, 'Have you left a *novio* back in London?'

Alexandra was taken by surprise. His question was bold and indiscreet. To her intense irritation, she felt herself blushing and looked away so that he could not see her confusion. The open challenge in his voice was baiting her but she refused to rise to it. They were slipping towards dangerous ground; the last thing she wanted was to be quizzed by Salvador about her personal life. In fact, there was not much going on in it, now that she came to think of it – apart from dear Ashley, of course. Anyhow, nothing of the kind he was alluding to. Shut away in a world of her own, she had been too busy writing romantic novels to give much thought to her own emotions in that sphere and, for some reason, she was reluctant to let him know that.

Mistaking her silence for resentment, Salvador laid a hand on her arm. 'Are you angry, Alexandra?' Placing two fingers under her chin, he turned her face towards him. His voice was soft and velvety, startling her out of her absorption. The steely-grey eyes fastened on to hers and she stared curiously into them. There was a compelling power there that made her forget her irritation and misgivings. He smiled at her uncertain expression.

'What are you afraid of?' he asked gently, echoing her earlier thoughts. She swallowed hard, transfixed by his nearness. Though his skin was smooth, underneath the golden tan she could make out the faint shadow of tomorrow's stubble. The set of his jaw and the line of his mouth appeared softer than they had in the moonlight, the night of the masked ball. His head bent towards hers, his mouth a breath away from her parted lips. She caught an expression in his eyes, vital and aware, as they took in the whole of her face. A current passed between them in the warm rose- and jasmine-scented air. It came like a gentle tremor, as though the invisible magnets of fate were drawing them together, building and engulfing them in a tidal wave, to drag them down into its depths, in a sea of unknown feelings.

The moment was transient. Without warning, he let go of her arm and turned away, once more unreachable. Alexandra stepped back too, her eyes clouding with confusion, unsure of what to feel. For a short while, the two of them stared out at the stunning gardens but Salvador's aloof manner didn't last for long. Regaining his good humour, he galvanized Alexandra, despite herself, into a different mood.

'And now, let's have lunch. I'm sure you're as hungry as I am,' he cheerfully declared.

He took her to the old Jewish quarter of Santa Cruz, a backwater of twisting streets and unsuspected byways, with fine old green-shuttered houses and whitewashed garden walls. At almost every entrance was a wrought-iron lantern; at every window a bow-shaped iron grille moulded with ornate rococo curls. The garden walls were splashed with overflowing vines and through occasional open doorways Alexandra caught glimpses of flagged patios filled with potted plants, copper urns and jugs, and a fountain tinkling in the centre.

They ate a hearty lunch in *Hasta Luego*, a quaint tavern in the middle of the quarter. Salvador knew the owner and although it was already busy, they were given an excellent banquette inside, where it was cool and more private in the pleasantly dim light.

He poured Alexandra a glass of sangria, studying her face and the delight in her eyes as she took in the surroundings, making mental notes to jot down in her notebook later. The tavern held a charming collection of dark mahogany tables and stools, pots and pans hanging from the ceiling; its walls of sherry-coloured panelling were covered with bright paintings and areas of patterned blue-and-white tiles; giant wooden wine barrels were mounted on shelves and displays of enticingly packaged Spanish delicacies were a feast for the eye.

Salvador leaned back in his chair. 'I've been watching you. You seem fascinated by Spain, Alexandra.'

'Yes, I suppose I am,' she conceded. 'My life in England is so very different. Here, there's colour and light and passion. The Spanish have an enviable gift for life and happiness. There seems to be a world of stories on every street corner.'

'You are a true romantic, a romantic hiding beneath a mask of English worldliness. But then again, every one of us wears a mask of some kind … You believe the best of people, don't you?'

'Should I not?'

Salvador smiled wistfully. 'Perhaps. People are unpredictable, the Spanish in particular. Yes, we are driven by our passionate nature but danger is often the bedfellow of passion.'

Was there a glint in his eyes as he had said this, she wondered, or again was it a trick of the light?

She glanced at him. 'I agree, passion can be dangerous,' she said as casually as she dared, though she could feel her cheeks warming, not purely from the effect of the sangria. It was impossible for her to resist the beguiling nature of his smile. 'But what do you mean, exactly?'

His voice softened. 'I mean, Alexandra, that here, things must be done in a particular way. In our country we have customs that are deep-seated and which govern our people, traditions that took root in this land centuries ago, which nothing and no one can destroy. Those ways can imprison us …'

'Only by choice. Every civilized person has a choice and the freedom to decide their own destiny, don't you think?'

'How provocative,' he said, as if to himself, 'a politician as well as a writer and musician. Is there no end to your talents?' He raised dark brows, his eyes sparkling.

'You're laughing at me.'

He grinned. 'Is it not good to laugh occasionally?' Pausing, he added thoughtfully, 'We have a great deal in common, you and me.'

'I cannot think what,' she answered, but was intrigued by his comment. 'We're from unimaginably different backgrounds.' Holding back from him seemed the sensible thing to do and yet she wanted to draw him on.

'We are both trapped behind masks, of course. Can you not sense it, *niña*?' There it was again: a glimmer of vulnerability beneath that confident masculinity. 'You yearn for something you don't have, searching for your identity and maybe even your destiny on this fiery soil of ours. Anyone who has heard you at the piano can see there is something restless and driven in you, another side that longs to take flight. You need to face who you really are, Alexandra.'

She blinked in surprise at his disarming frankness, her eyes questioning his sincerity. It was as if in a moment he had peeled away a layer to expose her vulnerable core. She frowned and looked away. He was dangerous – how fearful and fascinating were the days ahead going to be.

'Am I such an open book to you?' She tilted her chin a little stubbornly but could not help the thrill coursing through her at the thought of how he had got under her skin. That he could make her feel like this was almost frightening.

'You must forgive me if I lack your English diplomacy,' Salvador said, smiling at her reassuringly. 'Unfortunately, we Spanish speak our minds. But you know this, as you are essentially a true Spaniard.'

'Hardly. I've lived a very English life.' She looked at him and suddenly felt like she had indeed been trapped in a glittering prison ever since she could remember, her eyes closed in the dark, sheltered and closeted from the world.

'But you were born and nurtured under the Spanish sun, on Spanish soil, for the first years of your life. We are the blood that flows through your veins, Alexandra. The lifeforce of your passions ... which you clearly have in abundance, *niña*.'

His gentle tone surprised her and she made no comment. The dark, penetrating gaze held hers for a moment and slowly travelled to her mouth. Alexandra felt almost hypnotized as she tried to decipher its disturbing message. The heat intensified in her cheeks as he continued to look at her with ... she dare not believe what he was mutely telling her. Salvador's raw sexuality was overwhelming. He disturbed and excited her in equal measure; she recognized that now.

A Flamenco guitarist spontaneously began playing at the far end of the restaurant – loud, harsh, with a pulsing under-beat. With his long, unkempt hair, deep-set, jet-black eyes and gaunt face, the man looked like a gypsy. His song had a wave-like dynamic: soaring to passionate heights, dropping to a murmur, rising again. Waiters stopped and clapped softly or rapped their knuckles on tables as the hoarse, melodic voice of the guitarist echoed through the room. Like a drug, it was mesmerizing everyone in the place, including Alexandra. She soon forgot her embarrassment and became transfixed by the musician, letting the sound surge through her body.

It was then that she looked up. Emotion burned in Salvador's face as if a light had been turned on inside him. He sat without stirring, lost; forgetful it seemed of the woman who sat beside him. She felt a sharp desire to touch him, bring him back, slightly jealous of the music that had such power to take him away from her. Still, the plaintive sound of the guitar and the ardent words of the song were enthralling her too. When it stopped, Salvador looked at her, the emotion the song had inspired in him still burning in his eyes.

Alexandra spoke quickly to diffuse the intensity. 'I've never heard true Flamenco music played live, though I've always wanted to. I find its subjects almost too poignant, love and death.'

'Love and death are the two overriding Andalucían preoccupations. Indeed, more specifically, they are the two most important experiences of life.'

'But why couple them?' Alexandra protested. 'They don't go in pairs. One is the beginning – the *real* beginning – of life, the other is the end.'

Salvador smiled and shook his head at her. 'Spanish Flamenco is the embodiment of passion. Some people say that music is at its best when wild and unleashed. Flamenco is often like that, heels stamping, castanets clicking, skirts of the dancers whirling … But it was not the case with this singer; he sang a sad love song. Flamenco, and especially Andalucían Flamenco, is a force of nature … like love. The singer reaches deep down into his soul and that is what makes the notes so, as you say, poignant. What do you make of our Andalucían passion, as a writer, as a musician … or as a woman, Alexandra?'

Alexandra stared at him, realizing that he had subtly altered the sound of her name. Salvador's voice was low and caressing, making her aware of the deep potential of passion in this man, and she dared not look into his eyes.

'Music not only requires passion, but practice and dedication,' she countered, trying to steal back some of her composure, ignoring the unnerving fluttering sensation in her chest.

'And with dedication comes the release of true art, it's true. One day I'll show you the dance of Flamenco and, I guarantee, Alexandra, the Spanish part of you will be ignited.'

'I'm not sure I'm quite ready for that,' she said, unsure which part of his declaration she was replying to.

'You must say yes, Alexandra, or I will be forced to pursue you until you do,' he softly told her.

Under his steady scrutiny she became restive and her eyes wavered from his face. She could imagine how it might feel to have Salvador hold her tightly against him as they moved to the pulsating rhythm of the dance. To ease her dry throat she reached for the sangria. 'Flamenco is the music of the gypsies, I've heard. Is that true?'

'Some believe they invented it, yes. They have certainly appropriated Flamenco over the centuries and the wild, exciting nature of the music and dancing fits with their mysterious culture.'

'They sound fascinating, though they do have a notorious reputation worldwide. I've read about some of their more threatening ways, though like most things obscure and little-known, I suppose it's easy to paint a sinister picture and be quick to condemn. Do you know much about them?'

'A little.' Salvador's expression hardened. She could not read his face as he relapsed into one of his characteristic brief silences, his eyes gazing ahead, absorbed in his own thoughts. He returned to her and she saw the dark eyes regarding her gravely. She flushed faintly. 'They're a proud race, with a strong sense of honour ... And honour is, after all, one of the most important things that drive us: honour, revenge, love. What else is there?'

Alexandra laughed. 'Tolerance, decency, beauty ... honesty.' The solemn side of his Spanish nature had resurfaced in an instant, and she was trying to bring him back. It had worked and he shot her a provocative smile.

'Do you find me honest, Alexandra?'

He was doing it again, playing with the sound of her name.

'I find you completely exasperating.'

'So you're the honest one, I see.' Salvador threw his head back and laughed delightedly, the gleaming whiteness of his teeth as startling as the cobalt eyes that twinkled at her, animating his coolly handsome face.

Alexandra burst out laughing too and once again found herself totally at ease with this man that she knew so little about.

Meanwhile the music had died down to a slow strumming and the chatter from the diners had resumed.

'Perhaps we should get some fresh air and see more of Seville,' she suggested. 'There's so much I need to discover.'

'Of course, and much I have to show you,' said Salvador, and to her astonishment he took her hand and raised it to his lips in the same fleeting way he had done at the harbour. He paid the bill and soon they were back in the bright streets of Santa Cruz.

Later, they strolled through the maze of narrow white streets of this old Jewish quarter, under arcades garlanded with roses and jasmine. They lingered in plazas planted out with flame trees and acacias, and he bought her a superb shawl of thick silk, embroidered with myriad flowers and exotic birds. 'So that you will think of me every time you wear it,' he said solemnly.

He spoke to her about his childhood, about El Pavón, and his great-aunt, the *Duquesa*, whom he adored. Salvador had come to understand, and even admire, the dowager's quirks and respected her courage, both during and after the Civil War. It was a courage mixed with subtlety.

'I realized after the war that my great-aunt's cautious stance had been very wise,' he told Alexandra.

'Yes, I can appreciate even more now, having spoken to Ramón, just how terribly dangerous life in Spain has been over the last two decades. Grandmother must have been so brave to get the family through such horrors seemingly unscathed.' Alexandra gazed up at Salvador, frowning in concern.

'Ah yes. Ramón. He sees the world in such black-and-white terms. And, of course, sometimes he's right. The hatred and thirst for revenge that followed Franco's victory here have made the whole country a dangerous place. The de Fallas are one of the oldest of the noble families. We could have been viewed with suspicion and resentment by so many, but the *Duquesa* has navigated a shrewd path through it all. But let's talk of more cheerful things.' He smiled at Alexandra warmly and brushed his hand along an overhanging branch of bougainvillea above her as they walked. She watched a petal drift slowly to the ground and wondered at Salvador's sense of being a de Falla, and what she'd begun to detect in him: that, just as he'd remarked about her, he yearned for a freedom he didn't have.

'Yes, it's so beautiful here.' She lifted her face, basking in the warmth of the sun on her skin, and took in the impossibly azure sky, the riot of colour in the meandering, cobbled street. 'It's as if this place has been frozen in time for centuries.'

When he didn't answer, she looked sideways and almost blushed as his gaze found hers; the open curiosity of it was so disarming. 'Yes, beautiful,' he murmured. 'Andalucía is a blessed place. According to Islamic legend, Allah was asked for five favours by the people of El Andalus – clear blue skies, seas full of fish, trees ripe with every kind of fruit, beautiful women and a fair system of government. Allah granted them all of these favours except the last ... on the basis that if all five gifts were bestowed, the kingdom would become an unearthly paradise.'

'I like that one.' Alexandra was almost vibrating with the excited awareness of him next to her as they walked. 'Tell me another.'

He told her again of the legends and tales of ancient Spain, which reflected not only the traditions and customs of his country but also, indirectly, his own ideas, his principles, his aspirations, his ideals. Unconsciously he opened up to her and she listened, riveted, her eyes sparkling, drinking in his every word, eager to know more of the man she suspected lay behind those words. He was proud of his aristocratic lineage, mindful of the responsibility his status conferred, and was as deeply rooted in his country as he was in the earth beneath his feet. Yet today, he was like any other young Spaniard, playful and flirtatious, and the way he looked at Alexandra confused her heart and overpowered her body.

She wanted this day never to end. Salvador also seemed relaxed and happy. Passersby smiled, assuming them to be newly betrothed, as Salvador and Alexandra shared lingering gazes and laughed with such carefree spontaneity.

'I've not stopped talking,' he said at last in a somewhat embarrassed tone. 'I hope I haven't bored you with my stories.'

'On the contrary,' Alexandra replied enthusiastically. 'Your anecdotes are extremely interesting. Besides, you've given me a great deal of material for my book.'

Salvador smiled and glanced at his watch. 'In that case, you must visit Triana. Without it, your research on this part of the world would be incomplete. Triana is the poor suburb of Seville but I think it's typical of Andalucía. There is no better time to see it than at sunset, when it's packed with every kind of vagabond.'

'What's so special about Triana?'

'Triana is the haunt of gypsies, the home of popular song and folklore dancing. In the days of Haroun al-Rashid, it was the scene of magical Zambra festivals where they danced the "Dance of the Moors". Since then, Seville has become famous for musical culture throughout the Western world, and Triana the heartland of Flamenco. There is no place on earth I can think of where you can see so many bizarre and exotic characters. They are a different people, the Trianeros, with their unique traditions and a charm and wit all their own,' he added, his face alight. 'They have inspired the great musicians of the world. Rossini's bumptious barber, Bizet's bewitching Carmen and Mozart's frivolous Don Juan … all these characters are here.' Salvador spoke animatedly, his eyes gleaming with a singular fever. He walked at a brisk pace so that Alexandra had to hurry to keep up with his long strides. Once again, he was taking her breath away with his unpredictability. His drive was contagious and she felt her pulse race with unbridled excitement.

'Have you heard the legend of Triana?'

She laughed. 'No, Salvador, I think you can guess that I'm ignorant of that one.'

'Let me enlighten you then,' he grinned at her. 'Some people say that the goddess Astarte, amorously pursued by Hercules, took refuge at the bank of the Guadalquivir River.'

They stopped to cross the road. 'The goddess *who*?' Alexandra asked.

'Astarte, the semitic goddess of fertility.' He looked at her and a tingling heat rushed under her skin. 'The Greeks knew her as Aphrodite. She was so taken by the beauty of the riverbank that she thought it an ideal place to build a city, hence the creation of Triana. Astarte's dual influence of sexuality and war certainly seeps through the place, if you believe in that sort of thing.'

They walked back to the Plaza Hotel where they'd left the car. Something electric had sprung up between them now and the air crackled with tension. They drove down near the *Torre del Oro*, not far from the bridge straddling the Guadalquivir, where earlier they'd parted company with Sarita.

'We'll cross the bridge on foot.' Salvador got out first and held the car door open for Alexandra. 'That way you'll have a better opportunity to appreciate the local colour. Besides, no respectable car could survive the trip without damage.' There was an inexplicable look in his eyes as she stood beside him on the pavement. She could feel a strange excitement radiating from him too.

As they approached the bridge, the chorus of voices became almost deafening, some shrill, others boisterous, punctuated by the shaky rattling of carts, the tintinnabulation of tram bells, the flat, repeated cries of street vendors. And over in the distance, on Seville's waterfront, the dismal shadow of the Golden Tower, the old prison watchtower of the Guadalquivir, rose like some baleful omen of misfortune, casting its fiery reflection on the river's shimmering surface in the light of the setting sun.

Alexandra stepped off the pavement and glanced up at the tower, drawn by its threatening beauty. Suddenly a horn blared. She turned her head to see a moped speeding towards her. Frozen, she stared, horrified, at the oncoming bike. The next moment she felt strong arms around her waist, lifting her up and jerking her back to safety.

Salvador caught her as she stumbled against him, her hands gripping his muscular arms to steady herself. His embrace tightened, straining her to him. Her heart was hammering with almost suffocating unevenness. Trembling as much by sudden conflicting thoughts as by her stumbling, she lifted her face to say something and found herself paralyzed by Salvador's intense silvery gaze so close to her own. There was a question in their depths that she didn't understand – that she didn't want to understand – but before she could be sure of his meaning, he curved his hand around her cheek, tilted her chin up and his head lowered to find her mouth. Alexandra closed her eyes, welcoming the shudder of electricity that shook her as their lips touched. He kissed her lightly, softly, meaningfully. She could feel his strong torso pressing against her breasts; his lean, hard body telling her without words how he felt about her.

And now, as Alexandra's arms crept about Salvador's neck, his mouth slowly moved against hers, sensuously to start with before gradually building up into a more purposeful and desperate kiss. As his fire flowed into her, she was seized by a storm of wild feelings. Her innocence feared the strength of her own desire. He was burning through her, like nothing she'd ever experienced before. The power ebbed away from her mind as her body discovered a life of its own, leaping into flames, and her mouth gradually melted beneath his.

About them, the world seemed to stand still, even though the traffic blared and the pavement thronged with people; they were lost in the crowd, lost in their own crashing sea of emotions.

Time hung like a pendulum suspended. Nothing else mattered except the roar of their unleashed desire.

Alexandra's head rebelled against logic and caution. With wanton delight, she gave herself up to the rapturous bliss of the moment, startling that part of her which remained detached, that was watching her behaviour with shocked disapproval.

'Beautiful *señorita*, handsome *señor*, Paquita will tell you what the future holds for you ...' The voice came sharply out of the blue. A gypsy woman of uncertain age, with hooded eyes, hooked nose and unkempt, thick black hair like a witch's, had pushed out of the crowd behind them. Salvador almost leapt back in alarm. The *gitana* grabbed Alexandra's hand but the young woman pulled away, reeling with confusion at this violent interruption, her mind and emotions still caught up in Salvador's passionate kiss.

'What? Let go of me, I don't want to know,' she cried, glaring furiously at the fortune-teller.

But the harpy took no notice of her objections. 'Two paths ... I see two paths,' she went on in her deep, threatening voice. 'The first is difficult and tortuous, strewn with thorns and tears, but at the end of it you will find the paradise all young women dream of. The second is straight and easy, strewn with rose-petals and pearls. A cruel deception ... a castle built of sand. Careful, my beauty,' she rasped as she drew closer to Alexandra, waving a withered finger at her, 'do not delude yourself, do not be deceived, the devil is cunning.'

Turning to Salvador, her face clouded. 'As for you, my fine *Señor* with the sad face, wearing the tragic mask of death,' she hissed, clutching at his arm and digging her claws tightly into him, 'go, go in peace, and may God help you! Alas, each one of us has a destiny to follow and Paquita can do nothing for you today. The die has already been cast.' Then, all of a sudden, just as she had appeared from nowhere, she vanished, lost in the hubbub of the crowd milling around against the pink and golden backdrop of the sunset.

Alexandra was shaking, not so much in alarm at the gypsy's sinister predictions but more in anger at her forceful behaviour.

'Outrageous,' she exclaimed indignantly, though her hands were trembling. 'This is the side of gypsies I've heard so much about … these wild-haired witches who distract your attention and then steal your wallet. It's intol—'

She stopped short when she looked up at Salvador. His face had drained of all colour; his eyes were wide, for a moment, frozen in horror. Then his gaze clouded over and he shuddered as his long fingers raked nervously through his shock of black hair.

'Let's go back,' he muttered in a strained voice. 'It's getting late. Besides, Sarita will be waiting for us.'

'Salvador?' She wanted to know what had unnerved him so much, whether he gave any credence to the gypsy's words, but he merely shook his head.

'Let's just get going, Alexandra.'

They walked in silence along the wide pavement of the waterfront. Still pale beneath his smooth, copper-tanned skin, Salvador seemed lost in his world of ghosts and nightmares. Alexandra's mind, too, was disorientated by thoughts of the impulsive embrace they'd just shared and, despite herself, the gypsy woman's warning.

'It's odd,' he said in an almost inaudible voice, as if talking to himself. 'That woman, that gypsy, she always appears to me before some catastrophe. I remember now … she was there on the road to Granada.'

'What happened?' Alexandra asked.

Salvador half looked up at the interruption of her voice but instead continued gazing into the distance. 'She was standing outside a dilapidated caravan … I'll never forget that shrill voice. "Take care, young horseman! Before the day is out, your pride will be crushed to the ground." And she was right. A few hours later, an adder bit Centaur, my horse. He broke into a mad gallop and I was thrown into a ravine. They found me the next day, lying there unconscious next to my dead horse, and I was unable to walk for a long time afterwards.'

'That was only a coincidence,' Alexandra assured him.

'A year later,' he went on gloomily, paying no attention to her words, 'I saw the witch again as I was coming out of the Chapel of Santa María. I was still an invalid in a wheelchair and Isabel, then my fiancée, accompanied me. There she was once more, standing at the gate, selling some cheap trash. "Feline eyes, hair of flame, soul of marble, treacherous dame," I remember what she said. Two weeks later, Isabel broke off our engagement to marry the *Marqués* de Aguila.'

'How can you be so sure this gypsy is the same woman?' Alexandra asked, trying to sound logical and ignoring her needling irritation at the mention of Doña Isabel.

But it didn't matter what she said; Salvador was getting himself worked up. 'It's her, I *know* it's her,' he insisted with stubborn conviction. 'I wasn't sure to start off with, I couldn't quite make out her features, but now I know. I feel it in my bones. It's like the bell of fate is tolling again, for me.'

Rather surprised at Salvador's irrational reaction, Alexandra would have burst out laughing had she not realized how truly devastated he sounded.

'Don't be so ridiculously melodramatic,' she exclaimed. They were still walking in the half-light. The shimmering reflections of the waterfront's lamplights, which might otherwise have lent the river a romantic aura, now gave it a sinister, otherworldly enchantment that unsettled her. 'What you're saying is foolish, superstitious nonsense,' she continued. 'Surely you can see that? You're an educated man, Salvador, not an ignorant peasant. Don't let yourself be influenced by the groundless predictions of some evil hag whose only purpose, believe me, was to frighten us.'

Salvador gave her a tense look as he tried to school himself, but then grabbed her by the shoulders and wrenched her round, forcing her to stop and face him, his brooding eyes boring into her, imploring her to understand.

'*Go*, Alexandra! Go while there's still time. Leave before you're dragged down too. There'll be no turning back if you are.'

'What do you mean, Salvador? Why do you keep trying to send me away?' Alexandra was exasperated but his urgent tone was also beginning to alarm her, his hold on her almost painful. He looked at her intensely and dropped his voice, pulling her to him.

'For a moment I was mad. I thought, I hoped … but I see now that it would be futile and wrong … it's too powerful …' He trailed off, his eyes still fixed on her, and Alexandra searched his face, trying to understand, her body beginning to stir helplessly at his touch. Her chest was rising and falling, once more threatening to betray her to him. 'That witch Paquita is right, each one of us has a destiny to follow and mine has been traced already. Follow your own. Go, Alexandra! Leave El Pavón tonight, tomorrow may be too late.'

Salvador put out his hand and brushed her cheek softly. He was close, so close to her now that she could feel his warm breath on her face, smell the familiar fragrance of his soap, sense the fierce pounding of his heart. Hypnotized, her thoughts rioted out of control as they did every time he looked at her, touched her.

She stood on tiptoe and finding his mouth, pressed her lips longingly against his. This time they were still, unyielding. She felt him stiffen, but she didn't stop. Again she kissed him and again, softly, lovingly. She didn't care where she was or that anyone might see them. Salvador resisted for a few seconds more and then, gradually, she felt his strong, lithe body stir, his resisting lips move and claim her mouth in a passionate, fierce, desperate kiss. He held her tightly, crushing her against him, and she clung to him, dizzy and limp, eyes closed, her body vibrating to the furious rhythm of his need. Finally, he let go of her. Silently they stared at each other. His brows pulled together but otherwise his pale, handsome face remained expressionless.

*   *   *

As twilight fell on the city they picked up Sarita at the tram station. Salvador was generally a cautious driver but tonight he raced the car along the road out of Seville recklessly, as if they were being pursued by the devil himself, and in half the usual time the great wrought-iron gates were in view.

They turned into the drive of El Pavón. Barely a word had passed between them throughout the journey and, by now, the gloomy mood of the last few hours had caught up with Alexandra. She looked out into the night. Shadows of the stooping willow trees loomed on either side of the gravelled lane. In the moonlight, she could imagine their branches shedding lamenting tears into the opaque waters of the canal that irrigated the gardens and orchards of the hacienda. As they drove past, startled night birds flew up with mournful cries and insects, attracted by the light of the headlamps, hurled themselves pitifully at the car's windows.

Finally, at the turn of a corner, the ancient residence appeared at the end of the driveway, its imposing silhouette outlined against the horizon. Salvador pulled up a few yards from the house as someone came out of the shadows and rushed up to the car: it was Esmeralda. She snatched the door open and leant in towards her brother.

'Quickly, Salvador,' she uttered breathlessly. 'It's as you feared. It happened tonight, I'm sorry.' Esmeralda touched her brother's arm as he leapt out of the car, his expression bleak. 'You must go to her straight away. She's already there and they're waiting for you to start the ceremony. They're angry, they seem to think that this is God's revenge.'

'Revenge.' Salvador repeated the word emptily.

'Yes, because in their eyes you're guilty of a sin that you haven't tried to atone for.'

Forgetting Alexandra, brother and sister hurried off towards the back of the house. The young woman was standing there, wondering whether or not to follow them, when she was startled by a voice behind her.

'Doña Alexandra? Just the person I was coming to see … What a marvellous coincidence!'

It always gave her a nasty jolt to see the steward; he had the uncanny habit of appearing out of the blue.

'Good evening, Fernando,' she said shortly. 'What do you want?'

His smile was sly. 'I've come to offer my services, dear *señorita*.'

'Thank you, Fernando, but I don't need your services,' she retorted, starting to walk away.

The man regarded her speculatively. 'Allow me to contradict you,' he went on smoothly. 'I think that tonight you may need them more than ever.'

She turned to face him. 'Excuse me? Explain yourself,' she said, raising her voice a fraction in an attempt to sound authoritative.

Fernando Lopez appeared to consider her question. '*Patience, and shuffle the cards*, says an old proverb of ours,' he jeered. 'Keep calm, dear *señorita*.' He smirked, looking her up and down shamelessly. 'Forgive me if I bring this matter up. Your moonlight tête-à-tête with our beloved Count on the night of the masked ball was very touching. I feel it's only right to fill you in on what's really going on at El Pavón. My duty, in fact.'

Alexandra was angry and shocked at the idea of having been spied upon but she tried to keep her expression even.

She wasn't about to give the man the satisfaction of acknowledging what he was suggesting, or enter into a discussion with him about her affairs. Still, her patience was wearing thin at his blatant impertinence.

'I really can't see what you're driving at.' She turned away from him and started to make her way back to the house.

'I'm getting there, I assure you ...' His oily tone made her shudder but she kept walking. 'Come with me. We're going there together, right away.' Lopez caught up with her in two strides and seized her arm.

'How dare you! Let go of me, you scoundrel,' she flared, pushing him violently away. 'I don't understand your ridiculous riddles and I'd be grateful if you didn't involve me in your nasty little schemes. I warn you, if you persist in bothering me, I shall go to Don Salvador himself.'

'At this time, His Grace has more important fish to fry, *señorita*.' Lopez sneered insolently. 'He's paying for his acts of foolishness. We say in Spain: *The stink is still worse for the stirring.* There's been a big stink and an even bigger stirring and, trust me, the price is always high when gypsies are involved. You're deluding yourself, *señorita*, if you think you have any chance of worming yourself into his affections,' he scoffed as he watched her stride off towards the house. '*El Caballero de la Triste Figura* is up to his neck in the mess he's created.'

Alexandra was seething. Once in her room she paced furiously up and down for a good ten minutes, her eyes flashing with fury. She could feel a rising anguish that choked her. From the start, she had suspected Salvador was involved in some dramatic intrigue and she had promised herself to stay out of his private affairs, frustrating though it was not to know the truth. Whatever happened, these family troubles didn't concern her in any way. Yet she couldn't forget the harrowed expression on his face during their journey back from Seville. It was clear from the evening's events, and from Fernando Lopez's words, that he was threatened by some imminent danger. What should she do? Suddenly all caution, as well as her resolution to keep out of his affairs, gave way to a different feeling. An unknown emotion was driving her to his side; stronger than her instinct for self-preservation, greater and warmer than any sentiment she could remember. Her dilemma had evaporated.

Alexandra hastily threw the shawl Salvador had bought her that afternoon over her head and hurried out. At the front door, she hesitated briefly before deciding on which direction to take. Following her instinct, she rounded the house and went towards the far end of the back garden, where Agustina had told her the gypsies had their camp. As she moved across the lawns and past the groves, away from the hacienda, she could hear the sound of drums beating faintly in the distance. She stopped to listen, trying to work out how far away they were.

'I thought it wouldn't be long before your curiosity triumphed over your prim and proper upbringing,' Lopez breathed into her ear. She jumped at his reappearance behind her and shuddered with disgust as she felt his moist, hot breath on her neck.

'Leave me alone!' she snapped furiously, quickening her step along the path to escape him.

'Don't worry,' he shouted after her, his crackling laugh resounding in the night. 'I haven't the slightest intention of attending that mournful ceremony. Have fun, pretty *señorita*.'

Alexandra hurried past the groves and veered right at the cypress and sycamore trees, hoping the steward would not follow her. Finally, she reached the lower edge of the garden, which was fenced off. Slipping through the gate to the towpath beyond, she could hear distinctly now the sound of hands clapping rhythmically to guitars, drums and clicking castanets, punctuated at intervals by a monotonous chanting.

Alexandra crossed the small wooden bridge over the canal and suddenly the terrain dropped; there, below, encircled by rocky crags, spread a wide expanse of rough open ground. Starting towards it down a steep path, at the bottom she found herself in a small, arid valley dotted with the odd fig tree and knolls of hard clay, which nature had carved out into caves. She had the impression of being on the edge of an enchanted clearing, the den of some mythical creatures perhaps, illuminated by the glare of a huge campfire.

In the flickering light of the flames, old crones with lined faces sat at the entrance to their dens. Plump women, bare-breasted, nursed their babies; others, armed with enormous wooden spoons, lethargically stirred a gelatinous liquid contained in huge, black pots suspended above primitive stoves. She passed bright-eyed urchins squatting on the bare earth, poking the fire and fanning the blaze. Further away, coppery-skinned girls, barely out of adolescence, sang and danced to the frenzied rhythm of outlandish instruments. They wore brightly coloured skirts, with gold pendants in their ears and numerous clanking bracelets on their ankles and wrists. Bearded men with great manes of hair, sunburnt faces and enormous bushy eyebrows hiccoughed and laughed noisily, while mangy, lean-looking dogs prowled furtively in the shadows on the lookout for bones.

Alexandra had drawn her shawl over her head and no one paid her any notice, though her heart was hammering in her chest as she slowly walked through the camp. It was then that she caught sight of a crowd of gypsies gathered at the wide entrance to one of the caves, a hundred yards away from where she was standing. Unlike the others, this one glowed with flickering light. Alexandra carefully weaved her way through the cluster of people, trying not to draw attention to herself. Several of the gypsies were carrying candles, the ends of which were wrapped in paper, careful not to let the wax drip on to their hands. Salvador stood at the entrance to the cave, his face pale and drawn. Beside him was Esmeralda, stiffly upright, her mouth grave, her beautiful blonde hair partially concealed by a large silk shawl.

Further inside the entrance, men were crouched on the ground, drinking wine from goatskin gourds. One tall, hawk-eyed *gitano*, a scar deeply etched down the side of his face, was perched on a rock, sharpening a short-bladed knife with a stone and taking rough swigs of wine. Suddenly, the gypsies got up and started to dance. Their singing was a sort of raucous chant on a monotone, accompanied by castanets, the clapping of hands and the rhythmic tapping together of two stones. Then, as the men drew back into the shadows, the women came forward, forming a wild circle around an open coffin. Their sinuous bodies, wrapped in flowing loose dresses, wriggled in the eerie glow of the flames. They were swaying their hips like witches at an incantation and Alexandra half expected to see black cats appear at any moment, clinging to their backs with raised fur.

A trickle of gypsies went in and out of the cave as the chanting droned on. Alexandra took a deep breath and made her way closer to the entrance. The air was laden with smoke, the pungent smell of sweat and the nauseatingly sweet fragrance of dying flowers.

The coffin was decorated with camellias and surrounded by candles; inside lay a baby. At first, Alexandra thought he was sleeping, for his cheeks and lips, far from being livid, had a carmine hue to them as if they'd been unnaturally reddened. She stood there, horrified, staring at the little mite who lay in the wooden box, oblivious to the absurd orgy of shouting, dancing and stamping feet surrounding him.

A man pushed by her to get to the coffin, holding a gourd of wine in his hand; it was the scarred knife-sharpener. Alexandra froze and pulled her shawl closer around her head as he stared straight at her, eyes narrowing. At the crescendo of the chanting, the *gitano*'s blurry eyes shifted. He swallowed several mouthfuls and then, holding the gourd over the tiny body, sprinkled the child's face with the potent liquid, smudging the make-up. Tears ran down the infant's cheeks, making him look like some pathetic clown. This was greeted with cries of '*Olé*' and the capering and wild dancing started all over again. Alexandra let out the breath she had been holding.

Suddenly, Marujita appeared, twisting her youthful body and swaying her hips as her feet beat the clay earth in a continuous, frenzied rhythm. She moved her arms gracefully, turning her head from left to right, swinging her jet-black hair, which fell in disarray over her perspiring face. Her movements were so abandoned, so frenzied, that she seemed possessed by some cabalistic spell.

Alexandra felt as if she was in the midst of some hellish nightmare. Never would she have believed such barbarity existed; this spectacle went beyond the bounds of her imagination. It amazed her that only a matter of weeks ago, she'd been in England where life had been so much more civilized, so much simpler.

'Don't feel sorry for the child,' said a voice behind her. 'He's up there, in paradise, with the angels. He's lucky to have gone there so soon. What future is there for a bastard half-caste, born of a union between a *gajo* and a *Calés*?'

Alexandra turned sharply to meet the dark eyes of Paquita, the old woman from Triana, peering at her. 'And now,' went on the ragged gypsy as she took the young woman's hand, 'you, too, must dance the *Abejorro*, the bee dance. Do exactly as I do, and take care not to stop buzzing during the dance or else you'll die before the year's out.'

By then Alexandra was so taken aback by this bizarre ceremony and the old woman's sudden reappearance that this pronouncement barely made her flinch. Already the rhythm of the music had begun to accelerate and the guests had started to join hands around the coffin. Humming, they circled it, imitating the sound of bees.

Alexandra let herself be drawn into the dance. Her eyes scanned the alien gypsy faces, looking for Salvador. She spotted him holding Esmeralda's hand in the circle of guests, mechanically enacting the movements required by the strange ritual. He seemed to have aged astonishingly in the space of a few hours. Deep black shadows were visible beneath his stunned eyes and his ashen face had grown hollow. Esmeralda was holding his arm as if he needed her to guide him, and she kept giving him anxious glances. Why was he there, Alexandra wondered as she followed the steps of the circling *gitanos*, and how had he become mixed up with this wandering race? Salvador was the master here and they lived on his land, obligated to him for his generosity. Yet, somehow, these people and their curious superstitions seemed to have an extraordinary hold over him.

The bee dance came to an end. It appeared to mark the final stage of the ceremony and the gypsies were starting to disperse. As was her custom, Paquita had vanished into thin air. Even Esmeralda was no longer to be seen. Only Salvador remained, standing beside the small coffin, a tragic picture of grief.

Alexandra deliberated for a moment, wondering if she should slip out now without revealing herself, but she couldn't bear to see him with that pained look, whatever lay behind it. She wanted to hold him, and go on holding him to take away his pain but she knew she could not. Wrestling with her own fear and bewilderment, she approached him and tentatively laid a hand on his arm. Salvador started out of his torpor.

'*Madre de Dios*, what are you doing here?' he cried, aware of her presence for the first time. 'Can't you leave me alone?'

Then, turning to face her, he took her roughly by the shoulders and shook her brutally. 'Go, Alexandra, *go!*' His tone was almost savage. 'You're in danger here, don't you understand? If you have any sense at all, girl, go ...'

'*No escuchaste lo que dijo el Señor Inglés, chica?* Didn't you hear what the *Señor* said, English girl?' croaked a medusa in rags, who had just lurched into the cave. She was not particularly old, but life hadn't treated her well and her face held a kind of madness in it. Her eyes were feverish-looking as she stared at Alexandra, her hands compulsively flicking at the air as if swatting invisible flies. 'Yes, we know who you are. We *Calés* know everything that goes on. What are you doing here anyway, in this land so at odds with yourself? In your country of ice, one love consoles another, one lover replaces another ... feelings are light as the breeze, they pass and are soon forgotten.' She flicked her hands again and pushed at her unruly matted hair. 'Here it is the opposite. Our earth is like a volcano, it is a violent and bloody land, ruled by savage passions and cruel laws, and we are made in the image of our land.'

For a moment the crone gazed at Alexandra intently. 'Be careful the heat of our sun does not burn you.' Then she jerked her head dismissively. 'Go, pale *señorita!*' In the silence of the night, her shout echoed like thunder through the whole valley. 'Go back to your country of mists before the ground gives way under your feet and the erupting volcano swallows you up forever in its smoking lava.'

Added to Salvador's harsh words, this hysterical outburst of gibberish proved too much for Alexandra. Holding her hands to her ears, blinded by the tears that streamed down her cheeks, she ran towards the house while the shrew was still shouting oaths and warnings, and didn't stop until she'd reached her room.

She found Agustina seated beside the bed, waiting for her, an anxious expression creasing her usually cheerful face.

'I knew you would find out. You shouldn't have gone there, my child,' she remonstrated as Alexandra collapsed into her arms.

'Why, Agustina? … Why was he there? … And why does he put up with all of it?' she sobbed.

'It's a long story, *niña*,' said the servant as she poured some sort of herbal brew out of a teapot standing on the night table. 'Here, drink this and come and lie down on your bed. Agustina will try to help you understand.'

Alexandra did as she was told and gulped down the aromatic infusion that the housekeeper had handed her.

'You'll soon feel better.' Agustina helped Alexandra get ready for bed before sitting herself down at the young woman's bedside to begin her tale.

'Four years ago, Don Salvador became engaged to the very beautiful and rich Doña Isabel Herrera, whom you've met, I believe. Her father, Don Vincente Herrera, is a big wine merchant and owner of one of the largest *bodegas* in Andalucía. Both were young, handsome and had a great deal of money, which made them the envy of many people in their circle.

'A great ball was given to celebrate their engagement and everyone was talking about their being a perfect match. However, even though the old proverb says, *Marriages are made in heaven*, this one, it seems, was not to be. Some would say it was all for the better. Who knows? Perhaps it was but it's too soon to judge. The fire is not yet out and, even if it is, the cinders are still hot.'

Alexandra's heart gave an agonizing twist. Was Agustina inferring that Salvador still had feelings for Isabel? Perhaps the flame had already rekindled and it was only a matter of time before this ideal union was reforged. She desperately wanted to know but, for now, said nothing.

Agustina continued. 'A few months before the wedding, Don Salvador went to Granada to buy a new horse. He was brought home with a fractured pelvis and other injuries to his spine, which left him paralysed from the waist downwards. They said he would never walk again.

'Well, Doña Isabel visited less frequently after that. One day, out of the blue, we learned from the newspapers that she'd married the *Marqués* de Aguila. A titled man, for sure, respected in the whole of Spain, but nevertheless one almost three times her age, riddled with gout and arthritis. *Ay, qué vergüenza*, what a shame for our poor Don Salvador.' Agustina shook her head sadly and tutted as if the tragedy had befallen the young man only yesterday.

'Our Count was heartbroken and slipped into a deep depression. Doña María Dolores had lost all hope for him when a gypsy woman came to the gates of El Pavón and asked to speak to her. She was apparently part of the camp the *Duquesa* had allowed on the grounds. The *gitana* explained that her daughter, Marujita, possessed the *gracia de mano*, a healing power, and she had come to the hacienda to offer her services to the young Master.'

Mere superstition, Alexandra thought privately. Nevertheless, she interrupted Agustina. 'What exactly is this healing power?'

'Some people believe that a woman who has this power can rub life again into any creature, human or animal. Only one woman in two thousand has the power and she is born with a perfect caul covering her head and face. You know, some sea captains keep such preserved things in a jar on board their ship as a good-luck charm to protect them from shipwreck.

'Anyway, Her Grace, who'd tried every remedy without success, agreed to allow Consuelo and her daughter Marujita to try their cure on her nephew. Consuelo was a crafty one and Marujita, in spite of her young age, was already as provocative as a *lumiasca*, a harlot, with the looks of a goddess. Since her early teens, she'd hung around a good few street corners.' Agustina crossed herself and held up her hands. 'May God in heaven forgive me but they were like a couple of *cabronas putas*, pimped whores, those two, the way they came to the house, with the mother offering the daughter up for her services.

'Yet the magic in her hands worked the miracle. Not only did our young Count begin to live again but also he gradually began to walk. A year later he was riding around the estate on horseback and, *madre de Dios*, Marujita was carrying a child.'

Alexandra smothered a gasp. 'Oh God, the baby was his!' she whispered.

Agustina nodded, her hand on her chest. 'Sick with remorse, Don Salvador wanted to marry the girl but Doña María Dolores fiercely opposed this and rightly so. Finally, after many clashes between them, the *Duquesa* was able at least to prove to him that he had not been the first victim of the young gypsy's schemings. She could understand his being grateful to Marujita and, if he could not do without her, she would turn a blind eye to the girl remaining his mistress, but as for marrying her ...' Agustina shook her head.

'Consuelo and her daughter moved into the lodge at the bottom of the garden. The *Duque* had used it as a study while writing his memoirs. They knew this was a good set-up for those two, a bit of easy money. Some gypsies wander about and return to their camps from time to time, but others like four walls and a roof above their heads. Several months later, Marujita gave birth. From the start it was plain to see the little thing wasn't going to live long. The girl sensed that Don Salvador was slipping from her grasp. She panicked and began a campaign of quarrels and threats, stirring up trouble.

'Her brothers, who up until that time had stayed conveniently in the shadows, now suddenly came forward. They spoke of rape and duels with knives at dawn, for their sister's lost honour. It was all a cruel game but, nevertheless, one that could cause embarrassment and shame for the young Master's family. In principle, gypsies detest marriages between their people and *gajos*. In this case, Marujita had been granted a special permission from her *crayí*, or king, because of her status as a *curandera*, healer, and other powers of sorcery they claimed she had.'

The old maid sighed. 'Now, the Count is good and generous but he doesn't like his hand to be forced. Perhaps if the girl had gone about it in a different way, perhaps if the *Marqués* de Aguila hadn't died just at that time, freeing Doña Isabel ... or if Don Salvador hadn't seen your photo in his great-aunt's study. Yes, your *Duquesa* noticed his reaction – your grandmother is no fool – then it might have been otherwise. But I doubt it.' Agustina glanced knowingly at Alexandra as she spoke. 'The fact remains that, for whatever reason, Don Salvador decided not to marry Marujita, whatever the consequences. And in all honesty, he told the young woman and her family of his decision. He'd provide for the needs of Marujita and the baby, as well as for the hordes of relatives who had suddenly appeared on the scene, on the understanding that there would be no more talk of marriage or scandal.

'Then tonight the baby died. For these superstitious, ignorant people, this death is the wrath of God, a sign that the child was *maldito*, the accursed product of a damned union. A righting of wrongs needed to happen: by the Master marrying the girl, the curse could be broken now.' Agustina sat back in her chair and shook her head gravely.

Alexandra was filled with a painful confusion by this extraordinary tale; the revelation that Salvador had fathered a child with Marujita scraped coldly against her heart in a way that brought a new feeling of disquiet. What was she to make of his reacting to her photo before he'd even met her? It answered some of the questions that had been niggling at her, certainly. A yearning leapt up in her that she fought to suppress. Could it be that this had been enough to make him refuse to marry Marujita? Or was Alexandra just another amusing dalliance that paled beside the fact that Doña Isabel was now at liberty to marry again? She tried to push such tormenting thoughts aside and control her chaotic emotions.

Pushing her head back against the pillow, Alexandra stared up at the ceiling. 'I still can't understand why my cousin allows himself to be treated in this way. After all, this is his land and he would be completely entitled to ask them to leave,' she said indignantly, though her voice wavered.

'The dramas of these backward people are more dangerous than you can imagine,' explained Agustina. 'As I said to you not so long ago, it isn't wise to pick a quarrel with them. Gypsies are an unpredictable lot, handy with a knife and completely fearless of death. They live by their own *lachiri*, or justice, particularly regarding honour and marriage. If you break a promise to the *Calés* or go against their laws, you bring down *la venganza de Calés* on your head, and they will chase you to the ends of the earth. As they say, *os Calés abelan lachingueles pinrés*, gypsies have long legs.'

Alexandra fixed the other woman with a curious look. 'Why did you tell me all this tonight?'

Agustina smiled kindly and leant forward in her chair to place a hand on the bedspread. 'The Moors also had a saying: *In the depths of despair, never lose hope, for the sweetest marrow is in the hardest bone.* Don't despair, my child. I know you think you don't belong here, but remain at El Pavón. And one more word of advice … This is a big house, with lots of staff gossiping and whispering behind closed doors. Don't believe everything you hear, Doña Alexandra. People don't see with their eyes, but it doesn't stop them witnessing with their mouths. We once had a maid here, under my supervision it shames me to say, who was dismissed for her tongue wagging about the family. *Ay Dios*, a real mischief-maker. I gave her short shrift, I can tell you.'

Agustina's disdainful look at the mere memory caused a wave of guilt to wash over Alexandra. 'Yes, I suppose people are bound to talk about the family.' Her cheeks went a little pink as she recalled the woman on the train from La Linea who'd so freely offered her opinions on the de Fallas. She looked imploringly at the *duenna*, suddenly feeling the weight of everything she now knew. 'It's just all so confusing. I don't know what to think or what to do.'

'The truth can sometimes be slow to reveal itself. The sun sets every night but returns next day. *El tiempo es un gran curador*, time is a great healer. Is it not said that he is a great master who solves many things?'

Alexandra smiled grimly. 'But Salvador asked me to leave,' she said, huskily.

'Passion sometimes makes us think and do things we cannot control. Don't attach any importance to what he said in a moment of despair.' Agustina studied the young woman, deliberating. 'Would you like to know what fate has in store for you? The tarot cards can tell us what futures may come to pass, depending upon your actions.'

Alexandra hesitated. She did not believe in this superstitious stuff, she told herself, but an intense feeling was drawing her curiosity. Perhaps Salvador was right: perhaps she was more Spanish than she acknowledged to herself. She nodded.

Agustina took out a pack of old tarot cards, well worn from use, from her pocket. With nimble skill, which had clearly come from experience, she shuffled and cut them. Finally, she lay a few of them out in the shape of a horseshoe on the bed.

'The Knight of Swords,' she said as she placed a card face up on top of the horseshoe, between the eight others. 'There's a dark man riding a black horse at full gallop. Symbol of romantic chivalry ... definitely Don Salvador Cervantes de Rueda.'

She turned up the first card at the extreme right of the horseshoe. 'Here is the Fool reversed, dressed in his clown's costume. He is carrying a burden on his shoulders and a great stick in his hand. An angry dog is going for him. It describes the impulsiveness of His Grace, the consequence of his faults, and his atonement.'

Alexandra looked at the Spanish servant in alarm. 'A sinister beginning, isn't it?'

Agustina lifted her hand in reassurance. 'Not to worry, for the strength of this card is changed by the one placed alongside it: the Knight of Wands. It is also an important card. He is a messenger of hope. Though Don Salvador is surrounded by danger just now, he will nevertheless be saved, but he must still go through many tests, for the struggle is not yet over. Look here, at the heart pierced by three swords, the clouds and the rain on the next card. It foretells difficult times of sorrow, tears and even separation.'

'Separation? From whom?' asked Alexandra in a quiet voice.

But Agustina was not listening, totally absorbed in her fortune telling. 'Here comes the gypsies' wagon, pulled by two mules and carrying the branch of authority and of willpower. This means that the Count is still at the mercy of a power stronger than himself. He will have to overcome it with a greater effort of will and be stronger than the ones who confront him.'

As Agustina turned over another card, Alexandra held her breath.

'And now, the card of The Lovers,' exclaimed the servant, peering at the image. 'Once again he'll be called upon to make a choice. The struggle between sacred and profane love … the fight won't be an easy one … a crafty little vixen, possessed by a hundred devils. She has bewitched my master but, yes, love can conquer over evil.'

Agustina took a sip of water from the glass she'd set beside her on the table. She seemed unhappy at the turn her predictions were taking, and she looked out of the corner of her eye at Alexandra's drawn features. But she sighed with relief as she turned over the next card: it depicted a woman firmly closing the mouth of a lion. She wore a chain of roses about her waist and the cosmic symbol of eternal life over her head. 'At last!' Agustina whispered. 'That's the one I was waiting for – the card of Fortitude, an excellent omen. It's the triumph of love over hatred, the victory of good over evil.' She chuckled. 'Of course, it will all depend on the last card,' she murmured to herself. She took another sip of water and pondered over this final choice, her hands running lightly over the remaining cards, lingering on one, then another, while Alexandra fidgeted impatiently in her seat.

'Ah,' she said finally, as she turned over the card depicting the Tower. 'Interesting … neither good nor bad. See? The man and woman are being thrown from the Tower by a bolt of lightning striking the top. With lightning comes conflict, particularly between two opposing forces. This is destruction to form something new … a new direction or perspective perhaps. A greater power is at work … but personal transformation is needed.' She frowned thoughtfully and gathered up the cards.

'What does this mean, Agustina?' Alexandra was near exasperation. 'Transformation of Salvador … or me?'

'Fate and destiny must decide, but you must give them a helping hand and fight for what you want. That's what the cards are telling me. As we say: *Destino puede ser tomado porlos cuernos y impujado en la dirección correcta*, fate can be taken by the horns and pushed in the right direction.'

'Perhaps you're right, Agustina,' Alexandra sadly sighed. 'Yet I feel so worn down by all this fighting. I don't know how much energy I have to make my own destiny.'

The Spanish woman patted her arm, saying, 'Come now, get some rest. Sleep on it and trust in what tomorrow may bring.'

By now dawn was breaking on the horizon; the east was ablaze and bathed the room in a pale, rosy glow. Somewhere a cock crowed and was answered by its own echo. Agustina drew the curtains and tiptoed out of the bedroom. The herbal potion had done the trick: Alexandra lay fast asleep, her long hair spread out over the pillow.

CHAPTER 6

The following days were relatively quiet. Agustina's extraordinary disclosures had aroused mixed feelings in Alexandra. She wondered how much credence she should give to the *duenna*'s words. Why had the old servant imparted to her such private matters? After all, those were family secrets and she was sure most members of the family still considered her a stranger. Yet her desire to know everything had been inescapable. She'd not discouraged Agustina to speak openly and, admittedly, had pushed her to explain a good deal about the de Falla intrigues. Now everything was, at least, somewhat clearer. For that she was grateful, though no doubt Salvador himself would resent such confidences.

She didn't know what revelation cut her more searingly: the tragic secret of his love child with Marujita or the possibility that he still carried a torch for Doña Isabel. Before she had met this man, love and desire were things she wrote about from her imagination. Now they were physically and painfully real and she must decide how best to serve her own heart. The message of Agustina's tarot cards had whispered its way into her consciousness, despite the reluctance of her reason. Did she have the strength to push Fate in the direction she wanted and fight for Salvador?

An unreasoning impulse drove her towards him. She could not rid herself of the thought that, despite his bitter words near the bridge in Triana and later at the wake, Salvador had been tacitly reaching out to her before, trying to tell her something vital. Yet now he seemed to be avoiding her. Alexandra saw him only rarely, at mealtimes or when they happened to cross on the stairs or in the hall. When by chance their eyes met across the dining room table, his were indifferent. She began to fear that perhaps he'd misinterpreted the motive behind her presence at the gypsies' camp on the night of the wake, mistaking her fond concern for unhealthy curiosity, the instinct of the writer in search of a dramatic story. But surely he didn't think her capable of such heartless voyeurism? His secret was now known to her, he must have surmised. What did that mean to him? Did he even care?

At first she felt deeply hurt and upset. How could he have held her the way he had in Seville, vibrating with such hunger and fire, and now, just a few days later, offer her only coolness? Was it all a cruel game? Every time she thought of him and the gypsy girl, Marujita, together, her heart gave an agonizing wrench. She had never known jealousy could cut like a knife. To quash her yearning for him would be the sane and sensible thing to do, and yet it was hopeless: Salvador's complete masculinity, his sheer virility, succeeded in unnerving her whenever he was near, though she tried hard to fight her confusion and guard her pride.

Regardless of what her better judgement was telling her, again and again her mind had played over that embrace. She had returned his kiss with an ardour of which she hadn't known herself capable. Never had a kiss moved her so – not that she'd been kissed that often – and she had known at that moment if such heat, passion and euphoria could be ignited in her from this man's kiss, then she had never truly been kissed before.

As time went by, and daily she was faced with his continuous indifference, these feelings gave way to indignation. Soon she became resigned to it and tried to dismiss him from her mind. She carried on with her peaceful life at El Pavón and almost ceased to worry about his aloof manner.

Alexandra seldom sought the company of others. When she did, it was usually Esmeralda or Ramón. Ever since Esmeralda had admitted her secret love to her the night after the masked ball, the two cousins had begun to spend more time together; but Salvador's sister still seemed ever-watchful of confiding too much and Alexandra was equally guarded whenever Salvador's name was mentioned. Now and then, Ramón would drive Alexandra around, showing her some of the surrounding villages or dropping her and Esmeralda at Jerez to go shopping.

On one such occasion, Ramón left the two young women in the Calle Tetuàn to rummage around the town's main market, a few minutes' walk away in the Plaza de la Encamación. Like Calle Sierpes, which ran parallel to it, Calle Tetuàn was a narrow street, overlooked by balconies and teeming with bars and cafés, a charming conduit to the town's *mercado*. It was late morning and the sky was a glorious turquoise blue, making the brightly coloured awnings of the market stalls seem even more vivid. The sun was becoming increasingly hot and so, after buying a few postcards and decorative combs, Alexandra and Esmeralda found a café and had soon ordered a jug of iced sangria and were watching the Jerez townsfolk browsing among the tables piled with bread, *manchego* and chorizos, lace and painted plates, hats and other *curiosidad*.

Alexandra caught sight of a man in the crowd with overly long, blond hair, walking with a woman, and she tensed.

'Oh, no! Please tell me that loathsome man, Fernando Lopez, isn't here to spoil such a lovely day,' she said, sipping her sangria. She dreaded another encounter with the oily steward, and had managed to avoid him since the night of the bizarre gypsy wake.

Esmeralda raised a menu to her face. '*Ay Dios*, it's not him, is it?' She nervously lowered her voice, even though the man was too far away to hear.

Alexandra breathed a sigh of relief when the object of their concern turned round to kiss the woman on the cheek.

'*Está bien*, it's fine. It's not him. Does he give you the creeps as much as he does me?' Alexandra noticed that Esmeralda had gone even paler than usual.

'I'm sure he's seen me with ...' Esmeralda stopped, looking embarrassed, but then resumed. 'We thought we'd been so careful but Lopez is everywhere, and he makes it his business to know everything that goes on. I'm just terrified he's going to confront me one day.'

Esmeralda's lover, thought Alexandra. *What a terrible hold for that nasty piece of work to have over her.* 'Yes, I see. You think him capable of blackmail?'

'*Sí, sí*, Alexandra, I do. It's only a matter of time, I'm sure.'

Alexandra gritted her teeth. '*Abuela* should get rid of him. He's hateful.'

'Yes, indeed, but it's not that simple,' Esmeralda sighed.

'Why ever not?' interrupted Alexandra. She stirred the ice in her sangria, frowning. 'He's insolent, violent. I can't figure out why he's tolerated on the estate. I've been meaning to say something to *Papá* but he's always either locked in his study or disappearing off somewhere.' She suspected her father welcomed time away from Eugenia but wasn't about to admit that in front of Esmeralda. 'How on earth does he hold on to his job at El Pavón, I don't understand.'

'He was the steward of Don Eugenia's father, from his estate,' explained Esmeralda, her eyes still flitting around the crowd as if fearing the steward would appear at any moment. 'Eugenia brought him with her when she came to El Pavón, after her father, Don Fernán de Juni, died. Lopez was Don Fernán's "enforcer", if you like. Both men had a reputation for brutality. Apparently, Lopez used the harshest tactics for collecting rent from Don Fernán's struggling estate workers.'

Alexandra remembered the gypsy boy Pedro cowering in terror at the steward's feet. 'He probably bludgeoned it out of them,' she muttered, crunching on an ice-cube.

'Everyone at El Pavón hates the man. They know he's brutal to the gypsies on the estate and the de Fallas have a long tradition of being tolerant of the *gitanos*.'

'So why is he allowed to continue?'

'Because Eugenia is a powerful member of the household and she manages to pull the wool over the *Duquesa*'s eyes, so Lopez stays.'

'I'm sorry, Esmeralda, but I can't believe *Abuela* is that easy to fool.'

Her cousin shrugged. '*Quizás*, maybe. In any case, Eugenia has some power over her. She brought a huge dowry with her when she married your father and put a large amount of money and extra land into the estate and holdings. The *Duquesa* is no fool, as you say. El Pavón needed such financial support. You may have noticed, your grandmother tends to be frostily polite to Aunt Eugenia but never initiates a row.'

'Yes, I suppose that's true. Though Eugenia still seems to bow to *Abuela*'s authority.'

'*Por supesto*, but of course.' Esmeralda raised her eyebrows. 'She is the *Duquesa*.'

'And what does Salvador make of Eugenia's creature, Lopez?' Alexandra changed the subject smoothly.

'I think he would have the man flogged and thrown off the estate if he had his way but he knows your grandmother's predicament, and they are very close.'

'So Salvador knows how the gypsies are treated too?'

Esmeralda nodded. 'He avoids the man whenever he can, as much to save his temper from causing something he'd regret.'

Alexandra felt her stomach give a familiar, painful twist as she was reminded of Marujita, and suddenly she wanted to understand what kind of sway this girl and her people exerted over him.

'Do you think Salvador has some kind of special affinity with the *gitanos*?' Alexandra asked tentatively. 'I mean, he seems to do more than tolerate their superstitious ways. It's almost as though he's been caught up in the power of their beliefs.'

Esmeralda turned her sorrowful smoky-blue eyes on her cousin. 'I confess, I'm afraid for my brother. I have been ever since he became mixed up with the *gitanos*. I don't know what draws him to them. He's a proud man, and an honourable one, despite what happened between him and Marujita.' She looked at Alexandra, her voice softening.

'You must be aware of it, I know, Cousin. But remember, Marujita is a schemer. There's no doubt many young gypsy girls are experienced in the art of seduction, Marujita even more so than most. He was not himself when she found him: vulnerable, weak, literally a broken man. What that cold-hearted social climber Doña Isabel did to my brother when he was already debilitated was *desgraciado* … and then Marujita used whatever skills she's reputed to have to ensnare him. Salvador was told he'd be crippled for life but whatever the *gitana* did, she saved him. After that, his sense of honour kept him with her.'

Alexandra listened, though it was hard to hear. 'Do you think he'd have married her?' Her eyes searched Esmeralda's, her heart in her throat, so close was she to confiding in Salvador's sister everything she was feeling.

Esmeralda gave an enigmatic, sad smile. 'That's a good question.' She sighed. 'My brother's been plagued with bad luck when it comes to women, but it's not my place to advise him on who he can and cannot love.' At this, Alexandra became aware of her cousin's searching gaze. 'Ever since you came to El Pavón, I've thought you and Salvador would make a good match.'

Alexandra met her eyes, a pink hue rising in her cheeks. 'Really? Why is that?'

'There's something in your spirit that I think is the same in him,' said Esmeralda, hesitating. 'I'm not sure … but I can see a change in Salvador since you arrived.'

Alexandra gave a bitter laugh. 'I see changes in him all the time, it's hard to keep up with him. One thing's for sure, Salvador doesn't give me the time of day at the moment.' She looked down, tracing the edge of her glass with her finger. 'We seem to always be at odds with each other, so I hardly think we're well matched.'

'So you're indifferent to him?'

Alexandra glanced up sharply. No, she wasn't quite ready to lay herself open to Esmeralda at this point; Salvador was surrounded by a chaos too threatening to her own emotions and she needed to bide her time. Instead she chose blatant evasion. 'It seems that Salvador has enough complications in his life, as do I.' She arched an eyebrow. 'Surely you of all people can appreciate the difficulty of complications.'

Esmeralda shifted in her chair and Alexandra could see that her habitual detached air had returned. 'Yes, life is not always what you would have it be.' She looked at her watch. 'Ramón will be at the Iglesia de San Pedro soon. You might find it interesting. It's quite important during the *Semana Santa* because it's part of the procession route the penitents take.'

Alexandra drained her glass. Their conversation was clearly at an end. 'Yes, I have only a few notes on the *Semana Santa* at the moment, so that would be good.'

'It's about a four- or five-minute walk away, so we ought to go if you'd like to look round it first.'

Leaving some coins on the plate, the two women left the café and set off to meet Ramón. As they headed out of the market, a tall man bumped roughly past Alexandra in the crowd. Rather than apologize, he paused and turned his head, fixing her with a menacing stare. There was no mistaking the scar on his cheek, the hawkish black eyes that surveyed her with a look that sent cold shivers down her spine: it was the gypsy knife-sharpener she'd spied at the funeral.

'I've seen that man before. That night of … in the gypsy cave,' Alexandra whispered.

It was clear Esmeralda had seen him too. She tugged urgently on her cousin's arm as the *gitano* continued to stare at them both, lighting a long cheroot and squinting through the smoke. 'Come, Alexandra, we should leave. *Now!*'

*   *   *

Maybe it was the fear of crossing paths with the gypsy knife-sharpener once more, still, Alexandra stopped going into town for a while, though she was aware the *gitanos'* camp itself was closer in distance to the house. She spent days at a time without leaving El Pavón.

Increasingly, she would read to her grandmother: ironically, the one person she had thought she would most likely want to avoid during her stay, but who had turned out to be a good companion. They talked on the *Duquesa*'s patio, or sometimes in the garden when it was not too hot, and caught up on lost time. Ramón was usually somewhere around the hacienda, of course. Faced with an obnoxious sister and a father who was nowhere to be seen half the time, she was thankful for her sparky-eyed cousin whose cheerful and thoughtful nature lifted her spirits. Still, more often than not, Alexandra spent hours by herself: she worked at her desk, writing letters or endeavouring to shape her notes into some kind of structure for her novel.

She liked to walk through the extensive grounds of the de Falla estate. Sometimes Ramón accompanied her but for the most part she went alone. As a child, Alexandra would often happily roam the acres of parkland at Grantley Hall on her own, or invite her friends over for impromptu all-day tea parties on the front lawn. Sometimes, the quiet and gentle Ashley would come and stay and Aunt Geraldine let them have the run of the house. On warm summer nights, she would frequently stock up on ginger beer and *Girl's Own* comics and head down to the garden to spend the night in a tent, reading by torchlight and gazing up at the stars. Her notebook was always close at hand, where she would write down new ideas for stories that she later passed round the other girls at school.

Here, at El Pavón, she was more careful in her wanderings. She never ventured near the gypsy camp, for fear of some unpleasant encounter; the gypsy with the scar on his cheek and the witch-like fortune-teller were never far from her mind. Although she had gained only a fleeting glimpse of the *gitanos'* seemingly barbarous customs, part of her was still burning to understand the life of these wild people.

One day, while on one of her solitary rambles, Alexandra had discovered a small octagonal summerhouse overgrown with red bougainvillea, and adopted it as a hideaway where she went to read or think, away from the suffocating atmosphere of the hacienda. Apart from when she was alone with her grandmother, she felt her every move judged and maybe even discussed. Besides, she had always loved losing herself in nature and welcomed her escape to the vast gardens of the property. Not for the first time it struck her how surprisingly different the wild and exotic El Pavón was compared with the lush green surroundings of Grantley Hall. With both she revelled in discovering new secret places.

Writing didn't come easily to Alexandra now. Since her arrival in Spain, she had amassed an extraordinary amount of material for her novel and yet, strangely enough, she was reluctant to use it. Previously, she'd never experienced the slightest difficulty in putting her ideas into words. She had written her first novel in less than three months and her second in little more than that but, with this one, she found herself unable to sketch the most vague outline of a plot. Something had shifted inside her, transformed by a silent storm. It was almost as if she were afraid to formulate her thoughts now lest they betrayed some insidious inner feeling, forcing her to face up to a reality she was eager to ignore. Was she falling in love with Salvador or was the kiss they'd passionately shared the reason for her troubled thoughts?

One morning, after breakfast, she escaped to her usual hideout. Salvador had been particularly exasperating. During the whole meal, he'd deliberately avoided speaking to her, though once or twice she had felt his surreptitious gaze, and Alexandra was greatly relieved when she was finally able to get away from the electrifying tension in the air.

Two hours later she was sitting in the summerhouse surrounded by mounds of crumpled paper, nervily chewing at the end of her pencil, when a rustling of leaves startled her. Somebody was watching her, hidden in the bushy foliage of the coppice. This was not the first time her intuition had warned that she was not alone. She remembered that evening not so long ago, when she thought she heard someone prowling outside her bedroom; and the night in Esmeralda's room when someone had been listening at the door. On several occasions after that she had caught the sound of furtive footsteps again, and sensed the presence of an intruder.

Suddenly, Alexandra realized she was entirely defenceless in this isolated spot; her cries for help would be useless as no one would hear them. Her pulse quickened as a cold tingling broke out in the nape of her neck. She became rigidly still, rooted to the spot, refusing to believe what her senses, sharpened by fear, were telling her.

Was that the flash of something moving that she glimpsed out of the corner of her eye? A high-pitched, yet almost imperceptible hiss was followed by a soft rush of air as a projectile shot past her, brushing her cheek lightly. Her eyes widened. A few yards away, a quivering arrow had embedded itself with a *thunk* in the wooden beam of the gazebo. She gasped and pushed back her chair.

Still dazed by the speed of events, she distinctly heard this time a rustling of leaves and the rapid patter of someone running. Coming to her senses, Alexandra rushed from the summerhouse and into the clearing outside. Now, she could hear the distinctive sound of feet hurrying away at top speed, and she ran through the coppice in pursuit, outrage, rather than fear, firing her steps.

With a sudden surge in energy, she stepped up the pace, stumbling over the long unmowed grass and weaving her way through the maze of shrubs. Soon, she spotted the prowler ahead: it was Pablo, Marujita's young brother, whom she'd saved from Fernando Lopez's hands not so long ago. He was scurrying away like a hare, aware that the young woman was on his heels. Alexandra was gaining on him, her heart racing, when suddenly she crashed into a man's broad chest and found herself prisoner of two strong arms that encircled her tightly.

'Salvador!' she gasped, her eyes flashing green fire, at once powerfully aware of her captor. 'You shocked me!' She struggled, trying to break free from his hold.

'Where are you going? Why the mad rush?' Gone was Salvador's icy façade. The young man now regarded her with a curious, twinkling gaze.

'Let me go! I nearly caught up with him,' she cried, panting, still attempting to free herself.

'Catch up with whom?' He questioned her without relaxing the pressure of his arms around her, pulling her instead against his lean, powerful body.

'Pablo!' She was trying to recover her breath and ignore the sudden stirring inside her, triggered by Salvador's close contact.

'Pablo?'

'You must have seen him, you must have passed him a few seconds ago,' she insisted, her chest still rising and falling fast, the shrillness of her tone ringing almost hysterical in her ears. She babbled out the whole story in a trembling voice, her mind so blurred that she was barely coherent. It was not the arrow that had come so close to hitting her that alarmed her now, all she could think of was the strength of the arms clasping her and the warmth of the virile, hard body that towered over her.

Eventually, after she had finished, Salvador released his grip, his eyes holding hers. 'Very mysterious. Your story is rather intriguing ...' He was trying to keep a straight face but there was amusement in his voice, which immediately provoked her. Did he not believe her?

All of a sudden Alexandra was angry. Her cheeks tinged a heated red. How dare he doubt her word! His mockery incensed her and, glaring hopelessly up at him, she said, 'You seem to think I've made it all up, or that I simply have a vivid imagination. The arrow is still there, buried in the beam where I left it. Come and see for yourself.' She dearly wanted to dent his colossal arrogance.

Salvador let her lead him to the summerhouse. All was silent save for the happy warbling of a finch and, sensing her hesitation, he took her arm and steered her into the shady little house.

He looked around him. 'So this is where you hide out ... this place certainly seems to inspire you, Alexandra. Never in my life have I seen so much crumpled-up paper in one spot.' He grinned widely at her, his tone softly mocking.

Alexandra managed a tight smile as she fought back the angry tears welling up inside her. One moment he hardly wanted to look in her direction and the next he was talking to her again, but only to laugh at her. Why did Salvador have this crushing effect on her feelings? She blinked at the grey-blue irises staring down at her with such intensity.

'Come now, *niña*, what has brought tears to those beautiful eyes?' he said, now regarding her with concern. He placed an arm affectionately around her shoulders.

Alexandra moved away. 'Please, don't,' she whispered. Her nerves were already on edge and his proximity did not help. Every time she had been close to him they'd ended up locked in each other's arms, and she was not about to go down that path again, however much a part of her longed for it.

Salvador frowned. 'Here, dry your eyes,' he said gruffly, ignoring her curt rejection and handing her his freshly ironed handkerchief. 'Show me this arrow that's so alarmed you.' Again, he'd adopted the patronizing tone that so exasperated her. Where was the man she had glimpsed briefly in Seville, who kept appearing and disappearing like a mirage?

Irritated at herself for being so emotional, Alexandra gazed at the spot where the projectile had embedded itself. She stared wide-eyed: the arrow was no longer there.

'It was there,' she muttered disconcertedly to herself, pointing at the beam where a few moments ago she had left it quivering. 'I didn't dream it.'

She glanced anxiously at Salvador. The brief drawing together of his brows showed that he believed her. Obviously he had noticed something. In two strides he reached the wooden post. He bent his dark head to examine more closely the hole clearly made by the fine point of a dart or an arrow.

'Have you any idea who could have been responsible for this?' He straightened up and turned to face her, worried now. 'Did you actually see who fired it?'

'No, but clearly it's someone who wants me to leave.'

'Just then, you mentioned Pablo. Surely you don't suspect him?'

'I can't be certain,' she admitted hesitantly. 'However, I did see him scurrying off. But why would he be running away if he wasn't guilty? And what would he have against me?'

'Indeed,' he sighed, raking his hair with long, supple fingers. He shook his head. 'How many times have I asked ... no, how many times have I *begged* you to go ... to leave this place? I have good reason to believe that you're not safe here, Alexandra. Why are you so determined not to listen to me?' He looked away but she could sense his concern.

The last trace of the fear that had gripped her earlier vanished.

'And Salvador, why are *you* so determined not to tell me what that reason is?' Alexandra spoke softly now, knowing he wouldn't answer her.

He had moved away from her, his head held high, shoulders straight, hands thrust deep in his pockets. Standing there, his Grecian profile unmoving, proud, reserved and secretive, Salvador was without doubt a puzzle. Time and again, Alexandra had been baffled by his complex personality; it reminded her of a mysterious dark cellar she felt tempted to explore, but did not dare to do so. Suddenly he looked incredibly alone, tired and vulnerable. A wave of tenderness swept over her and she realized she would never forget his strong, brooding face as it appeared now. The impulse to help him that gripped her in this moment was far stronger than the one that told her to run away.

Aware that she was watching him, Salvador turned, shifting his gaze towards her. He remained silent but his expression was disturbingly intense. In the shadows of the gazebo, his eyes were deep blue and seemed sad.

'I do believe, *niña*, that you're feeling sorry for me,' he said softly, that familiar enigmatic smile floating around his lips.

He had caught her by surprise. 'No, Salvador,' she whispered after a few moments, looking away so he could not see the emotion on her face, 'I don't think what I feel for you can be called pity.'

Perhaps he would have pushed the conversation further but, at that moment, there was an exclamation outside.

'There you are at last, Salvador! I've been looking for you for more than an hour,' cried Mercedes, bursting through the foliage. Their time alone was at an end. Alexandra wondered how long her stepsister had been there, hidden in the coppice, and what she had overheard. Mercedes would have no qualms about eavesdropping on a conversation not meant for her.

Turning towards the newcomer, Salvador's face lit up; he grinned broadly and Alexandra suspected he was somewhat relieved by the interruption, which put an end to a situation he no doubt found uncomfortable. A slight lump came to her throat.

Mercedes threw her arms around her cousin's neck and kissed him.

'What can I do for my mischievous sprite this morning?' Salvador asked, placing his arm around the young girl's slender waist.

Mercedes gazed up at him adoringly, nestling closer to him. 'I wanted to go for a ride with you,' she cajoled.

'What a marvellous idea,' he said enthusiastically. 'Let's go then.'

Mercedes pouted. 'But you know it'll soon be lunchtime. *Abuela* would never forgive us for being late.'

He laughed. 'Well then, we'll have to postpone our delightful ride until some other time.'

'I don't believe you, you're as slippery as quicksilver,' Mercedes sighed. 'No one ever manages to make you do anything against your will.'

'Come now, little Mercedes, be truthful! Have I refused to go riding with you?'

'No, *little* Salvador,' she went on, mimicking his tone. 'But as Agustina always says: *Truth is not a beautiful woman hidden at the bottom of a well, but a shy bird which only guile can entrap.*'

They both laughed at this and Salvador gently cuffed the side of her head.

Alexandra, feeling so obviously *de trop*, shifted her gaze from them. Slowly she walked away, attempting to escape also from the alarming emotions that fermented inside her. Unable to stop herself from glancing back, she caught Salvador's parting glance over his shoulder, so quietly intense, her stomach fluttered. Then he was laughing again as Mercedes babbled on, and so she left the cousins to wander off together arm in arm towards the house.

All through lunch she was thoughtful and scarcely touched her food. Mercedes was bewitchingly feminine with her wide black eyes, dimples at the corners of her rosebud mouth and her impish pointed chin. When she thought no one was looking, she cast a look at Alexandra, clearly wanting to indicate that a point had been scored. Alexandra had no doubt that one look at the girl made most men want to protect her and Salvador was no exception. She couldn't help watching the two of them covertly during the meal. They were relaxed, talking and joking under the doting gaze of Doña Eugenia, who seemed delighted with her daughter's performance. Don Alonso, as usual, was quiet and lost in his own world, not seeming to notice what was going on around him. A sudden pain stabbed Alexandra's chest and her heart sank: could she possibly be jealous of her stepsister? Her whole being recoiled from the idea; it was a ridiculous and uncomfortable one. Mercedes was merely an immature child.

At that moment, Alexandra glanced up and caught Esmeralda's eye. She was sitting opposite, gazing at her inquisitively. Whereas normally she appeared to regard Mercedes' antics, and indeed her whole family, with little interest, now her eyes were unusually alert. Alexandra felt for the first time that her cousin was watching her and had noticed her edginess. Had Esmeralda read the jealousy written on her face? Or worse, had Salvador mentioned what had happened earlier at the summerhouse? Either way, even though she and Esmeralda had made a tentative connection, Alexandra was still too confused to allow anyone to glimpse her vulnerability.

She hastily looked down and pushed the food around on her plate distractedly with her fork. The morning's incident must not be made known to anybody. She felt a fool, regretting the circumstances that had forced her to tell Salvador, since he seemed to have already forgotten her existence and was back to his old mercurial ways. It occurred to her that he might not have believed her after all. Perhaps he thought she'd invented the story to excite his interest. Yet, had he not confessed that he feared for her safety, begging her to leave the hacienda as soon as possible?

What was he playing at? Her mind was trapped in a maze of questions, and thoughts flew round and round in her head like caged creatures looking for a way out. Every time it seemed she had come a little closer to him, he had acted disconcertingly. He was so unpredictable, indulging in some cat and mouse game, the rules of which were only known to him.

Had Ramón intended to warn her against her cousin when he'd described Salvador's difficult character? She tried to remember what he'd said, but the first evening she had spent in Spain seemed so far away now.

'Is anything the matter, my dear child?' enquired Doña María Dolores tenderly as her granddaughter was leaving the table. 'You seem preoccupied today.'

'It's only a touch of migraine, *Abuela*. I'm just going to lie down. I've probably caught too much sun. It was rather warm today and I didn't wear my hat.'

As Salvador abruptly pushed back his chair and passed by her, his jaw clenched visibly. For a fleeting moment she thought he was going to turn to her and say something, but he had obviously changed his mind and quickly moved on. The *Duquesa* had followed Alexandra's gaze. Her eyes narrowed slightly, like a cat noticing its prey.

'Salvador,' she called out as the young man reached the doorway, 'I'd like to speak to you.'

Salvador followed his great-aunt to her apartments. Alexandra went upstairs to her room. There, she remembered that she'd finished her book and needed something new to read. Coming back downstairs, she headed towards the library, across the hall from the *Duquesa*'s apartment. She was about to open the door, when a murmur of voices caught her ears.

'…What is it with you and Alexandra? I can almost feel the tension crackling in the air whenever you're in the same room together.'

At the mention of her name, Alexandra stopped. The door to her grandmother's room wasn't shut properly and through the small gap she could see Salvador sitting in an armchair facing the *Duquesa*. He was studying the tips of his shoes, his long legs stretched out in front of him; his eyes, hidden by his lashes, were impossible to read. Alexandra could detect some of what he was feeling, though, from his pale, set face and the determined fold at the corner of his mouth.

She pressed herself back against the wall and breathed deeply. What was she doing, creeping around like a thief? She could hear her aunt's disapproving voice, saying, *Eavesdroppers never hear any good of themselves.* If she was discovered, the humiliation would be terrible, and her grandmother wouldn't take kindly to such behaviour. And as for Salvador … She shuddered at the thought but an impetuous curiosity kept her rooted to the spot.

Salvador hadn't answered, still absorbed by the tips of his shoes, and though Alexandra couldn't see her grandmother, she guessed that the *Duquesa*'s eyes were watching him closely.

'Salvador,' she said at length in a calm voice, 'I have not long to live. As the days go by, I can feel death stealing up on me. True, it comes slowly, but the years roll by and I'm not getting any younger.'

Salvador tried to protest, but she must have signalled him not to interrupt her.

'My dearest wish, as you are well aware, is to see you married to a woman who loves you, who understands you, who will give you the support required by a man of your birth and rank, and help you shoulder the responsibilities and problems associated with that status. If fate has been unkind and unjust towards you for some time, why not give it a chance now? Things may not be as bleak as they look. Alexandra loves you, of this I'm sure. If she's not conscious of it yet, she soon will be. You're not indifferent to her either. I know you well enough and can recognize the signs.'

Salvador was silent.

'Why do you refuse to look the facts in the face? Do you wish to bring disaster down upon yourself?' persisted the old woman, trying to break through her nephew's stubborn shell. 'Why not reach out for this new love? Why not accept it with joy and grasp happiness instead of groping at shadows?'

But Salvador shook his head slowly without looking up. 'Because it was doomed from the start,' he said in a flat voice, as though to himself. He shifted in his chair, leant his head wearily against the back of the seat and shut his eyes.

Alexandra stood helplessly outside the door, humiliation washing over her, yet unable to tear herself away.

'I can't understand this determination to condemn a love before it's even been born,' exclaimed Doña María Dolores impatiently. 'You're both adults, quite capable of taking the situation in hand. Face up to the problems together, if there really are any problems. In my opinion, this business with

Marujita has assumed ridiculous proportions. It's up to us now to put an end to this affair, which I will no longer tolerate.'

'I have a debt towards Marujita, which I must pay off,' Salvador said. He had raised his eyes and was looking at his great-aunt in earnest.

'We have all paid off that debt,' retorted the dowager. 'And besides, a debt is paid in kind or in money. What more can you do for her now?'

A bitter laugh escaped from her nephew's lips. 'Sometimes, dear Aunt, I think you forget the harsh customs of our people. You know none of us can escape them.'

'I admit the gypsies have violent ways and live by the *navaja* ... and this reputation they have for dark practices and uncanny powers has always been feared. But they're also poor, and avaricious too, and therein lies the answer to your Marujita problem.'

Faced with her obstinacy, Salvador seemed thoughtful for a moment. Then his eyes clouded over. He rose to take leave of the dowager.

'I'll think about what you've said,' he promised as he embraced her. 'I'm sure we can resolve this problem. Don't you worry about it any more, *Tía*.'

Hearing him heading for the door, Alexandra darted into the library opposite, shutting the door as quietly as she could and pinning herself against it, heart thumping in her chest. Salvador's steps echoed briskly down the corridor. After a few moments she heard another set of footsteps descend the marble staircase and move across the hall, slower and more measured this time. Opening the door slightly, she saw Agustina arrive at the apartments of her mistress. Alexandra had a burning desire to know what they were saying. She heard low voices coming from inside her grandmother's room as she tiptoed back out into the corridor. At first she could not make out what was being said, though the *Duquesa* was clearly pacing up and down the room.

'… I know him all too well, he'll do just as he pleases. But I must do something to put an end to all these ridiculous dramas.'

'You've spoken your mind,' replied Agustina. 'Leave him for now, he's already too unhappy and you'll accomplish nothing.'

'Wise and faithful Agustina,' sighed the dowager, sadly. 'You're always right. What would I have done without your advice through all these long years? Since tragedy struck my dear Salvador, I've learned to dread what the next day has in store but you're always so reassuring, always telling me that better days will come.'

'Don't worry, have confidence. The rainbow isn't far,' insisted the old servant.

'You've been promising me rainbows for so long.'

'Remember the road is long and His Grace has already travelled a long way back to us.'

'Still, how many steps are there to climb?' answered the *Duquesa* in a quiet voice, as though to herself.

Alexandra suddenly heard a noise from the corridor and scurried quietly up the staircase back to her room, afraid she might finally be caught eavesdropping and feeling guilty at what she had already done.

Upstairs, it was Alexandra's turn to pace her room. Once the humiliation she'd felt at overhearing the discussion had ebbed, she was besieged by questions. They span around her head like a tornado; there was so much to think about. She was taken aback that the *Duquesa* thought she was in love with Salvador. What had she said or done to make her grandmother believe such a thing? Was this what she was feeling? Was she so transparent? Moreover, did she dare to think Doña María Delores was right and Salvador loved *her*? Yet Agustina's cards had seen a threat from Marujita who had apparently 'bewitched' Salvador.

There was an unpleasant tug at Alexandra's heart at the thought of the two of them together. Agustina had urged Alexandra to fight for him but what was he afraid of? Bringing down the revenge of the gypsies? Whatever the truth, the situation was making Salvador truly wretched.

In the meantime, Alexandra decided that it was time she took matters into her own hands. To do so, she needed to get to the bottom of who'd tried to shoot her with an arrow.

*   *   *

Alexandra walked briskly towards the stables on the lookout for Pablo. Confronting the young lad would hopefully remove any doubts she had about his involvement in this morning's episode. Common sense said that he had not shot the arrow. He may be a liar, as Lopez had said, perhaps even a petty thief, but she had difficulty in believing he would deliberately want to harm her. After all, she'd rescued him from Fernando Lopez's hands, and the boy had seemed grateful. However, he had clearly been near the summerhouse when the arrow had been shot, and even if he'd not actually seen the person who was to blame, at least he must have a good idea who it might be.

She reached the stables and walked round them. No one was about. Further along, she found the old gardener, Miguel, lying stretched out against the trunk of a tree, a red-and-white checked handkerchief covering his face. He was dozing peacefully, oblivious to the cloud of flies buzzing around him.

Alexandra hesitated, debating whether or not to disturb him. Siesta time was certainly over.

'Miguel,' she cried out. 'Miguel, wake up!'

The man started, removed the handkerchief from his face and blinked in the light. Recognizing Alexandra, he leapt to his feet, apologizing profusely. '*Buenas tardes, señorita*,' he mumbled, embarrassed that she should have found him asleep. 'It was hot and I lay down for a while … uh … what can I do for you?'

She came straight to the point. 'Where's Pablo?'

Miguel had a vacant look. '*Pablo?*' he enquired, as though hearing the name for the first time.

Alexandra sighed impatiently. 'Yes, *Pablo*. Pablo, the stable boy.'

'Oh, *sí, sí*, Pablo,' he said after some hesitation, and with the expression of someone who'd just seen the light. 'Pablo Gomez, *yo sé*, I know, uh … I've not seen him since this morning. Uh … no, no, *lo siento*, since yesterday evening,' he corrected, wringing his hands. 'Ah, *señorita*, the lad's a good-for-nothing. He's lazy, a liar, a thief and …' Leaving his sentence hanging in the air, he shook his head disapprovingly, and walked off a shade too quickly towards the stables. Alexandra went after him. Determined to find Pablo, her instinct told her Miguel knew the whereabouts of the young gypsy. She followed the old gardener into the stables.

'Where do you think I can find him?' she persisted.

He had started to shift some hay and gave her a sideways glance.

'I don't know,' he reluctantly replied. 'I've already told you, he's a *vagabundo*, vagabond. Today he's here, *mañana* who knows?' he waved vaguely without looking at her.

'He has a family, doesn't he?' she continued.

'He's the sort of lout who doesn't care about his father or mother. He goes to all sorts of no-good places and keeps bad company. You're wasting your time, *señorita*.'

'Isn't he Marujita's brother?' she added, playing her last card.

The expression of alarm that swept over the man's face was fleeting but unmistakable. Alexandra would have missed it had she not been expecting a reaction of this sort. Marujita was the kind of gypsy feared by the likes of Miguel.

When she repeated her question, he did not reply but busied himself raking and filling his bucket. His face was stony and Alexandra knew that their interview was over. Nothing now would induce him to talk.

She strolled back pensively. It was late afternoon and the heat of the day had died away, leaving the air cool and scented. Alexandra loved the garden at this time, when the sounds of nature, the very light itself, took on softer tones before reawakening to greet the night. The conversation with Miguel was niggling at her more than she wanted to admit. It was the man's withdrawn and wary attitude, rather than the seriousness of his words, which perplexed her. Alexandra had never before encountered shiftiness and deceit quite like this.

She didn't know what to think any more and wondered whether Pablo was hiding, and why. Somehow, despite Miguel's reticence, she could not bring herself to believe that the young gypsy was guilty. Instead, instinct told her to look elsewhere for the culprit, though who could it be?

Lost in thought on her way back to the house, she had inadvertently followed the stone wall that marked the boundary between the hacienda and the gypsy camp, unaware that her footsteps were leading her to the very part of the estate she had avoided during the week. After a long detour, she found herself facing Marujita's cottage.

The dwelling had a deserted air about it. Turquoise shutters were pulled to and, as dusk approached, only the warbling of birds in the shrubbery disturbed the silence. In its mute and abandoned solitude, the squat white-stone house with its cape of golden mimosa appeared even more secret and mysterious to her.

She was about to leave when the door flew open and Salvador marched out. His face was flushed, eyes shining with anger. Alexandra had scarcely time to hide behind a bush. He stalked by without seeing her and stormed off towards the big house.

Alexandra watched him disappear. Once she'd recovered from her surprise, she pondered whether or not to face Marujita now that she was here, and finally get an answer to the questions that were tormenting her. She hesitated briefly. Reason urged caution, reminding her of the frightening consequences of her nocturnal escapade to the wake. On the other hand, her feelings for Salvador, her curiosity and her reckless nature, pressed for a more daring approach. She had fallen in love, she knew that now: shouldn't she grasp the opportunity to defend that budding love, as Agustina had encouraged?

Looking around uncertainly before making up her mind, she took a deep breath and strode firmly to the door; she crossed the threshold. There, it was done! Her heart was racing, her palms clammy. There was no thought in her head of what she might say or do once confronted with the gypsy girl; she was there and, for now, that was all that mattered.

Inside, the wide, low-roofed room was gloomy, lit solely by two paraffin lamps. A rancid smell of oil and damp filled the place. The walls were whitewashed and bare, with the exception of a few sacred pictures. The furniture was simple and scant: a divan by one wall, with a rocking chair beside it. A rustic wooden table and three chairs filled the space in the middle, while an old deeply carved chest that served as a storage place had been pushed away to the far corner, next to the window, where the black cat snoozed peacefully.

The house was still; shrouded in silence; it seemed deserted. Alexandra thought of Salvador's dead child and morbid images of the wake swam into her head, making her shudder. Fear and doubt crept back like a cold finger on her spine. She asked herself what she was doing there. Surely she must flee this place and its ghosts; she was being foolish and unreasonable. The cat opened its phosphorescent eyes, narrowed them to green slits, and closed them again.

Alexandra had almost turned to leave when a muffled sound caught her ear. Her eyes, which had grown accustomed to the dim light, could only just make out the shadow of a huddled heap in the right-hand corner of the room. Cautiously, she approached it. Pablo was squatting there, tears streaming down his face, his thin arms folded around bony knees.

'Pablo,' she uttered gently.

Recognizing Alexandra, the lad was seized with panic and began to gabble at her. '*No fui yo*, it wasn't me! I don't know anything. I *swear* it wasn't me.'

'Listen to me, Pablo,' she interrupted. 'I know you didn't shoot the arrow, but I also know you saw who did.'

'I don't know anything. Don't ask me anything, *por favor señorita!*' he implored, reaching up and grabbing hold of Alexandra's hands, attempting to kiss them in a desperate gesture.

Disconcerted, she was momentarily thrown off-guard but then she knelt down beside the boy, seized his thin shoulders and shook him gently. 'Stop this at once, Pablo, and listen to me,' she said firmly. 'You must …' Alexandra stopped short; someone had come into the room. She turned to see Marujita standing behind them.

'What is a *busno* woman doing in our house?' the gypsy asked her brother, not deigning to look at Alexandra.

'I've come to talk to Pablo,' said Alexandra, placing a protective arm around the young lad's shoulders.

Marujita considered her opponent with contempt, hands on hips, her head with its rich raven-black hair thrown slightly back in a stance that epitomized the scornful arrogance of her people. Briefly, the two women assessed each other defiantly, the gypsy girl's eyes dark and fiery, Alexandra's glittering with restrained anger.

'You are not welcome under this roof,' the young Romany stated with cold disdain.

'So I gather,' Alexandra retorted sarcastically and stood up. 'But I'm not going before I get what I've come for.'

Half-smiling, Marujita countered, 'We'll see about that!' Then, with the lithe speed of a young panther, she threw herself on to her adversary and, claws out like a wild cat, grabbed her by the throat. Taken by surprise, Alexandra struggled, trying without success to free herself from the long iron fingers that were strangling her. The strength of the *gitana* was staggering; choking and fighting for air, the more Alexandra moved, the more the vice around her neck tightened. Suddenly, she jerked her head backwards and the gypsy girl's hold loosened slightly. Alexandra managed to free herself for a few seconds before her opponent's hands caught her again – long, gripping fingernails digging into her shoulders, penetrating the fine material of her blouse and drawing blood.

Marujita, though scarcely out of adolescence, was by far the stronger and more agile of the two women, with the advantage of being used to this way of settling a quarrel.

'You will pay, *gajo*, for all the trouble you're causing,' Marujita's eyes blazed as she wrestled with Alexandra. 'You think you're more *honrada* than me, because you're a *busno*, huh? Because you're one of his family?' She swung her forearm under Alexandra's chin and wrenched her backwards in a choke-hold. 'You'll never have the power over him that I do. I am pure *gitana*, pure Spanish, more woman than you'll ever be, and he knows it.'

'You're nothing ... but a harlot ... and a witch!' Alexandra gasped between breaths.

'*La mujer que no ha pecado es bruja, le juro a Dios*! The woman who has not sinned is a witch, I swear to God!' The gypsy girl hissed in Alexandra's ear. 'You want to know how the people of this land settle their disputes?' In a few moments, without knowing quite how, Alexandra found herself lying outside on the cottage steps, bruised and bleeding, while the young gypsy, arms folded, leant against the door, her dark eyes burning with hatred.

'Go back to your cold and colourless land,' Marujita hissed. 'There's nothing for you here. The *Conde*'s mine and there's nothing you or anyone can do about that.' Hands on hips, she looked down at Alexandra, her eyes glittering malevolently. 'This is only a warning. Next time you may not live to tell the story.' Her voice was loaded with contempt.

Smouldering with rage, Alexandra was beyond listening. She lifted herself up slowly and set about straightening her clothes with careful deliberation under the unwavering stare of her adversary. Then, quick as lightning, using all her strength, she delivered an almighty punch, catching her rival in the eye. Turning coolly, she started back to the house. As she went, she could hear the string of insults, threats and curses that the young Romany hurled after her. But she didn't care. She had never felt so good.

Night had fallen. The air was cold and a breeze whispered in the trees. The great leafy branches swayed gracefully with a swishing sound that reminded her of soft footfalls as they threw fantastic shadows over the pathway, dimly lit by a wan moon. Alexandra shivered and quickened her step. In spite of the humiliation she'd suffered, she smiled to herself. A new sense of power swept over her, finally making her feel that, in some small way, she had just taken back control. What was happening to her? Even a month ago, she would never have contemplated such a brazenly physical response and she wondered what Salvador's reaction would be when he heard about the catfight. Alexandra pushed that thought to the back of her mind; it was a problem she would have to face later.

When she arrived back at the hacienda all the lights on the ground floor were on; they had company. A car was parked in front of the house and, as Alexandra drew closer, she recognized it as Doña Isabel's. She sighed; no doubt the young noblewoman was visiting Salvador. This is what it must have been like to fall in love with Casanova, she observed wryly.

Before she could ring the bell, the door opened and Doña Isabel, accompanied by Salvador, appeared on the steps in all her splendour.

'Ah, there you are Alexandra.' Salvador greeted his cousin with a broad smile. 'We were looking for you. The bullfighting season started a few weeks ago at Castellon de la Plana and Doña Isabel has come to invite us to the next big *corrida* on Sunday, at La Plaza de Toros in Ronda.'

'It's a rather special occasion,' explained the *Marquesa*, still gazing up at Salvador, 'because my father will preside at the bullfight in which my brother Felipe will take part. Felipe is one of our most famous *toreros*, and the bulls used during the *temporada* are the bravest and most ferocious. It promises to be an exciting spectacle.' She gave Alexandra an affected smile, her eyes wandering over the young woman with disdain.

'Thank you for your kind invitation, Doña Isabel,' said Alexandra. 'I look forward to seeing Don Felipe in the ring and discovering the pleasures of bullfighting. And now,' she added, a little too hastily, hoping her cousin would not notice her torn blouse, 'if you would excuse me, I must dress for dinner.'

'Just a moment, Alexandra,' murmured Salvador, taking her arm as she passed, 'you've hurt yourself.'

'It's nothing,' she said, avoiding his eyes. 'I slipped into a bush.'

Thankful that he didn't pursue the matter, Alexandra fled across the hall to the big staircase, ran up the stairs two at a time and went to her room. But she barely had time to assess the damage caused by her skirmish before there was a knock on the door. Guessing who it might be, she ignored it: she had neither the energy nor the courage to face her cousin.

There was another knock and this time Salvador called out. Alexandra hesitated a few seconds more before reluctantly letting him in.

'What's the matter? What do you want?' she asked sharply.

'You disappear all afternoon, you don't come back until after dark, your face is scratched, your clothes are in a sorry state, and you ask *me* what the matter is?'

'I wasn't aware you were my keeper.'

'I was worried about you,' he confessed flatly.

Alexandra shook her head without replying.

'Where were you?' His voice was now soft, concerned.

'It's no business of yours.' She looked at him indignantly.

'But it is, *niña*. You're here under my roof and therefore under my protection. I'm responsible for your safety. You still have much to learn about our ways, this is a …'

Alexandra interrupted him heatedly. 'Spare me your lectures, Salvador, and don't get all patronizing and pompous on me. I learned from an early age to stand on my own two feet. I've done pretty well so far without your help, thank you.' Salvador frowned but didn't answer and, because she feared a scathing reply, she continued relentlessly, her green eyes sharp with defensive pride: 'And if my attitude at times has led you to believe that I was calling on your chivalry, trust me when I tell you you're flattering yourself.'

'Alexandra,' he sighed, 'must we go on like this? Can't we have a truce?' Salvador's voice was low, husky. He stared at her, his brows knitted in a puzzled frown; his handsome face otherwise expressionless. Alexandra stared back silently, trying to decipher any hidden message in his eyes, but once again the hypnotic power he exerted over her was robbing her of her senses. Her mind clouded and she had to struggle to control the irresistible desire to throw herself into his arms.

Looking away, she went to the window and took a deep breath.

'I was at Marujita's,' she told him at last.

There was a pause. 'And …?' he whispered hesitantly, as if fearing to hear more.

Though tempted, she refrained from telling Salvador that she'd seen him storm from the cottage. Instead, she said, 'I went looking for Pablo this afternoon and found him there, but before I had the time to question him, Marujita turned up. She asked me to leave. I refused and we came to blows.'

There was a moment's silence. Finally, Salvador spoke.

'You're even more reckless and foolish than I imagined.' His voice was icy, bitter now. 'It may be how the English behave but, I can assure you, it is not our way.' And before she could turn to face him, he had left the room.

His words rasped in Alexandra's ears, sending a sharp pain through her heart. She knew that, somehow, she had failed him. Her throat tightened. 'Salvador!' she called out in a strangulated voice, but he didn't hear her.

CHAPTER 7

The day of the trip to Ronda dawned fresh and clear. They left Jerez in the early hours of Saturday morning in two cars. Doña María Dolores had suggested they went by train instead; although it would take them twice as long to get there, it would be more comfortable and safer for the ladies, the road being so steep and stony. However, Salvador had opted for the more adventurous route across the mountain roads, arguing that the journey was shorter and more private by car. Anyway, he argued, it would be of much greater interest, despite being somewhat hazardous. Besides, they were setting out more than twenty-four hours before the *corrida*, giving them time to stop on the way at places that would be helpful for Alexandra's research. He assured the dowager that the two drivers he had hired especially for the occasion were experts at this route, which they travelled regularly every week.

Mercedes and Esmeralda rode with Salvador, while Alexandra and Ramón brought up the rear in the second car. Now regretting her spat with Marujita, Alexandra would have preferred to make the journey with Salvador so that she could explain herself, but she had not been asked to join him. Quite plainly, he had decided to avoid her company again.

The days following Alexandra's argument with him had unfolded predictably. In the mornings, she went for long walks in the countryside around the hacienda. Her afternoons were more productive. Somehow, her writer's block had been lifted. Alexandra didn't know if it was due to her liberating tussle with Marujita or perhaps some deeper, more gradual change in her psyche that had suddenly found its way to the surface. Everything had begun to flow again and although she had not spent much time on the book itself at last she could put down her thoughts, describe her feelings or sometimes, when she felt particularly creative, she would indulge in some poetry writing. The mad gypsy woman at the wake had at least been right about one thing. This was a vibrant, passionate land: the heat, the colours, the flamboyance of the people, the wild and mythical feel of the mountainous scenery, even the spectacular rise and setting of the sun. Everything took on dramatic proportions, leaving her senses buzzing.

Alexandra's own feelings had never been so vivid, so intense. Her outlook on life and her view of people had altered noticeably: if before she had been inclined to be slightly judgemental and stiff in her dealings with others – no doubt a result of her upbringing – her exposure to this highly demonstrative culture had now not only made her less so, but she also found herself bolder and even somewhat audacious. Spain had seeped into her blood, peeled away layers that had been suffocating her and, what was more, she liked this new, alive person she was discovering within herself.

Meanwhile, Salvador had retreated into his shell. Usually absent during the day, he often failed to put in an appearance at mealtimes, a tremendous feat at El Pavón. When their paths did cross, from time to time, he neither spoke to her nor did he look at her. It was as if she didn't exist; and although Alexandra had now grown accustomed to his volatile moods, she couldn't help but feel frustrated. She knew he was angry. Not only had she engaged Marujita in an undignified catfight, putting herself at risk, she had been perhaps more cutting in her comments to him than intended. Nevertheless, she found it unfair that he should judge her silently without giving her a chance to justify herself. Maybe in the heat of the moment, her embarrassed exasperation had come across somewhat petulantly. Still, that was no reason to treat her like an emotional adolescent. Did he think her so immature that she wouldn't be able to conduct a civil conversation? Twice, she had glimpsed him alone on horseback, riding through the grounds of the hacienda. She had wanted to go up to him and confront him but his fierce aloofness had intimidated her and in the end she dared not make the first move.

Alexandra stared out of the car window at the rugged scenery of wild shrubbery and herbs, framed against a cobalt sky, and seethed with frustration. *The Devil take him!* she thought with a sudden burst of pride and indignation.

She made a valiant attempt to shake herself out of her mood; after all, it was a fresh sunny morning with spring budding in the air, she was on her way to attend a bullfight for the first time, and she had nothing with which to reproach herself. Even though things weren't going the way she might have hoped, she wouldn't waste any more energy worrying about Salvador's fluctuating moods. But her mind refused to relax, and she wondered what conversations were going on in the car ahead, and whether Mercedes was being her usual coquettish self. 'You haven't uttered a word since we left,' remarked Ramón, who had been observing her frowning at the landscape for some time.

She forced a laugh, turning to look at him. 'I'm not very chatty at this hour of the morning. I'm still pining for my pillow.'

'I wondered if you were feeling carsick. I couldn't believe it when Salvador stubbornly insisted on this madcap route through the mountains. We'd have been travelling in comfort by train if he hadn't been so determined to impress you.'

Alexandra raised an eyebrow.

'Why else do you think we're both being shaken around like beans in a jar?' Ramón grimaced as the car flew over yet another bump. 'At least you would have been able to doze off in the train.'

She gave a look of mock contrition. 'So I should apologize, in that case, for depriving you of a smoother ride.'

Ramón narrowed his eyes, slanting her a wry look.

'I know what's bothering you. It's our charming cousin, isn't it? Don't deny it, I only have to look at your faces. You're a strange pair. Half the time, you both behave as if you were in love, the way you look at each other, and yet …'

'Ramón, let's forget Salvador today.'

He chuckled. 'Nothing would please me better.'

Alexandra gazed out of the window once more. 'What's Ronda like? I've read that it's one of the oldest cities in Europe.'

'Ronda is the city of outlaws and bullfighters. And if you want to see a bullfight, of course Ronda is the place to be.' Ramón nudged Alexandra, offering her a flask of water. 'Needless to say, the *corrida* is a very important part of Spanish culture. If you're here in September, you could see the *feria* Goyesca. That would be a real Spanish spectacle for your book, *mi primita*. Do you know Goya's paintings?'

She sipped some water and returned the bottle. 'Some. A few of his portraits are in the National Gallery in London.'

'You won't have seen his bullfight paintings then. Very realistic, even today. And at the *feria* Goyesca, everyone dresses in traditional eighteenth- and nineteenth-century costume. Some as *toreros*, others are spectators. There are parades, eating, drinking, dancing … it's all quite flamboyant. I think it would appeal to the romantic in you, even if you didn't care to see the bullfight.'

'You're probably right, it does sound fascinating.' Alexandra looked thoughtful. 'Tell me more about the *corrida* we'll be attending. Why does Felipe Herrera do it? He must be rich enough not to have to earn his living at such a dangerous sport.'

Ramón shrugged. 'He does it for fun and for fame. He's been at it for five years. Felipe has great courage and outstanding talent, I'll give him that. Added to which, one has to admit he looks like an ancient god in all his glittering finery. It's no wonder he draws huge crowds whenever he fights.'

'So he's famous round here?' Alexandra asked.

'Very much so. The people also like him because he's a philanthropist: he gives the huge purses he wins to the Church. A shrewd gesture under this government, given he's such a public figure in Andalucía.'

'He certainly sounds like an impressive young man.' Alexandra's eyes sparkled with excitement. 'I've never been to a bullfight. As a spectacle, it's supposed to be incredible. I can't wait to see what it's really like.'

'Well, you couldn't have found a more talented or courageous bullfighter to introduce you to our national sport,' Ramón told her, happy to note his cousin was smiling again.

'Before leaving England I read a marvellous book about Spain. A whole chapter was devoted to bullfighting. It'll be interesting to compare it with the real thing and gather some local colour for my novel.' She glanced at Ramón playfully. 'I hope you'll introduce me to the handsome Don Felipe?'

Ramón slanted a mischievous look at her. 'If that's what you'd like, I will certainly do so, dear Cousin. You'll have ample time to get to know him at the evening reception his sister is holding in his honour after the *corrida*. I'm equally sure that Don Felipe won't miss the opportunity to seduce such a charming and beautiful young lady as you. He's a notorious womanizer and has broken many hearts, so be warned!'

Alexandra smiled at her cousin's characteristic impishness. She remembered when she had glimpsed Don Felipe at the masked ball that Ramón had labelled him a heartbreaker. Were all handsome Spanish men Don Juans in disguise? Still, the attentions of a dashing *torero* appealed to her sense of romantic intrigue, and it was hardly an unwelcome prospect, particularly if Salvador was bent on ignoring her for the whole trip.

The landscape began to lose its sparse, wild vegetation; soon the road was running through a rocky plain, even bumpier than before; rough and barren as pumice. In late spring, Ramón told her, a carpet of wild flowers would cover this scorched land. Thyme, broom and lavender would spread their aromatic scent through the air but at this time of the year, traces of greenery were still scarce. Only gnarled olive trees and other evergreens dotted the countryside. What an overwhelming contrast this arid wilderness presented against the lush brilliance of El Pavón.

They drove for hours through winding tracks in a dust-filled mighty landscape of strange rocks, which rose grotesquely on all sides, peak above peak, honeycombed occasionally with gaping caves. Suddenly, as both cars rounded a sharp bend, they met a small truck travelling at speed in the opposite direction. Quick as a flash, the driver of the car in front steered the vehicle sharply out of the way, aiming towards the edge of the road to avoid a collision. The truck, bouncing along at full pelt, missed Alexandra and Ramón's car by a hair's breadth.

The car swerved abruptly, tyres squealing, as the driver slammed on the breaks. It began to spin out of control. The engine stalled, and it screeched to a halt right at the very edge of a cliff, with one of its rear wheels hanging precariously over the sheer drop into a deep ravine.

Alexandra froze, her scream dying in her throat. Their driver had been hurled from his seat but, luckily for him, had rolled out of the car on to the stony verge. Alexandra, meanwhile, was huddled in the corner of her seat, too terrified to move. Suspended over the drop, on a crazy tilt, she stared at her slanted view of the ravine, wondering how she and Ramón, who was backed up against the opposite door, could possibly escape before the car plummeted to the bottom of the cliff. For a few seconds, all was strangely quiet.

'Alexandra, are you all right?' Ramón's voice was shaky.

'Yes, I'm fine ... I think,' she told him though her heart was pounding.

'I'm sorry, I can't move towards you. If I do, I'll tilt the car over,' he added.

Meanwhile, Salvador had leapt from his car. Shouts could be heard as he ordered Mercedes and Esmeralda to stay put, while the driver of their vehicle helped his colleague to his feet, making sure he wasn't hurt.

Salvador rushed to the other vehicle and peered anxiously through the open window. 'Is anybody hurt? Are you all right?'

'No one's hurt,' Ramón reassured him, 'but I think it's going to be difficult getting out of here.'

'Keep calm, don't move. Stay where you are until I've worked out how to get you out safely.' Now, Salvador rounded the vehicle. It was clear that Ramón couldn't leave it first or it would only tilt further as he shifted his weight. Alexandra must be helped out first.

Leading almost vertically downwards from the edge of the cliff, there were narrow ledges on the mountainside in stair-step fashion. Directly below Alexandra's door, a few feet down the slope, a short bushy tree with tightly-knit branches clung to a small patch of clear ground. Alexandra would have to jump out of the car, allowing the tree to break her fall; it would serve as a buffer between her and the ground.

Salvador came back to the window. His eyes settled on Alexandra's pale face as he stroked his lean jaw. 'I'm afraid you're going to have to get out first and it will involve a few acrobatic feats,' he told her with an uneasy lift of his eyebrows. '*Pero no te preocupes mi bella dama*, but never fear my fair lady, your loyal knight in shining armour here will catch you,' he added, half-joking and half-reassuring; but the strain she glimpsed on his face told her that he was desperately trying to mask his concern.

She felt a tremor of fear run through her body but somehow managed to pull herself together and look cheerful. 'Don't worry about me, Salvador. Just tell me what to do and I'm sure I'll be fine.' She laughed nervously before adding, 'I was quite good at gymnastics at school.'

A smile touched Salvador's mouth. '*Espléndido*! I've worked out a plan.' His face then became serious again, his tone peremptory. 'Listen carefully to what I say, and do exactly as I tell you.'

His last words were so true to character that, despite the critical situation, Alexandra couldn't help the spirited twinkle in her eye. 'Your orders are my command,' she said with a hint of wryness, while Ramón gave an amused, if nervous, snort.

Ignoring the jibe, Salvador went on with his instructions.

'Can you see the tree that stands directly beneath your door?'

'Yes, I see it.'

'I'm going to stand right under it. Once I'm down there, I want you to open the door, *very slowly*. If you feel or hear the slightest movement of the car, stop immediately. Once you have a clear view of the tree, you'll have to jump on to it. Don't worry, the branches are dense and will hold your weight. In any case, I'll be there to catch you if anything goes wrong. Do you think you'll be able to do that?'

Alexandra swallowed hard. 'I guess so,' she said in a small voice. She was not particularly fond of heights.

'*Excellente*,' he said, before rounding the car once more and starting his descent down the hillside. He reappeared a few minutes later, standing on the flat patch of ground under the tree.

'Can you hear me, Alexandra?' he shouted, hands cupped to his mouth.

'Yes, Salvador, I can hear you. I can see you too.'

'Go very slowly, *mi primita*,' Ramón said beside her. 'You don't want the car to move.'

Alexandra opened the door as slowly and cautiously as she could, taking care not to shift her weight too abruptly. The drop, and the ground far below, made her suddenly dizzy. She paused and closed her eyes. Her heart was beating quickly, knocking violently against her ribs; her mouth went dry. She really didn't like heights.

'What if you don't catch me?' Alexandra instantly regretted those words as soon as they were out of her mouth. She sounded unnerved and loathed to admit her fear to Salvador.

'Alexandra, *querida, no tenga miedo*, don't be afraid, you must jump now. I'm here to catch you.' She heard Salvador's voice through the haze of her fear. *This is no time for histrionics*, she admonished herself, *where is your English gumption, girl?* And then, with her eyes closed, she jumped.

She almost fell through the branches to the ground but, true to his word, Salvador was waiting for her. He drew her to him, grabbing her with both arms and pulling her against his powerful chest with a bruising strength. Under his bronzed tan, Alexandra could detect a fearful pallor, and she could see the tension in his harrowed features.

Alexandra was still a little wobbly when he set her down. She met the dark blue eyes, which were fastened intently on hers.

'Are you hurt?' he enquired softly as he put an arm around her shoulders, drawing her close to him. Instinctively, she leaned into the strength of his muscular body.

'Shaken but not broken,' she replied with an uncertain laugh, hoping it wouldn't sound too false.

Even in the midst of this frightening experience, Salvador's dark good looks, his vitality, his self-control overwhelmed her. She faltered, her heart beating ferociously; not from fear this time, but with the sudden surge of raw passion she felt for him.

'I'll help you climb back up.'

Salvador took her hand firmly in his and slowly they scrambled up the graduated side of the cliff. '*Lentamente, mi ángel, lentamente.*' His tone was deep and gentle as he helped her slowly negotiate the rocky path.

Alexandra felt a riot of emotions skitter along the surface of her skin, which was reacting to his touch in a way she couldn't seem to control. A warm breeze blew a couple of locks of hair that had slipped over her brow. It played caressingly around her neck, and for a split second she found herself fantasizing that it was Salvador's fingers stroking her.

He stopped and looked down at her, still clasping her hand tightly. Had he felt her tension? Their eyes locked, as if he knew all about the tumult going on inside her body.

'*Por Dios,* by God, if they were jewels, those green eyes of yours would be worth a fortune strung on gold,' and, bending his head, he leaned closer. Mesmerized by her mouth, he paused a breath away from her before taking her lips in a slow-moving kiss. Her entire body flashed with heat, and all the while his fingers were twining between hers. The heady masculine scent of him filled her as the smooth texture of his lips finally lifted their pressure, brushing over hers as lightly as a feather.

Quickly, but gently, he pulled away. Alexandra's cheeks burned, not only because all her senses were crying out for more but also with the thought that they might have been seen from above. Reading her mind, Salvador shook his dark head reassuringly but his ardent stare, ocean-deep, remained a few seconds more on her face before they resumed their climb.

At the top they were greeted by the girls and Ramón, who had somehow managed to ease himself out of the other door once Alexandra had jumped. He now held out a hand to help them up the last steps.

'That was a near miss …' He heaved a sigh of relief. 'It's good to be back on firm ground. Alexandra, are you all right?'

But Alexandra was far from feeling that she was on firm ground and wasn't sure if she was feeling all right either, but she wasn't about to elaborate truthfully on either count. She felt Salvador's hand slip from hers and smiled at Ramón. 'Yes, thanks to Salvador, I'm fine.' She turned to her rescuer, not quite able to meet his gaze. 'I'm sorry if I made a bit of a fool of myself earlier, but I've never been good with heights. Thank you for being so patient.'

There was a glimmer of emotion in Salvador's dark eyes that she couldn't quite interpret. 'You did everything perfectly, Alexandra. Clearly your gymnastics stood you in good stead for dramatic car crashes.' For the first time, she saw him relax and the expression lighten.

Ramón stood with his arms folded, watching them both. He nodded towards Salvador with a wry smile. 'And you too did everything perfectly, Cousin, as always.' His jovial enough remark held a slightly mocking edge, even though Salvador had clearly saved the day.

Beside Ramón, Esmeralda regarded her brother with glowing eyes, clearly proud. Next to her, Mercedes was watching Salvador and Alexandra, a mixture of excitement and jealousy flitting across her face in equal measure. Alexandra had no doubt that her sister would have loved to have had the starring role in this highly charged adventure, not to mention having Salvador's arms wrapped around her.

It wasn't long before the drivers had hauled the car back on to the road with the use of some rope. They tested it, reporting that it was in good enough shape to continue the journey to Ronda.

'I think it would be wiser if you travelled in the first car with Mercedes and Esmeralda. Ramón and I will bring up the rear in this one,' Salvador told Alexandra. However, she wasn't listening, too busy recovering from the effect his unexpected kiss had had on her. The shock of the near-plunge down the side of the steep ravine was now setting in too. She was shivering, despite the heat of the sun, and was feeling dizzy and light-headed. Salvador, who had turned towards Ramón to issue his instruction, now abruptly turned back and she almost collided into him.

'Are you sure you're all right, Alexandra? You seem very pale.' He placed his hands on her shoulders, his touch once more igniting an awareness between them. 'You're trembling,' he murmured, a concerned furrow between his eyebrows. 'Come, let me help you into the shade of the car. You're not accustomed to our scorching sun. Its heat is quite unforgiving.'

Uncomfortably conscious of his closeness, Alexandra let him guide her back to the vehicle, his arm around her shoulder. She could feel the warmth of his body brushing against her corsage, making her heart beat erratically. In an attempt to free herself from this physical and psychological bondage, she pulled away from him but only managed to stumble unsteadily and he caught her swiftly. *What a fool he must think me*, she told herself, as she gripped his arm to steady herself.

Salvador settled her down comfortably in the back of the first car and poured some water from a thermos he brought out from under the seat. 'Here, drink this, it will refresh you,' he said in an overly gentle tone of voice, which Alexandra suddenly found infuriating. Her mind was beginning to clear. What had just happened between herself and Salvador? After ignoring her for days on end he had now pulled her into a kiss full of tenderness and slow fire. Had he misread her tension as fear and was merely trying to calm her down with an arrogant male response? Worse still, perhaps he thought she was some silly schoolgirl who had lost her nerve, and he felt sorry for her. She wished he would just go and leave her alone. Embarrassed now, she despised herself for so easily falling back under his spell, and for giving everyone the spectacle of her acting like a weakling.

'I've absolutely recovered now,' she insisted firmly, hoping he would be convinced and that they could get on with the journey.

'We're not far from Ronda,' Salvador informed her, studying her face and leaning his elbow on the open car door. 'Another twenty minutes and we'll be there. Do you think you can manage that?'

The implication that she was faint-hearted grazed Alexandra's pride further, but she gritted her teeth, determined not to create another scene. Lifting her chin, she smiled coolly. 'I expect so.' With that, she rested her head on the back of her seat and closed her eyes dismissively, as if by blocking him out of her sight she was erasing him from her life.

The driver rose to his feet, having examined the car. 'I'm afraid this wheel won't take us far, *señor*,' he announced grimly. 'We'll need a new one to take us to Ronda.'

Salvador frowned. 'How far will this one get us?'

'We're only a little way from Arcos de la Frontera. It should last long enough to take us there safely, provided we move slowly.'

'Very well then, we'll just have to stay there tonight. Let's get going.'

It was late afternoon when they finally rolled into Arcos de la Frontera, a small town not far from Ronda. The ancient bells in the church of Santa María were sending their age-old message to the inhabitants as the cars stopped in front of the inn Fonda la Felisa, the only respectable *posada* in the vicinity. Tomorrow morning they would travel on as planned to the more refined lodgings of the Parador de la Luna in Ronda.

Alexandra had the strange feeling of stepping into a different era as she entered the large inn. Like most buildings in Spain, it had numerous shaded patios, a broad wooden central staircase and long dark corridors. A cauldron simmered in the massive fireplace of the main hall, filling the place with the cloying aroma of a country stew. The pale glimmer of the oil lamps failed to pierce the shadows lurking in the recesses of the vast room. Flycatchers and wagtails flitted among the beams of the high ceiling, catching insects. This was not a smart hotel, to say the least. No electricity *and* bugs but it would have to do.

The shaken travellers were soon taken up to their rooms. By now, Alexandra was exhausted. She had feigned sleep through the remainder of the journey, in the hope of being left to her brooding thoughts. Now, the last thing she wanted was to join the others for supper but, not wishing to be rude and collapse straight into bed, she went downstairs to say goodnight.

She found the others seated at a long table in the main hall that ran from the corner of the room to the fireplace, where the *posadero* of the inn was dishing the contents of the cauldron into wide bowls for the guests at neighbouring tables. Half-full now, the room had taken on a far cosier atmosphere than when they had first arrived. The murmur of voices and clinking glasses mingled with the sound of a guitar playing somewhere. In the huge fireplace, flames were crackling, flickering light on to the rough walls as people milled about between comfortably huddled groups.

Alexandra almost regretted her decision to retire early but if she had been tempted to stay, one look at Salvador made her long to be back in her room and not so close to him. He was sprawled in a relaxed fashion on a high-backed wooden bench running the length of the table, trousers stretched over muscled thighs. A brooding expression glittered in his eyes.

'I think I'll get some food sent up to my room and have an early night. It's been an eventful day,' she announced. Her gaze flicked to him, then away again.

'Cousin, surely you'll stay for some sangria?' Ramón beamed at her, holding up a glass invitingly.

'Yes, Alexandra. Why don't you stay for one drink? It'll relax you after your ordeal. Ramón here has found its reviving properties effective, haven't you?' Salvador arched a brow at the young man, his lips curving with a trace of amusement.

Ramón grinned again and lifted his glass in a nod to Salvador. 'Yes, indeed I have. I will always stand by the reviving properties of sangria.'

'There you are, Alexandra. Now you cannot refuse.' Salvador filled a glass and pushed it towards her expectantly, fixing her with a look that made her struggle to hold his gaze. Her glance fell to his shoulders and then to his hands, which even in repose had a dark appearance of power in keeping with his face and athletic form.

'How are you feeling now, Alexandra?' Esmeralda gestured towards the empty chair at the head of the table, between herself and Salvador. Alexandra smiled tightly. *Why could there not be a seat further away from that stare of his?* She caught a whiff of fragrant tobacco mixed with soap as she took her place between brother and sister; it was a smell so particular to Salvador she would have recognized it anywhere. It played havoc with her senses for she was flooded with the recollection of those few times they had been intimate. Her heart was pounding against her breastbone and she could feel her spine tensing.

Esmeralda gave Alexandra a wide-eyed, sympathetic look. 'It must have been a shock for you. I would have felt so scared, leaping from the car like that. I know I wouldn't have been so brave.'

'Oh, Esmeralda, don't be so wet!' Mercedes' huffy voice cut in next to her. Clearly, she was still piqued that all the attention was on her sister, not to mention that Alexandra had enjoyed the benefit of a dramatic rescue from Salvador. She stared at her peevishly. 'I would have got out perfectly well on my own, unlike my dear sister, who found the perfect excuse to jump into Salvador's arms.'

Alexandra felt Salvador stiffen slightly beside her.

Ramón nodded with mock seriousness. 'Indeed, Mercedes. Something tells me rescuing you would have been a far longer and noisier affair.' He laughed loudly. 'Plus we would have been hearing about it for months afterwards. *La peor gallina es la que más cacarea*, the worst hen is the one that clucks the most.'

As was usually the case in her dealings with Ramón, Mercedes had no blistering retort to hand and merely resorted to pouting in silence. Alexandra, too, sat without speaking and sipped her drink.

'You know, it's a shame, for the sake of Alexandra's book, that we didn't travel past La Peña de los Enamorados, Lover's Leap,' Esmeralda noted airily, ignoring Mercedes' and Ramón's little spat. She looked her usual dreamy self but Alexandra could have sworn there was a hint of sly interest in Esmeralda's eyes as she glanced between herself and Salvador.

'No more an outlandish route than the one we took, I suppose,' muttered Ramón.

Alexandra was curious. 'What's so special about that place?'

All the while, Salvador had been silent, though the air between him and Alexandra throbbed relentlessly as her heartbeat. Now he broke in.

'La Peña de los Enamorados is attached to a local legend about an impossible love affair,' he explained.

Alexandra drove her gaze towards him. For an instant, something warred in his eyes as he looked at her; was it longing, regret? The force of his personality struck her like a hurricane, sending her head spinning. She struggled not to betray the effect he had on her, conscious that everyone's attention was on them both.

Salvador tapped a finger gently on the side of his glass and looked down into its contents as he continued. 'Lover's Leap is an enormous crag of limestone overlooking the town and valley of Antequera. The rock provides the setting for the tragic finale to the lovers' story. Legend has it that a young Christian man from Antequera and a beautiful Moorish girl from nearby Archidona were driven to the top of the cliff by Moorish soldiers. Rather than renounce their love, they chose to hurl themselves into the abyss. The rock remains a symbol of their eternal love.' His eyes were on Alexandra again, his features brooding. It felt as though his gaze was scorching her skin and she put a hand to the base of her throat, where she felt her pulse thudding beneath her fingertips.

Salvador paused, taking his time as he lit a cigarette. The air filled with the aromatic smoke, creating a halo around him. At this point, the others began chatting about the bullfight. Under his breath, Salvador went on: 'A romantic novelist's dream story, wouldn't you say?'

'Yes,' Alexandra conceded, lifting her chin. 'There's nothing more romantic than eternal love.'

'And nothing more foolish, perhaps.'

'Passion and fidelity are foolish?' She shot him a fierce look. 'Being prepared to die for love only makes it more powerful.'

'It is the stuff of romantic fables. And even there, the obstacles of real life soon show themselves. Those soldiers of misfortune chase most poor unfortunates to ground in the end.' He drained his glass and set it down abruptly without looking at her. 'Passion can be an affliction.'

But Esmeralda had caught the tail end of their conversation and was moved to speak: 'Salvador, that's a little harsh, I think.' She looked almost hurt at his pronouncement. 'Surely you can't condemn true love as foolish?'

Alexandra forced a laugh. 'I'm afraid your brother has a doomed view of life, Esmeralda,' she said, before he could answer. She was trying to make light of it all, but inside her emotions were churning. Is that what Salvador really thought about love and passion? Was he giving her a clear message that he regretted what had passed between them only hours before? Why did he keep pulling her one way, then another? His eyes were dark and impenetrable; her inability to fathom what strange truth lay behind them made Alexandra keenly aware of Aunt Geraldine's warning that, like her mother Vanessa, she too would find herself among strangers whose whole culture and way of thinking would be unfamiliar. Suddenly an overwhelming weariness descended, sapping her of all energy.

Salvador smiled wryly. 'Yes, I'm a lost cause, I suppose.' He then leaned forward slightly, seeming to sense the change in Alexandra.

'And so am I now,' she muttered, rising from her chair. 'I think I really do need my bed.'

'Yes, of course.' Salvador rose quickly too. 'I'll see you to your room.'

Her brows drew together. 'Salvador, that's really not necessary.'

'I insist, Alexandra.' He gave her a smile. 'After what you survived today, we must make sure you at least get there in one piece.'

Alexandra relented, deciding it was easier than protesting further. Salvador motioned to the *posadero* and asked for food to be sent up to the room. Saying goodnight and leaving the others to their bowls of stew, which had just arrived on the table, Alexandra made her way up the stairs with Salvador, both of them silent.

She was thankful for the scrupulously clean sheets and the washbasin in her room, as well as the hot stew that the waiter carried upstairs. If she had a good night's sleep, she would be a new person in the morning, she explained to a concerned Salvador as they said goodnight at her door.

'I learned long ago that sleep is the best remedy for many an ailment,' she could not resist telling him pointedly. For a moment she thought her subtlety was lost on him for he merely looked back at her, his brow slightly furrowed. But as he leant into the door-frame there was something in his gaze that she was unable to decipher.

'Sleep and mend,' he said almost gruffly. 'You look exhausted.'

'Thank you for your concern, Salvador. Now, please, go and join the others and enjoy the rest of your evening.'

At this she saw his eyes cloud over and he stepped back. She sensed that he was silently donning his armour again. Before closing her door, for the briefest of moments she watched his tall figure disappear down the corridor. Then she went inside quickly, not wanting to see if he looked back.

*   *   *

The following afternoon, La Plaza de Toros in Ronda was drenched with the blinding white glare of a fierce sun. Since the end of the eighteenth century, the huge, tragic amphitheatre with its floor of red sand, reminiscent of the Roman arenas of old, had been the scene of many a bloody and barbarous combat between man and beast.

There was a roar of applause as Don Vincente Herrera and his guests entered the President's box, reserved for the most important *aficionados*, the devotees of bullfighting. The Herreras, like other great Andalucían families, had survived the civil strife of the 1930s through a mix of caution and cunning. They now enjoyed the enviable position of being popular, not only with the Spanish people who loved the young *torero*, Don Felipe, but also with the Franco regime.

Fascinated, Alexandra watched people from all walks of life pack on to the crowded terraces that sizzled in the baking sun. There were foreigners passing through, onlookers simply curious to see the spectacle, and committed lovers of bullfighting.

Aristocrats and respectable middle-class men squeezed in with workmen and peasants. Another group of *aficionados* ate and drank noisily a few boxes away, while elegant women and pretty *señoritas* in flamboyant clothes, their arms laden with flowers, chattered as they looked for their places, or simply sat in their seats expectantly. They were there to take part in this fierce entertainment, mingling regardless of social class and oblivious to the heat and dust.

Alexandra had been given the honoured position on the right of Don Vincente himself; Ramón was on her other side, Salvador almost immediately in front of her. She could see the side of his chiselled, handsome face, and was so close to him that she could have reached out and touched his thick dark hair. The thought made her quiver slightly with a frisson of excitement, which she quashed hastily for the events of yesterday were still a confused whirl in her head but she was determined to block them out.

Doña Isabel was seated on the other side of Salvador. A fleeting pang of jealousy scythed through Alexandra as she noted the possessive way in which the *Marquesa* was leaning over him, and how dazzling she appeared in her magnificent dress of fawn-coloured organza and a matching feather hat, which, although old-fashioned, suited her aristocratic looks. Alexandra was acutely aware of the plainness of her own ensemble: the pale yellow silk dress with its delicate lace bodice and her wide-brimmed hat decorated with camellias. What she had deemed elegantly simple now appeared almost dull next to the *Marquesa*'s outfit.

Esmeralda, on her host's left, looked as ethereal as ever in a pearl-grey silk suit, which set off her fair complexion and unfathomable grey-blue eyes. She seemed further away than ever and, not for the first time since they'd left El Pavón, Alexandra wondered how long it would be before she plucked up courage to flee the ancestral home. In the row behind, two young members of the Spanish nobility were competing for Mercedes' affections and she was clearly enjoying the attention.

'The Plaza de Toros is the most ancient bullring of the Peninsula,' explained Don Vincente to his guest. He was a stocky man with a thick moustache and black hair that was swept back from his forehead. His chest in its brocaded jacket was puffed out, and he had never once stopped extolling the virtues of his son, Don Felipe, or boasting about his estates since Alexandra had first been introduced. She was relieved that his endless stream of conversation had at last settled upon something other than his family.

'It is entirely built of wood and dates back to 1784,' he continued. 'Legend tells the story of a young soldier who completely demolished it on the day of its inauguration, by toppling a column in the same way as Samson destroyed the temple. La Real Maestranza de Caballería, the oldest equestrian corporation in Spain, rebuilt it and used it to celebrate its games and tournaments.'

'Are there many bullrings in Andalucía?' Alexandra was not particularly keen to engage Don Vincente in another detailed discussion, but she was aware of the need to appear polite. Out of the corner of her eye she saw Doña Isabel place a hand on Salvador's shoulder and laugh extravagantly at something he'd said.

'Yes, indeed, and my son has fought in many of them.' Don Vincente's expression darkened slightly. 'Though Felipe has been careful not to fight in the Estremadura capital of Badajoz, where the bullet holes of a civil war massacre are still visible in the old bullring. My son prides himself on being identified with no political side, you understand. He is the people's hero.'

Alexandra smiled dutifully and turned her gaze back to the colourful crowds. Doña Isabel's loud, distinctive laugh sounded again. Alexandra did her best to ignore the small pantomime going on under her nose, certain it was being staged for her benefit. She felt foolish and small; out of her depth once more. To cover her wounded feelings, she turned to Ramón, suddenly feeling the need for his light banter.

As the clock struck three, Don Vincente waved his handkerchief. Thundering applause met his signal; a trumpet blew. From the patio, two mounted men in King Philip II outfits galloped across the ring and stopped opposite the President's box. They doffed their caps and bowed low. Alexandra watched Don Vincente nod, and then they rode back to their place.

Ramón leant over. 'They are the *algacils*,' he whispered in her ear. 'The President's orders are transmitted through them. The *paseo* is about to start.'

A deathly hush filled the arena. The ceremony was heralded by a fanfare of bugles, marking the solemn entrance of the bullfighters and their assisting *cuadrillas*. At the head of the procession rode the two *algacils* on horseback, followed by the *matadors* on foot, wearing dazzling brocaded jackets decorated with gold tassels. Then came the *banderilleros* and the *picadores*; and finally, bringing up the rear, the *areneros*, mounted on mules adorned with little bells.

As this bright cortège paraded round the arena, Alexandra was reminded of gladiators' processions in ancient Rome. It stopped to salute the President and the *toreros* exchanged their ceremonial capes for working ones. At this stage, Don Vincente stood up and threw the key towards the red door of the bulls' enclosure. An *algacil* caught it in his plumed hat, his dexterity meeting with a clamour of appreciation from a relieved crowd.

Ramón inclined his head towards Alexandra. 'It is said that if the key to the *toril* falls to the ground, the bullfight will be a bad one,' he explained.

The ring cleared, the clarion sounded, and heads turned towards the *toril* entrance. As the two red doors fell back, all of

Alexandra's previous distractions dissolved; she held her breath in eager expectancy and the first bull was released into the ring to the frenzied acclaim of the public.

It was a magnificent animal, black and glossy, with an enormous head and smooth, sharp horns – a real brute with the spirit of a fighter. Alexandra recoiled a little in her seat as the beast hurled itself into the middle of the arena. Two *banderilleros* ran across his course, trailing a cape. The bull charged and missed.

Don Felipe, meanwhile, who had been standing behind a barrier watching his adversary, now strutted haughtily over the reddish sand of the arena. He was wearing the dress of the *matador*: black silk breeches drawn in at the hips and a bolero in gold brocade, decorated with sequins, tassels, studs and epaulettes, which set off his golden hair, sun-tanned complexion and his proud bearing.

Taking the large red cape in both hands, he waited. The animal paused, sniffed the air, and then charged, head down, in a bold attack, horns gleaming.

Don Felipe stood motionless, defying his opponent. He leant slightly forward until the last moment and then, just as the horns were about to strike the cape, he moved his arms slowly in a sweeping motion, pivoting lightly on the balls of his feet, causing the head and body of the bull to pass by him.

His *veronica* was greeted by enthusiastic shouts from the masses. It was plain to Alexandra that Don Felipe was the star of this lethal duel, in which man and beast confronted each other in a game of skill and death. She found herself curiously entranced by the sheer charisma of his performance. True, he didn't have the immediate effect on her that Salvador had. At that thought, she couldn't help but glance at the man sitting so closely in front of her. Only yesterday those broad shoulders had towered over her and that muscular arm had pulled her to him for a kiss she could still feel on her mouth ... Now it was the

Marquesa who seemed to be delighting him with her winsome smiles and flashing eyes, clutching his arm at every charge of the bull, every gasp from the crowd.

Now the second fanfare resounded. The *picadores*, dressed in their short jackets, chamois leather trousers and wide *castoreno* hats, entered the arena astride their blindfolded horses. Alexandra wondered what sad fate awaited those poor, grotesque creatures equipped with padded mattresses strapped around their girths.

The *picador*, Miguel Pereda, sat motionless astride his mount, facing the bull. Suddenly, he drove his lance into the animal's neck and a large red stain spread across it. The beast charged once, twice and then, mad with rage, rushed brutally, horns down, towards its opponent. At this the horse reared up and staggered back on to its hind legs, neighing shrilly. The *picador* fell and the bull swept upon him in fury.

The cry that went up from the crowd seemed to Alexandra to be merely the expression of her own, which was caught in her throat. A terrible nausea swirled in the pit of her stomach and she would have left her seat, had she felt able to stand.

In a second, Don Felipe strode briskly over and was using his cape to keep the fierce creature from the fallen man. In one swift movement, the beast turned and charged right at him. Calmly, and majestically throwing out his chest, elbow bent, his eyes fastened on his adversary, the *matador* waited motionless for the assault, diverting it with a simple twisting of the hips before thrusting his *pic* victoriously at the last moment, *al quiebro*, into the bull's shoulder.

Mad with enthusiasm at the sight of such bold, hand-to-hand fighting, the crowd started to shout hysterically, throwing flowers, hats and handkerchiefs into the arena.

The clarions trumpeted a third time, announcing the third and final death match, the *tercio de la muerte*. Don Felipe, taking the sweeping scarlet *muleta* and the sword, went over to the grandstand to salute the President.

It was the first time Alexandra had seen the young man close up. On the night of the ball he'd been wearing a red mask that had screened part of his face. However, she had been too preoccupied with her mysterious 'stranger' to take note of anybody else.

Don Felipe suddenly stopped in front of her, a brilliant smile lighting up his hard features. He peered at her through long, dark eyelashes that only partially concealed the smouldering look in his eyes. Against the blondness of his hair, his eyes appeared almost unnaturally black. He bowed low, then, his gaze becoming more intense, in a theatrical gesture he threw Alexandra his black velvet hat, thereby dedicating the bullfight to her. In a moment, he turned to face the danger alone, walking deliberately up to the bull, his sword hidden under the scarlet folds of his *muleta*.

Caught up in the whole drama and overflowing with emotion, Alexandra failed to notice the bleak expression on Salvador's face as he watched the *torero*'s manoeuvres.

'He's offered you his life as a gift,' whispered Ramón beside her, nodding at the velvet hat clutched in her lap. 'It's the greatest homage a bullfighter can pay a woman and Don Felipe doesn't hand out his attentions lightly. Usually, he dedicates his fight to the whole arena.' Ramón paused and leaned further towards her. 'And don't look now but I think his sister is none too pleased. The expression on her face could sour milk! Anyhow, tradition demands that at the end of the combat you give him back his hat with a gift inside it.'

Alexandra's eyes widened. It was intoxicating to be the centre of such attention from the *matador*, though inside she felt confusion warring with her rescued pride. She watched him stalk across the arena. Alexandra disliked seeing animals suffer; still, she couldn't help but follow the ceremony with fascination, holding her breath for this hero who waltzed with death.

Facing the bull, his right leg extended, arm outstretched, and holding his *muleta* low in his left hand, Don Felipe began his performance with the reckless courage that had made him famous, pushing bravery to the borders of suicide. Time and again he made the scarlet cloth fly between left and right hand in a continuous passing motion. With scarcely perceptible movements of his body, he parried the repeated attacks of the furious creature, each time tracing quarter circles with the cape to dodge its sharp-ended horns.

Alexandra's hands were clenched. Fingernails cut cruelly into her palms but the spectacle in the arena gripped her so intensely that she did not notice the pain. Her attention was riveted on the brilliant figure of the *matador*, her heart beating wildly, and she felt a strange tingling run up and down her spine.

All of a sudden, Don Felipe flung the *muleta* back, completely uncovering his torso, which had as its only protection a shirt of such thin material that a pin could have pierced it easily. The exasperated beast rushed forward in frenzy and Alexandra noted with horror that only a hair's breadth separated the young man's chest from the cusped horns. Thinking he was done for, she buried her face in her shaking hands but Don Felipe was ready for him. Swift and dextrous, he struck the bull in the chest with the blade of his sword, which found its way smoothly to the creature's heart.

Covered in blood, the bull fell with a thunderous bellow that was drowned in the stamping of feet and cheers of joy from the crowd. Don Felipe had brought off the very difficult, notoriously dangerous and rarely seen manoeuvre, the *recibir*.

Under a rain of flowers and handkerchiefs, and to the hysterical ovation of the crowd, who were demanding that he be given the ears of his victim, Don Felipe went up to the grandstand, this time to reclaim his hat.

He walked slowly and with dignity, carrying his head high, his thin lips drawn into an almost cruel smile. For a fleeting moment, he made Alexandra feel uneasy. Yet, as this god of the arena, who had dedicated his bull to her, stood there before her, spotted with sand, sweat and blood, she was mesmerized.

Suddenly, she remembered Ramón's words: the gift to the *matador*. Her pulse throbbed furiously as she impulsively tore off a quirky-looking ring she'd worn since the day she had picked it up at a flea market in London, and slipped it into the black hat, which she now returned to its owner.

The solemn *matador* nodded in gratitude. 'From this day on, I will keep this ring close to my heart, in memory of the most beautiful and delicate being I've ever seen,' Don Felipe said, staring intently at her through the fan of his thick eyelashes.

Alexandra smiled nervously back at him but then found her gaze skidding over to Salvador. She sensed with some satisfaction that he looked uncomfortable. Motionless, his jaw was clenched and a little blue vein throbbed almost imperceptibly in his right temple. Was he showing signs of jealousy, she wondered momentarily? Was that an irritated look Isabel was casting in his direction? Then a fresh wave of exuberant shouting went up from the masses and her attention was drawn back to the show.

Already the mules were hauling the carcass out of the arena to the frenzied whistling of the crowd, while the *areneros*, armed with rakes, cleaned and smoothed the surface of the ground, throwing fresh sand on the splashes of blood.

The trumpet sounded once more, the red gates fell back with a crash and in rushed a fresh bull amidst a cloud of dust. But Alexandra had had enough: though this game fascinated her, she also found it somewhat repellent. Fight after fight would be played out in the same setting, the first act of a scenario where form and content are always the same, yet the outcome remains uncertain. Which of the two adversaries will die: man or beast?

Alexandra knew she would never again attend another bullfight.

There were six bullfights that afternoon: six fights and six killings. Alexandra had never in her life witnessed such monstrous butchery. After the last fight, led by Don Felipe with his habitual charisma, his delirious fans rushed into the arena. There, they hoisted their idol on to their shoulders, preparing to take him around the town to the '*Olés*' and cheers of the crowd.

Not once during the performance had Alexandra shared a single look with Salvador. Only now – when the maestro was but a tiny gleaming speck, silhouetted in the light of the setting sun as they carried him out of the arena and everyone was rising from their seats – did her eyes meet those of her cousin. His regarded her with an ill-concealed irony that went straight to her heart. As Doña Isabel linked her arm firmly with his, Alexandra glared at Salvador furiously. She turned away and rejoined Don Vincente who, now a few seats away, was explaining to Ramón, with much gesticulation and a good deal of facial expressions, the many complexities and skills of his son's technique.

CHAPTER 8

That evening at the Casa de Acacias, the home of Doña Isabel on the outskirts of Ronda, a great fiesta was held to celebrate the fifth anniversary of Don Felipe's debut as a bullfighter.

After his resounding triumph at La Plaza de Toros that afternoon, some two hundred men and women had come to pay tribute. Their hostess, Doña Isabel, was every bit the glamorous mistress of ceremonies in her dress of purple crepe. The amethyst necklace that adorned her neck reflected in her eyes, making them look deeper and more mysterious. She stood on the landing, at the top of a flight of marble stairs, framed by Don Vincente and her brother, radiantly greeting her guests.

Alexandra arrived on Ramón's arm. She appeared almost ethereal in a floating gown of pale green voile, which revealed just the vaguest outline of her graceful form. Her lush chestnut hair, set off by two deep-yellow carnations, was piled high on her head, enhancing the purity of her profile and the elongated line of her delicate neck.

Don Felipe spotted her as soon as she stepped out of the car. Aware of his unabashed, scrutinizing gaze, Alexandra felt her cheeks burn but, holding her head high, she stared back at him, almost defiantly. However, the velvet-black irises of the *matador*, for all their ardour, did not have the disturbing power that the steely glitter of Salvador's eyes always managed to exert over her.

The thought of Salvador brought a tightness to her chest. He had preceded her in another car with Mercedes and Esmeralda, and no doubt was already at the party. Determinedly, she drove him from her thoughts. Her gloomy Romeo was easily replaceable and tonight she would prove that to him.

Alexandra reached the top of the steps and was greeted icily by Doña Isabel and most cordially by Don Vincente. No doubt the *torero*'s sister was even more hostile than usual after her rival had been singled out in that afternoon's triumphant spectacle. Alexandra managed a dignified smile for the *Marquesa* and glided swiftly past her to where Don Felipe stood. Slightly embarrassed at his burning stare, which had never once left her face since she climbed out of the car, she was about to congratulate him on his success at the *corrida* that afternoon when he forestalled her.

'Allow me to express my admiration for the most beautiful and graceful creature that ever moved my soul,' he said effusively, taking her hand and drawing it slowly and ceremoniously to his lips. Don Felipe looked both magnificent and suave in his elegant dark suit, and Alexandra couldn't help but feel flattered by his attention. He was an impossibly dashing figure, and such exotic behaviour merely fuelled her heightened sense of romance. She blushed slightly and gently pulled her hand away as other guests behind her hovered keenly to offer their congratulations to the *matador*. Don Felipe's eyes continued to burn into Alexandra, but then he tilted his head in a chivalrous nod, allowing Ramón to lead her away.

She followed Ramón into the mansion, through the vast hallway and on to a terrace that led to the artistically floodlit garden, where the sound of Flamenco guitars mingled with bubbling chatter. A sophisticated array of glamorous men and women strolled to and fro in a rainbow of kaleidoscopic colours and shimmering materials, sipping chilled sangria and fino sherry, and nibbling dainty tapas presented to them on silver platters.

The cousins found Salvador in the company of Mercedes and the two flirtatious young men who had been part of their small group at the bullfight.

'Ah, there you are at last,' Salvador said as they joined him. 'We were wondering where you were.' Turning to Alexandra, he stared for an instant before giving her an appreciative look. 'That colour suits you to perfection. How many hearts do you intend to claim this evening, dear Cousin?' His eyes glittered mischievously though he could see that she was not amused. Flashing her a brief sardonic smile, he added, 'Can I get you a drink?'

'No, thank you,' she said coolly. 'I think I'll wait.'

'I've just the drink for the *señorita*,' said a voice behind her.

Alexandra turned and met Don Felipe's velvety gaze. 'Sangria is a mixture of fruit and wine, a favourite drink in Spain, and this one is our special Herrera recipe,' said the bullfighter as he handed her a glass of the rosy-coloured punch. 'It isn't a very potent drink, but it quenches the thirst during our hot, sultry evenings.'

'Not very potent? I wouldn't take much notice of that description if I were you,' scoffed Salvador. But Don Felipe seemed unfazed by this comment and kept his eyes fixed on Alexandra.

She smiled graciously. Ignoring Salvador's remark, she took a sip of the fragrant punch. 'This is exactly what I need.' Childishly, she was enjoying scoring points over Salvador, whose eyes narrowed fractionally at her rebellious expression.

'Since no one seems inclined to introduce us,' Don Felipe said, studying her intently through his long brown eyelashes. 'Let me give you a name of my own, a name out of Greek mythology: Aphrodite. This evening, just for me, will you be this Goddess of Love who rose from the waves, white and beautiful as foam, seated in a shell of mother-of-pearl?'

Alexandra laughed to hide her embarrassment and confusion. 'I see you're not only an extraordinary bullfighter but also an accomplished poet.' She wanted to look away but his disturbing dark eyes were inexorably holding hers, waiting for an answer. At the same time she felt Salvador's stare boring into her. 'Yes,' she heard herself utter, totally hypnotized by this game, 'for this evening, I shall be happy to be Aphrodite.'

As she moved off on Don Felipe's arm, Salvador called after her, 'Careful, *niña*, the devil is cunning.' There was an edge to his voice. He drained his glass, gazing after them with a frown, but Alexandra was already far away, transported into a new world of fantasy to which the God of the Arenas had introduced her.

Don Felipe did not leave her side for the next two hours. At dinner on the terrace outside, he made sure to invite her to his table. As she knew no one seated around her apart from Don Vincente, who was holding forth to a group of his son's cronies, the *torero* monopolized her unashamedly, regaling her with tales of his bullfighting exploits, which to Alexandra seemed indescribably dangerous but also thrilling to hear.

As they sipped on sangria and ate wonderful food, she found herself responding to his open overtures of interest with shy smiles and flirtatious banter. She began to relax into this rather chivalrous dance they seemed to be engaged in. Occasionally, she glanced over at the facing table, to where Isabel had cunningly steered Salvador as soon as dinner was announced. The *Marquesa* had been fawning over him in a way that Alexandra was beginning to find faintly ridiculous. If Salvador was intent on indulging such behaviour, then so be it, she thought with mounting irritation. It only made her welcome Don Felipe's straightforward attentions all the more. Still, frequently she found Salvador's brooding gaze on her, and despite herself her stomach gave a familiar flutter.

After dinner, Doña Isabel announced that chairs had been set out in the garden for the entertainment.

'Have you ever seen the Flamenco danced before?' enquired Don Felipe, as they left the table.

Alexandra paused, struck for a moment by the memory of the Flamenco music in Seville, before putting it firmly out of her mind. 'I've read about it, and heard the music, but never actually seen the dance performed.'

'The group you are about to watch tonight has among it some of the best Flamenco dancers in Andalucía.'

Alexandra laughed happily. 'Then I'll have been initiated to two of your traditions today. Thank you for making me so welcome.' Light-headed, merry and carefree, she felt like a butterfly in some enchanted garden, dazed and intoxicated by the flattery of her handsome partner, and in no small degree by having drunk too much of that oh-so-harmless sangria.

Don Felipe guided Alexandra away from the terrace towards the garden and they walked in silence, savouring the balmy atmosphere of the night.

'Doña Alexandra, what do you think of our country?' the young man asked suddenly in a tender voice.

'I think I like it,' she said in earnest, 'although I feel a total stranger to its customs and curious traditions. They're so different to ours in England.'

'In what way?' He folded his hands behind his back as they strolled across the lawn.

'I find them moving but I can't always understand them, despite being half-Spanish myself. It's probably this difference that attracts and yet frightens me at the same time.' She thought for a moment. 'Here, everyone lives with such intensity. You're all so conscious of death that it seems to be the inspiration for living, as though each step you take in life is a step that brings you closer to death. In England we find this attitude strangely disquieting. I suppose because it's so opposed to our own philosophy.'

'What you say is right,' said Don Felipe. 'The Spanish confuse life with death, and death with life. Perhaps the key to the soul of our people is to be found in the words of Socrates, who said that "the wise man doesn't fear death and the pious man doesn't regard it as a final end. It induces the first to make the most of life and the second to live in hope of a better world. For each, death becomes life."' He gazed solemnly up at the night sky as they neared the edge of the garden. 'We are essentially a religious people, who have learned wisdom by suffering and by our firm trust in fate. It's the Eastern philosophy of the "*maktoub*", what is "written", bequeathed us by our Moorish ancestors and rooted in our character.' He smiled, motioning her towards some seats where a few of the guests were beginning to assemble. 'Do you understand us better now?'

For the first time that evening Alexandra grew pensive. Don Felipe's words illustrated so well Salvador's blind submission to his own destiny. 'Yes, when you put it like that, it seems easier to accept.'

'Oh, Salvador,' Doña Isabel's laughter suddenly resounded a few yards away, 'how can you think that? But I forgive you because you're so devilishly handsome,' she purred.

Alexandra's spine stiffened. She didn't bother to look round at the pair. Why could he not find somewhere else to flaunt his attachment to the *Marquesa*? She raised her chin. But what did she care? She had the attentions of a man women swooned over and who was certainly the perfect romantic hero. Suddenly her irritation bubbled over. She deliberately touched Don Felipe's arm and raised her voice a fraction.

'*Torero*, poet, philosopher … is there no end to your talents, Don Felipe?'

Don Felipe raised his brows and smiled suavely, pleased at her compliment. 'I like to think that I have a few more, Doña Alexandra,' he responded, his eyes intent on her lips.

Isabel's laughter could be heard very close now. 'I'm sure your skills are consummate in all things,' she found herself saying, adding quickly, 'Your reflexes in the arena are certainly incredible.'

'Well, today they were challenged more than usual due to one ravishing, tormenting distraction.'

She felt her cheeks burn, unable to think of a reply. Then Salvador and Isabel stopped in front of them.

'I see you're enjoying yourself this evening, Cousin.' There was no mockery on Salvador's face now; in fact, his expression had taken on more of a scowl, Alexandra noted with some satisfaction.

She looked at him boldly. 'Yes, I am, very much, Salvador. Don Felipe here has been wonderful company. The time has simply flown.'

Salvador's jaw tightened.

'Felipe, you are incorrigible,' piped up Isabel, as if Alexandra hadn't spoken. 'You really mustn't neglect your other guests, you know. They're all here to see you this evening. I'm sure Doña Alexandra is capable of entertaining herself.' She passed a fleeting glance up and down Alexandra and smiled slyly.

Alexandra met the other woman's haughty regard. 'Of course you are right, Doña Isabel, and I wouldn't want to keep your brother from his guests. You seem not to have had the chance to speak to anyone else this evening either. Isn't it terrible to have such good company that we neglect our duties?'

The *Marquesa* simply stared. 'Well, I hardly think—'

'Isabel, I think Alexandra has *dado en el clavo*, hit the nail on the head,' interrupted Salvador. He inclined his head towards her, a dangerous light flickering in his dark eyes. 'Distracting company can often make us neglect what is important. I only hope, my dear Felipe, that you're looking after my cousin.' Though, as he spoke, his gaze was still only on Alexandra.

'*Amigo*, what else would you expect?' came the *torero's* courteous reply. '*Estar seguro*, rest assured your cousin is safe with me.' As if to emphasize his point, he took Alexandra's hand and placed it on his arm.

Salvador's gaze travelled from Alexandra's arm to Don Felipe's face and for a moment something approaching a challenge passed silently between the two men, like the glare of stalking animals.

'Come, Salvador,' said Doña Isabel fractiously. 'We really must be finding our seats before the dancing begins.' She tugged on his arm. He stared for a moment longer at the *torero*, then nodded brusquely and strode off.

Don Felipe's expression changed instantly and he flashed a smile at Alexandra. 'Doña Alexandra, I've reserved a space for us where you'll have the best view.'

Despite her proud demeanour in front of Doña Isabel, Alexandra was feeling nervy. She pasted a buoyant smile on her face and, raw with confusion inside, followed him across the grass.

They were sitting a little apart from the other guests, on wide cushions covered with rich embroidery, under an early-flowering flame tree. The round stage, which had been placed against the garden wall for the performance, was set only a few yards away.

This part of the garden had been cleverly arranged as a picturesque miniature theatre, with rows of straw-bottomed chairs, brightly coloured quilted cushions and leather pouffes stuffed with horsehair. Most of the guests took up their seats with glasses of sherry, *manzanilla* or sangria, which they sipped as they waited for the show to begin.

The music started softly. Alexandra listened to the strumming notes of the guitars and felt as though she were being gently rocked in a hammock.

A gypsy family, seated in a semicircle to one side of the stage, began to clap their hands rhythmically, faster and faster, louder and louder, the rate of the tempo matching the level of sound.

'Hand-clapping is a most necessary prelude to our singing and dancing,' whispered the *matador*. 'It's the gradual crescendo of clapping that frees all inhibition.' And so it was. Suddenly, as if by magic, the group of dancers, guitar players and singers came to life. They formed a single body, vibrant with a sense of collective excitement.

The first dancer to leap to her feet and occupy the centre of the floor was a young girl. She seemed barely thirteen, a fragile creature in her dress of white muslin spotted with red, a crimson shawl held tightly around her slender shoulders. Her dance was tempestuous. Coiling up and waving the flounces of her skirts, she beckoned to one of the male onlookers sitting on the other side of the stage to join her. All the time, the other members of the family, and some of the audience, stamped their feet, clapped their hands and interjected with cries of encouragement.

Alexandra was mesmerized by this vibrating show, and by the wild music. It seemed to call to something deep within, goading her, playing on all the simmering emotions that she was trying so desperately to hold on to. Beside her, Don Felipe too was clapping to the rhythm, nodding to Alexandra and smiling, but she couldn't bring herself to take part in the revelry, despite the *matador*'s encouragement and the elation of everybody around her.

Now, as a second dancer – a man – came into view, the first withdrew to her place. He began a series of jumps, pirouettes and great leaps into the air. Then, throwing his wide-brimmed hat on to the stage, he performed a dance around it that was almost primitive in its ferocity. His frenzied movements had a certain supple grace, echoing the sensuous, pulsating music. The haunting rhythm of his stamping feet was truly contagious.

All of a sudden, Alexandra's natural inhibitions melted, and she found herself being swept away by the spirit of merriment and the orgy of noise. Along with the rest of the audience, who were now on their feet, she leapt up and joined the throng, stamping her feet and clapping her hands. Red-faced, cheeks burning, she cried out '*olés*' as though she were a true *gitana*.

Suddenly she felt an arm pulling her into the crowd. She looked up, startled, to see Salvador's face close to hers, his arm now tightly around her waist.

'*Bailar el flamenco conmigo*, dance the Flamenco with me, Alexandra.' It was a whisper, no more, in her ear – a command, not an invitation – and he drew her in one fluid movement hard against his length. Salvador's eyes, shining almost cobalt-blue in his tanned face, bored into hers. She could feel his heart thundering against her breast, echoing the insistent rhythm of the music and driving the drumming beat through her already electrified body.

'What are you doing? Let me go,' she murmured, her emerald eyes flashing in a mixture of anger and desire. Her hands pushed against his chest in a half-hearted attempt to free herself. But he jerked her waist even tighter against him, his gaze even more burning. She could feel the contours of his body in such a way that made her throat so dry she had to lick her bottom lip.

'I said, dance the Flamenco with me,' he growled, his eyes on her mouth.

People were moving around them, skirts swirling, hands and feet clapping and stomping.

'I can't, Salvador. I don't know how to …'

Alexandra looked at him ablaze, though she was confused and light-headed, her pulse racing; his eyes held her enthralled and she caught her breath as he drew her swiftly among the dancers. He turned her in his arms, holding her against his warm strength, sweeping her away into his almost primitive world of fevered excitement, a world that had been waiting for her all her life.

With one arm still around her waist, he took her other hand and raised it up above their heads. 'Yes, you can. Follow me, and your instincts.'

Her instincts were telling her that nothing felt so natural and perfect than his body so close to her.

'Look at me, *niña*, *sólo a mi*. This is a subtle dance, Alexandra ... sensuous, passionate but strictly controlled.' His eyes seemed to burn even brighter. 'First, lift your arms, like an eagle ...'

He stepped away from her slightly and she began to mirror his movements, her arms arched above her, head held high to one side.

'*Sólo a mi, niña*.' Salvador swooped back close to her and his hand moved down the side of her body, making her shudder as an almost angry desire flashed between them, electric and heated.

She could see the pleasure and surprise reflected on Salvador's face when she began to move in perfect accord with him. With proud stamping steps they surrendered themselves to the mounting urgency of the rhythm and the precise evolution of the dance like a thin veil suspended above smouldering fires, threatening to erupt into flames at any moment. The same feeling of intoxication that had gripped Alexandra at the restaurant in Seville was now taking over her whole body as she flung herself wholeheartedly into the passionate *canto hondo* and *canto grande*, the traditional dances of Andalucía. Salvador's dexterous long fingers spun Alexandra away from him and pulled her back, curving her arm high over her head.

From time to time, a sudden drawn-out cry of wild, pure notes filled the atmosphere, and a thrill ran through Alexandra from head to toe. It was an indescribable sensation, enhanced by Salvador's intense blue gaze that never left her face, urging her on, faster and faster. She was acutely aware of his nearness, of his superb physique, of his magnetism. From time to time, his eyes flickered with an odd expression – it was as much arrogance as desire, this innate part of his proud people, which Salvador personified more than ever when he danced, and which seemed all at once to add to his powerful allure.

And then his expression changed. One moment, he was spinning her round; the next, he held her to him, searching her face as if struggling to say something. Then he was gone, swift and silent, swallowed up by the crowd of shouting, stamping dancers around them.

Alexandra stared ahead of her, disorientated. What had happened? She thought about going after him but at that moment an arm caught her.

'I lost you in the dancing, Doña Alexandra. Where did you get to?' It was Don Felipe. He was studying her face keenly with a look of concern. His hand still gripped her arm firmly. Something that made her uncomfortable gleamed in his eyes, making her want to pull away, but then it vanished. He released his grip and stepped back.

'I'm sorry, Don Felipe … As you say, I got lost in the dancing,' Alexandra managed to stammer, still breathless from her unexpected sensual interlude.

'Flamenco can have an overpowering effect on the uninitiated.' He regarded her pensively.

She added hurriedly, 'Shall we watch the rest of show? I'm rather hot now and could do with a rest.'

His attentive warmth returned: 'Of course, Doña Alexandra. You must get your breath back. We cannot have Aphrodite wilting before the evening is through.'

She flashed what she hoped was a winning smile and allowed Don Felipe to guide her back to the front of the audience.

Soon, among the jubilant shouts and stamping of the crowd, a third dancer languidly stirred from the shadows. Then all at once, springing into life, she took up her position in the centre of the dancefloor. Noble, proud and insolent, she strutted around the stage, just like an exotic bird showing off its plumage. The cascading flounces of her dress moulded the shapely line of her body to perfection and emphasized the curving flow of the dance. Every muscle of her young limbs throbbed, vibrating to the hypnotic magnetism of the rhythm. She kept her eyes closed and in the wan moonlight, her skin, usually a golden copper, seemed to have turned the colour of alabaster. Her movements were composed of sudden transitions, of spasmodic and syncopated gestures. Now and then, she would punctuate them with a long, plaintive cry that cut in piercingly and then continued in a yet more poignant tone.

The dancer's face was not yet in full view, but already Alexandra had guessed that she was the gypsy, Marujita. Instinctively, she looked for Salvador again but he was still nowhere to be seen.

'Is anything the matter?' enquired Don Felipe, sensing the abrupt change that had come over her.

'No, not at all.' She was trying to relax and concentrate on the show, but the spell was broken. Her head was spinning in confusion. She didn't know what to think any more. Preoccupied with the predatory *Marquesa*, she had forgotten the equally threatening presence of the gypsy girl in this complicated situation with Salvador. Right now she felt drained, and she wanted to go home.

Marujita ended her dance to enthusiastic cheers from the audience and, with great relief, Alexandra saw Ramón reappear.

'Wonderful party, eh, *mi primita*?' From the twinkle in his eye as he grinned at a couple of young women, who were giggling and waving goodbye, Alexandra could see that Ramón had clearly enjoyed his evening.

After they had thanked their hosts and bade them goodnight, Don Felipe accompanied his guests to their car.

'Will I have the honour of seeing you again?' he asked as he folded Alexandra's hands in his, scanning her face intently through his thick lashes.

She turned to her cousin. 'I think we're returning to Jerez tomorrow, are we not, Ramón?' she said quickly. Where the intensity of the *torero*'s attentions had enchanted her before, now it made her uneasy and she felt pressured.

'Yes, we leave tomorrow at first light.'

'Then may I call on you at El Pavón, one day next week? Perhaps you'd be interested in visiting our *bodegas*.' But she ignored his insistence and simply smiled demurely as he put her hand to his lips. 'Thank you for this marvellous evening, beautiful goddess,' Don Felipe whispered, helping her into the car and closing the door after her. 'I look forward to seeing you soon,' he called out as they drove off.

Ramón eyed her mischievously. 'You certainly have made a conquest, Cousin. Quite the charmer, isn't he?'

'Do I look charmed?' she retorted, nettled by the young man's insinuation.

'No, you look grumpy, though I can't think why.' He grinned to himself, unperturbed by her mood. 'But you know what they say ... A diplomat should always think twice before saying nothing, so my lips are sealed.'

He raised his eyebrows with a smirk and they drove in silence for a while. Alexandra had not yet recovered her sense of humour and wasn't ready to be teased. She felt quite irritated with the whole world, but mostly with herself.

'Where are the others?' she asked finally, trying to sound casual.

'They left before the show finished. I'm afraid it didn't go down well with our hostess, but for once Salvador behaved sensibly. Things could have become rather complicated with that young gypsy hanging around. I'm sure her presence wasn't a coincidence. Did you have a nice time?' His voice softened with sincerity this time. Without waiting for a reply, he added, 'When I last looked at you, you seemed to have entered the party mood and were enjoying yourself thoroughly.'

'Yes, it was a good show,' she admitted, forcing some enthusiasm into her voice, but her heart was not in it. The euphoria that had swept over her during the evening had evaporated, leaving her weary and depressed.

*   *   *

Set in ten acres of beautiful terraced gardens, the Parador de la Luna was perched on a lush hillside overlooking whitewashed hill towns and the dark El Tajo ravine that cut through the town of Ronda. At the bottom of the gorge, over five hundred feet below, the Guadalevín was a distant slender stream. The ground-floor rooms of the picturesque *posada* opened on to a broad terrace supported by porticoes. A large veranda, shaded by awnings, led off the upper-floor bedrooms; designed to give shelter from the scorching heat, it boasted an intimidating, precipitous view of the surrounding countryside.

The night was hot; a heavy and oppressive Spanish heat. Not a breath of air came down from the Sierras to relieve the atmosphere, and Alexandra was unable to sleep. She felt edgy. Thoughts of Salvador and the young gypsy girl pushed themselves to the forefront of her mind even though she had promised herself to keep them at bay. The prospect of the *Marquesa*'s wily designs on Salvador were almost eclipsed by what she knew he had already shared with the *gitana*. Her stomach lurched. Did he care for the gypsy girl? She shook her head as if to rid herself of such a taunting notion.

In the few magical hours they had spent together in Seville, a small, naïve part of Alexandra had thought that she and Salvador would be able to see past their differences, overcome whatever it was that forced him to be so guarded. Now that she knew more about him, she was still no nearer to figuring him out – or understanding what was happening between them.

Salvador had ignored her most of the evening and then swept her off her feet with such barely suppressed, heated passion that her senses were still reeling from the encounter. Feelings that were strange, exciting and dangerous had taken root in her, body and soul, as they danced together. And then, as quickly as he had pulled her into his arms, he had abandoned her. She wasn't sure whether to be relieved or insulted.

Forcing herself to think of something other than the mercurial young man, Alexandra recalled the flamboyant *matador* who had entertained her so delightfully. Don Felipe was gallant, attentive, and obviously quite taken with her. She had openly flirted with him, encouraging his advances, even enjoying them. The sangria had helped, admittedly, providing the necessary haze.

It occurred to her that the earlier part of the evening had seemed perfectly pleasant. Then Salvador had disappeared and flirting with Don Felipe hadn't seemed half as exciting with her audience gone. All through dinner, she'd been conscious of those steel-grey eyes of Salvador, following her everywhere, cold and impassable. No doubt disapproving of her behaviour. He had only spoken to her once throughout the whole evening, before the music began, and that was to express his obvious displeasure at her enjoyment. Still, she had enjoyed niggling at him, with the distinct impression she was inciting his jealousy. She wanted to hurt him as he had her. Instead, he had taken his revenge on her emotions and senses again; made her feel on fire when he placed his hands on her body and forced her to drown in silent, seething desire.

Damn him! Who did he think he was, storming into her life and making her feel this way? He was playing with her as if she were a puppet on strings. She would not stand for it; she didn't need a man like that in her life … But what was this hollow feeling that tugged at her stomach? She was miserable and wretched, no denying it. Would she be forced to admit she was falling in love with a man who, right from the start, had made it quite clear that they should not become involved? She quickly banished that thought from her head; it only made her increasingly restless.

Her mouth was dry; she felt suffocated and needed some air.

Alexandra slipped a dressing gown over her flimsy raw-silk nightdress and went out on to the terrace. Earlier that day, when they had booked into their rooms, she had looked over the parapet at the groves and whitewashed villages which seemed to shimmer haphazardly in the misty rays of the midday sun; she had suffered a sudden wave of vertigo as she stared down at them in the sunlight. Now, there was nothing but the bottomless void, the vast darkness spreading outwards, and above, a vaulted midnight-blue sky strewn with myriad stars.

A livid moon was up. In the vast shadows of the landscape, she could just discern the outlines of the arena on the edge of Ronda. Further off stretched the town centre; the windows of its houses were small, twinkling pools of yellow light scattered in an otherwise velvety blackness. From somewhere far away, the echo of a sobbing guitar floated through the sultry night air, like a whisper caressing her ear.

Alexandra sensed his presence even before seeing him. She wondered how long he had been there, leaning against the wall, the tiny glow of his cigarette a single, luminous point in the shadows.

The strains of the guitar mingled with the undulating hum of crickets in the night air.

'Is that you, Salvador?' Her voice was barely audible.

'*Buenas tardes, niña.*' Salvador approached the three-foot apology for a balustrade barely separating the two balconies. A pair of arresting blue eyes appraised her coolly and thoroughly, making her heart beat a little faster.

'Did you enjoy the party?'

Alexandra deliberately looked away. 'Why did you leave so suddenly?' she asked, ignoring his question. 'I hardly saw you all evening, and then—' but she couldn't bring herself to go on.

Salvador raised his eyebrows. 'I don't need to explain my actions to anyone. Still, before that, you seemed to be having such a good time, I'm surprised you missed me after I left,' he remarked sarcastically.

'Yes,' Alexandra snapped. 'I was having a *wonderful* time!' She glared at him, then added, 'Don Felipe made a charming partner, not only courteous, but considerate too. I had an excellent evening, thank you.'

His gaze was direct and needle sharp. 'Are appearances that important to you, Alexandra?'

'I don't understand what you mean.'

Salvador's mouth hardened. 'Don't give me that!' His eyes blazed as they flitted over her. 'You were swept off your feet by the dazzling façade of your host. Admit it,' he said harshly.

She flushed and jerked her head up. Unwilling to acknowledge his accusation, she tried to deflect it. 'What do you have against Don Felipe?'

'This conversation is not about Don Felipe.' His tone cooled as he looked at her broodingly.

Anger was beginning to build up inside her. Who was he to make pronouncements on the way she behaved? Green eyes glittered with indignation. 'How dare you interfere in my life!' she said vehemently. 'What entitles you to—'

'I agree, I have no right to interfere in your life,' he interrupted calmly, suddenly sounding tired, 'but I care about you, and would be sad if the slightest harm came to you.'

'Are you warning me off Don Felipe?'

He nodded gravely. 'I suppose I am.'

'I really don't understand what you're driving at.'

Salvador shook his head and sighed. 'You do make things difficult, Alexandra.'

He was making her feel like a capricious schoolgirl, and a swift rush of heat flushed her cheeks. She glared at him furiously, searching for some wounding retort.

'You know nothing of Don Felipe's reputation as a womanizer,' he went on, before she had time to answer. 'You've been taken in by the smooth affectation and the glossy, rather obvious charm, all of which I'm afraid are designed to conceal his true character. He looked at her reproachfully. 'Your encouragement of his attentions was unwise. Despite your twenty-five years, *niña*, you're still very naïve.'

Alexandra's face was now burning with hot indignation. Without giving herself time to think she looked fiercely at him.

'How dare you patronize me! How dare *you* judge *me*?' Her voice shook a little. 'I wouldn't start pointing fingers had I been credited with an affair as sordid as the one you've been having with that gypsy girl.'

Alexandra caught her breath, suddenly aware of what she'd said. Salvador had mortified her and she'd wanted to hurt his pride, to make him feel some of the humiliation she herself was feeling at his allegations, but instantly she regretted the harshness of her words.

Salvador's mouth twisted contemptuously. Alexandra had seen that expression before; he was holding his emotions in check. There would be no outburst of anger but an arctic comeback. He did not disappoint her.

'Again, Alexandra, this is not about me.' His face was in shadow, but she could see the steel in his blue eyes flash in the darkness. 'Are you still so ignorant of our ways?'

'I have done nothing wrong,' she insisted stubbornly.

His brows drew together in an exasperated frown. '*Dios en el cielo!*' he swore under his breath. 'Maybe, but you're playing with fire.'

Alexandra decided not to argue. Salvador appeared to be in a foul mood and, though her instinct was to protest against his unfounded accusations, his chilly contempt forced her into silence. He turned away from her, wordless too. It was a silence that contained so much for neither was willing to acknowledge what had passed between them during their electrifying dance. A hostility that she had never sensed before had crept in and made her feel uneasy. Suddenly they were unable to talk like rational human beings.

Tension vibrated in the air. Both had said enough for one night. The last thing Alexandra wanted now was to provoke a fight. She was tired and her brain did not feel that sharp, certainly not enough to say what she truly felt. Perhaps it was the fruity punch making her head feel fuzzy; in fact, it had been more alcoholic than fruity and she was not in the habit of drinking much alcohol.

Salvador stared distantly over the darkness of the ravine to the horizon, where one after another the twinkling lights had faded into oblivion. Alexandra watched him and yearned for those rare moments when they had been close and he'd seemed so relaxed and happy.

An owl hooted, breaking the heavy silence that hung between them. Salvador moved his head to look at her. He scanned her face, his eyes glowing like torches, searching Alexandra's shadowed features as though suddenly reaching out to her. When he spoke, his voice was calm and gentle.

'I was wrong to interfere in your affairs. I'm neither your father nor your brother and, though I can't help but regard myself as a little responsible for you, I had no right to intrude into your private life. I can only apologize for my irrational behaviour. It was meant with good intentions.'

Her heart rose to her mouth; the caressing tone of his voice stroked down the angry hackles urging her to hurt him.

'Are you upset with me?' she whispered.

'I'm not upset with you so much as irate at Don Felipe's behaviour. He should know better.' He paused. 'But that is another matter,' and though he had spoken in a low voice, Alexandra was aware of the thick undercurrents of smouldering fury.

'What are you worried about?'

'As I've said, Don Felipe has the reputation of being a ruthless womanizer. He will stop at nothing to get what he wants and his intentions are not always honourable. I wouldn't like him to hurt you.'

'Why don't you stop treating me like a child? I'm sensible enough to recognize danger and defend myself, if necessary.'

'That may be so, but I still feel I should warn you.'

For a while they were silent again, looking out at the dark hills and savouring the still of the night.

'Did you know Marujita would be dancing this evening?' Alexandra asked faintly, at last.

Salvador stiffened. 'Yes,' he said simply.

At this she glanced down, afraid he might see her heartache. 'Does it upset you to see her make such an exhibition of herself in public? Is that why you left?'

Salvador laughed. 'How imaginative you are, Alexandra.' He watched the smoke curling from the end of his cigarette and shook his head. 'Actually, it doesn't upset me to see her dance, quite the reverse. It puts things into their right perspective. The reason I left during the show was because …' Salvador paused. Alexandra turned to look at him and thought she would drown again in the world of intense possibility held in his gaze. 'Because I have a horror of scenes in public, and I didn't want to give anybody an excuse for making one this evening. Has that answered your question, *niña*?'

Alexandra hesitated a few seconds before the intimacy of the night gave her the boldness she needed. 'Are you going to marry her?'

Salvador appeared to consider her question. 'I don't know,' he sighed.

She looked at him mutely and swallowed back the painful lump in her throat; she needed to know. Moments passed before she went on stubbornly. 'Do you love her?'

'I feel grateful towards her … but feelings are so much more complicated than that …'

Was it complicated? 'If you don't love her, now that … now that …' Words failed her but then she heard herself say with a harsh impudence she hadn't thought herself capable of, 'Surely there's no longer any reason for you to stay with her?'

A muscle jerked in his cheek. 'How simple you make it all sound,' he replied wistfully. 'You see life in bright colours. Alas, ours is a world of darker shades.'

She glanced up at him in time to see his rueful grimace.

'You can't spend the rest of your life paying for a mistake for which circumstances alone were responsible,' she said vehemently. She wanted so desperately to understand why he insisted on punishing himself when his feelings seemed to be fighting to be free. After all, she had seen it in his eyes when he held her, when he danced with her.

Sadness swept across Salvador's face and his shoulders hunched slightly. He seemed exhausted.

'You're being very compassionate towards me, *niña*, but not too realistic. Once the cork is drawn, you have to drink the wine. The slate can never be wiped clean. I'm no longer a teenager. When a man of my age has an affair, he is fully aware of what he is doing and must be prepared to bear the consequences of his actions. Have you read *Don Quixote*?'

'No,' she admitted.

'I'll lend it to you when we get back to Jerez. Cervantes' proverb is often quoted in Spain: *He who plays with cats must expect to get scratched.*'

Alexandra thought back to Agustina's tale of the *gitana's* appearance after Salvador's accident. Suddenly, she felt close to him, imagining what it must have been like for such a man to be rendered so weak in every way, and her heart melted.

'You were sick and easily manipulated. Surely, you cannot be held fully responsible for your actions? Apparently, Marujita knew exactly what she was doing. You're too hard on yourself.'

'I'm not hard on myself, I'm simply seeing things as they are. I have no illusions about myself and even less about others.' He shook his head and blinked out at the night. 'Anyhow, I shouldn't be discussing this with you, or with anyone else for that matter. This is my personal life and my problem. It's for me to sort out.'

Alexandra frowned, perplexed. Her mind was a maelstrom of confused thoughts and emotions. She drew a sharp breath and hugged herself. A shudder ran up her spine and she struggled to control the terrible sense of foreboding that rose bitterly again in her chest.

Salvador reached out and gently touched the long chestnut hair that fell over her shoulders in such suggestive disarray. Alexandra looked up at him with wide green eyes where so many mute questions begged to be answered. Her pink lips parted slightly, glistening. He turned away.

'It's getting late,' he said, discarding his cigarette and crushing it with a sort of pent-up violence. 'A long journey awaits us tomorrow.' He lifted her hand, gently turned it over and brushed her palm with his warm lips. Then, closing her fingers slowly over his kiss, he bade her goodnight and started back towards his room.

'Salvador,' she whispered huskily.

As he turned she saw the fire leap in his eyes; Salvador looked back at her, loving and pleading in an erotic call of desire. He uttered a string of oaths in Spanish. Within seconds, she was drawn towards the warm vigour of his chest. His arms tightened about her and she let out a long, shivering sigh of delight as his mouth claimed hers, scorching, demanding and fiercely masculine. The fury of constrained jealousy and desire, which she knew had gnawed at him through the *corrida*, and been embodied in their sensual dance, was buried in his kiss. She could feel his desperate need and she would be his salvation. He had touched a chord deep inside her. When he held her, or his mouth brushed her lips, it was as though paradise was on her doorstep. The questions warring in her head paled at the searing contact of his skin. Alexandra's arms found their way around Salvador's neck, entwining her fingers in his raven-black hair, and her burning lips gave him the answer he craved.

They were caught up in a dream. She was trembling, slightly delirious. He was breathing rapidly. She could feel the pounding of his heart against her breast, or was it hers that raced at lightening speed? Brimming with love for him, her body ached for this man with such intensity it became a deep pain inside her.

Alexandra's robe slipped off her shoulders and his strong, gliding hands found the curve of her breasts. He cupped them, revelling in the way they hardened under the manipulation of his long, tanned fingers. Toying with them, he teased the little pink peaks between his finger and thumb and they rose, hardening in response, as he led her along the razor edge of desire. She wanted him to possess her, to be inside her, to feel the soft, damp core of her, and she knew he hungered for it too.

His caresses became increasingly urgent, his hands skimming up to her throat and then down again, gliding erotically over each curve of her body, his kisses almost primitive, branding her with the wild fire that tortured them both. With wave upon wave of pure yearning as never experienced before, she shook and moaned his name again and again as he claimed her heart and soul. Lost to the sensual vibrations in her blood, she gasped with pure pleasure as an urgent longing flooded her loins, the look in her eyes vulnerable with naked desire.

'Salvador ... *Salvador ...*'

'Alexandra, my pure, sweet angel! *Dios mío* ... I cannot ... I must not ... This beast that rages inside me ... I must kill it.'

'But I ... There's something in me too and I can't stop it ... I've never felt this way about any man before. ... There's only you, there's only *ever* been you!'

Her passionate words resonated in the silence of the warm night and had the sobering effect of a cold shower on Salvador. Quickly he moved away, releasing her, his eyes still glazed with need, his body trembling with a powerful desire. He took a few steps backwards, his irises dark and dazed, his face harrowed with pain, staring at her as if seeing her for the first time.

'I'm sorry,' he whispered low, his voice thick. 'I'm so sorry, *niña. Perdona me querida*, forgive me, *querida*. You are so beautiful, so desirable, I couldn't help myself.' He raised his hand, as if in surrender, and shook his head, then turned abruptly and disappeared into his bedroom.

Alexandra nearly called after him, wanting to stop him, but the sound died in her throat. She pulled her robe back up and clasped it over her chest. Her eyes filled with tears of disbelief.

Not for the first time since she had arrived in Spain, she wished for a better understanding of the male species.

Salvador must love her. He couldn't have held her, kissed her and touched her in the way he had done just now if he did not return the passion she felt for him. For a moment, she toyed with the idea of following him into his bedroom, but she knew that was a bad idea. She would have plenty of time to talk to him in the days to come. Reason and exhaustion had won the day.

It had been a long and eventful twenty-four hours. Climbing into bed, she fell into a deep sleep and did not wake up until Esmeralda knocked at her door, late the next morning.

Salvador had left early by train for Granada, where he had to attend to some sudden urgent business, leaving Alexandra and the others to make their own way back to El Pavón. He was running away and there was nothing she could do about it, except be patient and wait for his return.

Chapter 9

Almost two weeks had gone by since Alexandra and Salvador's romantic tête-à-tête at the Parador de La Luna; a fortnight during which she had barely set eyes on him. Salvador was clearly avoiding her and her wounded pride forbade her from seeking him out. He was often away on business, and when he did show up at the hacienda, he made sure they were never on their own. Alexandra had glimpsed him a few times in the company of Doña Isabel and she knew, like everyone else in the household, that Marujita had access to his apartment. Her stomach gave a sickening wrench every time she thought about it. Was the gypsy girl still his mistress? Did Salvador hold her and caress her, did he kiss her with such tenderness and aching intensity that it made the world grind to a standstill … *as he had with her?*

Alexandra's emotions were in riotous disarray. In the days following the trip to Ronda, she had struggled with an onslaught of anger, guilt and confusion. She had let Salvador touch her in a way that no man had ever done. Why had she allowed him to break down her defences again, making her want him with such disconcerting intensity? She tried to blame it on the *sangria*, on the febrile Flamenco dance they had shared at the *corrida* party, and on the frenzied *fiesta* atmosphere; still, deep down she knew that the way she was feeling had nothing to do with all that. She despised herself for letting it happen, but it was time she admitted that whenever she was alone with him, she seemed to act in a way quite foreign to her. When Salvador looked at her, touched her, she felt herself weaken, her mind cloud.

The young man seemed determined to torture them both with this flame of desire that leapt between them, playing a game of cat and mouse with her senses, and then pushing her away. And now a seed had broken open inside her and a reckless hunger had taken root. Salvador's hypnotic grey gaze haunted her mind and his burning touch filled her fevered dreams. Even though what she had told him was perilously close to a declaration of love, again he had walked away.

Alexandra's blood pulsated with a longing she never knew existed, but her feelings were in torment. Her mind seethed with questions. Salvador was an intelligent, educated, energetic man, but when it came to taking control of his destiny he seemed totally overpowered by a dark fatalism. If only she knew how to shake him out of his inertia.

Yet for all her anxiety and confusion, she had never felt so alive. The raw truth of her love burned through her, although she had not been able to say the words to Salvador, and her heart ached with a pain she could hardly bear. Clutching her chaotic emotions tightly to herself, she had escaped into her world of writing, trying to release the storm that raged within her, not knowing how to deal with this impossible situation. At least, for now, she didn't have to deal with Don Felipe coming to El Pavón to renew his attentions, which would only have added to her troubles. The *torero* had been called away on other business and he'd sent her an apologetic letter, promising to visit her at the earliest opportunity on his return.

It was Holy Week. Festivities marking the occasion of *Semana Santa* had already started and would last until Easter Sunday. The walls in the town had been freshly whitewashed, and trellises hung with greenery had been erected and adorned with pink, white and yellow flowers. There was a sense of mounting exhilaration in the air. The streets were thronged with pilgrims wearing long, loose coats and hoods, and everywhere, people seemed to be connected in one way or another with the Easter processions.

Alexandra had read about the magnificent *pasos*, the floats of riotous colour and movement symbolizing the drama of the Passion, and she was excited at the prospect of travelling to Jerez with the family the next day to witness the de Fallas' tableaux in the procession.

For days now she had helped Doña Eugenia and Esmeralda attend to various wardrobe jobs. Their skilled fingers embroidered Jesus's and the Virgin's vestments that would be displayed in the procession. Meanwhile she and Mercedes mended the penitential hoods and tunics worn by the members of the de Falla Brotherhood. These were dramatic-looking and similar to those that would be worn by many other large Spanish families. The solemn nature of their work seemed to bring an uncharacteristic reticence to Doña Eugenia and Mercedes, though their quietness might also have been due to the prospect of the *Duquesa*'s displeasure, should they choose to stir up any unpleasantness. Either way, Alexandra found this close activity tolerable enough, and when she spoke it was largely to Esmeralda. While they worked on the costumes, she thought that her cousin seemed even more tense than usual, but she put it down to excitement at the thought of the forthcoming parade, which promised to be spectacular.

The four women arrived in Jerez at half past four, just as families were beginning to take up their positions to wait for the procession. Places had been reserved for the de Fallas in the main plaza and they had seats on the corner, giving them an excellent view. Doña María Dolores had remained at El Pavón, the journey considered too arduous at her age; Salvador, Ramón and Don Alonso had left earlier, as they would be taking part in the event.

Coloured folding stools were lined up at the roadside so spectators could rest during the day. Crowds watched from windows and balconies and filled the canyon between houses, leaving a channel just wide enough to allow the passage of the *pasos*, the floats holding the heavy, imposing wooden sculptures depicting scenes from the Passion. Threading their way through the throngs of spectators, hawkers called out their wares: a motley assortment of flags, prayer books and sweets.

The air breathed orange blossom and overhead the sky was azure blue. Tall palms waved gently in the fragrant breeze and their green foliage glinted in the late afternoon sunshine.

As they waited for the procession, Alexandra didn't participate in conversation with the other three; instead, she entertained herself watching the people around her. Holy Week was plainly a time for families. They arrived in small groups of five or six, wearing their Sunday best or a special outfit made for the occasion. Some of the children were dressed as angels, others as Jesus on his way to Calvary, with long purple robes and crowns of thorns. The young women held rosaries and wore black silk dresses, with *mantillas* adorning their heads, gracefully kept in place by large tortoiseshell combs.

Alexandra had nearly worn a similarly beautiful Spanish addition to her own outfit. That morning, after breakfast, she had been asked to join Doña María Dolores in her apartments. The old woman had taken out of the cupboard a *mantilla* in fine black lace, and an exquisite embroidered manila shawl. 'These belonged to my grandmother,' she told her, smiling. 'I hope you will enjoy wearing them. It's been a while since I've used them. You will look every bit the Spanish beauty, *mi querida nieta*, my dear granddaughter. A true de Falla *para la Semana Santa*.'

Alexandra had been deeply touched by the dowager's affectionate gesture, but she'd worried that certain members of the family would take umbrage at her having being given yet another precious heirloom, so she had carefully folded them away in her drawer.

At one of the balconies decorated with palms, Alexandra noticed a bevy of young girls in their late teens, dark red carnations in their hair, giggling and whispering. From time to time, they would give out little cries of surprise and satisfaction. Alexandra wondered what was making them so excited, and then she caught sight of one of the girls throwing nuts and sweets into the street, aiming for a group of shy young men gathered outside a tapas bar. When one of the missiles hit its target, the girls cheered and laughed noisily.

'I've never seen anything like this,' Alexandra told Esmeralda. 'There must be thousands of people here.'

Esmeralda smiled. 'Of course, *querida*, everyone comes out for Holy Week, all over Spain but more so in Andalucía. *Semana Santa* has been like this for over four hundred years. It's a very passionate, emotional time for us.' Her features became pensive. 'We mourn the pain and suffering of Christ but there's joy in the resurrection too.' As she spoke, Esmeralda's eyes moved over the crowd, settling on Eugenia and Mercedes, who were speaking to some strategically well-placed Spanish aristocrats further along their row of seats. She turned to look at Alexandra. 'You will not fail to be moved by the spectacle, I assure you, Cousin. You are no stranger to passion, I think.'

'Given my profession, I'd like to think not,' Alexandra answered with a half laugh. Again, she wondered how much Esmeralda knew or guessed about her and Salvador.

Esmeralda fixed Alexandra with a look that seemed to read her mind. 'If you would allow me to give you one piece of advice, *querida*, stay true to your passion and it will stay true to you.'

Alexandra was about to ask her what she meant when they were interrupted by the sound of drums in the distance, heralding the *pasos*, and so the question died on her lips.

'Here they come,' Esmeralda whispered as the first marchers appeared. A great murmur stirred in the crowd and those watching from nearby balconies and windows leaned forward to get a better view.

From her vantage point, Alexandra had clear sight of the procession as it went by, stepping in time to the tattoo of the drums and the eerie call of trumpets, stopping every hundred yards or so to allow the bearers to rest. The great puppets of Christ and the Virgin Mary had a surreal, life-like appearance, she thought. They seemed to be moving alone, without human help, lifting their arms or nodding their heads slowly, in rhythm with the men who carried them.

'Here comes our float, Santa María de Concepción,' Esmeralda told her as a dazzling tableau of the Holy Mother came into view. She was clothed in a blue robe, richly embroidered with gold and silver threads. A great train spread out behind her, falling in harmonious cascades over the back of the *paso*. With a jewelled crown surmounting her face, she looked radiant amid a sea of glowing candles.

As the float reached Alexandra and her party, it paused. The thirty men carrying the load on their shoulders set down their burden, kneeling on one knee as they did so. Heads appeared from beneath the heavy cloak that hung over the *paso*, to claim a drink from the water-carrier.

She immediately noticed Salvador. His pale face glistened with sweat; the skin taut over his prominent cheekbones and his hollow eyes made him appear like a flesh-and-blood embodiment of the wooden figures in the procession, seeming to reflect, like them, the agony of the Passion.

All of a sudden, a drawn-out wailing sound came from out of the crowd, searing the evening air with its harrowing and mournful notes. Alexandra shuddered, startled, and saw several women cross themselves, while others threw themselves on the ground. She had read about these impromptu prayers directed to the Virgin Mary, which could burst forth, uninhibited, from someone in the congregation. She turned her gaze to Salvador. Kneeling there, he looked drawn and exhausted. As she watched him gulp down a draft of water and nod his thanks to the water-carrier, it struck Alexandra how he so epitomized the tragic soul of this fervent people. She wondered if she would ever get used to the colour and drama of Spain. Tragedy, blood and death surrounded her. Yet she could feel that this land had stirred something inside her from its sleep, that was reaching out to the passion of these people and, with a force now gathering momentum, gradually claiming it as her own.

As the shrilling *saeta* drew to an end, a signal was given. The lighted image was moved smartly into position; the bearers returned to their place under the drapes, where they straightened their backs and continued bravely on their way. More floats passed by, and with them the sound of drums and trumpets, which died away as they moved into the distance. Finally the penitents came – by far the largest group in the procession – a glittering bank of candles, silent, mysterious and solemn. They wore long, loose coats girdled with thick cords, and high-peaked hoods of every colour and description, concealing their identity, save for two holes allowing them to see their way.

It was getting late. The crowds were beginning to show the first signs of weariness. Bread and tortillas had emerged from napkins and baskets; people peeled oranges, bananas and mandarins, or chatted, now and then casting a cursory glance at the show that had been the original purpose of their outing.

Children, muffled in great shawls, cried as they tried to stay awake, in spite of the attempts on their parents' part to keep them quiet.

It was time to go back. Doña Eugenia and Mercedes, together with Esmeralda, moved off in the direction of the car in silence, still under the spell of the spectacle they'd just witnessed. Alexandra, hanging back, noticed Esmeralda glance over her shoulder one last time, her eyes deep and melancholy. Wanting to be by herself for a little while, Alexandra started back on her own, blending in with the crowd, her heart brimming with a new fervour.

*   *   *

It was a beautiful sunny morning, tempered by a breeze blowing from the north, which bore with it the scent of wild flowers and herbs. A week had passed since the Easter festivities. Salvador had remained out of sight for most of that time. He only appeared for meals and still shunned Alexandra's company – always civil, but cool and offhand. Out of pride and a sense of self-preservation, she didn't go out of her way to speak to him either, and largely tried to pretend he simply wasn't there.

One day she was coming back from her daily walk along the avenue of oaks that stretched across the grounds at the back of the hacienda when she caught sight of him. He wore his riding breeches, an open-neck shirt and polished brown boots. Instead of heading for the stables as was his custom, he strode to the coach house on the opposite side.

An impulse seized her and she called out his name, darting off the path as she did so. Hedges of laburnum and lilac in the full bloom of spring screened her from his view. Alexandra remained hidden for a few seconds, taking pleasure in watching him without being seen.

'Hey, Alexandra!' he shouted, cupping his hands to his mouth. His eyes were casting around, and then he glimpsed her through the branches, laden with yellow clusters, and rounded the hedge to meet her.

'*Buenas dias, querida*,' he said, taxing her with his most charming smile, his smoky grey irises alive with some unfathomable emotion.

'Isn't it a beautiful day?' she replied, her heart fluttering like the wings of a moth. Alexandra had no idea why she had chosen this occasion to stop avoiding him but she was here now and, to her amazement, he was beaming at her, his face so painfully handsome that the fluttering in her chest became a beating ache.

'I'm on my way to our dressage school,' he declared. 'Would you care to join me?' Like quicksilver, he had switched back to his beguiling persona and Alexandra didn't know whether to be delighted or nervous.

She felt the colour rush to her cheeks. A spontaneous smile lit her delicate features but she paused, not wishing to fall straight back into this game. Last time they had spoken, she'd made herself more vulnerable with him than ever before.

He must have sensed her apprehension and took a step towards her, adding sheepishly, 'I've been a little … preoccupied lately. Sorry if I've neglected my duty as host. Besides, this visit would give you more of an understanding of how things run at El Pavón, and perhaps there'll be some material there for your book. Horses are very important to us in Jerez.' Salvador's eyes glittered and Alexandra felt herself falling helplessly into their abyss once more. She was lost, and knew only her compulsion to be with him.

'I can't think of anything that would give me greater pleasure,' she said, all the while hoping the sudden surge of feeling that burned her face wasn't too obvious. She added quickly, 'And you're right, it would be useful for my notes. Do I need to change?'

His eyes ran quickly over her slim body clad in a sensible cotton dress. 'You look lovely, as always, but I thought we could go riding afterwards. I don't mind waiting if you want to change.' Salvador met her self-conscious gaze, the glow in his eyes making her feel light-headed. He smiled broadly and continued, 'You haven't had much occasion to go beyond the boundaries of El Pavón, so why don't we remedy that? There are some very beautiful spots in the region and nothing would please me more than to be your guide.'

Was this a sudden change of heart? Salvador seemed in an unusually sprightly and attentive mood. Would she ever get used to his whimsical states of mind? They changed like quicksilver, always extreme. She wondered if he, too, was still thinking about that night at the Parador de La Luna. Suspended as she was in a constant state of uncertainty, Alexandra found her emotions ridiculously impulsive, and she hated that her reason had become unreliable too. Still, her misgivings were drowned in the elation she felt at the thought of spending a few hours alone in Salvador's company.

As she dressed and fixed her hair into a more practical chignon, Alexandra had to admit that although she was thrilled at the idea of spending time alone with Salvador again, she was not overexcited at the thought of going riding. Up until now, she had managed to avoid it; her father's suggestion, when she first arrived, that they should go riding together was never taken up: he was so rarely at the hacienda these days, choosing instead to travel on estate business most of the time. (She guessed this was a ploy to keep out of the way of his wife and the awkwardness he must feel at her frequent jibes at Alexandra.)

Aunt Geraldine had insisted that she be initiated at an early age both to the practice of a musical instrument and to riding. Alexandra had taken to the first like a duck to water but she had to recognize that the same hadn't been true for the latter.

'You can't live in the country and not know how to ride,' Aunt Geraldine had told her niece firmly when the child had aired her fear of horses. Even now, her aunt rode to hounds every season and, as a teenager, Alexandra was forced to go hunting with her from time to time, as well as attend endless dressage classes, though she would much rather have been up in her room penning a story. It was yet another way in which she had found it difficult to conform. Finally, to her great relief, everybody had to admit she had no affinity with horses, and that riding was not for her.

But now was not the time to be negative, she reprimanded herself. Finally she was going on an outing alone with Salvador and, if nothing else, perhaps this time they could get along like adults and have a civilized conversation. If that meant she had to do a little riding, then so be it.

Salvador was waiting for her at the front of the house with the small open carriage that was normally reserved for the hacienda's daily errands. He held out his hand to help her up and settled himself in the seat next to her, brushing her leg with his thigh as he did so. Alexandra's heartbeat quickened. She could hear it thundering in her ears as she watched his long suntanned hands take firm control of the reins and, at the same time, she detected the familiar fragrance of soap that mingled with the leather of his jacket. His whole masculine being was redolent of animal magnetism and his proximity, as usual, sent her mind and body into a chaotic whirl.

The school was ten minutes away from the hacienda by carriage. Perched high on the gig, Alexandra had a full view of the countryside. Colour dominated the scene: the brick-red and chocolate-brown of the soil, the many shades of green and yellow in the trees, the dense banks of hibiscus hedges stretching for miles on end, the whole lot blazing under a permanently brilliant sky. It was enough to take her breath away and distract her momentarily from Salvador's disturbing closeness.

He told her of his work, which he also regarded as his hobby. 'Spaniards, and especially those from Jerez, have an inborn affinity for horses,' he said as they came in sight of the school.

'I've noticed that,' said Alexandra. 'In the town, there are always so many men on horseback or riders in carriages like this.' She decided not to mention her own less than impressive experience with horses.

'Indeed, and for centuries this town has been the centre for breeding the *cartujano*.' Salvador flicked on the reins, caught up now in his favourite subject. 'It's descended from the Arab horse and was developed by the monks of Chartres. In the sixteenth century, the royal stables at Frederiksborg, in Denmark, were founded using our Spanish horse. Later, some specimens were exported to Austria, and from these were derived the famous Lipizzaners of the Spanish Riding School in Vienna.'

He spoke enthusiastically, with a vivacity that was new to Alexandra, and she listened to him without interruption, not daring to speak for fear of breaking the spell. She knew that horses were his passion and that riding wildly through the countryside released the emotions he held so tightly inside him. It was a part of him that she had never seen, and she was fascinated by this different side to his complex character. The carriage rocked from side to side as they trotted briskly along the road, and Alexandra was acutely aware of the heat of Salvador's body whenever it collided gently with hers.

Suddenly conscious that she was staring at him in silence, he broke off, slanting her an embarrassed smile that somehow made him look younger. 'But I'm boring you with all these stories. Please forgive me, I always get carried away when on the subject of horses.'

'Do go on,' she insisted, flushing slightly at the thoughts she was trying to conceal. 'I grew up with horses, my aunt has stables, but I'm embarrassed to say, I know very little about them. I liked hearing you talk about the history of the Spanish horse.' And then, as an afterthought, she ventured to add, 'I appreciate their beauty, of course, but don't quite share your passion for them.' Salvador steered the carriage off the main road and they turned on to a dirt track that led them to an imposing two-storey stone building with a terracotta-tiled roof. They drove through an archway into an inner courtyard with a circle of grass and a cobbled turning area. Alexandra was impressed: this was not just a stable-block, it was a veritable temple for horses.

A groom rushed out of the building to greet them. After exchanging a few words with the young lad, Salvador helped Alexandra out of the carriage. His hands felt warm and strong, and she was aware that he was watching her intently.

'*Ácqui estamos*, here we are: the Cervantes de Rueda Riding School. Let me show you around,' he said, gently taking her arm and leading her across the grass circle into the main barn. Together they walked down the central aisle inside, on either side of which were open-backed stalls. In each stall a horse, tied to a wall ring and wearing a head collar of the finest leather, stood quietly munching hay. 'Further down, we keep boxes to house mares with foals, the colts and sick horses,' Salvador explained, 'On the upper floor we keep the feed and hay.'

Over the years, Alexandra had visited many stables but she had to admit that none had been fitted out quite as extravagantly as this. The state of upkeep was far superior to anything she had come across in England: evidence of the extent of care and money that had been lavished on the place.

They came out of the other side of the barn into the sunshine. Here a sand *manège* had been built, with the same disregard for expense and a similar attention to quality and detail as everywhere else. On either side lay paddocks where colts grazed the spring grass, unfettered and content under the blazing sun.

They walked towards the wooden fence of the *manège* to watch three young horses trotting on the lunge rein. Salvador motioned proudly towards the handsome animals.

'Look at our *cartujanos*. Over the centuries, their bloodline lost its purity and was injected with new strains that have made it stronger. Today, not only does the blood of their Moorish ancestors run in them, but also that of the Nubian horse, which the Romans used in their chariot races.' He folded his arms and watched the horses being taken through their paces. 'Last year, we introduced thoroughbred strains from England.'

'I'm really very impressed, Salvador. You clearly have a great passion for these horses. I can tell how much time and care has been put into maintaining the school.'

Salvador's voice was a sensual, throaty purr. 'I take great care with everything I'm passionate about, Alexandra.' She looked up, meeting his intense silver gaze. Warmth flooded her cheeks and his mouth curved into an enigmatic smile. 'You must have plenty of fine thoroughbreds in England,' he added, politely moving the conversation back to safe ground.

Alexandra looked at the spirited young creatures with their striking long shiny manes. Though not as big as hunters, they seemed strong and intelligent, as well as graceful.

'We keep hunters and thoroughbreds at our stables in Kent and some of our friends breed Arab horses for racing but, I must confess, I've never come across such handsome and healthy animals,' she told him, recovering her composure. 'No wonder every sovereign and gentleman in the last century who has had a portrait painted of himself on horseback has been depicted seated upon one of these lively *cartujanos*.'

'It's the cross-breeding and injection of new strains that have made the *cartujano* what he is today.' He turned to stare ahead at the *manège*. 'A pure-bred horse, just like a human born of a dynasty founded on intermarriage, has a tendency to become degenerate.'

Alexandra's clear laugh rang out. 'Do you mean that you're against marriage between relatives, *señor*?' she teased.

'In certain cases, of course, especially if they are very close and if similar marriages have occurred over generations. In fact, did you know that this very thing gave rise to the expression "degenerate"?' He leaned his elbows on the fence, his long body appearing even more lithe and powerful. 'Of course, mixed marriages make the most handsome children. Aren't you the living proof of that?' At this he looked at her askance.

She felt herself blush again under his teasing gaze. 'Whether or not I agree with you on this point isn't important,' she said carefully, not wishing to mar the moment by entering into that sort of personal discussion with him, 'but I do understand your passion and your pride in such an achievement.'

Salvador laughed. 'You're eluding the question but I forgive you because I'm in such a good mood and because you like my horses.'

Alexandra glanced up at his face, which was in profile. For the first time since their stroll round Seville, he seemed relaxed, at peace with himself, happy. His complexion, usually pale in spite of his tan, was flushed and his eyes, often so sad, now sparkled with excitement.

'You really do adore your horses,' she remarked, giving him her brightest smile.

'For once, *querida*, you've guessed right,' he said, beaming at her. 'Of all the creatures I have known, their character is the noblest. They are intelligent and easy to train and, above all, big-hearted.'

'What do you train them for?'

'For the cavalry, the show ring and competitions but also, in small numbers, for the arena, where they have to face the bull, of course.'

The words came as a physical shock to Alexandra. 'Oh, no!' She was horrified. 'Poor creatures!' All this care and attention lavished upon them and then Salvador sent them to be slaughtered in the ring. Was that how he treated the things he loved?

'It's a very honourable death,' Salvador insisted.

'It's cruel,' she went on, glaring at him, 'cruel and barbarous! And hiding behind the hypocritical "honourable death" bit doesn't make it any less so.'

'Ah, there you go again, my sentimental little cousin.' He favoured her with a patronizing grin.

Infuriated, her chin came up. 'My reaction has nothing to do with sentimentality, *señor*,' she retorted heatedly. Shadows of old apprehensions loomed in her mind. 'I dislike cruelty and you seem to revel in it.'

Salvador laughed shortly, without humour. 'I didn't see you objecting to anything at the *corrida* the other day,' he retaliated, obviously nettled by her remark. 'On the contrary, you appeared to be enjoying yourself.' He gave her a sidelong glance. Alexandra could read a hint of mockery in his eyes but also something else … She felt trapped. She'd asked for this. Her gibe had been unjustified and, though impelled to defend herself, she realized that, if she wasn't careful, their casual conversation could degenerate into another heated argument, one that would destroy the pleasurable morning they had enjoyed so far.

'*Touché*,' she said good-humouredly instead, and quickly changed the subject. 'Has the family been training horses long?' she asked, slipping back to his favourite subject.

Salvador smoothly recovered himself. 'No, this riding school is all my own work, my dream, but the family has been breeding horses for two generations. My father and his father before him reared stallions, which they sold to the riding school at Jerez. Eleven years ago, with the help and encouragement of my great-aunt, I set about founding a training school. It was a lot of hard work, but today we can boast a professional riding school with a very good reputation in Andalucía.' His expression relaxed. 'It's the one thing the de Fallas are expert at.' he continued. 'They know about horses.'

'What does the training consist of?'

'It's essentially about the co-ordination of movements between horse and master. Our riding masters are both grooms and riders who take full responsibility for their mounts. There builds up a certain understanding between the man and his mount and they come to complement each other. Look over there,' he said, pointing to a bay being led along by a young man in a yellow shirt. 'That colt is in the very first stages of training. His instruction will be carried out on the end of the *cuerda*, until he learns the meaning of an order. This must be done gradually and gently. I suppose it's much the same as teaching a child to walk.'

They watched silently while the riding master exercised his four-legged pupil, holding the end of the rope, trying to get the animal to walk slowly round him. Now and again the colt backed up jerkily, head high, shaking his mane nervously to free himself. Unruffled, the master brought his pupil to order by giving a sharp tug on the rope, which had the effect of quieting the animal. Alexandra had seen this done once in Hampshire, with New Forest ponies.

'Your colt isn't happy,' she observed, laughing.

'Perhaps not, but he must learn who's in charge.' Salvador straightened up, resting his hands on the fence. 'He's now being taught how to walk, trot and canter. In a few months he will be fitted with a girth, then a saddle. Only when he has satisfactorily assimilated all these stages will he be mounted. A horse can be ruined if any are neglected or missed out.'

Alexandra looked up at him, eyes brimming with admiration. 'It's a wonderful thing to feel such passion for one's work. It must bring you so much joy and fulfilment.'

He gave a bitter apology for a laugh. 'I don't know what my life would be like without my horses,' he admitted. Then he turned his head towards Alexandra and his expression changed. He grinned at her, the lights in his eyes flickering with something warm but unreadable. 'But let's not dwell on that. I've promised to show you the neighbouring countryside and that's exactly what I'm going to do.'

Salvador waved at the young groom, signalling him to bring out the mounts he had saddled up for them. If Alexandra had harboured any misgivings about riding that morning, they vanished as soon as a grey mare and a bay horse emerged from the stable block and were led towards them. 'El Cid and Reina,' Salvador said, pointing at each of the animals. Once again she marvelled at their beauty and grace. As the groom handed her the reins of El Cid, she suddenly felt exhilarated at the idea of mounting such a creature and her pulse quickened in anticipation.

'*Gracias*, Diego,' Salvador said. 'I'll give the *señorita* a lift up,' and before she had time to realize what was happening, he had helped her up and into the saddle. 'Are you comfortable?' he asked, letting his hands linger just a moment longer than was necessary on her waist.

'Yes,' she breathed, paling at his touch. Their eyes met and something passed between them in a flash, a brief and vibrant emotion that left her disconcerted. He had turned away in no time and she watched as he hoisted himself into the saddle of the grey with the easy elegance of the *hidalgo* he was. As he patted the side of the powerful animal, Alexandra was aware of his strong, masculine hands and she couldn't help but think of how they might feel on her again. With that thought, her mouth went dry.

They set off with the late spring sun behind them, through avenues of eucalyptus, the hot, still air made fragrant by the fallen leaves and button-like fruit that carpeted the ground for stretches on end. They cantered gently past orange groves and grey-green olive plantations. At intervals where there was shade, they would see an old man or woman standing motionless, or herding a few goats. Small, dark-faced children playing on the side of the road stared fixedly at them with their bright, black eyes. Sometimes a passer-by, carrying a tool or driving a mule laden with maize, would raise his hat in greeting.

'The Spanish are so polite and friendly,' Alexandra remarked, as a man sitting in the doorway of a whitewashed cottage half-lifted himself from his stool on observing their approach.

Salvador lifted an enquiring eyebrow. 'Is that not the case in England?'

'No, I don't think so. Anyhow, not in the same way. We run a much more equal society. These days, there's no longer the same deference and courtesy in England.'

His blue-grey eyes glinted teasingly, his expression momentarily boyish again. 'I'm glad that we meet with your approval then.'

As they rounded a bend, the soil became sandy with banks of prickly pear and cactus plants studding either side of the road, with open fields stretching as far as the eye could see.

They stopped their horses under the deep shade of a jacaranda tree to watch the peasant women in their black scarves and voluminous skirts, plodding barefoot up and down the arid soil, attempting to work the land. On a trodden patch of hard earth and stone, a patient blindfolded ox turned and turned. Its pole was attached to a toothed wheel of primitive wooden cogs carrying a chain of buckets that repeatedly drew up water from a wide, shallow well to tilt it out between the lips of an irrigation channel. They watched in silence, savouring the enchanting hush. For Alexandra, the scenery, like everything she had encountered in Spain, was suggestive of a bygone age redolent of romance. This was a land of dreams; Salvador was next to her, relaxed and happy. What more could she ask?

And then, all of sudden, El Cid, stung by a horsefly, bucked and surged forward. Alexandra gave a sharp scream as the bay tore off into a wild gallop. He went at gale-force speed, churning up sand into her eyes, gathering momentum by the second.

She tightened her grip on the reins and tried desperately to hang on to the pommel, her old riding instructor's words revolving in her head: '*Keep calm, don't panic, keep calm, don't panic …*' She could hear the thundering hooves of Salvador's mare as he rode hard on her heels, trying to catch up with them. Soon, they were riding side by side. In an instant, he had reached out for the reins, snatching them up and curling them round his fingers in a tight grip, before skilfully pulling the horse to a halt in a cloud of dust and sand.

In a flash, Salvador slid off his mount and rushed to Alexandra's side. She had wasted no time in dismounting, stumbling as her feet touched the ground, her whole body shaking from shock.

'Are you all right, *querida*?' Salvador stared down into her pale face, and gripped her shoulders to steady her, his strained features betraying his concern.

'Shaken, but not hurt,' she managed to say faintly.

Alexandra felt the warmth of his breath on her cheek and the pressure of his strong palms through her riding habit. Her breathing had become ragged. She hoped that he would put this down to the riding incident; only she knew it was not, as she gazed into his worried cobalt-blue eyes.

He raised a hand to brush away a rebellious strand of hair that had escaped from the net holding the neat chignon at the nape of her neck. There was such gentleness in his gesture, so much tenderness, that she felt her head swim. She shut her eyes momentarily and reason deserted her as the physical awareness of him engulfed her entire body.

Once again she felt vulnerable. She could tell that Salvador was conscious of her need, silently urging her to release the pent-up dam of their mutual longing. His eyes were like molten silver, burning into hers, and in them she saw his noble intentions struggling with raw desire.

Salvador ran his thumb slowly over her bottom lip and a strange tingling sensation rippled along her skin. He gazed at her with a fierce hunger that made her tremble uncontrollably. As he drew her to him with a deep sigh, her hands instinctively met behind his back. Wrapped in his embrace, feeling the hard contours of his lean body against hers, she intuitively arched, surprised, almost afraid by the powerful physical response she felt in him. He pulled her against him again, almost ferociously, his eyes never leaving her face, and she gave a soft gasp at his obvious arousal. Once more she was enthralled, at the mercy of the unbridled call of her desire, alive, on the edge of an unknown magical world, never wanting this moment to end.

And then suddenly he was avidly claiming her lips, her willing surrender stimulating his urgency. Passion exploded between them like wildfire. Still ravaging her mouth furiously and encircling her waist with his arm, he let one hand brush over the swelling curve of her breasts so that she felt their centre pulsate under his butterfly touch. He stroked and massaged sensually, his powerful fingers erotically provocative, until, aching with desire, white-hot flames licked through her and Alexandra's entire body was consumed by this terrifying inferno that Salvador had lit within her. She could not get close enough to him, returning his open-mouth kiss with a feverish abandon that matched his own.

Finally, they reluctantly disentangled their embrace, tearing their mouths from each other, panting, trying to release themselves from the fire that consumed them and from the compelling influence of their hands. They knew that soon they would be crossing the point of no return and though their bodies drew away, each could still feel the burning imprint of the other.

Salvador gazed silently into her green eyes as Alexandra tried desperately to fathom the meaning in his. For a fleeting moment, she thought he was going to say something but he shook his dark head, clenched his fists tightly at his side and turned away, still breathing raggedly.

The horses had moved off a little and were happily munching grass and weeds. Salvador brought El Cid over and she let him help her back into the saddle, blinking slowly as his hands dropped away.

His smoky grey eyes were deep but brooding as he looked up at her. 'Are you going to be all right?' he asked with concern. He offered to walk by her horse but she shook her head.

'I'm quite capable of handling the journey back, thank you,' she said softly, though her hands were trembling a little.

They rode side by side in silence, each recognizing that something wonderful had just passed between them, knowing they could not ignore the towering rage of emotion they had shared.

Still shaken and bewildered by the experience, Alexandra knew, more than ever, that what she felt for Salvador was not sheer uncomplicated lust. Like their bodies, their souls had touched, and though she was still not convinced, she had the notion that he burned with an equal fire. The power and strength in his kisses … the piercing sweet demand … these were not the lightly given caresses of a man acting merely at the whim of his senses.

How could he make love to her with such life-giving warmth if his feelings were not so passionate and all-consuming as hers?

Surely it was love she'd read in his eyes when they had pulled back from that scorching kiss? Had he not been trying to ask or tell her something important? A look, a kiss, a caress from Salvador said so much more than words could ever do. Would the fantasy end with their kiss, as it had in Ronda? And would reality then intrude, once again tearing them apart? He was what she wanted; he was everything she had ever wanted; and somehow she knew that if he only let her, she would prove to him that she was what he was looking for.

They arrived back at El Pavón in the afternoon, having missed lunch. As they came into the hall, José informed them that the *Marquesa* of Aguila and her brother, *Señor* Felipe Herrera, had called at the house that morning and would come back again in the late afternoon.

'Instruct the cook that there will be two additional places for dinner,' Salvador instructed the major-domo as he strode off towards his apartments without a backward glance.

Alexandra's heart sank. Salvador had been less than talkative on the way back to the hacienda and she had hoped to catch him alone in the afternoon, or after dinner, for a serious heart-to-heart about what was happening between them. Besides, Doña Isabel and her brother were the last people she fancied seeing tonight, even though, not so long ago, she had admittedly enjoyed the attentions of the dashing *matador*. After such an eventful morning, she needed to think things over quietly and found the prospect of facing polite conversation all evening quite unbearable. There was also the question of Don Felipe's expectations to deal with. Tonight she would need to tread cautiously.

In her bedroom, Alexandra thought carefully about what to wear. She chose a simple long dress in soft orange silk, the rippling shades of which ranged from maroon to pale peach, enhancing the warm colour of her green eyes, making them seem wider. It was a slightly more daring dress than those she usually wore: the deep V-neck of her corsage showed off the gentle curve of her breasts. Before washing her hair, she had worked into it a creamy substance made from oils and plants that Agustina had given her. Now it looked lush and shiny as she piled it up on the crown of her head, showing off the delicate oval of her face. As the sun that morning had given her skin a healthy-looking hue, she wore no make-up except for some lip gloss, a little eye-shadow and mascara. Ordinarily, she didn't spend so much time on her appearance, but she wanted to look her best for Salvador that night. When she had finished, she was not displeased with her reflection in the long mirror.

Alexandra came down just as José was ushering their guests into the drawing room. She paused for a few seconds on the bottom step of the staircase before crossing the hall to join them.

'Ah, there you are, my dear,' exclaimed Doña María Dolores as Alexandra appeared in the doorway. 'I was a little concerned you might have caught the sun this morning but I see our weather agrees with you. You look particularly radiant tonight. Did you have a nice time?'

Alexandra bent to kiss the *Duquesa*'s forehead. 'Good evening, *Abuela*. And yes, thank you.' She smiled at the old lady.

'I think you've already met my granddaughter, Doña Alexandra de Falla,' said the dowager, turning to the *Marquesa*, who was sitting in an armchair next to the fireplace.

'Indeed,' said the latter with a chilly smile. 'I've met Doña Alexandra on several occasions.' Alexandra was conscious of ice-blue eyes surveying her insolently, and her hand itched to swipe that superior expression off Doña Isabel's aristocratic face.

'I am delighted to see you again, *señorita*,' Don Felipe, impeccably dressed in an oatmeal beige suit and standing behind his sister's chair, gave an elegant bow. Just before he did so, Alexandra was aware of his velvety gaze moving smoothly over her body, as if those dark, gleaming eyes intended to strip her to the soul. Although self-conscious and ill at ease, she managed a gracious smile.

Alexandra was on the point of seating herself next to Esmeralda on the sofa when José announced dinner was served. Instinctively, her eyes searched for Salvador. He was standing on the other side of the room, looking devastatingly handsome in a crisp white dress shirt and a black suit. Alexandra willed him to look at her but his face remained impassive. He didn't even glance at her as he made his way over to Doña Isabel, offering his arm so they could go into dinner together. With a pang she registered that the *Marquesa* was leaning a little too close to him, almost clinging to his arm, and was casting him coquettish looks and smiles. He, on the other hand, was unreadable, neither overtly responding, nor trying to get away.

As though her grandmother's piercing grey eyes had penetrated her soul, Doña María Dolores chose that moment to tell Alexandra that the *Marquesa* had suffered a fall that morning while walking in the grounds, and had twisted her ankle.

'Fortunately we were able to send word to Dr Perez, who came over immediately and assured us that it is only a benign sprain.' Then, much to the annoyance of Don Felipe who was making a move towards Alexandra, the dowager turned and held out her hand to him. 'Let us lead the way,' she said pointedly, before he had time to offer his arm to her granddaughter.

They went into dinner and took their seats. Alexandra let her eyes wander round the table. The family were all there. Salvador was at the head, with Doña Isabel on his right. At the other end sat the *Duquesa*, with Don Felipe on her right. The others were seated in the order dictated by etiquette and Alexandra found herself placed next to the *torero*.

There was electricity in the air; Alexandra could sense its undercurrents quivering in the atmosphere. Conversation was stilted. Doña María Dolores was courteously reserved, particularly with Don Felipe, in keeping to general topics, but Alexandra, who by now knew her well, was aware of a certain impatience in her manner. Doña Eugenia, her features fixed in a permanent artificial smile, unobtrusively observed her daughter and seemed rather worried. Mercedes had indeed lost her usual vivacity and was eating her paella in silence like a sulky child. Now and again, she would cast a stormy glance at the *Marquesa*, who, unconcerned, could not keep her eyes off Salvador. Her cascading laugh erupted every time the young man gave her the opportunity, filling the room with its characteristic tremolo, the inevitable effect of which was the irritation of most of those present. Don Alonso and Esmeralda hardly spoke and when they did it was fleeting. Only Ramón seemed completely at ease. As usual on such occasions, he had difficulty in keeping a straight face, and more than once tried to lighten the atmosphere by telling a joke that invariably fell on deaf ears.

Alexandra could not say whether Salvador was aware of the awkwardness his guests had caused. He appeared uninterested in her, detached, exercising his duty as host. Or was it more than that? Not once did he look across the table at Alexandra; not once did their eyes meet. Could he not have spared her just one telling glance to show that he had been as moved as she by their passionate embrace that morning? She knew he was deliberately avoiding her again. Was he already regretting it?

A tremor ran through her body as the memory of his touch suffused her mind. Alexandra ached for him, despite the coiled and remote air he was displaying tonight; but she was upset by his repeated determination to hurt her. She knew the powerful pain gnawing at her insides was jealousy and she was deeply ashamed of it. Still, she could not help herself.

Looking at him now, sitting next to Doña Isabel, she had to admit they formed a very handsome couple and the *Marquesa* was certainly well-suited to him. They'd had a whirlwind romance and Alexandra reflected achingly that first love is often the strongest. Perhaps, in toying with Alexandra, Salvador had been merely salving an old wound, channelling his broken feelings for Doña Isabel into his purely physical attraction for Alexandra – or even Marujita, for that matter; playing with them both in an ultimately meaningless dalliance. Her heart gave a painful squeeze as she watched Doña Isabel murmur something to him and smile. There was an undeniable intimacy between the pair and it hurt to watch.

The *Marquesa* was beautiful, rich and titled; above all, she belonged to his world, initiated to the ways and traditions of this exotic and flamboyant land. How could Alexandra possibly compete? That morning, she had been aware of a deep synchronized tuning between herself and Salvador, and she had thought she could make him happy; now she was not so sure. She was weary of this inscrutable dance, for which she didn't know the steps, and in which she so often stumbled and fell.

'Doña Alexandra, would you like to visit our *bodegas* in Puerto de Santa María next week?' Don Felipe's question reached her through the fog of her thoughts.

'Er … yes, yes, of course,' she heard herself answer absentmindedly.

After having exchanged small talk with his hostess for decorum's sake, the young *torero* had given his full attention to Alexandra. Unaware that her mind was elsewhere, he had set about telling her the history of the sherry industry in Spain, and particularly the role his family had played in developing it in this part of Andalucía, hence his invitation to Puerto de Santa María. But she had not been listening, absorbed as she was in her obsession.

And now, suddenly, Alexandra was angry: angry with Salvador for ignoring her, with Doña Isabel for making her feel so ordinary and inadequate but, most of all, angry with herself for being such a fool. She was behaving like a mixed-up, gauche adolescent and she despised her own weakness in allowing the pair of them to sap her self-confidence in this way. Being in control of her thoughts and feelings had never been a problem in the past and yet, suddenly, she was assailed by all sorts of emotions that made her feel small and cheap. She would prove to Salvador he was not the only attractive man in the world and that it was so easy for her to do without his attentions.

Turning to Don Felipe, she began to encourage his assiduity with renewed enthusiasm. She couldn't be certain but she fancied she saw Salvador's jaw tighten; she began to feel slightly better.

After dinner they went into the drawing room to have coffee. The *Duquesa* had found the meal trying so she excused herself and retired for the evening. The older members of the family followed suit, while the others remained.

Conversation centred on trivialities. Old José came in somewhat unsteadily, holding a heavy salver laden with cups of fine china and baroque silverware. Esmeralda rose to pour the coffee. Mercedes suggested a game of charades.

'Charades, when we have a virtuoso among us?' Ramón cried out, putting his hands to his chest in a dramatic gesture, pretending to be horrified. He turned to his cousin. 'Alexandra, would you play the piano for us?' Mischief danced in his eyes as he watched Doña Isabel stir uncomfortably in her seat, looking daggers at him.

'I haven't played seriously in years,' Alexandra protested, feeling the colour in her cheeks.

'Nonsense,' Ramón went on. 'I've heard you play several times in the afternoon when you thought no one was listening.' Then, turning to the others, he added, 'She's a very talented young lady, you know.'

'What a marvellous idea!' Don Felipe said emphatically, crossing the room and holding out his hand to Alexandra with a flourish. 'Please,' he whispered huskily, 'it would give me such pleasure to hear you play.' She put her hand in his, rather embarrassed by this public display of effusive chivalry. He pressed it to his lips before leading her to the piano. She couldn't help giving an inward smile at the thought of Salvador's reaction.

Don Felipe ran his fingers over the richly varnished surface and, before lifting the lid, turned to his host. 'Will you permit me, Don Salvador?' he asked in a sugary tone.

Salvador, aloof and impassive as ever, nodded. 'Go ahead, please,' he said coolly, his eyes narrowing only slightly.

The *torero* raised the lid slowly and lightly touched one of the ivory keys, then another and another. 'It would give me much pleasure to hear you play,' he repeated, turning to Alexandra, his velvety-black eyes caressing behind their curtain of dark lashes.

'We would all love you to play for us,' Esmeralda assured her, leaving no alternative to the others but to join in.

'I'm really a mediocre musician,' Alexandra told them with an apologetic little shrug as she seated herself on the satin-upholstered stool. However, she quickly set about sorting through the pile of music lying on top of the piano, picked out a sheet and placed it in front of her.

She chose a familiar piece by Chopin. The rhythmic and somewhat rousing melody brought back childhood memories of when she was a young girl in long plaits with red ribbons, scampering happily over the wide expanses of Hyde Park, or through the dark woods of Kent where she sometimes went with her Aunt Geraldine to gather wild mushrooms and strawberries.

As the first notes of the mazurka flooded the room, Alexandra noticed, out of the corner of her eye, that Salvador had left his armchair and moved across to lean against the mantelpiece, from where he had a perfect view of her. She could feel the intensity of his enigmatic gaze resting on her and was aware that it was the first time that evening he had so much as acknowledged her presence. Every now and again she allowed herself to glance up. His eyes held a silent hunger, his lovemaking unspoken in his every look.

Alexandra congratulated herself on having chosen such a light piece. She had played it so often to entertain Aunt Geraldine during the long wintry evenings that her fingers now ran effortlessly over the keys. Otherwise, she would have faltered under Salvador's powerful stare. Why did he have to make things so difficult? He was at it again, blowing hot and cold, engaging in his fickle game of read-me-if-you-can.

As Alexandra struck the last notes of the finale, her audience applauded enthusiastically.

'Magnificent!' Don Felipe exclaimed warmly. 'Absolutely magnificent! Would you do us the honour of playing for us some more, Doña Alexandra, and will you permit me to choose something a little soulful this time?' he asked as he flicked through the pile of music.

'My dear Felipe, I'm sorry to drag you away from your entertainment,' said Doña Isabel as she rose from the sofa, giving Alexandra no time to reply. 'It's been a long day. We mustn't abuse our host's hospitality.' Her brother glared petulantly at her but she clearly wasn't concerned, wanting to end the evening as quickly as possible. Tense and irritable-looking, her demeanour looked very different from the relaxed and laughing self she had displayed over dinner. The *Marquesa* bade her hosts goodnight, thanking them for their friendly and generous reception. She expressed her gratitude especially to Esmeralda for calling a doctor so promptly after she had injured herself that afternoon and for providing emergency supplies but her smile changed to one of contempt as she came up to Alexandra.

'Thank you, my dear, it was kind of you to amuse us.' Her condescension was horribly blatant. 'Although, I always think those lightweight, easy pieces are perhaps best kept for the schoolroom.'

'You mustn't take any notice of my sister when she's in this mood,' the *torero* interjected hurriedly, casting a glare at Isabel. He took Alexandra's hand and brushed her fingers lightly against his lips. 'You played magically,' he declared fervently, 'truly magically! I hope you'll do me the honour of playing for me again soon.'

'It's very kind of you to say so.' Alexandra endeavoured to give a gracious smile, determined not to allow Doña Isabel the satisfaction of thinking that her spiteful words had hit home.

'I will be in touch soon about the visit to our *bodegas*.' Felipe dropped his voice a little and fixed her with one of his salacious looks, before turning to Salvador. 'I have spent a most enjoyable evening, *señor*. You're very lucky to have such talent in your family,' he stated emphatically. Salvador acknowledged his comment with a nod and the shadow of a smile. His eyes flicked across to Alexandra but the expression in them was unreadable. 'I'll walk you to your car,' he offered, giving Doña Isabel his arm. Together they strolled into the garden and Alexandra hurried up to her room without a word.

*   *   *

Alexandra woke up with a start, shuddering from an incoherent and confused nightmare in which gypsies were guests at a masked ball in a strange castle and a *torero* was chasing her into the dungeons. Her chest felt constricted. Panting, she reached for the lamp on the bedside table and turned it on. A pale shaft of light flooded the room. Dazed and half-asleep, her screams still echoing inside her head, she slid out of bed and staggered to the window. Outside, a crescent moon was faint in the half-light of morning and the first sounds of the dawn chorus had begun.

Alexandra stepped out on to the small balcony. The distant accents of a string adagio trembled in the air. She strained her ears; the music was barely audible, its sad melody a sultry whisper in the silence. As she leaned over the balustrade, she saw light spilling out on to the terrace from the drawing room below. Who could be playing the violin at this hour?

Alexandra went back into her room and glanced at the clock. Half past four. She wouldn't get back to sleep now: the fresh early-morning air had caused her to feel wide awake. On impulse, she slipped on her dressing gown and crept down the staircase. By the time she reached the bottom, the music had stopped. Though the drawing-room door was shut, a weak bar of light shone underneath it. Alexandra moved forward and paused, her hand resting on the doorknob, uncertain whether or not to breach the privacy of the person on the other side. She opened the door but didn't walk in.

Straight away she saw Salvador. His back was to her and he was leaning against the frame of the open window, smoking quietly, gazing into space. His head shifted a little as the door creaked, but he didn't turn.

Alexandra stood on the threshold staring at him. He obviously hadn't been to bed as he was still wearing the same clothes he'd worn at dinner, though he had shed his suit jacket and tie. She couldn't help but admire the strong lines of his profile, his long, straight, masculine back and broad shoulders clearly visible beneath the white shirt. Suddenly she felt at a loss, not knowing whether to leave or what to say if she stayed.

Salvador remained motionless for a few moments more, looking out into the budding morning. The cigarette in his hand was no more than a stub. After tossing it brusquely on to the grass outside, he turned at last.

He was pale, his features drawn and his brow furrowed with fine horizontal lines that she didn't remember noticing before.

His eyes had the same glazed, desperate look they'd had on the night of the wake and his mouth was set in a thin, hard line. If there had been any residue of anger in her, it melted when she saw his expression. She ached to run to him, to take him in her arms and relieve him of his demons. But just as suddenly as she had felt that urge, she felt helpless again. Salvador, with his baffling silences and offhand behaviour, had built such high walls and barriers between them, so many insurmountable obstacles, that she stood there, paralysed. Once more, her own pride, and the fear of rebuff, left her tongue-tied.

They stared at each other across the room. Salvador didn't seem surprised by her presence. Nor did he seem to feel the awkwardness hanging so palpably in the room. Finally she found the courage to speak.

'You never told me you played the violin,' she said, unsteadily. 'What a beautiful melody, I don't think I've heard it before. Who's the composer?'

'He's unknown,' Salvador answered flatly, shutting the window and placing the violin in its case.

What should she do? Standing there alone with him in the small hours, she had to find something to say, some way to ford this chasm, she told herself. But what was the use? The dark, impervious look on his face suggested that he was far from approachable.

'Speak to me, Salvador,' she said softly, instantly regretting those words the moment they left her lips.

But he shook his head obstinately. 'It will do no good,' he sighed, without looking at her. 'I've endlessly repeated all there is to say. I have nothing more to add.' His tone was final, his eyes shuttered. Alexandra moved tentatively across the room and stood next to him as he put the violin case in a cupboard.

'So we're back to where we were … again?' She took a deep breath. 'But why then, all those times … what about the night at Ronda and this morning?' she whispered, trying to get him to look at her, once more her deep-green irises searching his face for some clue.

'They meant nothing.' Salvador leant an arm on the cupboard door and ran the other hand through his unruly hair.

'Nothing?' Alexandra stared in disbelief.

'Why must you always challenge me, Alexandra?' He spoke without looking at her. 'You're a very beautiful woman. No hot-blooded man would be able to resist you. Can't you see that?'

He turned on her, his eyes blazing, and with his free hand pushed her firmly by the waist against the cupboard. She gasped, her pulse leaping. Their bodies were so close now that she could feel the heat radiating off him, his warm breath against her mouth, his eyes searing her own. It brought back to life all the yearning she had strived to keep under control. Her breasts were rising and falling unsteadily against his chest as his gaze travelled over her lips.

'Don't pretend you're not aware of how provocative you are,' he growled, his hold tightening on her waist. Alexandra's pupils widened and he gave a bitter laugh. 'Don Felipe could hardly keep his hands off you tonight.' Scorn twisted his mouth but the look he gave her was sharp with tormented desire and some kind of deeper pain. He looked down at her flimsy dressing gown and closed his eyes. When he opened them again, his expression had become cold and aloof. He stepped away from her. 'The flesh is weak, Alexandra. Forgive me if I gave you the wrong impression.'

His answer was so brusque and unexpected that Alexandra looked at him blankly, her heart slowly breaking. She shook her head. 'You're lying,' she muttered, forcing back a sob.

'Perhaps I am.' Salvador met her accusing gaze impassively. 'But that is my prerogative.' His voice roughened. 'You don't look well. You should go to bed, get some sleep. You'll feel better in the morning.' He crossed in front of her and briskly left the room.

Trembling, her back still against the cupboard, she finally caved in and began to cry.

CHAPTER 10

Once in her room, Alexandra knew it was pointless to go back to bed. A soft, luminous brightness bathed the garden. Dawn burned through the trees at the edge of the hacienda and over the orange and lemon groves. The happy choir of birdsong had given way to the incessant hum of cicadas, heralding a scorching day. At this hour, the garden glowed with timeless enchantment. Alexandra wondered how many generations had stood at the same window, year after year, enjoying the tranquil view at daybreak, and would continue to do so for aeons to come. People would come and go but nature's meticulous clock ticked on eternally, unchanging and immutable. She sighed. Much good it did her to philosophize.

He can't treat you like this, she thought. *Where is your pride?* The encounter with Salvador the previous night had wounded her in ways she could not begin to understand. Angry, but most of all hurt, she gave in to the wave of self-pity that swept over her. A bleak sense of desperation filled her heart; the memory of her mother's abandonment surfaced with the pain of a wound being reopened. Desertion seemed fated to be her lot in life: first her mother, then her father, and now Salvador.

Still, with Salvador she felt trapped in a hopeless situation and she was beginning to believe it was of her own making. Tears of humiliation welled in her eyes. She had been wrong, utterly wrong from the start. Salvador didn't need her, let alone love her. He was physically attracted to her; that she could see. However, she had mistaken the drive of his libido for deeper feelings, conjured by her own fertile and romantic imagination. After all, it was common knowledge that sex drives were totally different, she told herself. A man's was not only stronger but much more straightforward; certainly this was so with Salvador. Alexandra, like most young women of her age, had always been led to believe that sexual desire in a woman was mostly emotional, rather than physical; though if this were true, the frightening power of her own newly discovered needs and desires caused her even more confusion and guilt.

On top of this, Salvador had now made it perfectly clear that he considered her an argumentative and immature female who had obsessively thrown herself at him, and he would be much relieved if she kept out of his way, and yet ...

There were times when she had been aware of a harmonious bond between them, as well as moments when he had vibrated with an intensity of feeling that equalled her own. Only yesterday he had displayed an ardour that belied his indifference. Still, she had to admit that, right from the start, her spells of happiness with Salvador had been made up of fleeting moments and were always punctuated by far longer bouts of aloofness or outbursts of anger on his part; and always by regret.

He had made it quite clear the first time they'd met, on the night of the masked ball, that she had no place in Spain. She should have taken his advice then and fled; but already she'd fallen under his spell, even back there on the terrace; she knew it now. The setting, the scenery, the atmosphere, the ambiguous personality of the man had all conspired to create a situation that appealed to the passionate and adventurous side of her nature.

She had blinkered herself, clutched at every cliché, wanting to believe in the big romance. Now she herself was captive of those same circumstances in which the heroines of her novels had so often found themselves, with all the pitfalls and dramas that made her own books bestsellers. How ironic ... What a fool she'd been. Her anger rose again, and with it new resolve. *I am a woman, not a child. I won't run away.* Besides, a deeper feeling had been triggered inside her and she could not ignore it now; it kept her here, waiting for something to happen that she could not understand yet. Time passed as she sat there in the sanctuary of her bedroom, lost in introspection, musing on how the events of the past few months had changed her.

The sun was up, a swollen golden globe above the treetops. Gradually, its warm rays crept into the room, banishing the purple hues of night and with them Alexandra's sombre thoughts. She breathed in the morning air, trying to absorb some of its tranquillity. How invigorating it felt.

Alexandra shrugged; it was pointless to brood, she would dress and go for a walk. No doubt that would help untangle her emotions and clarify her confused thoughts. Perhaps there was a way for her and Salvador to be friends, if she could only set aside her romantic notions and become less sensitive to his mercurial ways. Besides, he'd always indulged in these childish moods so what was different this time?

She put on a pair of jeans and a white cotton blouse and slipped her book into her bag. Almost used to the Spanish sun by now, Alexandra decided against a hat. Missing breakfast was a good idea too, even if that meant breaking the sacrosanct 'meals rule'. For once, she would be the elusive, moody one; it would teach Salvador a lesson. Then, perhaps, he would be loath to play silly games in the future.

There were charming corners of the hacienda Alexandra had not yet explored so she drifted down to the east side of the grounds. She turned into a pathway shaded by jacarandas and planes, where orchards and gardens extended on either side as far as the eye could see. Roses, wild jasmine and sweet-smelling herbs filled the morning with their aromatic scent.

The day was heating up; it was still quite early, but already the sun was blazing down, like most mornings in the south of Spain in late spring. There wasn't a ghost of a breeze. Alexandra took her time winding her way through the exquisite gardens, edged with elegant cypress trees, often stopping to sit and read her book or scribble down a few notes in her notepad. After that, beyond the borders of the gardens, she walked for more than an hour, meandering back and forth across acres of fruit trees, soaking in the beauty of the light and heady fragrance of orange blossom in the air.

But she was becoming hot and weary. Maybe leaving her hat behind was not such a good idea after all, she thought, as she crossed an unshaded path and walked down the side of one of the apple orchards. She paused just long enough to catch her breath. This was a place to laze and abandon all idea of exercise. The air itself was persuasive, and it took an immeasurable amount of effort not to surrender to its wiles; but the walk was doing her good, clearing her mind of the shadows that often accumulate in the silent darkness of night. Indulging in a short siesta this afternoon would be just the thing to recuperate.

Soon, a little ahead on the right, the ground dropped slightly into a small grove. Through the foliage Alexandra noticed a tool shed, its walls covered in a huge crimson rambling rose, dazzling under the beating sun. Carefully, she made her way down the steep slope of red soil. The floor of the glade was covered in white blossoms that exhaled a tart fragrance as she walked. Spying an old bucket at the foot of a tree in a patch of shade, she sat down on it and leant against the tree trunk, watching a solitary puffy white cloud drift slowly into the distance. Except for the rasp of the cicadas, it was totally silent. A hawk, his wings spread wide, hung in the blue sky, gliding smoothly round and round until he too disappeared out of sight.

Alexandra was about to get up and resume her walk when she heard a rustling of leaves and the faint sound of muffled voices coming from the other side of the tool shed. She looked around in a panic, not knowing what to do. Eavesdropping was not a habit she wanted to acquire, but she was trapped. To get back on to the pathway or go deeper into the grove meant that she would have to come out into the open. Either way she would be seen and intuition told her that wasn't a good idea.

'This time there should be no accidents,' said a woman's voice. 'The aim is to make her life unpleasant and force her to go back to England, not kill the girl.'

'Leave it to me,' snorted her partner.

Although they spoke in whispers, Alexandra could easily hear what was being said. Furthermore, she was in no doubt as to the identity of the pair. Clearly she had come upon a conversation not meant for her ears.

'The last time you told me to leave it to you, a disaster almost happened. Don Salvador got involved and it was only by sheer luck you weren't discovered,' retorted Doña Eugenia icily.

'Bah!' the man's laugh jarred against Alexandra's ear. 'That was all exaggerated. The young lady came to no harm, as far as I know.'

'None of this concerns me,' hissed her stepmother. 'I am only warning you that should anything unfortunate happen, should somebody get hurt for any reason, you, and you alone, will suffer the consequences. This conversation never took place.'

'Of course it didn't,' sneered the steward. 'Perish the thought that the aristocracy should be seen to get their hands dirty!'

'Spare me your impertinent comments. If it wasn't for me, you'd have been sent packing years ago. And I've made sure you're well paid.'

'Not *that* well,' he retorted derisively. 'But I'm not a greedy man. Perhaps you could let me have a little payment on account, to help me overcome any scruples I might have.'

'Here, this is the last you'll receive before the job's done. Don't waste it and, remember, be careful this time!'

After this, Alexandra heard Doña Eugenia hurrying off into the grove. Seconds later, Lopez appeared from behind the tool shed, making his way nonchalantly towards the pathway she had earlier ventured along. He stopped and pulled a wad of banknotes from his pocket. Breathless, she was suddenly aware that she was in full view; if he turned, she would be discovered. Lopez counted the money avidly before replacing it in his pocket. '*Las brujas*, bitches,' he muttered under his breath but loud enough for her to hear. 'Young, old, rich, poor … they're bitches, the lot of 'em.' Then he took a packet of cigarettes from the top pocket of his shirt. Lighting one, he drew a few puffs and then, to Alexandra's relief, strolled off.

Still shaken, Alexandra pressed her fingers to her throbbing temples. Her head ached and she felt sick at heart. What was she to do now? Would anybody believe her story? Without proof that Lopez and Doña Eugenia were behind the arrow incident, it would be her word against her stepmother's. It was obvious she didn't stand a chance. If she said anything, the family would put it down to her overactive imagination. Worse still, they might accuse her of maliciously trying to drive a wedge between her father and stepmother. Still, Alexandra refused to be beaten and had no intention of running. Had she been tempted to leave Spain after the previous evening's episode with Salvador, now, more than ever, she was determined to stay.

Nevertheless, she knew she needed an ally at El Pavón, if only to have someone she could trust to watch her back. But for that she must tell her story, which meant making accusations. She would need to tread lightly.

Alexandra made her way back to the hacienda, mulling over the various members of the family. The first person to eliminate was Doña María Dolores. Strangely enough, she thought her grandmother would be the most likely person to lend a sympathetic ear without accusing her of spinning a tale, but she was loath to burden the old lady. She considered telling Salvador but instantly dismissed the idea. In taking him into her confidence, she would only be giving him proof that his fears for her safety had been well-founded all along, even if he'd been mistaken about those threatening her. It wasn't *la veganza de Calés* of which she should be wary but her father's second wife. Either way, Salvador would be perfectly within his rights to put her on the first plane to England and then he would have won. It was no use speaking to Esmeralda either. Alexandra was sure that, on this occasion, the young woman would have no qualms about going straight to her brother. Then there was Ramón. Of all the family, he had been by far the nicest but, in such a serious situation, she very much doubted he would be reliable.

So it would have to be Don Alonso. After all, it was his own wife hatching plots, his own daughter in peril. Wasn't a father the most natural and obvious protector? Hadn't Alexandra every right to call on his support? She didn't believe he could have been involved in the shenanigans, even slightly. In fact, she was convinced he had not the barest inkling of what was going on. It was true, since her arrival in Spain, that he had not given her much of his time or attention; he had so often been away and, whenever he was present at mealtimes, he spoke little and usually took the first opportunity to hole himself up in another part of the house. He was weak, and for a quiet life would let his wife have her own way more often than not. Nevertheless, Alexandra was convinced that he loved her deeply and was incapable of being party to such malevolent games.

Alexandra reached the house just in time to change for lunch. Everyone was present at the dining table except for Salvador, which didn't surprise her. She managed to get through the meal without manifesting any change in her behaviour and avoided looking at her stepmother in case her eyes gave her away.

Immediately afterwards, when everyone had retired for their siesta, Alexandra went looking for Don Alonso. During the afternoon usually he shut himself away, either in his office when he had letters to write, or in the library, where he most of the time remained until dinner, reading enormous old history books. She found him there, sitting in one of the large wing-backed chairs, engrossed in a great leatherbound volume. His face lit up. 'Ah, Alexandra!' He seemed truly happy to see her. 'Are you looking for a book?'

'No, *Papá*, it's you I was looking for,' she said, coming straight to the point.

'I see.' He smiled and then peered more closely at her. 'You seem upset,' he remarked. 'What can I do for my little girl?'

Encouraged by his tone, Alexandra relaxed.

'*Papá*,' she said, seating herself on a leather pouffe at his feet, 'there's something unpleasant I need to tell you but I don't know quite where to start.'

'You must start at the beginning,' he told her gently, taking off his spectacles and shutting the tome on his lap.

Alexandra hesitated a few moments more. Then, choosing her words with care, she told her father what she had heard. She related the incident of the arrow and described how since her arrival she had felt on several occasions that she was being watched.

Don Alonso listened silently, his elbows on the arm of the chair. A look of shock gradually gave way to confusion and concern. When she had finished, he passed a hand over his face.

'Are you sure you didn't misunderstand what you overheard?' he asked.

She shook her head. 'Absolutely not. I could hear every word they said.'

Alonso frowned and for a moment said nothing. Then he let out a deep sigh and gazed bleakly at his daughter. 'Eugenia has always been jealous of Vanessa, even the memory of her. She knew how much your mother meant to me, I think it was always plain to see. And because of that, she was always going to be threatened by you too ... my pretty eldest daughter, *Vanessa's* daughter, stealing the show from Mercedes. I suspected she was up to something but didn't think she would go to these lengths.'

'I felt her animosity from the first moment she laid eyes on me. I showed respect and courtesy towards her when I arrived but she seemed determined to provoke me from the start.' Alexandra drew her feet up on the edge of the pouffe and hugged her knees tightly. 'I don't know if there's any other way I could have behaved with her, played it differently ...'

'Dear child, you must understand that my wife decided long ago that Mercedes would marry Salvador. Your sister is in love with him and, as far as I can see, he isn't entirely indifferent to her. But my mother, who has always taken it upon herself to organize our lives as she sees fit, has decided otherwise. You must have realized she has taken a great liking to you. In her opinion, you're the only member of the family suitable to support the heir of El Pavón in the running of the estate. Mother is a strong and wilful woman, and has always had her own way ... and that, I'm afraid, is at the root of all the trouble. You've been caught up in family politics but I never thought—'

'Family politics... is that all it is to you?' Alexandra said vehemently, cutting him off, 'All this because "the heir of El Pavón" needs a suitable wife? I suppose, in your despotic and reactionary world, this behaviour seems quite normal to you.'

Her anger had been building gradually and now was ready to burst. On what grounds did these people imagine they could scheme, plot and meddle in her private affairs? What gave them the supreme right to manipulate her life, just as Salvador was always doing, pulling strings as though she were a puppet with no say in the matter?

Don Alonso sighed again. 'No, no, you misunderstand me, *querida*. Though I know Eugenia can be difficult and fiercely protective of Mercedes, I didn't imagine she would try to scare you like this …' Once more he looked pensive. 'It seems more likely that the plan was Lopez's.'

Alexandra was nearly bursting with exasperation at her father's refusal to grasp the situation. He was clearly so under his wife's thumb that he was incapable of admitting that Eugenia would go to any lengths to scare her, and certainly not on her own. She shook her head incredulously. '*Papá*, can't you see what's going on under your nose?'

The emotion in her voice made him look up. 'I can understand your anger,' he said, his gaze resting on her face. 'Eugenia and my mother have always fought a silent battle for supremacy as far as El Pavón is concerned, and Salvador being its heir …' He paused, fumbling for the explanation that seemed to be eluding him. 'I know that our ways are often strange …'

'Strange?' she retorted, jumping from her seat. 'I can see why *Mamá* couldn't bear to live like this. Is it also part of your "ways" to indulge in ridiculously underhand and threatening behaviour to get what you want? All this has nothing to do with the traditions of your country but with the dictatorial and downright ruthless nature of certain members of this family.'

She was shaking now, mutiny etched on every feature. 'I don't know what folly made me come here in the first place,' she cried out, her hands clenched. 'But I won't be threatened and manipulated into leaving until I'm ready to go. And I will certainly not play into the hands of my stepmother, my grandmother, or anyone else for that matter. I'll …'

'Gently does it, my child, gently does it,' whispered Don Alonso, raising his hands, whether in an attempt to pacify his daughter or to fend her off, she didn't know. 'This is a delicate matter that needs much thought and tact,' he added calmly, though his brow was now furrowed. 'Leave it to me, I'll deal with it. From now on you'll have nothing more to fear from your stepmother, I promise, and even less from that scoundrel, Lopez. I know that life has been difficult for you at El Pavón … we're not an easy family to live with.' He paused. 'Perhaps it would be worth your while considering a return to England if being here is making you unhappy. Let things blow over a bit.'

Alexandra felt as though she'd received a cold shower. Biting back the retort that quivered on the tip of her tongue, she shook her head mutely. She should have known this would be his reaction. Her father had always been weak and, in this instance, she had no doubt, the tide would be too strong for him to fight. The only time he made a stand for himself had been when he'd married her mother, and look how that ended. Alexandra had to face up to it; she was on her own. She managed a pale smile but couldn't hide the sadness in her eyes.

Her father's expression held sadness too, she noticed. Did he realize he had hurt her? Maybe, but it would make no difference in the end. She had no doubt he had difficulty imagining his daughter settling in Spain; after all, Vanessa hadn't managed to do so and he'd repeatedly told Alexandra she reminded him of her mother, the only woman he'd ever loved. It was plain that her father thought it best if she left and that Mercedes, despite her immaturity, would make a perfectly good wife for Salvador.

Standing up, Don Alonso said, 'Come, I'll walk out with you.' They left the room through the French doors and, as they emerged on to the terrace, they saw Marujita sauntering across it, her hips swaying provocatively as usual. It was obvious to Alexandra that she had come from Salvador's apartments. The gypsy girl was wearing a clingy dress of very fine silk, which emphasized the curves of her voluptuous young body. With her lustrous black hair swinging softly to her hips, she looked bewitching and alluring. Don Alonso stopped her as she was passing.

'Where have you been?' he asked in a severe tone Alexandra had never heard him use before.

'*Señor* Salvador's apartments,' replied the gypsy girl with a smirk.

'You're aware of the rules. Her Grace the *Duquesa* has strictly forbidden you to set foot in this house. You have your own quarters and simply no business here,' he told her coldly.

Marujita threw back her head in that defiant Amazonian gesture so typical of her people. Briefly, she looked Alexandra up and down. 'It was *Señor* Salvador himself who asked me to come,' she said, giving them a quizzical half-smile. 'He needed my services.'

'That can be done at your own place,' retorted Don Alonso, struggling to keep his cool.

'But he wanted me here, now, immediately,' she went on shamelessly, stressing each word in the slightly husky voice Alexandra had no doubt was enticing for most men. She felt her blood boil.

'I am here every night ...' The gypsy girl looked daggers at Alexandra, a sly glint of triumph in her eyes. 'I satisfy his hunger, quench his thirst. Without my warmth, my fire, his body lies cold and lifeless, tortured by a need only I can fulfil. He is my master and ...'

'That's enough,' cut in Don Alonso sharply, clearly shocked by the graphic, shameless impudence of the girl. 'I'll have you remember who you're talking to, girl. And I'll have your story checked, believe me. Go on, get out – leave now!'

Alerted by the noise, José hurried out and grabbed the girl by her shoulders. Marujita fought like a wild cat, scratching and stamping her feet.

'He'll never be able to do without me!' she shouted after them in a shrill voice as the major domo dragged her from the terrace. 'I'm the match that lights his fire. Without me, he's nothing, he's no good. And by the *Madre Santa* he knows it!'

After they'd gone, Don Alonso shook his head. 'This has gone far enough, it's getting quite out of control,' he sighed, as if to himself. Alexandra watched dumbly as, taking leave of his daughter, he retired once more to the sanctuary of his office. His ostrich policy had obviously served him well in the past and this was no exception.

She made her way to the front garden, a stream of sombre thoughts tumbling through her mind. This was the final straw. Hot anger smouldered within her as she totted up everything pitted against her: Salvador's casual and chauvinistic attitude to women, her father's cowardice, Marujita's effrontery … and that was the least of it. She strolled on to the front lawn. Enough was enough, she would no longer put up with it.

'Good afternoon, Doña Alexandra.' She jumped, rudely forced out of her deep reflection, to find Don Felipe at her side. Evidently she had been so wrapped in her thoughts that she hadn't heard his car draw up.

'Don Felipe,' she exclaimed. 'How lovely to see you. I'm sorry, I didn't hear you arrive.'

'I came by horse and carriage and left it further down the drive. I thought you might like to take a ride with me.'

She smiled as the young man brought her hand to his lips.

His dark, burning eyes scrutinized her face. 'You look very doleful today. Is anything the matter?' he asked.

'You're very perceptive,' Alexandra said, still smiling. 'I think I could do with some pleasant company at the moment.'

The idea of escaping the stultifying atmosphere of the hacienda, with all its intrigues, made the *torero*'s offer particularly appealing. Don Felipe had always been courteous towards her, and although he had perhaps been somewhat over-assiduous in his attentions, Alexandra saw no reason not to reciprocate his friendliness. It was difficult to make out why Salvador held him in such contempt. Certainly, he was flirtatious, and she imagined that sometimes the mischievous glint twinkling in his eyes might have landed him in trouble, but he was consistently cheerful and charming. And, quite frankly, today she needed someone to make her feel good about herself for a change.

'I was on my way in to Puerto de Santa María for my weekly visit to our *bodegas*, and wondered if you'd care to accompany me ...'

'You've taken me rather by surprise,' she said hesitantly.

'I'm quite aware that I should have dropped my card earlier and given you more notice,' he said apologetically. 'My only excuse was my eagerness to see you again.'

Alexandra hesitated a few seconds. Shouldn't she tell someone where she was going? Perhaps ask Sarita to accompany her? Suppose someone was to look for her? Aunt Geraldine had warned her against the narrow-minded bigotry of the Spanish and the de Fallas were no exception, as she'd now seen for herself. They were sure to condemn her behaviour: one did not go out in the company of a young man without a chaperone. She mentioned her reservations to Don Felipe.

'It's only three o'clock,' he reassured her. 'I promise you'll be back before dark, and well before dinner. Our *bodegas* aren't far, just a few kilometres between here and Santa María, on the sea.' He gave her his most engaging smile. 'Don't worry, I'm a trusted friend of the family. You'll be perfectly safe with me, I assure you.'

For a second, Alexandra thought of Salvador, whom she felt wouldn't quite agree on his 'trusted' epithet, but then she laughed and pushed her qualms to one side. After all, she wasn't a prisoner in this house and Don Felipe had promised she would be back by dinner. Anyhow, she doubted anyone would miss her. She had a habit of going out for long walks in the grounds and so far no one had ever come looking for her. If they did today, well then, she would just have to face the consequences …

'Oh, goodness, why not?'

'Wonderful!' The *torero* took Alexandra's arm and hurried her rather energetically down the drive towards the gig, whose horse was patiently waiting, munching on grass. 'We must leave straight away so as not to waste any more time.' He helped her into the carriage and took up his seat beside her.

'Thank you,' Alexandra said with a grateful smile. 'I really did need to get away.'

'Don't thank me, beautiful *señorita*, the pleasure is all mine,' he declared gallantly, with a crack of his whip.

The sky was azure-gold and hazy, the afternoon sun beating down on the fields both sides of the road, where vines stretched to the horizon. No wonder fruit and vegetables ripened here so rapidly. What else could they do under such sultry persuasion? This was the route Alexandra had taken with Ramón on that long-ago night of her arrival. It was *siesta* time and there were few pedestrians. To her right, almond trees edged the road mile after unbroken mile, their sweet-smelling blossom now coming to the end of its life, covering the ground like a snow-white carpet. *What an exquisite sight*, she thought.

'There's a legend attached to the almond blossom,' said Don Felipe, whose watchful eye seemed to have read her mind. 'It goes back to the days when we were ruled by the Moors, and tells the story of the sultan who brought a beautiful princess back from Scandinavia.'

Alexandra laughed lightly. 'I think I should be writing a book of Spanish legends instead of a romance, I've collected so many.'

'Then I hope this one will not disappoint you.' He fixed her with a suave smile.

'I'm sure it won't. I love to hear them.' She relaxed against the low-backed leather squab, letting the *torero*'s silky voice wash over her.

'When winter came, this fair lady took to her bed,' continued Don Felipe, his hands loosely on the horse's reins as the carriage jogged along. 'She pined and seemed to be fading away. No amount of cajoling, potions or entertainment seemed to do the trick. The Sultan consulted his viziers, his doctors and his magicians, but no remedy could be found.

'One day, a wise man from the East was passing by. As he sat in the town square, he heard the story of the ill-fated sultana. He presented himself at the palace and asked to meet with the desperate King. "May I suggest, your Majesty, that the Queen is yearning after the wintry ice and the snow of her native land," he said. The Sultan was surprised at such a suggestion. How could anyone prefer the bitter cold of the northern countries to the languorous air and warmth of Spain?' Don Felipe broke off, glancing at Alexandra.

She nodded and gave a half smile. 'Yes, indeed.' She went back to studying the sweep of vineyards they were passing.

'Nevertheless, he would do anything to save his beloved wife. According to the wise man there existed a tree the blossom of which, when in flower, would give the impression of snow. So the Sultan gave the order that almond trees should be imported from the East and planted on every inch of ground visible from his wife's windows. One morning in spring, the fair Sultana woke to a vision of purest white, a spectacle of snow-white blossom that reminded her of the icy flakes of her country. From that moment, she no longer yearned for the snow-mantled lands of Scandinavia and the almond tree became a popular species, planted all over Spain.'

When Don Felipe finished his story, they both fell into silence again, though Alexandra could feel the bullfighter's eyes on her frequently. She gazed out over the hot, intensely foreign landscape, thinking about the sad queen and the life that she herself had left behind in England earlier that year. So much had happened, where did she fit in now? She wasn't the same person who had left London in the spring, but still she wondered if she would ever truly belong in this strange country. The thought disturbed her.

They went through Puerto's main street, on either side of which the rich wine-merchants' mansions stood shuttered in the shade of acacias and jacaranda trees. In the reddish glow of the afternoon light, the sun-baked town seemed to bear the amber hue of Spain's famous sherry. Scattered about the town, the *bodegas* gleamed a spotless white in vivid contrast to their red-tiled roofs and emerald-green shutters, their arcades opening on to shady patios. Some of these wineries covered areas of several acres, forming whole districts.

It was a beautiful sunny afternoon and at Alexandra's side sat one of the most attractive and sought-after men in Andalucía. That she must be the envy of many women, Alexandra was in no doubt. Yet deep down, she felt disillusioned. No matter how hard she tried, she was unable to drive Salvador from her thoughts. He seemed to delight in hurting her and she couldn't block out the questions about him that circled obsessively in her mind.

Freshest in her thoughts was Marujita's alarming presence at the house. The gypsy girl seemed so sure of her hold over him. Could there be some truth in her words or was Salvador one of those men who had mistresses rather than a wife? That would explain his changeable and irascible attitude towards her, especially if he felt the tightening web of the *Duquesa*'s matchmaking plans looking to force him into finding a suitable wife to run El Pavón. Wasn't that what her father had intimated?

Equally as unsettling as Marujita's presence on the terrace that morning was the conversation she had overheard in the grove. Suddenly, events appeared to be conspiring against her in a way she was finding almost impossible to cope with.

Why was life not simpler? Or rather, why were people so complicated? She liked Don Felipe; in fact, in many ways she liked him a lot. He was handsome, smart, well-read and well-travelled, brave, with a good sense of humour. Furthermore, he'd been courteous and attentive to her needs. Why then could she not find it in her heart to enjoy the present?

'You're very pensive today,' remarked her companion, shaking Alexandra from her reverie. She smiled faintly, unable to answer. 'Is there something worrying you?' Don Felipe continued with concern. 'I can't believe that a young lady as accomplished as you doesn't have all she wishes for.'

Alexandra gave a little hollow laugh. 'I wish …' she sighed.

'We'll put an end to those worries right away,' he said determinedly, as the carriage turned into one of the narrow, twisting lanes that led towards the sea.

As the briny smell of the coast became stronger, memories flooded back to Alexandra of the picturesque fishing village, Puerto de Santa María, that first morning when she'd arrived at the railway station. She felt a pang of nostalgia tugging at her as she remembered the hope and excitement that had filled her at the idea of meeting her estranged family. How very differently things had turned out.

'We've arrived, and there's nothing a glass of our marvellous Jerez won't cure.' The bullfighter's voice, coupled with the jerk of the halting carriage, once more roused Alexandra from her grim thoughts. Don Felipe leapt out on to the roughly paved drive and went round to help her down. 'Welcome to the *bodegas* of Vincente Herrera and Son,' he said, bowing courteously and waving his arm in a wide flourish towards the building.

The *bodegas* of Vincente Herrera consisted of a huge warehouse and rows of outbuildings stretching as far as the eye could see. Alexandra could tell from the style of its architecture that the main building was ancient; it looked as if it had formerly been a convent. The present owners had gone to great lengths to preserve its unique character, down to the smallest detail. The passage of time had imprinted itself on each pillar, arch and flagstone.

'This place has such presence,' Alexandra murmured, looking around the walls, her voice echoing back to her. In fact, it felt slightly spooky, though she didn't admit that to her host. 'How old is it?'

'It was built in the seventeenth century, originally as a nunnery.' He glanced at her, as if reading her mind again. 'They say that it's haunted by the ghost of a nun who broke her vows of chastity with a monk. After the sentence of "*in vade pace*" was passed upon her, she was walled up alive in her cell.'

Alexandra's eyes snapped back to him. 'God, how grisly!' she declared.

'Yes, but fascinating all the same, wouldn't you say? That this young nun would risk such a fate for sexual gratification …' Don Felipe's eyes had darkened curiously.

'Has anyone ever seen her ghost?' Alexandra couldn't help asking, intrigued and appalled at the same time.

'No, but some people have heard scraping noises and despairing wails echoing around the old part of the *bodega*. Just think how long it would have taken her to die of starvation.' For a long moment he stared intensely into space. '"*Vade in pace*", "go into peace" …? I think not. Fascinating …'

Alexandra felt the stirrings of unease but then the *torero* flashed her a brilliant smile. 'I'm sure you don't wish to dwell on such macabre things. Besides I have much to show you.'

Don Felipe led the way into the nave. An atmosphere of gloom and mystery reigned, created by eternal dust accumulated over the years and of long-woven cobwebs. Along the whitish side aisles, piled one on the other, lay thousands of venerable casks of seasoned grey-brown oak, inside of which was the clear wine that filled the air with its delicious aroma. The floor of the cellar was damp calcareous soil and a chill rose from it. In the semi-darkness, a dozen workmen handled with great care the butts of this prestigious vintage, each containing more than a hundred gallons of the valuable sherry.

At the head of the group, an older man in a brown cotton overcoat was holding an *avenencia*, a ladle with an extremely long whalebone handle, at the end of which was a thin silver goblet. He moved among the rows, from barrel to barrel, giving an order here, adjusting a row there, tasting, muttering indistinctly, and spitting the wine into the dust.

Don Felipe took Alexandra's elbow. 'Come and meet Toma. He's nicknamed "*El Colonel*" because he rules this *bodega* like an officer leading an army,' said the *torero* with a grin. Alexandra noticed he was still carrying the horsewhip and she wondered why he hadn't left it in the gig.

Don Felipe beckoned the foreman over. A broad smile creased the man's weatherbeaten face into a hundred small wrinkles. Toma was in his sixties, yet in spite of his mop of grizzled hair, he retained in his muscular body and dark magnetic eyes all the vigour of a man still in the prime of life. There emanated from him a kind of innate nobility and elegance, which, had he been in another setting and dressed differently, would have allowed him to pass for an aristocrat.

Toma gave them a courteous nod. '*Señor, señorita.*'

'When the wine arrives at the *bodega*, and during this first phase of life, it is Toma's responsibility to classify and blend it in each barrel to reach the best quality and the finest taste,' Don Felipe explained.

Alexandra smiled at Toma. 'That sounds awfully involved, how do you do that?'

Though her question was directed at the foreman, it was Don Felipe who answered. 'We use an elaborate system called *solera*,' he said, his gaze fixed on Alexandra. 'This process requires great care and experience. I am a mere bullfighter, I enjoy a good glass of Fino, but I am totally ignorant of the complicated methods used to produce it.' Turning to Toma he added, 'Would you explain to the *señorita* this marvellous system that allows us to produce wines of such quality?'

Toma did as he was bid. In his gruff but melodious voice he described in detail the method used at the Herrera *bodegas*, which required that sherries of various ages be left to ferment and mature spontaneously in six tiers of barrels, without being disturbed for a number of years. 'During this process,' the foreman explained, 'a minute bloom grows on the surface. It's called the *flor, e le da un sabor de nuez al vino*, and gives the nutty flavour to the wine. The *flor* is formed twice a year, usually over a period of six years. After that it sinks to the bottom, leaving a clear wine. This is the wine we draw from for blending. It is then replaced in the barrel by the next oldest wine directly above it, and a younger wine is added at the top tier, and so on.'

'Gosh, that sounds like a long and painstaking process,' said Alexandra, genuinely impressed. 'How long does it take?'

'The time of fermentation depends on the type of grape, its ripeness and how much natural sugar is in it,' replied Toma, clearly pleased that Alexandra was taking an interest in the art of his sherry making. 'Once this is done, it's up to us to develop the character of the sherry by introducing the properties of an excellent established wine into the new ones.'

Don Felipe interjected. 'At the end of the seventeenth century, three brothers, my ancestors, developed our mother wine. For two hundred years we have drawn on it to blend and improve the production of our young sherries, that is what gives them their unique flavour,' he proudly informed her. 'Classification is a real art: the casks are carefully labelled by category. These labels say whether they contain a young wine or one less young, whether it's a pale wine or one with more body, if it's considered a good wine or not such a good one,' he explained.

Alexandra couldn't help comparing his passion for the family business to that of Salvador when he had spoken of his horses. And yet, there was something more of the obsessive perfectionist in Don Felipe. Where Salvador's eyes held the deep warm glow of fiery passion, those of the other man glittered with a darker flame. *He must be like this inside the arena too*, Alexandra thought as she watched the *torero*. *Without that kind of keen eye for detail, a matador could easily lose his life*, she reflected.

She noticed too that, increasingly, his mood was tinged with an edgy, pent-up energy. Every now and then he absentmindedly coiled and uncoiled the whip as he spoke, flicking it gently across the floor. Ordinarily, Alexandra might have found such a gesture unnerving but instead she dismissed it as the strutting affectation of a *matador*.

Tomas led them to a dark corner where a single barrel stood in the dusty darkness, dramatically adorned with garlands of spider webs. 'Solera 1800,' he announced proudly. Taking out the bung that sealed the enormous cask, he solemnly plunged his *avenencia* into the dark depths of the receptacle, dipping below the frothy top layer to reach at the cool wine beneath. Then, holding the ladle high in the air, he transferred a thin golden stream of liquid to two small glasses without spilling a drop, all at once freeing the heady aroma locked in the wine.

Don Felipe took his glass from Toma, lifted it to his nose and breathed in. Alexandra followed suit, taking in the strange fragrance. Hesitantly, she ventured a sip. The taste was even more surprising than the scent. There was about it an almost dusty dryness that was not unpleasant; it carried with it the distinct flavour of grapes but without being too sweet.

'It has an unusual taste but it's quite delicious,' she observed, taking a second sip, then a third. In seconds, she had drained her glass. Normally, she wouldn't have consumed alcohol so quickly but again she was rebelliously ignoring her usual rulebook. Don Felipe seemed to exercise this effect on her, she noticed. Gripped by a longing to be free of her previous dark mood, still stalking her insistently, she threw herself into the proceedings with heedless recklessness. Her head had begun to spin slightly and, by the time she emerged from the temple of Bacchus half an hour later on Don Felipe's arm, she was filled with a gentle euphoria and an overwhelming, but not unpleasant, feeling of dizziness.

'Doña Alexandra, I'd love to show you more of the grounds, if you'd like that?'

Alexandra looked up at his hooded gaze. She could read nothing in those jet-black, gleaming eyes of his, but all the same they seemed to burn with a hypnotic intensity. 'Yes, very much so,' she answered through a slight haze.

They had come out into the tranquil courtyard. A vaulted gallery, supported on Doric columns and surmounted by magnificent sculpted capitals, surrounded the internal quadrangle. Alexandra found she had to hold on to Don Felipe's arm a little more firmly than she intended as her senses shifted in and out of focus.

As they made their way slowly across the courtyard, Alexandra became aware that the capitals above the columns were adorned with carved faces of animals, the expressions of which shifted constantly with the interplay of light and shadow. Here, where the light was intense, a lion smiled broadly; there, in the shade, the same smile seemed transformed into a fierce snarl. Near it, a monkey with a comic little face grimaced mischievously in the sunlight, while on the shadowy façade of the covered walkway, he took on an almost sinister expression. Though the air was hot and heavy, Alexandra gave a tiny shiver.

The quadrangle was quiet, lying golden beneath the sun, while under the plane trees dwelled pools of grey-blue shadow. A fountain of pink granite warbled gently in the centre, surrounded by tubs of miniature lemon and orange trees, dwarf roses and other scented shrubs. Alexandra was still feeling distinctly as if she were floating rather than walking, and her unsteady vision took in the myriad fleeting colours in the courtyard, shifting with each turn of the light and shade. She looked back at one of the columns: a fox who had seemed to be dozing in the semi-darkness of the walkway now watched the couple with a smug grin; and a snake, languid in the shade, was flicking out its forked tongue in the sun, as if ready to attack. Alexandra turned her head away from them and kept moving, blinking against the light.

After they had visited the gardens beyond the courtyard, she allowed herself to be guided by Don Felipe towards a twisting path to the right of the building. It meandered through a cluster of low rocks to the cliff edge, and then to a descending stone stairway, perhaps one cut into the rock by Christian slaves under Moorish rule, she mused. The thirty steep steps were oddly flanked by freestanding granite columns and led down to a mosaic terrace below.

Unlike the meticulously maintained quadrangle, this part of the property had been abandoned to the mercy of the weeds that grew all over it: couch grass, buttercups and bindweed lived together in joyous profusion and gave the spot an air of gothic decay. Here the landscape was hazy and silent, almost hauntingly so. Only occasionally did the staccato chirping of crickets disturb the solitude.

The melancholy desolation of the place hung like a flimsy shroud over everything. A sudden sadness swept over Alexandra and her concentration shifted; she missed a step and slipped, but before she could fall headfirst down the steep flight of stairs, Don Felipe caught her. He tightened his grip.

'Lean on my shoulder,' he said in a hoarse voice. 'These steps are dangerous. If it wasn't for the fact that the view of the neighbouring towns is so spectacular, I wouldn't have brought you down here.'

Finally, they reached the terrace. Perched on top of a rock, and dangerously projecting over the sea, it was a masterpiece of architecture, one that retained a certain grandeur despite the crumbling stone and brambles. Four pink granite columns, placed at the corners of the monument, were topped with capitals delicately sculpted with mythological flora and fauna. Mirroring the columns on the stairs, they soared dramatically skywards, as though in supplication to some mythic deity.

The floor was entirely covered by slabs of mosaic depicting the twelve signs of the Zodiac surrounded by various heavenly bodies, geometric patterns and demonic monsters, which enhanced the atmosphere of pagan archaism. Alexandra shivered again.

'Where are we? I feel there's something almost evil about this spot,' she murmured, as she looked around her. Not for the first time since her arrival in Spain, her sixth sense was whispering to her, warning her to get away from this place.

Don Felipe appeared not to have heard her comment or, at least, chose to ignore it.

'Alexandra, come and look.' He drew her attention to the magnificent landscape that stretched out beneath them.

Indeed, to the west of the bay, the fortified town of Rota presented them with all the ingredients of a vibrant, quaint picture. Vividly painted boats bobbed cheerfully on the shimmering waters or dozed on the golden sand. Salt marshes gleamed in the distance, while further on, a white semicircle of modest houses with green shutters winked in the afternoon sun.

The writer in Alexandra had no difficulty in embroidering this canvas still further with her inner eye. Hers was a rich tapestry, where brightly coloured laundry hanging at the windows flapped and snapped in the wind; where a busy population of tanned fishing folk spread out their nets on the ochre sand, while swarms of copper-skinned children gambolled in the white foam of the waves that came and went, snaking their way along the shore.

'That is Cádiz,' said the *torero*, as he pointed to a rocky peninsula rising out of the ocean to the south; not quite an island, it was poised like a white lily in the middle of the sea. 'The Moors compared it to a "dish of silver in a bowl of blue". It really is an exceptionally lovely city, maybe the most beautiful in Spain, well worth a visit. My mother has a house there, where she spends her summers. My sister and I often visit her during August. Maybe you'd care to join us this summer.'

Bewitched, Alexandra merely nodded absentmindedly, busy taking in the magnificent view and distracted from her momentary unease. She wanted to inscribe every detail of this breathtaking setting on her memory so that she could translate its splendour on to the page when she got back. If only she could put pen to paper here and now.

'May I be indiscreet?' the *torero* asked, once again the first to break the silence.

'You may,' she said, without turning.

'How is it that such a charming and accomplished lady as yourself isn't yet married?'

Had she been in a different frame of mind, Alexandra would have found his bold question discourteous, even offensive. As it was, she felt somewhat light-headed; her sense of reality was disconnected, as though she were in a dream, and instead she was simply amused. What was it with Spaniards? She vaguely remembered that Salvador had also enquired about her marital status, or something to that effect, but hadn't he put it more subtly?

Alexandra shrugged and laughed. 'I suppose I haven't yet found my soulmate.'

'Is there no one special waiting for you back in England?'

'No one,' she glanced at him, then turned back to stare out at the sea, only giving Ashley the briefest of guilty thoughts. 'And that's just as well because, if there had been, I wouldn't have been able to prolong my stay in your amazing country.'

'You like our country then?'

'I do indeed, very much so. At times I find your customs and traditions a little bizarre … and certainly quite conservative, but that's only because they're alien to me. At least they were. Now I've become more or less used to them, I think.'

To the west the setting sun, huge and incandescent, was poised to plunge into the azure sea. Alexandra half expected it to emit a colossal hiss as it vanished into the ocean.

Time was marching. Her head was beginning to ache. Around her everything seemed to be swaying gently, as if she were in a boat. The sherry had been much more potent than she'd expected and she regretted drinking so much, so quickly. They should be starting back as she would be late for dinner but she simply couldn't tear her eyes away from the view. After all, it would be a shame to miss the sunset. A feeling of defiance swept over her again; what could possibly be wrong in enjoying it all? Enraptured, she turned, smiling, to find her companion's burning gaze upon her.

'I knew you would fall in love with this spot as I fell in love with you, Doña Alexandra, the moment I first laid eyes on you.' He moved a little closer. 'Do you think that you could have the same feeling for me?'

This was a dangerous game. She ought to have recognized the signs and put a stop to Don Felipe's outburst of passion there and then but for weeks Alexandra had been silently burning for Salvador. The fire that had been repressed, stifled by the combination of unfortunate circumstances and Salvador himself, was suddenly liberated under the influence of the wine, the magical setting and by the force of the bullfighter's ardour. The touchpaper had been lit and now the intensity of her feelings took on a power that seared through her inhibitions.

'I must say, I have never met anyone like you, Don Felipe. You're courageous, flamboyant, interesting … a prince among men. How could a woman not be sensitive to all that?' she exclaimed, giving free rein to her turbulent emotions and unconscious thoughts, hardly realizing that she was falsifying the situation, both in regard to herself and to her companion.

Had she been given a moment to let her thoughts untangle, Alexandra would have qualified her wild outburst. And later, once the elation of the moment had passed, once she had looked at things with a cool head, she might have regretted their shared moment altogether. Yet, for the time being, such regrets held no sway; in those chaotic few seconds even the memory of her love for Salvador was momentarily lost, carried away by the quiet sea whispering against the shadowy cliffs.

And then, before she could resist him, the *torero* had forcefully drawn her to him, pressing his mouth to hers. Horrified, she was abruptly jolted to her senses as she felt the warmth of his hot lips, the alcohol on his breath, and the probing tip of his tongue. She struggled helplessly, attempting, in vain, to push him away with both hands but he held her prisoner against his lean body. Panic rose in her throat; she was suffocating. She tried to scream, but his forceful kiss made it impossible. And then all of a sudden ...

'*Alexandra!*' The shout rang out in the twilight, startling the couple. She wrenched herself out of her captor's tight grip, realizing, quite suddenly, the compromising position she was in. Looking up, her eyes fell upon a dark figure that she would have known anywhere.

Salvador stood at the top of the stairs, fists clenched at his sides. Rooted to the spot, Alexandra felt her cheeks burn scarlet under his icy gaze. He was the last person she expected, or wanted, to see at this moment. His face was ghostly pale and his mouth formed a colourless line as he stared down at her in the waning light of dusk.

'So this is where you're hiding, my dear Felipe,' he said sardonically, his eyes narrowing slightly as he came down the steps. Alexandra could see that his mood was almost summoning a storm to break overhead. 'I should have realized I'd find you here. The criminal always returns to the scene of his crime ... You should have been locked up a long time ago ... As for you, young lady,' he added chillingly, barely looking at Alexandra, 'I thought you had more sense than to listen to the fairytales of the first Don Juan who whispered sweet nothings in your ear. Obviously, I was mistaken.'

'Come, come, *amigo*, what a holier-than-thou attitude,' scoffed the *torero*. 'To my knowledge, your copybook is hardly without blot. The whole of Jerez awaits with bated breath the next episode of the unsavoury saga with your gypsy lover.'

Salvador crossed the space between them in two strides.

'Scoundrel!' he roared as he leapt at Don Felipe and landed a crashing blow to the *torero*'s jaw.

'Salvador, *no!*' shrieked Alexandra, frozen in horror.

Don Felipe let out a grunt of surprise at the blow, but then returned it in a flash, sending Salvador staggering backwards. The duel had started, and on the terrace at the edge of night, under a sky still red from the seething sun, the two men fiercely squared up to each other, while Alexandra looked on helplessly.

Now the fiery orb had set and a reflected gleaming line crossed the cloudless sky like a second horizon. A breeze was beginning to wrinkle the surface of the water below which, up until then, had retained a glassy smoothness. Nocturnal shadows stole furtively from the west and slowly gathered round the trio on the terrace as though setting the scene for an archaic tragedy.

Although of different heights and builds, the two men were of equal strength. While Salvador was tall and well built, with square shoulders, long muscular legs and slim hips, Don Felipe was of average height with a lithe body, full of feline agility and velocity. He deftly warded off his rival's first blows, his almond-shaped watchful eyes anticipating Salvador's tactics from behind their long eyelashes, as he weaved and ducked, never once losing his balance as Salvador's fists came at him repeatedly.

With jaw clenched, his expression impenetrable, Salvador wasted no effort, choosing to stand firm and leaving it to the bullfighter to lead the fight. He gave short staccato blows, vigorous and regular, threatening to disorientate his opponent with their straightforward power and ferocity.

'*Please*, both of you, *stop!*' Tears were streaming down Alexandra's face as she inched her way around the two men, but they were oblivious.

Don Felipe suddenly went for his whip and Salvador leapt upon his opponent, knocking it from his hand. With a roar, he began pummelling his fists into Don Felipe's face. Bellowing with equal fury, Don Felipe managed to throw him off and Salvador landed with a sickening thud on his back. By the time the *torero* had come at him again, Salvador was already on his feet, blocking a blow with his arm and striking hard and fast below Don Felipe's ribs.

It was dark now. The moon cast an ashen light, while fifty feet below, at the bottom of the cliffs, the sea roared threateningly. The struggle had taken a curious and dangerous turn: for both men, this was now a combat to the death. Don Felipe had manoeuvred the fight so that they were on the narrow balustrade, the only thing between them and the precipitous drop to the black chasm of the ocean below. Alexandra was still rooted to the spot, terrified, not daring to move for fear of causing one of the men to fall. Then she saw with horror that Don Felipe had picked up the whip again.

Moonlight fell momentarily on the bullfighter's face. Don Felipe wore his arena look. Just as he had been flirting with death during those afternoons in the bullring, so too was he tempting destiny or the devil now. The whip cracked, making her jump. Salvador warded off the blow and reeled a little as he tried to rid himself of the whipcord that had wound itself round his ankle. Just as he had regained balance, the whip cracked again and caught him full in the face. His cry, like that of a wounded animal, tore the night and a trickle of blood appeared on his cheek. It cracked once more.

This time he was ready for it. He caught the cord in mid-flight and yanked it sharply towards him, toppling his opponent, who rolled over on to the terrace. Throwing himself on top of the *torero*, Salvador punched him hard, again and again. But Don Felipe, quick as lightning, turned his upper body swiftly to the left, shot out his right leg and smashed his foot into Salvador's knee, causing him to lose balance. With the exceptional agility he had acquired in the ring, the *torero* now sprang to his feet, his face covered in blood, and threw himself at the Count's throat. They wrestled savagely, each trying to bring the other down one more time.

Alexandra could no longer bear to watch. 'That's enough!' she screamed, shaking as much with anger as fear. 'Stop this right now!' Breathing heavily, she wiped her face with the back of her hand, staring at them both in a mixture of horror and disgust. 'You're nothing but a pair of brawling louts.'

The two men stopped dead. It was clear that in the heat of the fight they had forgotten Alexandra's presence. Pulled back to reality, they staggered apart, wild-eyed and dishevelled, breathing heavily.

Don Felipe's features, battered from the blows of his opponent, were almost unrecognizable. He had difficulty standing upright and it looked as if he must have had a rib or two broken by the force of the Count's punches.

At first glance, Salvador's condition didn't seem that alarming. The blood oozed from the gash on his right cheek and his left shoulder was bare, the skin badly torn. It was only as he tried to take a few steps on the terrace that Alexandra noticed he was finding it difficult to walk. He turned feverish eyes to her and she flinched from the disdainful, icy gaze she had never seen him use before, which left her shivering and on the brink of tears. Now that the reality of the situation had hit home, her anger at their fighting had dissolved into guilt and shame.

'Let's go,' Salvador growled. His eyes were sharp and focused on her in blazing fury.

'No,' rasped Don Felipe. 'Doña Alexandra came with me and I will see her home.'

He turned to her, his disfigured face twisting in the semblance of a smile. 'You're right,' he said contritely. 'Don Salvador and myself should have shown better judgement, settled our differences between us according to the rules of propriety. Our conduct was unworthy of gentlemen.' He tried to stand straight. 'And now, with your permission, I will accompany you back to El Pavón.'

But Alexandra realized she had caused enough grief for one day. She figured it would be wiser if she returned quietly to the hacienda with Salvador. Conscious of the bullfighter's pride, however, she placed a trembling hand on his shoulder. 'El Pavón is out of your way, it's too far for you to travel in your state. You need to see a doctor and get some rest.' She let her hand drop to her side. 'I think that I should go home with Salvador.'

Don Felipe looked at her momentarily, something fierce flashing in his eyes for a second before it was gone. He then nodded courteously and turned away, clutching his arm.

Alexandra looked at Salvador, hoping the storm had subsided, but instead met his diamond-cutting pupils.

'Come on, let's go,' he said gruffly, wiping the sweat and blood from his forehead with the back of his sleeve. He grabbed Alexandra's hand and dragged her back to the stairs like an errant child. With almost rigid composure, he led her in a painful climb up the steps, leaving the *torero* alone on the terrace, his back to them, staring out to sea.

Salvador had come alone in his Hispano-Suiza. Without a word or a glance, he opened the door for Alexandra. She climbed in and the door was slammed shut hard, making her close her eyes and shudder. Salvador eased himself into the driver's seat, wincing as he turned the ignition. With one hand he manoeuvred the car on to the main road, his left arm hanging by his side.

A lump rose in Alexandra's throat and her vision became blurred with unshed tears. She was so tired. It was all too much – this was certainly more than she'd bargained for when she decided to rediscover her relations in Spain. Never before had she been through such a kaleidoscope of wild and contradictory emotions. Her family and friends back in England considered her down-to-earth and logical. She had seen herself that way, too. Principles, and ideals about emotional propriety, had remained safely unquestioned. Only in her novels had she allowed her imagination to run away uncontrollably into fantasy, weaving romantic and exciting plots that reflected the more intense side of her personality she had tried to keep thoroughly in check. It was now as if the English side of her temperament was subsumed by the Spanish. Suddenly her beliefs were being challenged and her whole life was topsy-turvy.

They sped through the warm night in silence. Alexandra was huddled in the corner, desolate, making herself as small as possible. She found it hard to tell whether Salvador was suffering from his injuries for he provided no clue. He'd retreated into his solitary tower. Remote, seemingly indifferent to the pain, he drove pale-faced; his jaw set stubbornly, eyes fixed on the road ahead. His lean profile showed the gash in his cheek, streaked with blood, a mute reminder of her recklessness.

Had Salvador not been there, Alexandra would have given in to the surge of emotions that assailed her and cried her eyes out. Never had she found him more disturbing than at this moment. On one hand he rebuffed her, urging her to leave, seeming to favour a woman of easy virtue to whom nothing mattered but his money, and a titled socialite who'd already let him down once. Yet when Salvador held her, when he kissed her, all the magic of love, tenderness and passion she had ever dreamt of were contained in his touch. And tonight he had behaved with the blind and impulsive passion of a jealous lover. She no longer knew what to think.

Turning to him, she reached out a hand in an attempt to break the silence, or perhaps to tenderly touch the wound on his cheek, she wasn't sure which. But she drew it back. The words died on her lips as she noticed the bitter twist in the corner of his mouth. She couldn't see his eyes but because she was so familiar with their every changing mood, she knew how they must look. He was beyond anger for he had misinterpreted what he'd witnessed and chosen to condemn her.

A sense of impending doom and fierce anxiety clawed at her insides. Alexandra's hot-headed need for adventure had finally landed her in real trouble. Her reputation would now be in tatters. What would people say if it became known that she'd let herself be drawn into such a compromising situation? Could she ever make Salvador believe in her again?

Having burnt her bridges this time, she would just have to ride the storm.

CHAPTER 11

It was almost ten o'clock when they turned into the long avenue of willows leading to the house. Agustina, wrapped in a large flowery shawl, her arms folded across her bosom, was waiting for them at the front door. As the car drew closer, she hastened to meet it, gathering her shawl tighter around herself.

'Doña Alexandra, your grandmother's waiting for you,' she said urgently, resting her hand on the open window. 'Her Grace the *Duquesa* is very upset. She's horrified you went off like that with a young gentleman, without a word to anyone, and your getting home this late hasn't put her in any better mood either.'

Alexandra hastily climbed out of the car, avoiding Salvador's gaze. The tension between them was still palpable. He pulled himself slowly out of the driver's seat and Agustina gave a start when she saw the state he was in. Anticipating her words, he said quickly, 'Agustina, please tell my aunt that I'm tired and will speak to her in the morning.' Thereupon he went off, limping badly, never once casting so much as a glance towards Alexandra.

'I suggest you tidy yourself up before meeting with your grandmother,' Agustina advised. In the wrestling session with Don Felipe, part of Alexandra's chignon had come adrift and was hanging loosely down her back. As she hurried to her room to change, she was already marshalling her arguments in preparation for the showdown that was to come. She was determined to stand her ground; after all, she was a grown woman. If this had been England, no one would be making such a fuss, she told herself. And, combined with that, Salvador's cold and angry demeanour only heightened her rebellious frustration, which was gradually beginning to usurp her feelings of guilt.

When she was ready, she found Agustina waiting for her in the hall. The *duenna* placed a hand on her shoulder in support, then silently led her to the *Duquesa*'s apartments.

Doña María Dolores was seated in her wing-backed chair near the window with a book in her hand. She did not look up straight away when Alexandra entered the room, seemingly absorbed. After a few moments, she put down the book and removed her glasses, carefully replacing them in their case. Crossing her hands, she laid them in her lap. Her movements were deliberately measured. When at last her eyes met those of her granddaughter, their expression was icy.

'Well …' the *Duquesa* said at length, raising her eyebrows questioningly. 'I'm waiting for an explanation.' She had not asked her granddaughter to take a seat as she usually did.

'What sort of explanation?' Alexandra's stormy eyes fixed those of her grandmother defensively.

'I see that you're not only irresponsible but also impudent,' countered the old lady stiffly. 'I expected better of you.'

Alexandra tried to maintain her composure, despite the anger bubbling up inside her. 'Grandmother,' said the young woman calmly, reverting to the English address in an attempt to gain the upper hand, 'I really don't understand the big drama.'

'Are you saying you don't understand why a respectable young lady shouldn't wander off unaccompanied with the first braggart to show her some interest?'

'Don Felipe isn't a braggart! On the contrary, he's a respected gentleman. In fact, a hero among your people, whom I met for the first time here, in your house.' She didn't want to antagonize her grandmother after they had started to build bridges these past weeks, but neither did she intend to buckle under the *Duquesa*'s domineering nature, now showing itself in full force.

'Don Felipe is not only an insufferable braggart,' exclaimed the *Duquesa* passionately, deliberately choosing to ignore Alexandra's argument, 'he's also a rogue!' She waved a hand in the air. 'Oh yes, he seems carefree and quick-witted, a smooth talker when he wants to be, but any fool can see that he's a good-for-nothing scoundrel. Not an ounce of moral fibre in his body!' She paused a moment to catch her breath, her measured control now vanished. 'I have to warn you, Alexandra, although it concerns me you didn't have more sense. This man cannot be trusted when he's joking, and even less when he is being serious. At the slightest disagreement, he will turn on you like a wolf, you mark my words. Just like in the arena, he smiles as he wounds. If he's treated as a hero, it's because he's been able to hoodwink unsophisticated and fanciful people. And you, my granddaughter, in your extreme youth,' she held up a hand as Alexandra looked indignant, 'Yes, in your extreme youth and ignorance of the human race, you have allowed yourself to become caught up in his trap.'

Alexandra had listened to the old lady's tirade in astonished silence. 'I can assure you, Grandmother, that the picture you paint of Don Felipe is quite unfair,' she declared. 'We spent an interesting afternoon visiting his father's *bodegas*. We would have returned for dinner had Salvador not turned up unexpectedly, behaving quite bizarrely, and laid into Don Felipe with his fists.'

'Salvador went to look for you because I asked him to,' the *Duquesa* retorted, ignoring her defence of the bullfighter. 'Your cousin, my dear child, is a man of honour and certainly not bizarre, as you put it. Quite frankly, if he chose to strike that miscreant, I have no doubt he must have had good reason for doing so. As for you, it disheartens me to find you're still so naïve and ignorant of Spanish customs. May I remind you a young lady who cares about her reputation never goes off on her own with a young man under any circumstances, even Saint Francis of Assisi himself, without being accompanied by her *duenna*. You should have taken Agustina or Sarita. You aren't in England now, Alexandra.'

That was too much. Alexandra felt the blood rush to her face. 'I don't like to contradict you, Grandmother,' she said, trying to contain the tremor in her voice, 'but I'm almost twenty-six. No longer a child and quite aware of certain relationships that can evolve between a man and a woman. And yes, things are done differently in England. Happily, customs have changed since the war. Women are far more independent now. Not hampered, thank heavens, by outdated notions such as needing a chaperone. Believe me, I have deep-rooted principles of my own. I'm mature enough not to go rushing blindly into some casual liaison, and I trust my own judgement. Don Felipe feels very deeply for me, I'm certain of that. His intentions are honest, and besides, he can do me no harm since the feelings I have for him don't go beyond those of friendship.' She had spoken honestly, trying to reassure the old lady.

'To believe in Don Felipe's good intentions is to believe that the water of the Guadalete could flow upstream, my child! *Man is made of fire, woman of tow, the devil arrives and has only to blow.*'

The *Duquesa* looked at her granddaughter wearily, the severity in her eyes having given way to an expression of anxious affection. 'You're right,' she sighed, 'I can't stop you seeing whomsoever you choose. You are indeed old enough to make up your own mind and take what decisions you think best. At the end of the day, we all have to make our own mistakes, do we not? As the proverb goes, *Treinta monjes y su abad no pueden hacer un rebuzno de burro en contra de su voluntad*, thirty monks and their abbot can't make a donkey bray against his will.' She fixed Alexandra with a stare. 'Yet, your indiscretion will have its consequences. It is my duty to warn you of the risks you're taking in going with Don Felipe and by encouraging his friendship.'

'Grandmother, you don't seem to understand …' Alexandra broke in with frustration.

But Doña María Dolores stopped her with a peremptory gesture. 'I haven't finished, Alexandra. Whether you're interested in my opinion or not, you will have the courtesy and the good sense to hear me out. Sit down,' she ordered.

Leaning back, Doña María Dolores shut her eyes. Suddenly, she seemed so helpless and worn out that Alexandra could scarcely control the impulse to rush over to her grandmother and wrap her arms round those frail, bowed shoulders.

'I'm listening, *Abuela*,' she said softly.

'You must understand, Don Felipe has a certain reputation with women,' said the old lady.

'Yes, I know that. Surely, that's not surprising, given his status as a local hero?'

'No, no,' the *Duquesa* shook her head. 'This is different. Did you know he's been engaged no less than twice before?' She leant forward in her chair. 'That is almost unheard of in Spain. Each time it was broken off by the girl in question, under *circunstancias ambiguas* never explained. In Spain, a woman doesn't do that sort of thing lightly.' The *Duquesa* paused to check that Alexandra had taken this in. 'In Spain, once a woman's name has been associated so intimately with a man, her chances of marrying again after that are negligible, unless of course you have an independent fortune. Neither of these women did, and they were seen as second-hand goods afterwards. Whatever drove them to break off the engagement must have been serious enough to make them risk their future chances.'

'But there's no proof anything untoward happened. There could have been any number of reasons why Don Felipe was unlucky enough to have two failed engagements.' Alexandra looked at her grandmother as her mind turned over the possibilities. Wasn't the *Duquesa* biased against the Herreras because of the way Doña Isabel had treated Salvador? Didn't she want to steer her away from Don Felipe because she hoped Alexandra would make a fitting wife for the 'heir of El Pavón'?

Doña María Dolores sighed. 'I see I haven't managed to convince you, child. All I ask of you is to consider what I've just told you, before seeing this young man again. Talk to Salvador, when you've both calmed down. I'm sure he'll be able to throw more light on the subject.' She pursed her lips. 'At one time I'm afraid to say he was very friendly with the Herreras.'

'No!' replied Alexandra a little too forcefully. 'No, I prefer to keep my cousin out of this. Salvador overreacts and everything with him turns into a drama. Besides, he's been so bad tempered lately.'

Doña María Dolores gave her a sideways glance. '*No hay infierno en la tierra como la del corazón de un hombre infeliz*, there's no hell on earth like that of the heart of an unhappy man,' she said softly.

Irritated, Alexandra pretended not to have heard. '*Abuela*, I should go now. It's late, you look tired and I'm sorry to have kept you up. I'll think about what you've said.'

Affectionately, she kissed her grandmother goodnight. As she was leaving the room, seeing the *Duquesa*'s weary figure still slumped in her chair, a wave of regret at causing her so much distress swept over her. Deep in thought, she went back to her bedroom.

Climbing into bed, she gazed up at the ceiling. If she were truly honest with herself, she had felt a whispering of unease at the *bodega*. She had to admit that Don Felipe's behaviour had been rather too forward. He had taken advantage of her temporary weakness, but then he too may have been feeling the effects of the alcohol. But her thoughts continued to swirl around her head, with disquieting images. In her mind's eye she recalled the cruel mask that came over the bullfighter's face as he used the whip on Salvador. And the undisguised pleasure Don Felipe's features displayed as he realized the dangerous way in which the duel was developing. Still, the *torero* was used to fighting for his life in the arena. Could this have been no more than his instinctive thrill for combat, fuelled by damaged pride and the potency of the wine?

Her thoughts turned to Salvador. She could see that, of the two men, he was the one to blame for the fight. He had struck the first blow, and there seemed no solid argument in his defence. Why should a man, considered by everyone to be reasonable and balanced, act like a moody adolescent whenever a situation involved her? And start a violent brawl simply because he'd found her in the arms of another? That he may indeed love her seemed the only explanation. Alexandra's heart lurched keenly in her chest with a bittersweet pain. But if that were true, why did he continue to ignore her and brazenly pursue his liaison with Marujita under this very roof? Why did he flirt with Doña Isabel and Mercedes at every opportunity? Either he didn't want to care for her, or he didn't care for her at all. She decided that it must be the latter: Salvador didn't love her, he simply took delight in playing a pointless game, cruel sometimes, and unworthy of the gentleman he claimed to be. She had heard of men like that.

Exhausted, she finally closed her eyes and gave in to sleep. It had been a long day, and one that had changed things between herself and Salvador irrevocably.

*   *   *

Alexandra stirred in her sleep as sunbeams filtered through the heavy silk curtains, summoning her to yet another glorious day. Only half awake, she was vaguely aware of doors banging and general commotion on the floor below. A brightly coloured butterfly flew in and fluttered round for a few seconds before settling on the linen sheet next to her. Alexandra raised herself on one elbow and watched it through drowsy eyes, admiring the velvety texture of its delicate wings. She was tempted to stroke it with her fingertips and moved a hesitant hand towards the quivering creature but it was too quick for her. Abruptly taking off, it beat round the room in wide, alarmed circles as if stricken by a sudden panic at being prisoner of those white walls. Still numb and drowsy, Alexandra's gaze followed it for a moment and, as she remembered flashes of the previous evening, she too experienced a desperate need to feel less closed in. She climbed out of bed and drew the curtains back. The sun shone through, flooding the room with a brilliant light. A fresh breeze wafted into the room. The butterfly drifted gracefully towards the open window and disappeared into the clear morning air.

Alexandra returned to bed and snuggled into the warmth of her bedclothes. She cast a quick glance at the clock on the bedside table: it wasn't yet eight. The noise of which she'd been aware earlier had stopped. She wasn't sure how long she lay there, her thoughts floating in that state between sleep and wakefulness, when the mind confuses wonderland with reality and gives our fantasies a semblance of truth, yet it seemed only a few minutes later that somewhere a door banged and the rattling sound of a horse and carriage drifted up to her. In her drowsy state, she couldn't tell whether it was heading for the coach house or leaving El Pavón.

'Salvador,' she whispered. But what would he be doing at this early hour? Perhaps it wasn't Salvador but Fernando Lopez off on estate business. She recalled her cousin's lean profile and the bitter twist of his mouth the night before. What had her grandmother said as she wished her goodnight? Something to do with the heart of an unhappy man … Well, Salvador's fate was in his own hands. Anyway, what did it matter now? It seemed she was powerless with regard to him and, that being the case, she should simply look after herself. In daylight, everything became simple and ordinary again.

The sound of a light swish of skirts forced her eyes open. Agustina was standing there with a tray in her hands. Alexandra blinked, surprised. She wasn't accustomed to being served breakfast in her room.

'The house is all topsy-turvy this morning,' said the *duenna* in answer to Alexandra's raised eyebrows. 'I thought you might prefer to have breakfast in your room, instead of getting yourself involved in the uproar.'

'What's the matter?' enquired Alexandra, alarmed by the housekeeper's expression.

'She's finally flown the nest, gone. She couldn't put up with the lie any more,' Agustina announced gravely. Then, delighting in pushing the suspense to the limit, she added dramatically, 'What love is to the heart, so freedom is to the soul. You can't keep it prisoner, even in a golden cage.'

Alexandra raised herself up on the pillows. There was no doubt that the residents of El Pavón delighted in speaking in riddles, and pompous ones at that. Her whole conversation with her grandmother the night before had been strewn with strange sayings about fire, the devil, and monks being unable to get a donkey to bray. Now, the old servant was mumbling yet another proverb. It was far too early in the morning for such nonsense.

'For heaven's sake, Agustina,' she said brusquely, rubbing her eyes. 'Please get to the point. I don't understand a word of what you're saying.'

'I am talking about Doña Esmeralda,' Agustina explained, a little huffily.

'Well …?' prompted Alexandra who, by now, was beginning to guess what would follow.

Agustina set the tray down in front of her. 'She's eloped with the man she loves. Your grandmother is beside herself. In all my years in service at this house, I've never seen her so distraught. Even when your father married your poor mother she didn't take it this badly. She's made herself ill and Don Salvador had to call the doctor to prescribe a sedative. Now he's gone to the ranch in the hope of finding the lovers there.' Agustina shook her head. 'Going off with the hired help, even if he's from an honest family, is not what well bred *señoritas* do.'

Alexandra pushed the tray away sharply and leapt out of bed. 'Poor *Abuela*, I was the one to upset her last night and now this. I'd better go to her.'

Agustina watched her inscrutably for a moment and then left the room. Alexandra washed and dressed hastily, leaving her breakfast untouched. She was pleased for her cousin and almost envied her. How must it feel to have a man show such devotion that he would flout convention and risk a life of uncertainty for the sake of love? Perhaps it was not so foolish to be romantic after all. Esmeralda was finally free to follow her heart, free of El Pavón. Another disappointment for her grandmother.

Alexandra slipped into her shoes and hastened along the corridor. She was determined to do her best to reassure the *Duquesa*. Perhaps she could at least try to convince her to forgive Esmeralda's decision, even if she couldn't find it in her heart to accept such apparently indiscreet behaviour right now. She ran down the great marble staircase but before she could reach her grandmother's apartments, she found her way blocked by the horsy figure of Doña Eugenia.

'Good morning, my dear. Where are you going in such a hurry?' Her stepmother, eyes narrowed, looked like a poisonous salamander guarding its eggs. 'If it's to see Doña María Dolores,' she added, without waiting for Alexandra's reply, 'I'm afraid you're out of luck. The doctor has given strict instructions she mustn't be disturbed under any circumstances. Anyhow, I would have thought that after your little jaunt yesterday, you'd have the good sense, if not the decency, to keep out of sight for a while.'

'I was coming to—'

'The reason your grandmother has taken Esmeralda's elopement so hard,' Doña Eugenia cut in sharply, 'is because she was already deeply distressed by your scandalous behaviour yesterday. She knows now, as I've always done, that you could never fit in here. And I'm quite certain she wouldn't welcome a visit from you.'

'Let me be the judge of that,' retorted Alexandra, trying her best not to get upset.

'You've done enough harm already, and I won't let you make matters worse …' Doña Eugenia leaned in and lowered her voice. 'Do you think I'm not aware of the plans that are going on in your scheming head? That I don't see through your manipulation of your grandmother? The saying "*Como la madre como hija*, like mother, like daughter" has never been so true.' Her eyes were ice. 'Get out! Take your intrigues and leave before your true personality becomes clear to everyone and your disloyalty damages this family for good.'

There was something in Doña Eugenia's calm and cold delivery that made her venomous words more hurtful than had they been shouted furiously. Alexandra clenched her fists. 'I don't need to explain myself to anyone, least of all you,' she managed to say in a trembling voice. 'You vile, hateful woman!'

With as much dignity as she could muster, Alexandra turned and stalked off down the corridor, almost colliding with

Salvador, who was approaching in the opposite direction. He made to grab her by the arm, and threw her a questioning look, but Alexandra rushed past him and out of the house, her face burning, trying to hold back the tears of frustration.

Still running, she crossed the lawn and dived into the shadowy avenue of willows that bordered the irrigation canal. She stopped at last, out of breath, her cheeks crimson. Humiliation in the face of the completely unfounded but damning insinuations of her stepmother suddenly gave way to hatred. She was surprised by the violence of her resentment, which raged like an angry beast within her breast.

Alexandra sat down on the fallen trunk of an ancient willow on the bank of the canal, brushing aside a few wisps of hair that had slipped across her face. The serenity of the spot had something mystical about it, almost bewitching, and had a calming effect on her. Here, silence was king; there was not a sound, just the hush of the shadows. Alexandra picked up a few pebbles and tossed them into the canal, each one making multi-coloured ripples, like fleeting rainbows in the stagnant waters.

A mockingbird flew out of the undergrowth with a shrill screech, disturbing the peace. The beat of its wings startled her. A breeze brushed her cheek lightly and further rippled the surface of the water. With a faint sigh it swept through the weeping willows as though to share a secret with her, its confused whisper like the rustling of silk.

Alexandra passed a hand over her throbbing forehead. It felt as if a steel vice were squeezing her temples. A strange sadness swept over her. The intense loathing she had experienced towards Doña Eugenia a moment before gradually gave way to a feeling of total helplessness and desolation.

When she had first arrived at El Pavón, she had hoped to find in its residents the welcoming, caring and loving family that she had lacked in childhood and which her heart, hungry for affection, had yearned for all those past years. Instead, most of the family had been condescending or downright spiteful towards her; some had even been openly hostile. Her own father had often treated her as a stranger. His reaction to her distress the previous day seemed proof enough that his love for her was only skin deep, their relationship not the one she had hoped for. Only Ramón had offered his friendship spontaneously.

Doña María Dolores, true enough, had welcomed her into her home as a privileged member of the family. She had been attentive and interested in her granddaughter, had given without apparently expecting anything in return. However, now Alexandra could not avoid noting with cynicism the old woman's ulterior motives: the *Duquesa*, disillusioned with other members of her family, had turned to Alexandra in the hope that she would take on the tiller of the sinking ship. Her grandmother had spent the best part of her youth caring for the family and El Pavón. If no one were able to take over, then all the years of fighting, all the sacrifices, would have been for nothing. What a waste that must seem. Salvador was quite able to take on the job but he needed someone to shoulder the responsibility with him.

At that moment, Alexandra could see through her grandmother's eyes and all the things she was trying to achieve. Her granddaughter had been her hope and genuine comfort. Was that such a terrible thing?

I've disappointed her, too, she thought bitterly. *I'm no better than the others.*

Alexandra must have been sitting there for the good part of an hour when she caught sight of Salvador coming along the path. His leg couldn't have pained him much since he was now walking quite briskly. His head was bent, but as he reached the canal, he raised his gaze, as if by instinct. Had he noticed her? Alexandra's heart missed a beat as his eyes locked on to hers and

he made his way towards her. Her first impulse was to run away
– anywhere – to escape him. Yet she remained rooted to the spot
as if mesmerized by some invisible spell. Her heart was racing so
hard that she was afraid he would hear its uncontrollable beat.

'Good morning ...' His voice was unexpectedly friendly as
he approached. 'I didn't know you liked this spot.'

Alexandra attempted a smile. 'I came here by chance,' she
replied softly, her senses trained to be wary at his every change
of demeanour. They remained silent a while. He stood beside
her, and once again she inwardly cursed as her eyes couldn't help
but wander surreptitiously over his lean, sharply defined profile,
his high forehead, and determined jaw. She noticed, with a slight
jolt, the livid gash across his cheek. In daylight, the wound
appeared much worse than the previous evening and she felt a
pang of remorse.

Salvador bent down and picked up a pebble. Absentmindedly
he turned it over in his hand before tossing it casually into the
water. He remained motionless for a time, staring at an invisible
point beyond the undergrowth, deep in thought – stern, haughty
and aloof. Then he lit a cigarette. His hand trembled imperceptibly
as he drew deeply on it and contemplated the glowing tip.

'I think I owe you an apology for the way I behaved yesterday,'
he said roughly, his eyes narrowing a little. 'I was angry. I acted
on impulse and mishandled the situation,' he went on, in a voice
barely discernible, as if talking to himself. Then, raising his tone
slightly, he added: 'Can you forgive me?'

Turning to her now, she saw that the hard expression that had
distorted his features the night before had softened. Salvador
seemed strained and tired as he searched Alexandra's face. His
eyes had lost their metallic coldness, and the tenderness in them
set her heart beating faster.

Though used to his sudden changes in behaviour, she was not
accustomed to such humility on the part of her cousin and it

unsettled her. Alexandra shrugged her shoulders, feigning indifference in her confusion. 'What does it matter anyway?' she said, trailing her fingertip along the bark of the willow trunk next to her.

She noticed the dark rings deepening under his eyes. His expression looked nothing if not wretched. He shook his head and sighed, almost defeated: 'Alexandra, why do you so stubbornly refuse to understand me?'

'I don't *refuse* to understand you,' she scoffed. 'I just find it impossible to do so!'

Salvador gave a short, bitter laugh. 'Will you believe me when I tell you that I act always in your best interests?'

She stood up and tossed her head defiantly. 'Not really. Why should I?' she asked harshly, looking him in the eye before turning away.

Ignoring her scornful words, he went on: 'Don't you trust me?'

Alexandra hesitated and gazed round at him. He had moved away now, averting his gaze, and seemed to have once more withdrawn into his shell. Her anger was bubbling up again, but feeling him slipping away, she instinctively wanted to pull him back to her: this time there was something different about him.

'I don't know,' she admitted in earnest, hugging herself. 'I don't know what to believe when it comes to you, Salvador.'

A long silence followed. 'You're right,' he murmured at last, sadly. 'Yet if you'd listened to me, if you'd left when I'd asked you to the first time, all this wouldn't have happened. Do you remember that first night on the terrace, Alexandra?'

How could she forget? Memories of that faraway evening at the masked ball came tumbling back with a freshness and clarity that made her limbs weak, consuming her entirely as though all strength had drained from her. She could actually feel his burning lips on hers with a vividness that made her almost dizzy. Was he playing with her again, pushing her to the limits in the way only he knew how? No one but this man could make her feel such anger, desire and despair all at once.

Suddenly, innumerable sensations were assailing her, confusing her, so it was impossible to distinguish between them. Was it tiredness, passion, lust, anxiety, sadness or shame? Alexandra's throat constricted and her eyes stung. Closing them tightly, she tried to suppress the hot tears that threatened to spill over.

All at once Salvador was next to her, pressing her fervently against him. Through the thin linen of his shirt she could feel the wild thundering of his heart, that secret heart that hid its own truths and rejected her. He looked at her and his eyes seemed to hold myriad emotions, fighting one another for supremacy. Whatever iron control he usually exerted was palpably crumbling, as she too lost her resolve, falling into the hunger of his gaze.

'Alexandra,' his voice was husky as he whispered her name, searching urgently for her lips. His mouth closed over hers, his kiss fierce and so demanding it took her breath away. Her lips parted to the commanding thrust of his tongue, and she responded eagerly to the familiar taste of him, raising her arms around his neck, pressing her body sensually against his hard, masculine arousal, urging him not to stop. She moaned softly with pleasure, welcoming the fiery response to his touch, deep between her thighs.

She knew now, without doubt, that he wanted her as badly as she wanted him. It would have been so easy to let him make love to her there and then, under the willow trees, to give in to this storm of feelings that threatened to carry them both away to the point of no return. At that moment Alexandra no longer cared about what was right or wrong; she only knew that this all-consuming flame of passion was tearing them both apart.

Yet already Salvador was regaining control. He broke off from the kiss, his chest rising and falling fast, and brushed the top of her head with his lips. After breathing in the fresh, clean fragrance of her hair, he tore himself away, as if the very scent of her threatened to send his senses off on a new wild escapade. Gently, but resolutely, he stepped back a few paces, leaving her breathless and still trembling with insatiate desire.

He saw the look in her eye. 'No,' he said in a soft voice, controlled now, and devoid of emotion. 'This is wrong and unfair, *querida*. I mustn't deceive myself or you. I can't make promises, I can offer you nothing at the moment. It was callous and quite inexcusable of me to take advantage of you again. Please forgive me. You are—'

'There's nothing to apologize for,' Alexandra cut in. 'I wanted it just as much as you did.' She stared at him in disbelief, not understanding how he could suddenly distance himself from her, when she herself was unable to control this agonizing passion they shared.

He grimaced and ran his fingers through his hair. 'It's no use, you must leave El Pavón,' he said in a clipped voice, permitting no discussion. 'I've no right to drag you through this turmoil of scandal and vengeance. I'm a stigmatized man, we'd be tempting fate. You know nothing of *la venganza de Calés*. In linking your life with mine I'd be tarring you with the same brush, even putting your life in danger, and I'm too much ... I feel too much affection for you to be so irresponsible.'

'And this is truly why you want me to leave? Why you think we can't be together?' Relief, hope and exasperation tumbled together inside Alexandra. Salvador had never put it like this before, making himself directly the author of what might happen to her. In his mind, Paquita's warnings to each of them in Seville were bound together. He was trying to stop her sealing her fate with his.

'Salvador,' she said, walking up to him and placing a hand on his arm. 'You know that I'm not bothered about what people think, or any superstitious nonsense about gypsy curses.' Alexandra tried not to think about the threatening images of the wake at the gypsy camp or the dark forebodings of wild-eyed old Paquita.

He shook his head, unconvinced. 'I could never forgive myself if some harm came to you.'

Was he telling her that the paradise she had glimpsed whenever she was in his arms was a forever forbidden land to her? She could not, and would not, accept such defeatism.

'Then let's go away together, at least for a while, until your doubts and fears have died down. We could go to England, we could stay with Aunt Geraldine. Once I explain things to her, I'm sure she'll welcome you at Grantley Hall.' Alexandra spoke quickly, urgently, her voice pleading, hoping against hope to break through the wall that Salvador was once again putting up between them.

He gave a bitter smile, shaking his head slowly. 'How naïve you are, *niña*.'

'*No!*' she burst out. The forceful tone in her voice commanded his attention, compelling him to look at her. For a few seconds Salvador stared at Alexandra, as if seeing her for the first time. 'I'm not naïve, neither am I a little girl,' she cried out indignantly and stepped back from him. 'In case you haven't noticed, Salvador, I'm a woman. A woman who loves you …' She saw his expression suddenly freeze with a watchful intensity. '… Yes, loves you. Fighting against your stubbornness, your arrogance, and the figments of your twisted imagination.

'Since day one, I've put up with your cat-and-mouse games. You've done nothing but play on my emotions, unable to untangle your own and decide what you truly want. Our destinies are not dictated by superstition or the whim of others, we control them. You're so fond of proverbs … well, I read one just the other day that suits you admirably: *Fatalism is the lazy man's way of accepting the inevitable.*'

Salvador tensed, looking for a moment as though she'd slapped him, and then he stared at her, lost for words. A slight furrow formed between his brows, his pale face grew otherwise expressionless, and Alexandra was aware of the old gulf widening again between them.

'You know nothing of our country,' he said, a cold formality in his tone, 'nothing of its traditions and tribal customs. You're ignorant of the dangers that threaten those who don't conform to them, who disobey their rules or, worse still, people like you who arrogantly make fun of them.' He spoke without looking at her.

'What of your own sister, Salvador? Esmeralda left,' Alexandra countered defensively. 'She didn't care much for your traditions either.'

He lit another cigarette, drew in deeply and slowly exhaled before continuing in a colourless voice. 'Esmeralda's case is quite different.'

'On the contrary,' argued Alexandra, moving back to the tree trunk and twisting off a spindly branch in her hand, 'Esmeralda is a woman, and people here are forever telling me that a woman in Spain is not the mistress of her own life: she goes straight from her father's house to her husband's, without having any say in the matter.'

Faced with Alexandra's obstinacy in refusing to accept what to him was so obvious, Salvador's features grew tense. 'Nowadays that's becoming less so.'

'Clearly, Esmeralda decided there are more important things in life than what society tells her she can do as a woman.'

Salvador made a casual gesture with his hand. 'With Esmeralda, it was more a case of her will coming up against my aunt's. Personally, I have nothing against the young man she's chosen.

He's not an aristocrat, but he comes from an honest, middle-class background and will be able to give her a good life.'

Alexandra shredded a leaf between her fingers. 'Esmeralda thought you would disapprove.'

'Had I known about it, I would never have opposed their marriage. Quite the reverse, actually. I care deeply for my sister and wish for her to be happy. I'm sure that she didn't act on impulse. She did what she thought was right, and though some would perhaps criticize her conduct, I'd be the last to reproach her for it. In her place, perhaps I would have done the same. Who can say?'

'So, in her place you would have followed your heart, Salvador? You would have broken the rules too, is that what you're saying?' Alexandra was being deliberately provocative, but Salvador chose to ignore the challenge.

'You seem to be unaware that, in some cases, people are led by more than heartstrings alone,' he noted, a steely glint in his eyes.

'Yes, they are led by their own free will. I have a will of my own and I've been taught to think for myself. I don't need the sort of protection Spanish women seem to accept without question. I've not been shielded from the world to be handed over to a man before I have a chance to discover what life is all about. Why should a man be seen to have better judgement than a woman?'

'Men are logical.'

'And women are not?'

'Women are emotional.'

'And men are not?' Alexandra was in full flow and she could feel the heat rising in her cheeks. 'How would you describe your little scene yesterday? Where was the logic there?'

'A Spanish woman would have been flattered to have her honour defended by a man.' Salvador spoke in a controlled voice, though his eyes held a threatening glimmer.

'I'm not Spanish. I'm English and in England—'

'You are half Spanish, *niña*, and maybe our customs are different from those of England but while you're at El Pavón you'd be wise to respect them.'

Salvador's voice held a dangerous note, but Alexandra had bitten her tongue since they had first met and now she was on a rollercoaster of belligerence and self-defence.

'Obey your customs, which have neither rhyme nor reason?'

Salvador sighed. 'If you wish to put it that way.'

'I would call that tyranny, and it went out of fashion in civilized countries a long time ago.'

'You are one argumentative woman.'

'Why, because I question? Because I don't spend my time flattering you and massaging your ego?' She pulled another leaf off the stick sharply. 'What you're telling me is that you like your women to be submissive.'

'No, *niña*, I am not,' Salvador said calmly, as though Alexandra were a cornered animal he was trying to pacify. 'You would actually find it easier on yourself if you tried to fit in with our ways. Haven't the burning embers of a fire more warmth than the flaming blaze that is burnt out too soon by its own intensity?' Salvador's silvery gaze was steady.

'Oh, *please* … don't hide behind metaphors and clever words.'

'I'm not hiding, Alexandra. Merely trying to explain to you why I sometimes find your impulsive behaviour disturbing. It can be dangerous too. You just don't understand, do you?' he said softly, in a way that sent shivers down her spine. 'You're a very beautiful woman … whether or not you realize the effect you have on men, I'm not sure, but I know that around you, a man becomes aware of primitive instincts that have nothing to do with the way he's been brought up, or his station in life. *Niña*, it's all too easy for a woman, however worldly and sophisticated she might think she is, to walk recklessly into a situation beyond her control.'

The edge to his words seemed to cut away Alexandra's defences. Perhaps Salvador had a point. Wasn't that exactly what had happened with Don Felipe the day before? Despite this, she refused to allow him to sidetrack her into submission and instead steered the argument away from herself.

'And yet you don't think that Esmeralda is being a reckless, emotional woman in running away with her lover? She did what she thought was right, you said so yourself. She acted on her logic, which still led her to flout tradition and the rules of her family.'

'As I said, Alexandra, Esmeralda's case is different,' Salvador answered impatiently. 'Yes, she went against the wishes of the *Duquesa*. Your grandmother belongs to other times, another age. In her day, young girls stayed with their families and waited obediently for their suitors. It would never have crossed their minds to dispute their father's authority or even cast doubt on it. It is on the strength of such traditions that the great dynasties were founded.' He inhaled on his cigarette.

'And it is precisely because modern norms of behaviour are not so rigid as before that today we're witnessing the disappearance of the great families. A castle can't be built on sand. It's because we're living in these changed times, and ironically *because* Esmeralda is a woman, that she can turn her back on everything and leave.' He looked at her flatly.

'In my case, the situation is totally different: I am a man, I have responsibilities that hold me here, and as a man of honour, I must face up to them.'

Fury raged through Alexandra. There was no point in arguing with Salvador any more. He made everything sound so final. She threw the stick to the ground and tossed her head back dismissively, refusing to acknowledge any sense in what seemed to her a lame explanation.

'*Honour*? You're just a miserable hypocrite hiding a carnal passion for a gypsy girl beneath a tissue of excuses and lies!' she blurted out, storms blazing in her green, accusing eyes. She realized too late the significance of her words and wished she could swallow them back.

'The way I feel about Marujita is entirely my affair and not anyone else's,' he answered coldly. 'I meant everything I said, though I can't stop you from interpreting it any way you choose.' He met her recriminatory gaze without flinching. 'However, if that's what you think of me,' he went on, his voice now flat and toneless, 'then I fear you lack the sort of sensitivity I had thought you capable of.'

'Very well, Salvador, I will do exactly what you want, what you've always wanted. I'll leave,' Alexandra declared, doing her best to stop her hands from shaking. She hated the way he was making her feel, and was so desperate to regain her sense of balance, but she couldn't think straight. He always seemed to be one step ahead of her and now she wanted to lash out and show him that she wouldn't be beaten.

'I'll accept Don Felipe's invitation and spend some time in Granada,' she added, defiantly sinking deeper into the quicksands of her scorned pride. 'I'll visit him today, and tell him of my decision. I'm sure he'll be delighted.'

'Of that I have no doubt,' Salvador's face was ashen as he flung his cigarette into the murky waters of the canal.

He flashed Alexandra a final glance that froze her to the spot. She looked away so that he couldn't see her tears. Then, without giving her the chance to offer a retort, he turned on his heels and strode off towards the house.

CHAPTER 12

Alexandra let herself slide to the ground. Her head throbbed. She leaned it against the willow trunk and watched Salvador's cigarette butt float slowly on the water. What a mess! Why did conversations with him inevitably end this way?

She gave a long sigh. There was no going back now and she cursed the foolish pride and fiery temper that had made her say such hurtful things. But it didn't matter any more: she had to leave El Pavón now, if only to save face. Perhaps the trip would do her good; she really needed a change of scene.

In spite of the recriminations she had hurled at him, Alexandra now knew that Salvador's passion for her was genuine. Like the Flamenco of Andalucía, to which he had introduced her, their mutual desire raged like a force of nature. The way he'd held her, clinging to her possessively, feasting on her lips as though he wanted to drink up her soul, even his angry outburst of the night before … all of these things, she had to admit, were proof of his feelings.

And now he knew where she stood too: she had told him she loved him … but still he pushed her away. What more could she do? She felt exhausted and, for the first time, ready to give up, ready to leave El Pavón.

Heavy-hearted, Alexandra stood up. She still loved Salvador and wanted him with a passion that equalled his; but the fire of that passion was always a destructive one, burning them up in its angry flames. Even if she had shared his fear of the gypsies, or credited the superstitions almost everyone seemed to believe, she would still find it difficult to trust a man who had blown hot and cold from the very beginning, always evading an honest, open conversation with her.

Salvador had been right about one thing, though: this was no place for her. Alexandra had come to Spain hoping to acquire a father and a family but the de Fallas had never accepted her. To them she was, and would always remain, the foreigner, the cuckoo coming to rob them of Doña María Dolores' affection and a slice of their inheritance. Anyhow, she would never have been able to conform to all the strict laws and traditions ruling the inhabitants of El Pavón. She could see now how her mother had suffocated under them, why she had run away.

Still, Alexandra thought wistfully, it would have been such an amazing achievement, had things turned out differently: to have a caring family, so many people to cherish, roots that anchored her and the sense of belonging she'd always yearned for. She was strolling head down, deep in gloomy thought, when the sound of a car close behind made her jump. She turned to see Ramón at the wheel of the old Fiat in which he had picked her up on that very first day at the Puerto de Santa María. It seemed so far away now.

'Good morning, Cousin,' he called out cheerfully. 'How can I be of service to you today?' She managed a ghost of a smile.

'What's the matter?' Ramón frowned, alarmed by her miserable expression. 'Don't tell me you're upset by Esmeralda's prison breakout? If only she'd left a map of her escape route, some of us could have followed.'

But all Alexandra could manage was a sad shake of her head. The lump in her throat choked her, and she remained silent as she fought back the tears that were stinging her eyes.

Ramón opened the passenger door and motioned for her to get in. 'Come on, tell me what is making you so sad and we can try to put it right,' he said in a soothing voice. 'It can't be that bad. Let's take a trip into Jerez. That'll soon cheer you up, it always does.'

At times like this, Ramón reminded her of Ashley. Kind and faithful Ashley, always there to console, to listen to her troubles and offer a shoulder to lean on. Ashley … now he seemed like a ghost from another world.

'What would I do without you, Ramón? Yes, let's go into Jerez.' Alexandra managed a weak smile and climbed in beside her cousin.

'That's my girl. Now, tell me everything.'

Alexandra confided a little in Ramón. She didn't tell him everything, just that she and Salvador had argued, it had involved her going off with Don Felipe to his *bodega*, and that she couldn't understand why Salvador continued to allow himself to be caught up with Marujita.

Ramón listened quietly as they wended their way through the lush countryside dotted with vineyards, orchards and cattle ranches. 'Alexandra, I did try to warn you that Salvador was a law unto himself. Who can say why he does what he does? Our cousin is a complicated man, with a misplaced sense of honour. He's reckless as well as stubborn, which isn't a good combination. This business with Marujita is of his own making, and so is the solution. There's nothing any of us can do or say to influence him but as for you and Don Felipe, you should be careful of him.'

Alexandra cocked an eyebrow. 'So I should be careful of him and of Salvador? Are there any safe men in Andalucía?'

'Listen, *mi primita*, I feel some of this is my fault …' Ramón glanced at her as they sped alongside a field of high corn. 'I should have discouraged you at Don Felipe's *corrida* party. I was too busy having a good time myself to realize how much attention he was paying you. If I'd stuck closer to you, I could have told you more about him. I never thought I'd hear myself say this but, had I been in Salvador's place, I'd have given the man a good thrashing too.'

'Please, Ramón,' Alexandra laughed, momentarily finding her good humour, 'don't you lecture me as well!'

'No, no, I'm not lecturing you,' he replied. 'I'm only putting you on your guard against this Romeo. He's broken more than one heart in Jerez. There's been all kinds of malevolent gossip – who knows if it's true? – but one thing's for sure, his exploits have covered most of Andalucía.'

'So I hear. Look, as I keep telling everyone, I'm a grown woman. I promise I'm not about to fall into that sort of trap, Ramón.' Alexandra flashed him a reassuring smile. 'We're nearly in Jerez, let's talk about something more cheerful. You can tell me the best places to visit.'

They left behind fields of sunflowers and olive groves, and the road fed into the dusty suburbs of the town. Ramón began to tell her about it: Jerez de la Frontera, the capital of horsemanship, sherry and Flamenco.

'This is the season of the horse fair,' he explained. 'The town will be teeming with extra life and colour, there'll be lots to see.'

He left the car in one of the squares and, after a drink and some tapas, the pair parted company, giving Ramón the chance to pick up a few things he needed and Alexandra the welcome opportunity of exploring a little on her own.

She strolled haphazardly around the narrow *calles*. The breeze had dropped, the sky was serenely blue and there was a magical quality in the air, which was saturated with the heady fragrance of jasmine and orange blossom. Like that first afternoon in Puerto de Santa María, Alexandra wandered through the cobbled backstreets where the windows of the whitewashed houses were guarded by curved grilles rimmed with spikes. She couldn't help thinking of submissive women, kept prisoner in their golden cages; she wondered about their destiny and about her own mother, who couldn't bear to live that life. Then there was Esmeralda, born into wealth and status, who had nonetheless decided to spread her wings and fly out of the enchanted garden. For the chance of true happiness, Alexandra would have done the same in a heartbeat.

Lost in thought, she barely noticed that she had come out of a side street into one of the main thoroughfares, full of large crowds milling about. Many of the women were dressed in long, polka-dot ruffled skirts, with embroidered paisley shawls, flowers and *mantillas*, high combs in their hair. Horsemen strode through the throng, attired in white shirts and ties with wide-brimmed, flat-topped hats, tight-fitting jackets and soft leather boots. And then there were carriages and horses; everywhere Alexandra looked there were horses, the majority decorated with fancy harnesses in brilliant hues, brass ornaments, ribbons and bunches of flowers: the Jerez Horse Fair was in full swing.

Alexandra kept walking, taking in the festival energy of the town. There was nothing caged about this atmosphere, she mused. Here the women were more like birds of paradise set free, however illusory that might be, she noted cynically.

She drifted along the margins of the crowd, eventually coming to the fringes of the town, where the buildings, in faded dusty pinks and browns, had a rundown look. Alexandra continued to walk, absorbed in her own thoughts, until suddenly she found herself on the edge of an open space lined with palm trees, many of which had horses and mules tied to them. At the far end of this clearing, two corner walls of a ruined building, punctuated with arches, rose high into the air, and a cluster of tents was pitched in the shade cast by them. Her eyes were drawn to a large group of gypsies, jostling about in an abundance of music, dancing and laughter.

The *gitanas* were wrapped in shawls of dark red and fuchsia, the only splashes of colour against their black dresses or shabby white blouses. The men, who wore blue handkerchiefs around their heads, under their hats, stood in groups, shouting and laughing, gesticulating rapidly as they spoke, their bronzed faces creasing in a multitude of expressions. Elsewhere, mules were being handled by their drivers, who had deep blue sashes encircling their waists, while women called out from tables covered in baskets of oranges and wine gourds. There were horses everywhere, tied up together with ropes or being led round the dusty encampment under the sharp gaze of prospective buyers. The air was impregnated by their smell and the constant snorting and neighing.

Alexandra stood at the edge of the clearing a moment, mesmerized by the scene, drunk with the magic of the atmosphere. *A horse fair or a gypsy fête?* she wondered apprehensively, her hand resting on a palm tree. A horse and a couple of mules tethered to the next tree stood munching grass from an old hat on the ground, now and then blinking stoically at her. She was just about to turn and leave when she thought she glimpsed Salvador. Despite the unusual attire of patched shirt and baggy trousers, she was sure it must be him.

He stood at the entrance to one of the tents that was hung with coloured lanterns. Half-turned from Alexandra, he was towering over three gypsies, with whom he was talking. The first looked more Mexican than Spanish, with a huge moustache and an enormous pagoda-like straw sombrero; the second was thin and wiry, an older version of Pedro, with a *navaja* tucked into his belt. But it was the third, a hawkish-looking man with a deep scar etched into his weathered face, who stopped Alexandra in her tracks: it was the knife-sharpener.

The men seemed to be talking quite amiably with Salvador. Next to them, a couple of rabbits were roasting on a spit, which they turned occasionally. Two guitarists and a fiddler sat close by, thrumming their instruments. Crouched around a great fire, hung with cooking pots, a group of women and children were throwing pine cones and sun-dried branches over the flames, which leapt up from time to time, casting a rosy glow on their faces. Then, without warning, the trio of musicians stood up and started to play. Thrum, thrum, thrum, went the guitars, while across the deeper chords the fiddle with its strange tuning threaded a shrill pattern of monotonous arpeggios.

Three young dancing couples lined up, face to face, and began swinging to and fro. Soon they were joined by another pair. Alexandra's eyes were drawn instantly to the woman, who tossed her mane of raven hair, golden-brown shoulders gleaming against her white, low-cut blouse. Like a copper butterfly, she seemed to quiver with life, from her bare, beautifully shaped ankles to the tips of the glittering half-moon hoops that swung from her ears. With a pang, Alexandra recognized Marujita and she felt a hand grip her heart fiercely. Afraid she might be seen, she edged closer to the palm.

Now the dancing duel began. Marujita raised her hands and clapped them sharply above her head. Bracelets jingled on her arms, and her bare feet stamped the earth. Her partner was much older, dark-skinned and obviously Spanish, but Alexandra didn't think he was a gypsy. Indeed, he looked every bit the aristocrat in his expensive shirt and trousers. The rhythm of the music was pagan and exciting; Marujita's dancing had a wild beauty as her long hair nearly swept the dust, her slim body arching and swaying towards her partner, seemingly wanting to be touched even though she repeatedly eluded him. Even from this distance, Alexandra could see the passion in the *gitana's* eyes: she looked in love. Was Marujita trying to incite

Salvador's jealousy, or was she finally giving up her hold and turning to pastures new?

For an instant Alexandra was compelled to glance away from the dancers towards Salvador. What was his reaction? His tall, dark figure stood at the entrance to the tent, his profile visible through the shimmering air around the flames. He seemed unaware of anything but Marujita, his attention wholly captured by her. Instinctively, she knew that his eyes were unsmiling, damascened steel in his haughty face. What was he thinking? Why was he here with Marujita and the gypsies? Alexandra felt a rising sense of panic, a need to get away from this place. She didn't know how much more her weary heart could take. Her mind ached with confusion, to the extent that she felt completely numb. Still she remained as though mesmerized by some hypnotic spell.

Marujita and her partner finished their dance to hoots and claps from the assembled gypsies. Without so much as a glance at Salvador, she and the older man disappeared beyond one of the arches.

Alexandra moved away from the tree, and as she did so, she saw Salvador murmur something to the thin, wiry gypsy and pat him on the back in a farewell gesture before striding off. The gypsy watched him go before nodding to the knife-sharpener. At this, the scar-faced man stepped inside one of the tents. A moment later, propelled by a great kick from the gypsy's foot, a figure was sent sprawling through the opening. He landed on his knees, and Alexandra could see that his lank pale hair was plastered to his bowed head in bloodied clumps. All of a sudden the mood of the crowd changed, though it was no less intense. Instead of the jokes and laughter, she could hear hisses and catcalls.

The man had a rope tied around his neck and his shirt was in tatters, open to the waist. Through the ripped fabric, Alexandra could see reddish-purple bruises and bloody scrapes and she wondered, hand to her mouth, if he'd been dragged across the ground or beaten. A gasp escaped her when she realized that a bloody 'V' had been carved into the skin of his chest.

Alexandra's eyes widened in shock: *Fernando Lopez.*

What was he doing here? Did Salvador know? She thought not, judging by the way the gypsies had waited until he had left before bringing Lopez out. She watched in horror, not daring to move. Should she interfere or call for help? These were gypsies, she realized. What was it her grandmother had told Salvador: 'They live by the *navaja*'? If all she'd heard about them was true, she should leave well alone.

The knife-sharpener circled Lopez, who was cowering, breathing heavily, his ferrety eyes darting about, looking for an escape. Grasping a handful of the prisoner's lank hair, the *gitano* pulled out his *navaja* from the inside of his waistcoat.

'*No por favour*, no, please, I'm begging you. I'll just go, I'll leave you alone, I'll never come back. *Prometo*, I promise! Just don't …' Lopez's voice was almost a scream.

But the *gitano* merely sneered at him and sawed off a hank of hair. The crowd of gypsies roared in grim appreciation and slowly began to stamp their feet. Another handful of hair, another swipe of the knife … The stamping continued. Some spat on the ground and hollered. The knife-sharpener hacked away three or four times until what was left of the steward's hair stood in matted tufts.

'Oh yes, *gajo* scum, you'll *never* come back! And if you ever lay a hand on one of our people again, I'll string you up by the heels over the fire and roast you like a pig.' He paused to deliver a kick to the steward's kidneys. 'That would be proper vengeance but for now, you've got this to remind you …' And with these words, he picked up a bottle and poured a clear liquid over the bloody 'V' on the other man's chest.

'You've been protected for too long, Lopez.' His last words were almost drowned out by the shriek from the steward as the alcohol bit like acid into his open wound. 'Today, we've been merciful, very merciful indeed, but only because it suits us. If you show your face again, *hijo de la bruja*, you son of a bitch, you'll feel our *venganza* on more than your skin ... I'll rip you from ear to ear and feed your remains to my dog!'

With that, the knife-sharpener hauled Lopez to his feet. The steward took off, stumbling through the crowd of jeering men and women, some of whom threw bits of food or the contents of their cups at him as he passed, the rope still around his neck.

As if to signify that Lopez wasn't worth breaking the festivities for another moment, music from the guitars struck up again and the gypsies continued chatting and carousing. Alexandra watched as Lopez staggered across the clearing towards the line of trees where she was standing. She disliked the man intensely and couldn't help thinking he had brought this upon himself with his brutal treatment of these people, but the humiliating scene she had just witnessed appalled her.

It was only as he drew level with her, and paused to wrench the rope from his neck, that Lopez saw Alexandra. She took a step towards him. 'Fernando, are you—?'

'Get away from me!' he hissed. '*Le juro a Dios*, I hope they get eaten up by the disease they spread. Gypsy scum! I'll drink to their corpses.'

He made for the horse tethered to one of the palms and untied it. With some effort, he hoisted himself into the saddle. Bringing the horse's head around with a yank of the reins, he leant over and spat on the ground at Alexandra's feet. 'You bastards are no better. *Hipócritas y putas*, hypocrites and whores, the lot of you, under your high-and-mighty ways. Burn in hell, where you belong!'

And with a final sneer at Alexandra, Lopez galloped off.

She stood there, stunned. Would she ever escape this madness? At that moment, her determination to leave El Pavón gripped her more keenly than ever. Alexandra turned and quickly walked back the way she had come. She must return to the hacienda and make plans for her departure.

*   *   *

Once at El Pavón, Alexandra went to find her grandmother to inform her of her plans to return to England. She contemplated telling the *Duquesa* about Lopez, but thought better of it. It was unlikely the steward would show his face at the hacienda again, and she had no desire to complicate the already difficult conversation she was about to have with the *Duquesa*. It would be hard enough to deliver the blow that she'd decided to leave.

Her grandmother listened in silence but Alexandra was keenly aware of the distress she was causing. She tried clumsily and somewhat evasively to justify her hasty departure without much success. Using work as a pretext for leaving, she hoped her explanation would be plausible enough without having to go into the other reasons. It wasn't totally without truth: a few days earlier, she had received a short letter from her agent, asking how the new novel was going and when it might be finished.

'Is this anything to do with Salvador?' the dowager asked, eyeing her granddaughter pointedly.

'Of course not, *Abuela*,' Alexandra answered quietly. She had deliberately omitted any mention of him. 'My publishers are becoming concerned that I haven't yet sent them the new manuscript. They paid me an advance and I need to submit the first chapters for review,' she concentrated on holding her grandmother's gaze. 'Such things are better done face to face.'

Doña María Dolores nodded sadly but made no comment, obviously not taken in by her granddaughter's lame excuse, and when Alexandra, suddenly overcome with guilt, wrapped her arms around the old lady, she felt the *Duquesa* stiffen slightly.

On the pretext of a headache, Alexandra retreated to the solitude of her room and didn't go down for lunch. She had no wish to endure the searching glances and prying questions of her family, particularly her stepmother, who would doubtless be jubilant at the news of her imminent departure; nor did she wish to be the object of Mercedes' spiteful insinuations. This was hard enough without all their interference and meddling. Besides, she might run into Salvador. Just the idea of facing him was enough to make her want to flee although, knowing him, he would make himself elusive for the next few days, which would give her time to sort herself out.

In the early afternoon, she went down to the library to return the books she had borrowed during her stay. She hoped she wouldn't meet anyone there. It was siesta time, that sacred hour of the afternoon when Spaniards retire to the coolness of their rooms, blinds drawn, to escape the stifling heat. However, she was irked to find Doña Eugenia and Mercedes seated on the sofa, working at a large tapestry.

'Ah, there you are,' said her stepmother, on seeing Alexandra. 'I'm told you're leaving us.' She made no effort to hide a triumphant smirk.

'Yes,' Alexandra replied softly. She didn't look at her stepmother but went straight over to the bookshelves on the far side of the room, which held rows of leather-bound volumes, each one engraved in gold with the family crest. Alexandra was fond of this somewhat austere room. Many times she had come here seeking refuge when she was feeling lonely or homesick. Somehow it reminded her a little of home, and the thought that this was probably the last time she would ever set foot in it made her wistful.

'This decision to leave El Pavón is rather sudden, isn't it?' continued Doña Eugenia, with feigned surprise.

'I must deliver my manuscript in person,' Alexandra replied coolly.

'Nonsense! There's nothing wrong with our post. Where would we be if we had to hop on to a plane every time we needed to send anything abroad?' her stepmother continued relentlessly, still watching her closely.

'My dear sister doesn't want to tell us the real reason for her departure, I'm sure,' suggested Mercedes, with a surreptitious glance over her shoulder.

If Alexandra had been watching she might have noticed the glance, but instead it was the sound of rustling paper that drew her attention. She turned towards it and sucked in her breath. Salvador was sitting in a corner of the room, holding a newspaper, almost hidden from sight behind an antique Japanese painted screen. His presence threw her into confusion. She felt faint; the walls were closing in on her, and all she wanted to do was flee the stifling tension of the confined space that held them all, like mice in a cage.

'Such a pity you're leaving so soon,' Mercedes went on, cheerfully mocking. 'You'll miss the ball I'm having for my birthday.'

'How naïve you can be, *querida*,' snorted her mother. 'Those sorts of balls are only for the amusement of innocent young girls of your age. I'm sure Alexandra would rather be in London with its more permissive social scene.'

Determined not to rise to the bait, Alexandra hastily made for the door, not trusting her own tongue. But just as she reached it, Ramón came into the room.

'Ah, there you are, Cousin,' he smiled. 'I went up to your room to see if you were feeling better but you weren't there. Here, this should be interesting,' he said pointedly, as he handed her an envelope. 'It's just arrived for you. There's a messenger in the hall waiting for your reply.'

'For *me*?' Alexandra was genuinely surprised. Then, as Ramón gave her the letter, and she immediately recognized the Herrera family crest embossed on the grey envelope, she hastily shoved it into her pocket. She was uncomfortably aware that everyone else in the room had probably registered the provenance of the note too.

'Aren't you going to open it?' Mercedes said, bristling with curiosity. 'Or maybe you already know what it says,' she went on mockingly, a smile curling the corner of her mouth. 'Let me guess … has my sister a mysterious lover … perhaps someone we know … won't you give us a hint … or …'

'That's enough, Mercedes,' a deep voice cut in coldly. 'Act your age!' Salvador's face was in shadow but Alexandra knew that tone only too well and could imagine his expression.

Mercedes stopped dead. She wrinkled her nose mischievously like a recalcitrant little girl who had been caught doing something naughty. Salvador stood up, folded his newspaper, and let his gaze wander for a moment through the open French doors. Outside, in the golden light of the early afternoon, the lawn stretched like an emerald carpet as far as the blueish shadows of the willow walk. He sighed, placed the newspaper on the coffee table and walked out on to the terrace, but not without Alexandra noticing his eyes as they flashed momentarily at her; they were storm-coloured, a dark grey, like the threatening skies of a mythical sea when Neptune himself was in a rage, a look that filled her with dread. How had things reached this point, where the gaping chasm between them held so many unspoken truths, unresolved anger and painful misunderstandings she had to leave? Salvador seemed beyond her reach now, and the realization froze her heart.

'What's the matter with him?' Mercedes asked innocently, looking round the library. 'Everybody's so bad-tempered today,' she added, sticking out her lower lip in her usual sulky pout.

'I wouldn't take any notice, *querida*. You know how moody Salvador can be,' declared her mother. 'He'll soon be back, apologizing for the way he behaved.'

'Come along,' Ramón whispered in Alexandra's ear. She allowed her cousin to usher her from the room. He took leave of her at the door of her bedroom. 'A couple of malevolent *viboras*, vipers, those two in there. I wouldn't make too much of their words.' He laid a hand on her shoulder. 'Are you feeling all right? Look, *mi primita*, are you sure this decision to leave El Pavón is the answer to everything? You're not fooling me with this story about needing to go back to England to meet with your editor.'

She gave him a weak smile. 'Nothing gets past you, does it, Ramón?'

'Of course not,' he winked. 'I am all knowing, all seeing. Perhaps I have some circus fortune teller in me, as well as trapeze artist.'

Alexandra chuckled in spite of herself. 'I do have to visit my publisher, though not immediately.' Her smile faded. 'But yes, things have become too difficult here.'

'But you have me to help you.' Her cousin looked at her earnestly. 'You said you wanted to discover yourself. Isn't that what you're doing? It's not always a comfortable process.'

'I'm deeply grateful for your friendship, Ramón. You can't imagine what a difference it's made to me. Without your company to cheer me up I don't know what I'd have done. But, at the end of the day, I need to be alone to untangle my thoughts and sort my life out.'

'I suppose I can't blame you. Can't see how much longer I can stand this place myself, particularly now you're leaving too.'

'Where would you go?'

'I don't know, America probably. The Land of the Free, isn't that what they call it? Sounds like my kind of place.' He gestured to the letter she was still holding. 'What about the messenger?'

Alexandra looked thoughtful. 'Could you please ask him to leave now, and say I'll get a reply to Don Felipe later? If I write a letter, could I ask you to take it over to him once I've have left El Pavón? I really don't want to see him again.'

'Anything for you, Alexandra.'

For a moment, warmed by his good-natured smile, she let herself wonder why she never fell for the Ashleys or Ramóns of this world. Kind, dependable, always even-tempered, they were surely the sort of men who could offer her a good life.

'I'd be only too happy to help you send that slimy womanizer packing, although I'd like to have seen you turn him down to his face,' Ramón said wickedly.

'Ramón, that's slightly unfair. He really hasn't done any harm,' she protested. 'We both had a little too much to drink. But, still, it's probably better I don't see him.'

'That's my girl,' he said, patting her shoulder lightly. 'I'm only warning you for your own sake.'

'Anyway, you'd better leave me to get on now or tomorrow will be here before I've started to pack. Would you mind giving me a lift to Jerez in the morning to book my passage? I'd like to be gone by the end of the week.'

'Of course, but I do wish you'd change your mind … Has Spain been such a disappointment to you?'

'It's El Pavón I need to get away from, not your beautiful country, Ramón. In fact, I may do some exploring on the way back to the coast. I've hardly seen anything of the rest of Spain.'

'Well, maybe I'll come with you on the train. That way I can delay our goodbyes.'

'We'll see.' She smiled and shooed him away playfully. 'Now go!'

As soon as she was alone, Alexandra opened the envelope. It was quite a long letter. Don Felipe's writing was small and fine, reminding her of spiders' legs, with a marked tendency to flowery embellishment. The bullfighter wrote that he was not so badly injured as it might have seemed the evening of the fight but, because of two broken ribs, his doctors considered it advisable for him to rest for a time. He went on to say that, consequently, he was leaving for Granada, where he would convalesce, and was hoping that he would see Alexandra again soon. Maybe she would consider coming to stay? The family house was large, and both he and Doña Isabel would be delighted if she would agree to be their guest. Finally, he assured her yet again of the depth of his love and the honesty of his intentions.

Alexandra sighed, folded the letter, and placed it on the table. She went to the window and pressed her feverish brow against the cool pane before closing her eyes. This invitation was all she needed to complicate matters. However, if she and Salvador were doomed to find nothing but torture in each other's presence, she must pull herself together and move on, she knew that now. And she couldn't help but feel flattered by the undivided attention the bullfighter had showed her. It made such a contrast to her relationship with Salvador. Whether or not she was living out her displaced feelings for him through Don Felipe, she didn't know but after the exhausted emotional circles she had been following, it was such a temptation to allow herself to be courted and cherished.

Although she had always enjoyed more freedom than most of the unmarried girls of her age at home, her life up until now had been quite uneventful. Circumstances being as they were, a trip to Granada would be most welcome and Don Felipe's company a remedy to her injured pride. And, she told herself, if the warning bells about him refused to be silenced, that was a good thing. It would help her keep a decorous distance between them. She reflected that the dashing *torero* had perhaps been misjudged by everyone and had only been guilty of a little arrogance. Perhaps it was just his intense nature, coupled with the potent alcohol, that had led him to lose control at his *bodega* when he'd forced a kiss upon her? Would he have been the first young man to make such a mistake? And, moreover, was she completely blameless?

The thought of him conjured up a strange mixture of excitement and unease. For a whole hour Alexandra paced up and down her room, trying to work out what to do. Finally, she resolved to leave matters as they were for the moment. It was probably unwise to think of putting herself in such a compromising position again. Even avant-garde young ladies such as she knew better than that. Though the *torero* had mentioned Doña Isabel's presence at the family house, Alexandra thought the situation was still unacceptable. In fact, the prospect of seeing the *Marquesa* again was unappealing in itself, to say the least.

Half an hour later, her note to Don Felipe had been written. She had tried to avoid the subject of his invitation as much as possible, without appearing to be evasive. '*I must go to England for some time to deal with the editing of my new novel,*' she wrote. '*I would be delighted at some point to spend some time in Granada, as an essential part of my novel is set there and it would be an excellent opportunity for me to familiarize myself with the city. Perhaps my aunt and I will do some travelling in the autumn, or after Christmas, which is always a miserable time in England. I promise to let you know of our plans ...*'

She ended the letter by wishing the young man a safe journey, a rapid recovery and a pleasant stay in Granada.

* * *

Lying on the bed that evening after dinner, her head propped against a large pillow, Alexandra tried in vain to fix her attention on the book she had bought that morning in Jerez. She had hoped it would take her mind off things but she was wrong. Salvador's face kept coming between her and the printed page, making the whole exercise pointless. Finally defeated, she gave up, closed the book and shut her eyes.

She remembered the look in Salvador's eyes all the times he had held her, the way he clung to her so desperately, his whole body trembling with the intensity of his passion; and then there were his kisses. Time and time again, he had given into his own needs, but then wasn't that what men were like? Was that not why he kept going back to Marujita? That bitter thought overshadowed her memories. She chided herself for plunging recklessly into a situation that her romantic mind had dreamt up, clinging to the tenuous strands of the hope that he cared for her the way she wanted him to.

The bedside lamp threw monster shadows on the great white walls. It was hot. Through the open window came the scents and furtive sounds of night approaching. It was one of those airless Spanish twilights that Alexandra had grown to love but which, this evening, she found unbearable. She sat up and flicked back the sheet, feeling stifled, tired but restless. Her skin and her mouth were dry so she staggered to the bathroom and splashed some cold water over her face and neck. The reflection that stared back at her in the mirror wasn't flattering: she was pale, her cheekbones too pronounced and her eyes disproportionately large in her face.

How lonely she suddenly felt. London, Aunt Geraldine, Grantley Hall and Ashley all seemed part of a life that had existed thousands of years ago. Overcome by a dry-eyed despair, she cradled her face in her hands. Despite the days spent in soul-searching and self-reproach, in dissecting and analysing every situation and every conversation she had ever had with Salvador, she was no nearer a solution to her problems.

Where was he now? Had he guessed that the letter she'd received earlier that day was from Don Felipe? Of course he had. He'd been absent at dinner, which had taken place in almost total silence. A very disgruntled José had been forced to return whole dishes to the kitchen untouched. Alexandra sighed and went out on to the balcony. The night was dark now, with neither moon nor stars. In spite of the heat, she shivered. How many lonely hearts did this great house conceal? Her thoughts lingered a moment on the inhabitants of El Pavón. Don Alonso de Falla, her absentee father. Where was he tonight? She had found him witty and sparkling in London. The man she had rediscovered here was weak, taciturn, resigned to his lot. How great must have been his loneliness all these years, caught between a despotic mother and a dictatorial wife. Maybe that was why he was hardly ever at the hacienda.

What about Esmeralda? The beautiful, sensitive and fragile Esmeralda, who preferred scandal to the loneliness of her pretty gilded cage? At first, Alexandra had dismissed her as just another de Falla eccentric but now regretted that she had never had the opportunity to truly break through Esmeralda's defences. Despite their tentative confidences, her cousin remained essentially distant and aloof, seeming not to want or need the company of others.

Her thoughts returned inevitably to Salvador, her dear Salvador: passionate, tender, strong yet proud, irascible, inflexible; prey to his private terrors and his jealousies, and bound to a dismal future of his own making and, from which, apparently, he wasn't even trying to escape.

Finally, there was Doña María Dolores, the loneliest of all, an austere and tyrannical figure, but no less pathetic, holding on to outdated customs with the grim determination of a shipwrecked sailor clinging to pieces of his craft – traditions that represented a past she knew all too well was irrevocably lost.

'I saw a light under your door. Do you need anything?' Startled at the voice, Alexandra turned round. Agustina was standing at the door.

'Maybe you'd like a cup of tea or one of my special infusions?'

'Oh, Agustina,' Alexandra sighed miserably, and came back into the room from the balcony. 'I'm so mixed up. I've really made a mess of things and I don't know what to do.' She choked on her words as she tried to fight back the tears clouding her sight.

Agustina took Alexandra gently by the hand and sat her on the bed. She poured her a glass of water. 'Here, drink this,' she said. 'It'll refresh you.'

'Thank you, you've always been so good to me,' Alexandra said hoarsely. She sipped the water slowly. 'I really don't want to go, you know …' At that, the flood of tears she had held back for so long flowed in an uncontrollable stream down her cheeks.

The old servant gently took the glass from Alexandra's hand and sat down next to her on the bed. She put an arm around the young woman's shoulders.

'I love him but he wants nothing to do with me. He doesn't really love me. I thought he did … but now I don't know anything any more.'

'Has he told you he doesn't love you?' asked the old woman.

'I didn't need him to tell me that, I could read it in his eyes. Oh, Agustina, if you had seen the look in his eyes! So cold, so hard …' She broke off again, her whole body shaking with sobs.

'Ah, *niña*, if you knew how eyes can be made to lie,' replied the *duenna*, sadly shaking her head.

'Sometimes,' Alexandra went on, 'he seems to care about me and then suddenly this shadow passes over his face. He becomes this uncaring stranger again, distant and disdainful. He thinks we can't be together because he's haunted by superstitions that have nothing to do with reality.'

'Don Salvador *es un hombre de honor*, a man of honour,' Agustina tried to explain. 'He can promise you nothing before he has settled his own problems.'

'What problems?' Alexandra cried out passionately. 'Why can't Marujita and her family be paid off? Doña Eugenia herself, not so very long ago, said that the only way to solve such problems was with money.'

The old servant made a face, clearly expressing her opinion of Doña Eugenia's ideas. It was the first time Alexandra had seen her express disrespect towards a member of the family.

'*La venganza de Calés* is never settled with money,' she went on, her eyes grave. 'It is a tradition as old as the Sierras. Many men have scoffed at it, chosen to ignore it. Then, *ay*! Alas, they've discovered that the revenge of the gypsies knows no frontiers. It can be carried beyond oceans, over mountains; it can even reach the other side of the world. Believe me, *niña*, *la venganza de Calés* can only be satisfied by one thing: *que es la sangre*, and that is blood.'

'You want me to believe that the only way out of this is *death*?' Alexandra exclaimed, horrified.

Agustina waved her hand. 'No, *no*! There's another solution to the problem, but it's a long, painful and uncertain path,' she said, emphasizing each word. 'His Grace is well aware of it.' The *duenna* moved to the chair next to the bed, lowering herself into it with a sigh.

'And what is this path?' Alexandra asked, sarcasm in her voice.

'*La paciencia*, patience, my child,' the servant replied, looking her directly in the eye. Her tone was calm, but insistent: the voice of wisdom.

'Patience?' Alexandra asked again.

'As they say: *No por mucho madrugar, amanece más temprano*, no matter how early you get up, you cannot make the sun rise any sooner. The only person who can put a stop to this war is the offended party,' explained Agustina, 'in this case, Marujita herself. If Don Salvador plays his cards shrewdly, she will soon tire of him, reject him in favour of fresher pastures, and he'll be a free man again. At that point, he'll be able to offer a certain amount of money – as an encouragement, you understand – allowing her to live comfortably for the rest of her life. It's a tricky situation that requires self-control, patience and unshakable willpower. Already she is showing signs of boredom. There are rumours that her eye is already roving.'

An image came into Alexandra's mind of Marujita and the aristocratic man, with whom she'd danced so provocatively at the horse fair. Was he a serious rival or just the means of ensnaring Salvador all the more tightly?

'Supposing she doesn't tire of him, what then?' Alexandra asked.

'That's a risk His Grace considers he has no right to expose you to. All the more so since, if this business is not settled, your life, as well as his, would be in danger.'

'Put my life in danger? Why?' she cried out. 'I would have thought if anybody's life were in danger it would be Doña Isabel's. He spends much more time with her, and they were engaged once.'

Agustina let out a deep breath. 'The *gitanos* have a way of perceiving things about people. Perhaps it's down to the seers among them. Added to that, our world has no power over them. The gypsy lives by his book of rules and traditions, which is closed to all *gajos*, so who knows what goes on inside their heads?'

Agustina's fears seemed somewhat exaggerated to Alexandra, if not totally unfounded. Such strange beliefs were not unheard of among uneducated people, she told herself; they were an important element of the colour and character of a place. She was sure that many parts of her own country teemed with stories like this but they were just that: stories and superstitions passed from one generation to the next.

Yet Alexandra remembered only too vividly how fearful she had been during the wake of Marujita's child; how there had been a sense of some mysterious, powerful force at work that night. If Agustina had told her about those bizarre rites, even describing them in minute detail, would Alexandra have believed her without seeing them for herself? It was a world that had penetrated Salvador's fears, and on no account could she label him an ignorant, uneducated man.

Alexandra closed her eyes and lay back against the cushions on her bed. Perhaps she would have to acknowledge that these weren't fictitious barriers separating them but real and serious obstacles; dangers she had ignored because they'd seemed so alien to her own way of life. Maybe she was the naïve fool after all. Anyhow, there was precious little she could do.

At last she opened her eyes. 'What should I do, Agustina?'

'You must go away, *dejar*, leave,' replied the older woman. 'I hoped things would be settled here without you having to take such a difficult decision but, at the moment, going away is the only solution.'

'My leaving seems to be causing my grandmother so much grief.'

'At this time Her Grace is like a traveller who, after a long hike in the desert, finally reaches the river, only to discover she's forbidden to drink. You are this river and your tenderness is the clear water your grandmother needs to quench her thirst. In her family, other than you, the only one to feel a deep and genuine affection for Her Grace is Don Salvador. Most of the others are parasites, living at her expense; or worse still, they're like vultures waiting for the moment to swoop down on their prey.'

As she considered the *Duquesa* again, Alexandra's heart ached for her. She might play the despotic matriarch with her family but she had opened her house, and her arms, to Alexandra.

'Poor *Abuela*,' she whispered.

'Her dearest wish is to see you marry Don Salvador.'

Alexandra looked up in astonishment. 'Is she not aware of the dangers you've just spoken about?'

'Oh, she knows them well enough but *la gente está en contra de la razón cuando la razón está en contra de ellos*, people are always against reason when reason is against them.'

A deep sound vibrated through the silence of the sleeping hacienda. 'What was that?' Alexandra asked, her nerves once more on edge.

'Just the old clock in the hall,' Agustina reassured her. 'It's already one o'clock in the morning. You have difficult days and a long journey ahead, so you'll need all the rest you can get.'

Alexandra smiled gratefully. 'I don't know what I'd have done without you, dear Agustina. You've always been there for me whenever I've felt down.'

Colour spread over the *duenna's* plump cheeks. She patted Alexandra's hand fondly. 'Get some rest now, *niña*,' she said as she bent down to switch off the bedside lamp. 'And *que sueñes con los angelitos*, dream with the angels.'

And with that, silently, the old servant left the room.

CHAPTER 13

Alexandra was gazing out of the window at the snowy, tapering peaks of the Sierras that stood, colossal and immutable, a white silhouette against a sky of shimmering blue. The great mountain range, slashed with sun and shadow as if waiting for Judgement Day, had exerted a strange fascination over her these past few weeks while she'd been staying at the Hacienda Hernandez; it seemed to her that the appearance of its arid slopes changed with every nuance of light or wisp of cloud.

What was she doing here? What was she hoping for? Alexandra had asked herself the same questions ever since her arrival a month ago. She had made the trip to Granada on impulse, but as time went by, a thousand little things indicated she was becoming increasingly embroiled in a situation from which she would undoubtedly have the greatest difficulty extricating herself. And yet, she had stayed ...

When leaving El Pavón, she had decided against taking the train on her own, accepting instead Ramón's offer to accompany her to Gibraltar, where she was to board the ship back to Southampton. She could always explore more of Spain when she returned in the future, she told herself. Besides, she could tell that her cousin was going to miss her a great deal once she'd left and that he would welcome this last chance to spend time with her on the train.

She had asked Ramón to drop her off at the entrance to the waiting hall. 'I hate goodbyes,' she told him firmly. 'It was bad enough at El Pavón. I really can't go through all that again.' She laid a gentle hand on his arm. 'I'll be back sooner than you think. Besides, it would be better for you to catch that last train to Jerez tonight.' Ramón had finally given up insisting he wait with her, and left. It was only after having said goodbye to him that Alexandra had been informed her ship was delayed and she would have to wait ten days before she could embark. She tried to find another passage, but the only vessel with appropriate accommodation was already fully booked.

For a fleeting moment she had been tempted to return to El Pavón and put up with Mercedes' cruel mockery and Doña Eugenia's gratuitous spite, to brave Agustina's sinister predictions and Salvador's bitter reproaches but she was weary of these people she had never been able to understand, of disappointing the ones she loved and struggling to hang on to a fleeting happiness that promised no future.

Faced with a thorny situation, her English blood soon took over and, pulling herself together, she threw her shoulders back. *Buck up, old girl, don't be such a wimp*, she told herself. *This isn't the end of the world*. And it wasn't long before she had a plan: the couple who had been her travelling companions during the crossing to Spain earlier that year lived here in Gibraltar. She had their address to hand; she'd look them up. In the two letters they had exchanged during her time in Spain, they'd impressed upon her how much they would like to welcome her at their house. So why not? Anyhow, the temptation of staying a little longer in Spain was overwhelming. If she were able to stay with them, she could plan a whole month's tour of the country at her leisure. However, she was making her way out of the shipping office when a firm hand on her shoulder stopped her.

'What on earth ...?' she spun round with a jolt. Her eyes widened in surprise when she realized that it was Don Felipe. She'd not seen him since the night of the fight, and was relieved to note that he seemed to have recovered remarkably well from his injuries.

'Doña Alexandra, what a marvellous coincidence meeting you here,' he said, a dazzling smile lighting up his face. 'I didn't expect to see you again so soon. Doesn't fate work wonders?'

'Indeed.' She blushed a little and gave the *torero* a warm smile in return. It was so comforting to meet a familiar face that she wanted to hug him in her relief. She had almost forgotten how handsome he was.

'What are you doing in Gibraltar?'

'I came to say goodbye to a friend before starting out for Granada,' he explained.

Alexandra filled him in about her postponed journey and her intention to look up her friends.

'I know Gibraltar well,' he said. 'This address is quite far away, on the other side of the city. My car's waiting outside. It would be a pleasure to give you a lift. We could have lunch on the way and get there after the siesta, if you like.'

They had reached her friends' house in the early evening, only to be told by the housekeeper that the couple were away for a fortnight. This was turning into a nightmare. Tired and disappointed, Alexandra was beginning to wonder if she hadn't made a serious mistake in leaving El Pavón after all. Her mind rapidly cast about for a solution. At that late hour the tourist office would be closed. She was on the verge of asking Don Felipe whether he could advise on a suitable *parador* when he turned to her with his usual charming smile.

'What a happy twist of fate, Doña Alexandra, here's your opportunity to visit Granada. My invitation still stands, of course. Please, do come and stay with us.' His dark eyes seemed to hold nothing but innocent concern.

Her initial reaction had been to refuse, on the pretext that it would not be seemly for her to stay at his family's hacienda, even with Doña Isabel there; but she hadn't counted on the young bullfighter's ingenuity and determination.

'That poses no problem,' Don Felipe argued. 'You can stay with an old friend of my mother: *mi madrina*, my godmother. She lives in the property adjoining ours.' Just as Alexandra opened her mouth to speak, he continued, sweeping her up on his tide of enthusiasm, 'Even better, you can meet her then decide. You'll get on famously, believe me. She's here in Gibraltar, staying at her townhouse. We will stay there tonight before travelling back with her tomorrow,' he declared.

'But Felipe, I can't possibly ...'

'Doña Inés lost her husband a few years ago and lives alone in her large hacienda,' he went on regardless, gazing at her earnestly. 'Her three sons are now married and have moved away. She's often complained of loneliness. I know she'll be delighted to have your company, as will I.'

Alexandra hadn't taken long before she gave in, secretly relieved she would neither have to face the mortification of going back to El Pavón, nor spend time alone in a strange city. She had begun to realize that, as a foreigner, the experience of Spain could be daunting without the support of friends. At the time, she had justified her decision by telling herself that this strange concurrence of circumstances would give her a heaven-sent opportunity to gather more material for her book. Happily, she hadn't warned Aunt Geraldine of her imminent return so there would be no need to explain the delay or worry her about the plan. Besides, what was there to explain? Was there really anything unseemly in staying with Don Felipe's godmother?

'So you say your godmother lives alone?' Alexandra asked him once he had swung her bags into the back of his bright-red Pegaso Z sports car and slipped in beside her.

'Yes, her husband left her penniless. Don Ignacio Hernandez's company went bankrupt just before he died, a series of bad investments. Poor woman. Of course, I couldn't leave her to fend for herself.' He gave Alexandra a debonair flash of his straight white teeth as they sped out of the port. 'I bought her a comfortable house bordering ours in Granada, a modest townhouse here, and set her up with a small allowance.'

'That's incredibly thoughtful of you.' Her amazement at the generosity of this gesture was coupled with the reflection that her family had definitely got him wrong. But then a fleeting, less charitable, thought crossed her mind: was it really fair to discuss his godmother's financial situation with outsiders? Surely it warranted a certain discretion on his part?

He waved aside her compliment. 'Oh, it's nothing, I assure you.' Then he paused, before adding, 'I'm very fond of my godmother. She's always been a calming presence.'

Alexandra found herself wondering at Don Felipe's choice of words as they zoomed along the coastal road and into the main town of Gibraltar.

Doña Inés Hernandez was a handsome, middle-aged lady of medium height with a tendency to plumpness. In her youth she must have been a real beauty, as testified by the rare clarity of her complexion, her regular features scarcely touched by time, and the doe-like expression of her soft brown eyes. Her thick and lustrous black hair, strewn with occasional silver threads, was drawn back into a large bun at the nape of her neck.

She had greeted Alexandra at her elegant home with a twinkling, kindly smile. 'I'm delighted to meet you, Doña Alexandra. My godson has told me so much about you. I do hope you'll agree to honour me with your company in Granada. Felipe tells me you're a writer?'

'Yes,' replied Alexandra, instantly warming to her. 'In fact, my next book is set in your beautiful country.'

'How wonderful!' Doña Inés took her arm and gave her hand a squeeze. 'That's settled then. You can spend as much time as you like writing at the hacienda and I'll leave you in peace, unless you say you'd like company. Isabel won't be around, she's decided to go away to her cousin in Cádiz until Felipe's next *corrida*. So it will be just you and me. I'm certainly happy to act as a chaperone when Felipe is there,' she added, giving Alexandra a reassuring look. 'It'll be so enjoyable to have a young person around the house.'

The Hacienda Hernandez stood at the top of a hill, behind high walls and huge gates, in a courtyard shaded by the foliage of rare trees. A much smaller domain than El Pavón, its dusky garden was filled with colourful flowerbeds and herbaceous borders, and a picturesque arcade fronted the house, its elegant arches covered in red bougainvillea. Along the several paths that converged on the house stood huge terracotta basins planted with petunias, which spilt over the edges in riotous profusion. Behind them, ancient olive trees stood with twisted trunks and bewitched-looking branches bent to impossible angles.

The walls of the house were whitewashed, smothered under a cascade of climbing roses. Deep-set windows and the central courtyard, whose wrought-iron gates were thrown wide, appeared to welcome their guest with open arms. Inside, the high ceilings and beautiful coloured-marble flagstone floors lent an atmosphere of cathedral calm to the place that seemed to mirror the character of Alexandra's hostess. It was all so different from the stuffy, severe atmosphere of El Pavón.

Although Hacienda Hernandez was less grand than the de Falla estate, it was so much more inviting; this house spoke to Alexandra, took her into its bosom, something the family home in Jerez had never done. Her bedroom was large and airy, the bed itself comfortable. Like a caress, a light breeze scented with garden flowers and vine leaves moved about the property all day.

Doña Inés had welcomed Alexandra with a kindness and hospitality that never ceased to amaze the young woman, especially after her unfortunate experience with some of the members of her own family. Since she flatly refused any payment for her generosity, and didn't seem to need any help in the house, Alexandra often brought back tokens of her appreciation and gratitude: flowers from her walks in the countryside, little delicacies, small presents of silverware or other amusing trinkets she discovered on her exploration of the various markets in local towns she visited in the small car she had insisted on hiring. She was now glad that Uncle Howard had taught her to drive on the estate at Grantley Hall; she revelled in the independence it had given her.

Alexandra's thoughtful gifts and tales of her explorations delighted her hostess and she and Doña Inés soon became friends, spending long hours, in the evenings after dinner, talking without either one encroaching on the private life of the other.

Don Felipe spent most of his time visiting his *ganaderia*, the cattle ranch where many of the bulls were bred for the ring, or meeting *aficionados* and others involved with bullfighting. He was preparing for an important *corrida* less than a week away. Most afternoons, after the siesta, he saw Alexandra. Together they visited the stunning palace of the Alhambra and the beautiful Moorish gardens of the Palacio de Generalife, among other sights.

One afternoon, at the Hall of the Abencerrages, Don Felipe turned to her, saying: 'Do you know from what the name derives?' When she shook her head, marvelling at the exquisite vaulted roof decorated in glittering blues, reds, browns and golds, he continued: 'A tragic legend. Thirty-six members of the noble Abencerrage family were invited for a banquet by the Sultan Abu al-Hassan. The sultan wanted revenge after finding out that Amet, the chief member of the Abencerrage family, was courting his favourite concubine, Zoraya.'

'I can see this is going to end badly,' Alexandra quipped, glancing at him, but Don Felipe was gazing off into the distance.

'During the banquet, he had his guards come into the intricately carved hall and cut the throats of every member of the family. Afterwards, the victims' heads were thrown into the fountains. Legend has it that the stain, just visible at the bottom, is their blood. An indelible reminder of the massacre.'

'That's truly horrible!'

His eyes glittered. '*Sí, sí,* Doña Alexandra, truly horrible, but she was his *Gözde*, his favourite. Besides, a sultan's harem is a symbol of his authority. It was a different time, another era.' Don Felipe shrugged. 'Though what man wouldn't go to extreme lengths to protect what is his?'

Alexandra looked at him blankly for a moment and then gave an incredulous laugh. 'Thank goodness women don't have to live in the dark ages any more! But, surely, barbarity is barbarity, no matter what the era. As human beings, we should have an inbuilt abhorrence of cold-blooded violence. Isn't that what separates us from animals?'

'You'd be surprised how close we are to animals when we're threatened.'

'Perhaps. A few months ago I couldn't understand the strange perspective the Spanish have on love, passion and death. Now, although I'm not sure I'm comfortable with it, I'm certainly more familiar with it.' She shook her head and turned away, thinking how different she was now to the naïve girl who had been teased by Salvador at the *Alcázar* in Seville. Her heart gave a squeeze at the memory, but she refused to think about it; instead, she let herself be entertained by the solicitous, if slightly intense, *torero.* He was a cliché of the Spanish man: parading his masculine pride alongside impeccable courtesy and charm. But now she felt careless of everything: of Salvador, of her family. Something had detached within her and begun to float away, making her feel lighter, freer.

Meanwhile, Don Felipe continued to scrutinize her. 'Granted, our Moorish ancestors had rather severe solutions to their problems. And yes, for the Spanish, love, passion and death are inextricably linked.' A dark fire leapt deep in his obsidian gaze for just an instant before he smiled pleasantly and nodded. 'In any case, I'm glad you're more at ease with the Spanish view of things now.'

As time went on, Alexandra had found no reason to feel anything other than relaxed in his company. He was the perfect gentleman. Her pride had been bruised at El Pavón, and although the excitement of novelty that she had felt at first in Don Felipe's presence had now waned, his courteous attentions were still far from unwelcome.

Most afternoons, when they weren't out visiting the local sights, were spent lazing on the terrace of the Hacienda Hernandez or chatting over a glass of fresh orange juice and small dishes of tapas, always under the watchful eye of Doña Inés, who took her role of chaperone very much to heart.

For her part, Alexandra spent the mornings, and sometimes entire days, writing in the shade of a flame tree, among the flowering cacti and grey-green stems of aloes, inspired by the peaceful atmosphere and the incredible beauty of the place. In Granada, the writer in her had come alive; she had achieved a great deal of research and wrote copious amounts.

Sometimes, when she was short of ideas, she would stroll through the narrow and congested streets of Granada's old district. She wandered free, happy and relaxed, taking in the bright palette and quaint scenery that this popular quarter offered. Alongside the quaintness, there was a no less striking picture of poverty and dirt in the old town, with its flies, the clatter and noise of thronging life, and odours reminiscent of Arab *souks*. There were beggars squatting on pavements and gypsy tinkers hawking their clinking kettles and pans: so much on which to feast the eye. Numerous colourful stalls overflowed with delicious fruit and vegetables, meats, poultry and fish. There were little donkeys, their panniers loaded with bread and everywhere, hanging over the narrow streets, were balconies spilling crimson flowers and oleanders.

From time to time, Alexandra would pause to watch the blacksmiths at work, or to admire the weavers as they dextrously spun their gaudy but nonetheless spectacular shawls. She would stop at a stall to buy a few olives, nuts or the long sausages stuffed with peppers of which Doña Inés was so fond. It was a poetic setting, one that was always changing. Sometimes it seemed romantic and reflective, other times demanding and provocative, but always satisfying. Then, after her long walk, she would come back exhausted but fulfilled to the peace of the hacienda at the top of the hill, feeling as if she were cocooned from the rest of the world.

In spite of all this, Alexandra was conscious that she had acted rashly and unreasonably in accepting Don Felipe's invitation. As the days went by, she was increasingly aware of her compromising situation, an unforgivable indiscretion in the eyes of Spanish society. Certainly no unmarried young lady, aristocrat or not, would think of embarking on such an adventure. She knew that she enjoyed unusual latitude as a foreigner, and perhaps that was why the more cosmopolitan Doña Inés and Don Felipe encouraged her to stay, but there were certainly limits to the tolerance of most of the traditional people here, and she suspected she was coming close to crossing that boundary.

Several times during the course of the month she had thought about going back to England, though the prospect of taking up her old life – and of facing Ashley again – became less and less appealing as time went by. But her sojourn had lasted longer than she'd thought, and she didn't want to overstay her welcome at the Hacienda Hernandez.

When, on one occasion, she had voiced her thoughts about leaving, Don Felipe had assumed an injured expression. 'Has anyone harmed you? Have I offended you in some way?'

She had retracted her proposal laughingly. Of course, nothing the *torero* had done had caused the slightest offence. Never during her stay had he been anything other than courteous and respectful, avoiding the slightest word or gesture that might have made her uneasy or tarnished her reputation in any way and, for that, Alexandra was grateful. Now and again, when Doña Inés was out of earshot, he would try tactfully to steer the conversation towards more intimate subjects, but she had always managed to evade them astutely without hurting him and Don Felipe, with his customary consideration and tact, had never persisted.

Every time the subject of her departure had arisen, Doña Inés too had found convincing words that took away her qualms. 'Really, Doña Alexandra, you're simply doing necessary research for your novel. Plus, you're my companion, and a wonderful one at that. What could anyone object to?' Finally, with Don Felipe's help, she had managed to persuade Alexandra to postpone her travelling, at least until after the Whit Sunday bullfight.

So Alexandra stayed on. She loved this sun-baked country and its talkative people and had even begun to understand something of its strange traditions, which previously she had found distasteful and sometimes barbaric. Above all, though, if she were honest with herself, it was the thought of Salvador not being far away that had led her to stay so long in Granada. She knew he often came down to the city for his work. Despite the fact that she had left El Pavón largely to escape her feelings for him, deep down she hoped that by some fortuitous twist of fate she would bump into him at a bend in a narrow street during one of her frequent strolls. So she dreamed.

She dreamed and wrote, wrote and dreamed. Because she had now experienced for herself each word of love, each moment of fear, each sigh she described, with Salvador the hero and she the heroine, Alexandra's characters came to life. They throbbed with a new vitality and her novel was redolent with the flavour of authenticity – something she had never quite achieved before.

But now today, suddenly, events had taken an unexpected and complicated turn. That morning, Don Felipe had proposed. It came out of the blue, while they were walking in the garden. Unprepared for such a bombshell, Alexandra had been at a loss for words. He had assumed her silence signified consent.

'I've known that I wanted you for my wife since the first time I saw you. You're exquisite, *querida*, and no man can look at you without wanting to make you his. My life without you by my side is impossible to imagine. You've been happy here too, I'm sure. I will make you the envied head of a new dynasty. Come with me tomorrow, we'll take a trip to my *ganaderia*. What plans we shall make!'

Regaining her self-control, Alexandra had protested, trying to clarify the misunderstanding, but he had not wanted to hear.

'Shush, *querida*,' he'd whispered, placing his fingers lightly on her lips, his black, fiery eyes boring into hers insistently, 'not a word until after the *corrida*. They always say, never put a *matador* off his stride or he may be gored in the next. You only have forty-eight hours until the *corrida*, *mi princesa*. We will announce our happy news at the party I'll be giving in your honour, Alexandra.'

Now, a few hours later, Alexandra was standing at the window of her bedroom, studying the distant outline of the Sierras, lost in thought, as if those silent titans held the answer to her predicament. She sighed and turned away, moving to the table, where she began distractedly to tidy her papers. Why had she not managed to make her feelings clear to Don Felipe? In saying nothing, she had only managed to complicate matters. She felt ensnared in a sticky web and slightly ashamed at her part in the weaving of it. How on earth could she extricate herself?

Calm sense prevailed. Whatever she decided to do, it would have to wait until after Don Felipe's performance in the arena. She would never forgive herself if something untoward were to happen on the day of the bullfight. One painful thought to distract him, or a feeling of devil-may-care recklessness, brought on by her refusal, could make all the difference between life and death, and she didn't want that on her conscience. She dropped her pen on to the stack of neatened pages and gazed back at the far-off, enigmatic mountains. If the Devil was involved at all, she mused, he was still playing his pipe and laughing at how she was caught up in his tune.

She told herself that once the *corrida* was over, and she had cleared up the misunderstanding, she would go back to England and that would be an end to it.

* * *

That night, having pleaded a headache so that she didn't have to face Don Felipe at dinner, Alexandra couldn't sleep. She tossed and turned in the big four-poster, a hundred disturbing thoughts milling about in her head. Finally, she gave up and climbed out of bed.

Putting on her dressing gown, she went downstairs. It would soon be dawn but perhaps some hot milk would help her sleep for a few hours. When she stepped into the kitchen, she saw Doña Inés standing by the open door to the terrace, sipping from a steaming glass. She turned her head and smiled from the doorway.

'Alexandra. Can't sleep, my dear?'

'No, not really. You look like you're having the same problem.'

'I suffer from insomnia quite a bit these days and often come down to make myself some hot milk. Ignacio used to sweeten his with honey whenever he couldn't sleep, but I prefer mine plain.' She cast a look of gentle enquiry at Alexandra. 'You missed dinner, *querida*, which won't have helped. Here, let me make you some.'

'Thank you, I was hoping it would do the trick too.' Alexandra sat at the table and watched Doña Inés as she began heating milk on the stove.

'Shall we move to the terrace?' Doña Inés suggested when she'd finished. 'The kitchen's a little stuffy.'

Alexandra took the glass of frothy milk from her hand. 'I'd love that, thank you.'

It was a smaller terrace than the one they usually used when they sat together in the evening after dinner. During the afternoon this was always a shady spot, a refuge from the heat of the kitchen. They sat down in a couple of easy chairs and put their glasses on the small, marble-topped table. Tired and overwrought, Alexandra was grateful for the softness of the light gleaming from a couple of wall-mounted, conch-shaped amber lamps.

The night was full of subtle enchantment, the air warm and sweet, throbbing with the sounds of insects and amphibians, and fragranced by spicy breezes wafting up from the flowers and shrubberies.

'You really miss your husband, don't you?' Alexandra asked, as they settled back in their chairs.

Doña Inés smiled sadly. 'Yes, I do. Ignacio and I had a wonderful marriage. I was devastated when he died.' She paused, looking at Alexandra. 'He was completely bankrupt, you know. I didn't care, of course, being so consumed by grief. But I had nothing, no money to look after myself. If it hadn't been for Felipe, I don't know what I'd have done.' She waved a hand at her surroundings. 'He paid for all of this, and the house in Gibraltar too.'

'He's obviously a wonderful godson and cares about you a great deal.'

'I'll always be grateful to him,' Doña Inés paused. 'A lot of people don't understand him, but he's very loyal. Felipe is an intense young man and – how can I say it? – doesn't always have control over his passions. He's been like that since he was a boy.'

Alexandra met her direct gaze. 'Yes, I can see that.' She was tempted by the kindness in Doña Inés' expression to tell her about Don Felipe's proposal. Could she take the risk of confiding in his godmother? She seemed so wise and grounded. But what if she insisted on talking to him, or worse still, if she thought that Alexandra and her godson would make the perfect match? So far, confessing her troubles to other people had not brought Alexandra much luck, and had only made her feel more vulnerable. No, it would be better to handle this alone for now.

'My godson was always an affectionate child … but complicated,' Doña Inés went on, looking out over the garden. 'Funnily enough, it was to me he often came when he was upset or angry, not his mother. Perhaps that's why we have something of a special bond. He still values my advice, you know, even though he's a grown man … charming, popular, courageous.'

'The people's hero,' said Alexandra pensively, sipping her drink.

'Yes, the people's hero, but a hero with few real friends. I'm glad he's found a friend in you, Alexandra.' Doña Inés patted her arm gently, in a maternal way. It made her yearn to reach out to the older woman for comfort but she merely gave a wan smile.

The velvet sky was alive with stars and the moon's milk-white sheen. Where its beams fell, the garden was almost as bright as day, although the shadows were blacker. Alexandra shivered in spite of the balmy air: the idea of light and dark had brought to mind the two facets of Don Felipe's personality, an unsettling association. Feeling suddenly lost and lonely, she hugged herself.

'Are you cold?'

Alexandra shook her head.

'I'll fetch you a shawl.'

'No, really, I'm not cold. I think tiredness is finally catching up with me.'

The older woman nodded at Alexandra's glass. 'Why don't you take that to bed with you while it's still warm? I'll stay here on the terrace for a bit.'

'Yes, I think I'll do that. Goodnight, Doña Inés.'

'Goodnight, my child.'

As Alexandra padded back to the kitchen she glanced over her shoulder. There was a shadow of sadness on Doña Inés' face as she continued to gaze into the night.

Once in her room, Alexandra stood on her balcony and drained the last drops of milk from her glass. If only things weren't so complicated, she thought. If only she could untangle the knots inside her. Sighing, she breathed in the night air. She longed for a storm, with its cool rains to wash away this muggy night and, with it, the claustrophic feeling that everything was closing in on her. Finally, she crossed to her bed and crept under the sheets. She fell asleep as the first rays of the sun announced dawn.

Alexandra was awakened a few hours later by Juanita, the chambermaid, enquiring whether she would be joining Doña Inés for breakfast on the terrace or preferred to have it in her bedroom.

'Thank you, Juanita. I'm not very hungry this morning,' she confessed. 'Would you please convey to Doña Inés my apologies and tell her I'll be joining her on the terrace after my coffee.'

'The *señorita* looks tired this morning,' remarked the servant. 'Did the *señorita* not sleep well?'

'No, Juanita, not very well,' Alexandra admitted with a faint smile.

'If the *señorita* has a headache, Juanita can prepare for her a special herbal tea, a secret recipe known only to the gypsies.'

The mere mention of gypsies sent a nasty shiver down Alexandra's spine and she looked sharply round at the chambermaid. 'That's a kind thought, Juanita, thank you, but it's nothing a cup of coffee won't cure. I'll be back on my feet in no time,' she replied, a little too hastily. Was it her disturbed mind playing fancy tricks on her, or did she detect a momentary flash of mockery in the young girl's eyes as she left the room?

Juanita returned a few minutes later with a steaming pot of coffee and a bowl of fresh fruit on a tray as Alexandra was coming out of the bathroom, wrapped in her dressing gown. 'Thank you, Juanita. Just put it down on the chest of drawers, there, by the window.'

Juanita did as she was bid but remained standing there, hesitant.

'Yes?' Alexandra prompted.

'If the *señorita* pleases, I have a message to give her.'

Alexandra struggled to conceal the tension fraying at her nerves; she had a bad feeling about this. Picking up her brush she went to the mirror, avoiding the gaze of the young Spanish girl.

'I'm listening,' she said at last, brushing her hair vigorously.

'Paquita wants to see you,' announced Juanita.

Alexandra stiffened and drew a sharp breath. The strange fear that had lain buried inside her these past few weeks bubbled to the surface. Ever since her arrival in Granada she had been unconsciously waiting for something of this kind, a sign to show that the gypsies knew she hadn't left Spain. Even so, the very name filled her with dread. How did the maid know Paquita? Alexandra had no doubt that the gypsies were feared by many, and their influence was presumably widespread among the peasant and servant classes. Previous encounters with the Romany fortune-teller flashed vividly through her mind and she tightened her grip on the brush to control the quivering of her hand. The best thing was to remain impassive and feign ignorance. Placing her brush on the dressing table, she coolly turned to face the girl. 'I don't seem to recall the name,' she declared.

Juanita eyed her slyly. 'But Paquita knows *you* well,' she insisted. 'You're the *señorita* who used to live at El Pavón. I saw you there myself, with the gypsies on the night of the *velatorio*,' she concluded defiantly.

'Really, I don't know what you're talking about,' Alexandra maintained, without batting an eyelid. She never knew she had such capacity for lying, a trait she had always deplored in others. 'And now I'd be grateful if you'd let me finish getting washed and dressed,' she added, in a tone signifying the interview was over.

Juanita pulled a face and crossed to the door, her head high, swinging her hips nonchalantly. For a moment, Alexandra thought how seductive she looked despite the drab black dress, with that sensual beauty so like Marujita's. At the doorway, Juanita turned round abruptly. 'I must warn you that it's *disgracio*, unlucky, to go against Paquita's wishes,' she taunted, spite gleaming in her eyes. 'She will bring *un millón de maldiciones*, a million curses down upon you.'

Something snapped inside Alexandra's head and a rush of heat burned her cheeks. Clenching her fists, she swore under her breath. 'Tell your Paquita I'm not scared of her threats!' she said vehemently. 'Tell her as well,' she went on in a colder voice, articulating each word clearly to put the girl in her place, 'not only am I not afraid of her threats, but if she carries on bothering me like this, I'll report her to the authorities and have her picked up.'

The Spanish girl's fiery black eyes widened in surprise and then swept insolently over Alexandra, full of disdain. Then, turning on the balls of her feet, she strode out of the room, slamming the door behind her.

Alone, Alexandra began to shake violently, Juanita's threats ringing in her head. *Now calm down*, she told herself. *You aren't going to let a bunch of gypsies ruffle you this way.* She sat down on the edge of the bed, her face buried in her hands, forcing herself to think positively. It was no time to be pathetic, she lectured herself, hysterically running off to somehow placate the old fortune-teller was the last thing she should do. A relaxed, constructive attitude was the only way to smooth those ripples her being in Spain had caused.

Her coffee had gone cold. She poured it into the sink, without having touched it, and glanced at the bronze clock on the bedside table. Discovering with horror how late it was, she hurried to wash and dress. Not only had she promised her hostess she would join her on the terrace once she had finished her coffee – which should have been almost an hour ago – but she had also agreed with Don Felipe the day before that he would show her around his *ganaderia* at half past ten. She had just a few minutes to finish getting ready before he arrived.

Downstairs, she found a message from Doña Inés saying that she'd had to make an urgent visit to her lawyer and apologizing for not being able to accompany Alexandra to the *ganaderia*. She would, however, make sure she joined them later at the Hacienda Herrera, where Don Felipe had invited them both to lunch.

Don Felipe was waiting for her on the terrace. He greeted her with his usual friendly smile, hands outstretched. 'Good morning, *querida*,' he said as she came up to him. His brows drew together in a concerned frown. 'I was worried, Juanita told me you're unwell. Nothing serious, I hope?'

Alexandra smiled reassuringly. 'Only a slight headache.'

'Do you still want to visit my *ganaderia* this morning, or would you rather rest here in the shade? It's very warm today,' he said with his usual consideration.

'I'd be delighted to visit your ranch,' she said hastily, instinctively knowing it would be a better idea for them to be among people, talking about bulls and bullfighting, than be alone together. She knew that if they were to sit quietly in the shade of a flame tree, in the romantic Hernandez gardens, a more intimate conversation would be bound to ensue, one she wanted to avoid at all costs.

'Let's go then!' he announced cheerfully, attempting to take her by the arm. When she gently evaded his touch, he didn't seem to worry unduly, no doubt putting her gesture down to the headache.

'The *ganaderia* isn't far,' he explained, as they drove off in his red Pegaso Z. 'It's an integral part of the estate and borders our hacienda's orchard. You can see it from the top-floor windows of Hernandez, the ones overlooking the inner courtyard.'

'I haven't paid much attention to the scenery on that side of the house,' she admitted. 'I'm much too fascinated by the constantly changing views of the Sierras on the other side. I could look at them for hours.'

Other than that brief exchange, Alexandra and Don Felipe barely spoke during the short journey to the ranch. Soon, the car stopped in front of a big pair of iron gates, on which the Herrera family coat of arms was embossed in gold. Two wardens in sombreros, with lances in their hands, hurried to open the gates and the car passed through in a cloud of dust.

Bordering the drive was a stand of ilex trees, under which the herd was slumbering peacefully in the shade. As Don Felipe helped her out of the car, a breath of hot air caught Alexandra full in the face. Her head was throbbing from lack of sleep, as well as a growing feeling of anxiety, but Felipe seemed not to notice there was a tension in her quietness.

'As I explained to you before,' he said, while they strolled across the field of short, tufty grass, 'being a *ganadero* is to have a love and respect for ancestral traditions but also to belong to a long line of ranchers, which, in my case, starts only with me. However, I intend to remedy that. Together, Alexandra, we'll create a dynasty of the best *ganaderos*.'

Alexandra felt herself blush under the intensity of his gaze. He moved closer to her, obviously having taken the deepening pink in her face as a sign of girlish modesty. She edged away, wanting to put as much space between them as she could. Inwardly she cursed herself for having let things slip this far: it was not in her nature to deceive and she despised herself now for her duplicity. She was so tempted to tell him that she didn't love him and could not agree to marry him. Still, she hesitated for fear of causing some dreadful calamity; the earlier heated exchange with Juanita only fuelling her misgivings. Moreover, there was something hard as onyx in his coal-black eyes, and part of her quailed at discovering what might happen when she unburdened herself of the truth … a touch of cowardice, she admitted to herself, of which she was not proud.

'I bought this *ganaderia* six years ago with great difficulty,' Don Felipe explained, jolting her from her reverie. 'One cannot become a *ganadero* without buying the land, the herds and the family brand from the owner. I've now registered my own brand. I want my ranch and bulls to be wholly identifiable as mine, without being connected in anyone's mind with the family who had the place before. Two years ago, I was accepted as a member of our new Breeders Association and today I'm proud to be one of the suppliers of bulls for the *fiesta brava*.'

As he spoke, Alexandra's attention drifted again, enraptured by the sight of the distant Sierras. She forgot her headache, and was hardly aware of his words, as she gazed at the snow-capped peaks rearing up, level upon level, as if striving to reach the highest heaven with their silent prayer. Why did these mountains remind her so of Salvador? It seemed to her that their sublime muteness contained a message she needed to discover.

Aware of her fascinated gaze, the *torero* said tenderly: 'I'll take you to get a closer view of them soon. Would you like that?'

Amidst twinges of conscience once more, Alexandra swallowed hard and merely nodded, ignoring the quiet little voice in the back of her mind, telling her to come clean and get this ordeal over and done with.

'I would have liked you to attend a *tienta*,' the *torero* went on cheerfully, disregarding his companion's awkwardness and no doubt putting it down to her earlier malaise. 'Unfortunately, the season has passed, but we have all the time in the world to do these things together.'

Alexandra forced a smile. 'You must forgive my ignorance, Don Felipe, but I have no idea what a "*tienta*" is,' she confessed.

The *torero* flashed his brilliant smile. 'Please, you must call me Felipe now. The *tienta* is the test to which every cow between the ages of one-and-a-half and three years is subjected in order to find out if she is suitable for breeding. The experiment is carried out in a small arena on the farm. It tests the animal's courage, its fighting qualities and the boldness of its attack.'

'Did you say cows, and not bulls?'

Don Felipe beamed, obviously delighted by the interest Alexandra was showing in his pet project. 'You've hit upon the fundamental rule of the bullfight, how very clever of you … The *corrida* is the one and only time when man and bull meet face to face. When the bull comes out of the pen to confront the bullfighter in the arena, they're total strangers to each other. In addition, the animal has never been fought. For this reason, the bullfighter must have a sound knowledge of his adversary's ancestors, particularly its mother, to anticipate its likely reactions. Do you understand now?'

'Yes, I understand a lot better, thank you. But I must admit, I still find all this slightly repulsive and more than a little dangerous.'

He laughed. 'You have a faint heart, *querida*! Still, you're right, it is dangerous for the ignorant, but not for the maestro,' he concluded, his eyes shining with conceit as well as something Alexandra couldn't quite fathom.

The sun was beating down mercilessly now. A hot resinous scent came from the ilex trees. They had walked a short way, to the edge of an isolated field, encircled by a low dry-stone wall. There, in the midst of the green pasture, looming large in the white light of midday, was a magnificent bull: dark, hunched and threatening-looking.

'That's the bull I will be up against tomorrow,' the bullfighter announced proudly. His voice was slightly hoarse and, as Alexandra turned to him, she was shocked by the barbaric expression distorting his features. It was as if, forgetting her presence in proximity with the bull, something had been stripped away, laid bare, as he stared at the black snorting creature in the distance. And she was repulsed and a little scared by what she saw. His head was tilted slightly backwards, his eyes like those of an animal watching its prey. She shuddered. The *torero*'s face was an odious mask of arrogance and cruelty.

A wave of uneasiness swept over Alexandra. The sun was scorching yet she felt ice-cold and dizzy. She took a step forward and faltered; she would have fallen but with his usual alertness Don Felipe put out an arm and caught her.

'It's too hot for you.' His face was now a mask of kindly concern. 'You're not used to our weather and here am I lecturing you selfishly, without a thought to your wellbeing.' He helped her walk to a jacaranda tree, where he sat her down on the low stone wall in the shade. 'There, you'll feel better now. It's cooler here and there's a breeze blowing from the Sierras. It was very inconsiderate of me, I do apologize.'

Alexandra closed her eyes. She managed a shake of the head. 'No, no, no, it has nothing to do with the sun. I've not been feeling well since this morning. Really, it isn't your fault. I'm fine now but I do think we should be making our way back,' she suggested, easing herself up.

The dizziness had gone but the strange sensation that had swept over her earlier persisted until lunch. Fortunately, Doña Inés was able to join them at the Hacienda Herrera. Ever sensitive, she kept up an amusing conversation about her morning's session with her lawyer as they began the meal and so, for the most part, Alexandra was able to maintain a grateful silence.

For the first time, they were taking lunch in the dining room. Don Felipe thought it would be cooler than the veranda overlooking the south gardens, where they usually ate if they were having lunch at his house, especially as this room was north facing and, on some days, was blessed with a fresh breeze. The room was tastefully decorated with antique Moorish tiles on which were inscribed a number of Arab motifs and letters. The floor consisted of bare flagstones, which Alexandra assumed would need to be covered with carpets during the winter months to provide insulation from the cold.

Her eyes moved to the great white wall and remained there, transfixed. It was bare of everything but a display of ancient armour – long whips, a number of old swords and other curious archaic objects with hooks and spikes, which she could not immediately identify. The sight made her shudder. Why would the *torero* have such a perverse-looking display on his dining-room wall? She wondered, with a sinking feeling, if he ever took them down, handled them with those dextrous long fingers. She noticed that Doña Inés seemed unaffected by their presence. *Perhaps it's just me*, she concluded. Nonetheless, all through lunch, Alexandra struggled to stay focused and her eyes kept flitting to the wall.

They'd just finished lunch, and Doña Inés had left the room momentarily to fetch her hat, when Don Felipe said to Alexandra, as if reading her mind: 'They're a collection of old instruments of torture dating from the eleventh century. Some were used in the Inquisition.'

Alexandra had already guessed this, but hadn't wanted to admit it.

'Do they interest you?'

'No, not really,' she replied coolly.

'But I was watching you, *querida*,' he said softly. 'You were staring at them during the whole meal. They fascinate you, don't they?' His tone was velvet, but there was an eagerness there.

Alexandra felt uncomfortable under the *torero's* gaze. 'I admit I was looking at them,' she answered calmly, trying to ignore the unpleasant quickening of her pulse. 'But it was out of curiosity rather than real interest. I've never seen such strange devices and wondered what they were for.'

The bullfighter walked up to the wall. Alexandra followed him unwillingly, dismayed but not wanting him to notice this. Why did Don Felipe suddenly inspire in her such repulsion, even fear? And why was she now so anxious to flee this place? What was this bizarre feeling she had, of being gradually drawn into a deep and threatening abyss? Surely she was being ridiculous, she told herself. This was the same man she had always found considerate, kind and respectful. Why the sudden change of heart?

Seen at close hand, the display of whips and lashes, of chains and irons of all sizes and thicknesses, as well as the other more complicated instruments from the Inquisition, left no doubt as to their nature and function. In a flash, Alexandra remembered the blood-curdling moonlight battle between Don Felipe and

Salvador. A chill ran up her spine and a longing to see Salvador again flooded her heart.

The voice of her host reached her through a mist. 'I've heard these objects have come into fashion again ... for ... how should I put it ... other purposes.' Alexandra couldn't look at him now and wanted more than anything to be somewhere else. She dearly wished that Doña Inés hadn't left the room. What did she think of these distasteful objects? Maybe she was simply inured to them.

'Most of these pieces are originals. They've cost me a small fortune,' Don Felipe was saying, his eyes darkening. 'They're very dear to me.' Then, seeing how pale Alexandra had become, he added solicitously, 'You should have a lie down, *querida*. It's my fault, I shouldn't have dragged you with me this morning.'

'No, no, I should have taken the precaution of wearing a hat ...' she protested quickly, 'but I think I should have a rest, back at the hacienda.'

'Yes, you should. Have a long siesta, a good night's sleep and a lie-in tomorrow morning.' There was something in his tone that brooked no argument. 'The *corrida* doesn't start until the afternoon. You have plenty of time to relax and take it easy. Wear a large hat at the bullfight. Even though the seats are in the shade, you'd be wise to protect yourself against our vicious sun. You want to be well tomorrow evening to greet our guests.'

Had she heard correctly? Had he really said 'our guests'? She instantly felt as if the walls were closing in on her. How far would this ridiculous masquerade have to go? It was one thing to be dealing with Don Felipe's attentions face to face, quite another maintaining the deceit in a roomful of guests at a party. Her mind searched wildly for a way out. The *corrida* would have ended by then. Yes, once the spectacle was over she'd be able to be quite candid with him. He must be told the truth before the party, even if that meant her appearing callous and ungrateful. For now, she would simply have to keep quiet and stay out of the way.

To Alexandra's relief, Doña Inés came back in just then. 'You're quite pale, my dear,' she remarked with concern. 'Is something the matter?'

'Alexandra's been overdoing it a little and has probably caught a touch of sunstroke,' the *torero* hurriedly interjected. 'I'm afraid I'm to blame, *Madrina*. I haven't been looking after my guest as I should.'

'I'd like to have a lie down now,' said Alexandra, whose uneasiness was growing by the second.

'I'll drive you,' Don Felipe said. 'It's much too hot for you to walk and …'

'No, that's all right,' Alexandra interrupted quickly. She turned to Doña Inés, imploringly. 'Doña Inés, if you don't mind, I'd rather walk. It will only take us a few minutes, we can keep to the shade. Besides, the stroll will do me good.'

The Spanish woman regarded Alexandra with concerned eyes.

'Of course, my dear. I must admit, I could do with a walk too,' she said cheerfully. Faced with the young woman's insistence, and his godmother's acquiescence, the *torero* was forced to reluctantly let Alexandra go, and the two women took their leave.

Doña Inés' home was only a short walk from the Hacienda Herrera; the two properties shared a communal wall. During lunch her attentive gaze had noticed the sudden awkwardness and change in Alexandra's conduct. Now, she anxiously watched her young charge out of the corner of her eye.

'You seem troubled, my dear. Yesterday evening you went to your room without any dinner. This morning, as far as I know, you only had a cup of coffee for breakfast, and during lunch today you scarcely touched your food.'

Alexandra smiled weakly, inwardly debating whether or not to take Doña Inés into her confidence. During her stay, the *duenna* had always been kind and generous towards her, showing her at times an expressive motherly affection which Aunt Geraldine, despite her obvious love for her niece, had never quite managed to display so openly. But still Alexandra kept her silence.

'Don't be afraid to talk to me, Alexandra,' her companion continued solicitously. 'I'm not trying to pry or be indiscreet but I feel there's something seriously worrying you and I would like to help if it's in my power. I think of you as my own child, you know. The daughter I so wanted but God refused me.'

They sat down in Doña Inés' summer room, looking on to a cool, shady patio. There, while her hostess busied herself with some embroidery, Alexandra opened up to her friend. At last, after weeks of torment and soul-searching, she was able to unburden herself, her tangled thoughts and feelings tumbling out in a liberating torrent. She spoke of El Pavón and her love for Salvador, of how she had ended up in Granada, and of her various clashes with the gypsies. Finally, she told Doña Inés of her irresponsible behaviour towards Don Felipe, of his proposal of marriage and the misunderstanding which followed.

Doña Inés listened to her in silence, nodding at times approvingly, and at other times grimly shaking her head.

'And that's where I stand today,' Alexandra at last concluded. 'I really have got myself into an awful mess.'

Doña Inés looked up from her handiwork. 'Yes, I can see you've landed yourself in a rather complicated situation,' she said softly. 'I hadn't realized things had gone so far with young Felipe.'

'Neither had I,' admitted Alexandra. 'His proposal took me completely by surprise. I knew he felt an attachment towards me … and I felt a certain admiration for him, but to ask me to marry him … I suppose I was flattered by the attention of such a charismatic personality, but that's really no excuse, and

I'm not trying to acquit myself of any blame. I realize now how frivolous and foolish I've been.' She didn't mention her growing unease about the cold cruelty she had begun to witness in the *torero*. Naturally it wasn't something that seemed appropriate to discuss with his godmother. 'I've no idea what to do now,' she continued. 'I know that this is probably difficult for you but I would dearly appreciate your advice ...'

Doña Inés remained silent for a moment, as though considering what she was going to say. 'I'm grateful for your confidence, Alexandra, and you can rest assured that our conversation won't go further than this room. You understand,' she went on, picking her words carefully, 'Doña María Magdalena, Don Felipe's mother, was my best friend and I've known Felipe since his infancy. To complicate matters, I'm also his godmother, and because of that he holds a special place in my affections. Obviously, I wish the best for him and, in choosing you, he has shown excellent judgement. Still, as I was telling you earlier, I've grown very fond of you over these past weeks, and the fact that you've trusted me enough to come to me with your problems puts me in a somewhat delicate position, you might say ...'

Doña Inés concentrated on her embroidery for a while in silence. The only sounds were the gentle cooing of doves and the babbling of a fountain outside. But Alexandra noted the hesitation on the older woman's face, and waited for her to continue.

'My dear child, I find it truly difficult to advise you without feeling that I'm betraying the son of my dear friend, a young man who has been so very generous to me. I love my godson but Felipe has a difficult side to him ...' She paused. 'A hot temper, for one thing ... and, true, his courage can sometimes lead to an unfortunate arrogance. I have always wished he would find someone like you to bring a stabilizing influence to his character.' She smiled sadly. 'However, for your own good, you must put an end to this situation as soon as possible.'

Doña Inés let her arms fall to her side in a gesture of helplessness. 'Go and find him, after the *corrida* tomorrow, before the reception, as you intended, and explain to him that there's been a misunderstanding,' she suggested. 'But don't approach him before his fight. *Nothing* must distract him. It would unman him to hear such news and might be fatal. Then, after you've told him everything, you should immediately leave Granada.'

'But I can't go back to Jerez,' Alexandra cried out in sudden panic.

'No, you cannot. I will accompany you to Gibraltar,' the *duenna* reassured her, 'and wait there with you until you find a passage to England.'

Alexandra felt a huge weight lift from her shoulders. 'I'm so grateful to you, Doña Inés. How will I ever be able to repay your kindness?'

'The company you have given me over these last weeks has been repayment enough. Your departure will leave a big gap,' declared the older woman, shaking her head. At these words, Alexandra's eyes misted. 'Don't be sad, my child.' Doña Inés patted her hand. 'Maybe one day, when your problems with your handsome count have been ironed out, you'll come back.'

'Do you think I have any hope with him?'

'I have only met Count Salvador Cervantes de Rueda once, and that was a long time ago, when he was engaged to Isabel Herrera. The terrible accident that laid him low just before his wedding happened here in Granada, and I remember my good friend, Doña María Magdalena, being very upset by it. I can't recall too well the events that caused the engagement to be broken off. I seem to recollect that it involved a young gypsy and the scandal made ripples for a while among the Andalucían *beau monde*. My husband died around that time, so my heart was full of my own problems.'

Alexandra listened avidly in the hope of finding out something new that would throw some light on Salvador's ambiguous character. But it seemed Doña Inés had pretty much withdrawn from the world at that time, in mourning, and had little else to add.

'However,' she continued, 'one fact remains certain. The young count has always been considered a man of honour by those who know him. Even the rumours resulting from his relationship with the gypsy girl have never managed to tarnish his reputation, I can assure you. These scandals crop up from time to time but no one takes them very seriously.'

'My feelings for Salvador run so deep,' Alexandra whispered desperately. 'How will I ever be able to forget him?'

'Go back to England,' advised Doña Inés, placing her embroidery on the table in front of them. She smiled at Alexandra, leaning forward and placing a reassuring hand on her arm. 'Who knows? Maybe later some happy combination of circumstances will bring you together again. Fate will give you both a second chance. The world is full of the unexpected! There is some truth in the old Moorish saying: if it's *maktoub*, written in the unknown, that you are meant for each other, then neither the oceans, nor the deserts, nor the whole universe will be able to keep you from one another. And you will meet again.'

Soothed by these words, Alexandra went up to her room. The discussion with the *duenna* had clarified some of the questions niggling away at her and had confirmed, moreover, that she must at all costs avoid a confrontation with Don Felipe until after the bullfight.

Tomorrow, before the reception, she would go to him to clear up the misunderstanding. Determined to be humble and take all the blame for misinterpreting his intentions, she would stress her admiration for his skills, as well as her gratitude for his hospitality and kindness during the past weeks; then, she would strongly advocate friendship and beg his forgiveness for having unintentionally misled him and hurt his feelings.

Alexandra would have preferred to write a letter, one that would be delivered once she was miles away from Granada so that he wouldn't try to come after her, but she realized that would be unfair and cowardly. Whatever his faults, Don Felipe had always been considerate towards her, while she, in return, had only been deceitful. At the very least she owed him an honest explanation.

That night, before going to bed, she composed a short note to Don Felipe, requesting a meeting immediately after the *corrida*, and gave it to Juanita, asking her to deliver it first thing in the morning. Finally, she turned out the light, thankful that she would be extricating herself more or less unscathed from a tricky situation. By this time tomorrow she would be on her way to Gibraltar.

Chapter 14

Alexandra woke up with a start, momentarily unaware of where she was. Juanita was drawing back the curtains of her bedroom window and sunshine flooded the room, its warm shafts caressing her face.

'I hope the *señorita* will forgive me,' Juanita said as Alexandra lifted herself up in bed, bleary-eyed. 'I did knock, but the *señorita* didn't answer. I was afraid the *señorita* would be late for the *corrida* this afternoon. It's already ten o'clock.'

It had been a terrible night. Alexandra had hardly slept, assailed by doubts and overwhelmed by confusion. Finally, in the early hours she had fallen into a deep sleep.

'That's all right, Juanita, you were right to wake me.'

'Would the *señorita* like me to iron her evening dress?'

'No, thank you, it's already packed.'

'No, *no*,' the servant shook her head vehemently. 'I'm sorry, but the *señorita*'s evening clothes need ironing again.'

Alexandra frowned. Was the maid trying to be difficult again? 'I won't need any evening outfits today, since Doña Inés and I are leaving for Gibraltar this afternoon after the *corrida*. Thank you, Juanita, that will be all,' she declared, slightly irritated. Yet the maid stood there staring intently at her with her great dark eyes. 'Thank you, Juanita, that will be all,' she repeated. Feeling increasingly uneasy under the Spanish girl's penetrating gaze, she pushed herself further up against the pillows. 'You can go now.'

'Forgive me *señorita*, but maybe the *señorita* doesn't know that the journey has been postponed,' Juanita announced with a pert smile, scrutinizing Alexandra's face for the effect produced by this titbit of news.

Alexandra's heart sank and she swallowed hard. What had gone wrong? Whatever it was, she didn't want the maid to see her anxiety. 'I don't know what you're talking about,' she muttered, fighting to keep a blank expression. 'Run along now and let me get dressed, otherwise I'll be late for the *corrida*.'

'But *señorita*, you don't understand ...'

Just then, there was a knock at the door, and Doña Inés hurried into the room, looking agitated.

'Good morning, my dear, I have some bad news,' she said, coming straight to the point. Then, noticing Juanita, she asked the maid to leave them alone and close the door behind her. The girl cast a lingering glance at both of them before she left. Doña Inés hovered about aimlessly for a few seconds before settling herself in the armchair opposite Alexandra's bed. A frown wrinkled her usually smooth forehead. 'There's been an outbreak of summer fever in La Línea de la Concepcíon. For the time being, the town is under quarantine and the authorities in Gibraltar are not letting anyone across the border.'

'What do you mean? How did you find out?'

'I heard it on the radio after you'd gone to bed last night. And close friends of mine called this morning. They've just arrived from Algeciras and were full of the news.'

'It might just be a rumour,' argued Alexandra. She thought back to Aunt Geraldine's comments about communications in Spain. 'Are you sure the reports are reliable?'

'I can't be sure that the town is still in quarantine today but it's highly likely. I've tried to ring various friends who live in that area but all the telephone lines are busy or down. It's impossible to get through to anyone. I do think it would be unwise to risk setting out today, unless we hear any news to the contrary.'

She looked at Alexandra's worried face. 'And I'm afraid, my dear, that's not the only piece of bad news,' she went on grimly. 'Don Felipe came round early this morning to apologize that he won't be able to meet you straight after the *corrida*. He received your note, but he has some business to attend to with a couple of *aficionados*. Apparently, they're coming all the way from Toledo to see him.'

This was just about the last straw. Wearily, Alexandra sank back into the pillows on her bed and closed her eyes. 'What am I going to do? I can't go to that party and act as if everything is all right,' she protested, 'Felipe is planning to announce our engagement!'

Doña Inés stood up and made for the door. 'Listen, Alexandra, you mustn't worry, you're not alone in all this. I'll be at the reception too, and one way or another, we'll deal with the problem together,' she said resolutely. 'Now, my dear, I must let you get ready and I need to finish dressing myself. Time is marching on, we should be leaving in an hour.'

Alexandra felt trapped. There was an odd sense of inevitability about all this. It was as if invisible influences were at work, inexorably playing havoc with her life, preventing her from leaving Spain. This was the second time that fate had interfered with her plans. She thought of the Moor's *maktoub* and of the gypsies. Was all of this 'written'? Maybe there was some truth in those weird superstitions after all. Her stomach churned at the idea but she swiftly admonished herself. *No, no, absolute nonsense!* She was just the victim of a coincidental combination of circumstances. Rousing herself

from these unwelcome thoughts, Alexandra slipped out of bed
and began preparing herself for the afternoon's event.

*   *   *

There was a lively atmosphere on the terrace when Alexandra
and Doña Inés arrived at the Hacienda Herrera that evening,
after the *corrida*. Several lanterns adorned the trees of the garden,
which was artistically floodlit for the occasion.

Despite the beautiful setting, and the party mood around
her, Alexandra was decidedly nervous. All afternoon at the
bullfight she had been tense, her mind endlessly going over the
conversation she planned to have with Don Felipe. It didn't help
matters that thoughts of Salvador continued to distract her. She
remembered that first time in Ronda at the Plaza de Toros. It
had been such an intense day. Salvador had been there, with
Doña Isabel. Alexandra remembered how she had looked at
Don Felipe through rose-tinted glasses then, finding him
exciting and dashing. And later, Salvador introduced her to the
Flamenco with a fire she would never forget. Afterwards, at the
Parador de la Luna, the enthralling day had culminated with
their achingly passionate embrace … It seemed so long ago and
now Alexandra was a world apart from those happy memories,
and from the man she loved. All she felt now was dread.

In order to boost her morale, she had taken special care
in choosing her gown for that evening. She also knew that
Doña Isabel would be there, attempting to outshine her guests.
Don Felipe's sister had just returned from Cádiz and although
she had managed to avoid her at the *corrida*, tonight would
be more difficult.

Alexandra had opted for an elegant Schiaparelli gown, an
ivory-and-gold long Grecian dress which Aunt Geraldine had
bought her in Paris, and which she had worn only once before to

go to the opera. The tightly cinched-in waist and flaring flounces of cream-coloured chiffon showed off the elegant contours of her slender, willowy figure and brought out the warm glow of her skin; the golden tan she had acquired after days of exploring the markets of Granada gave her a healthy radiance and accentuated the green of her eyes. With her bare shoulders gracefully peeping out from gossamer frills, the low V-neckline of her close-fitting bodice emphasizing the firm line of her breasts, she was reminiscent of some ancient diva as she glided through the drawing room, straight and tall, picking her way carefully among the selected crowd of socialites beginning to fill the place.

Don Felipe immediately spotted them. He was at the other end of the room, greeting guests with Doña Isabel. Alexandra could have sworn she saw his smouldering ebony eyes narrow slightly, although his mask-like features broke into a smile. She was still aware of his powerful but inscrutable feline beauty, but as he made his way across the room towards them with that characteristic lithe grace, bringing to mind the double-faced stone animals at his *bodega*, she realized that everything about the *torero* had now taken on a slightly repulsive aura.

She felt Doña Inés squeeze her arm. 'Try to get Felipe on his own soon, my dear,' she murmured, 'before he's tempted to make his announcement. I'll be here if you need me to talk to him afterwards.' When Alexandra shot her an anxious look, Doña Inés simply patted her hand reassuringly, telling her, 'Only you can speak with him first. Now smile, and go with him. I know you'll choose the right words.'

Alexandra had to fight the instinct to back away from the *torero* when he took her arm. As he led her off to introduce her to some of his friends, she couldn't help but glance nervously over her shoulder at Doña Inés. She thought she saw a flicker of apprehension behind the older woman's kindly features.

Alexandra's head buzzed with a dizzy fever. All she could hear was a staccato chattering, punctuated every now and then by a sharp laugh or exclamation, and the eternal rustling of fans, like the fluttering of moths in the warm evening air.

'You should always wear your hair this way, *querida*,' whispered the *torero* in her ear, his eyes travelling over the mass of auburn coiled locks dressed in a high chignon at the crown of her head, a style that accentuated the pure oval of her face and her high cheekbones. Alexandra made an effort to smile.

'Are you still suffering from a headache?' he asked, sensing her stiffen.

'Yes, a slight one,' she said softly. Indeed, it was stifling in the brightly lit drawing room and her head was beginning to feel as if it were being squeezed in a vice. If she didn't speak to him now, it might be too late, and concentration would fail her.

'Felipe, there's something I must tell you …'

He put a finger to her lips, his other hand still grasping her arm firmly. 'Enough, *querida*, there'll be plenty of time for talking later. There's nothing, I'm sure, that cannot wait.' There was a controlling urgency in his voice. His velvet black eyes were staring at her intensely as he made a sweeping gesture with his hand. 'Look, so many guests who are dying to meet you.'

She had no desire except to run away from this throng of waxen, richly attired dolls, through which she was now being paraded on the arm of a man from whom she recoiled almost with revulsion but the *torero*'s grip was tight. Anyhow, her legs felt heavy, incapable of responding to the simplest of commands.

Before Alexandra could protest any further, a plump, bald man with a bushy moustache beckoned to the bullfighter. Don Felipe made his apologies and followed him. Together they disappeared among the guests and Alexandra hurried off, relieved at the chance to get some air. She would go back inside in a few minutes and find Doña Inés, she decided. Together they would work out how to tackle Don Felipe again.

Leaving the terrace, she went down the steep steps to a cobbled footway lined with flowering shrubs, cacti and aloes. The very feel of the balmy night air invigorated her; already her headache was receding. She knew the Hacienda Herrera quite well by now and walked quickly along the sweet-scented path, distancing herself from the merry chatter and laughter of the crowd until it had died away. Soon she came to a gently sloping plateau on the edge of the garden, set with cypresses, across which was an incredible view of the Sierras soaring above the rooftops of Granada.

Sunset smouldered over the orange groves and olive trees. In the distance, the Sierras loomed with a strange foreboding in the fading light, their summits fiery and menacing. With the fragrance rising from the nearby tobacco plantations, the evening air was as intoxicating as opium.

Alexandra stared at those mute giants, so far away, towering impassive and unshakable, braving the harshness of wild nature with silent courage. Suddenly, the message of the Sierras came to her in this clear twilight: like them, Salvador faced life, distant, impenetrable, inflexible in his resolution, determined in his actions, confronting his fate with stoicism – a fate, like the night winds of winter howling through the mountains, that was unleashing itself against him with unrelenting fury.

She leaned against a cypress tree, her heart filled with an inexpressible melancholy, trying to take in for the last time the incredible beauty of the place. As she did so she felt her soul slowly wither in despair, along with the dying sun. Soon she would be leaving and every experience she had tasted there – all her hopes, her sorrows, these beautiful landscapes and the strange sensations that Spain had awakened in her – would be nothing but the cold, grey ashes of memory.

The sun plunged behind the mountains. Although the temperature had dropped a little, it was still hot. Soon it would be night. Alexandra took one last yearning glance at the sad purple summits, and then slowly turned, preparing to go back to the party.

And that was when she saw him. She froze. Salvador was standing on the edge of the garden above her, just a few feet away from the trees, his tall, dark figure looking out to the horizon. Their gaze met and locked. Alexandra's eyes widened, and he stared back at her, his lips parted in shock. Her mouth went dry. There was an instant of silence, a brief lull in time when the world seemed to have stopped.

Then, with a stifled exclamation, they were in each other's arms again, their long-denied yearning driving them, the old chemistry exploding back into flames. Salvador's mouth closed over hers as he greedily pulled her against him. His kiss was demanding, savage, almost primitive in its ardour, and went on until the last shards of reason fled from her and only the consuming flames of passion remained. He was devouring her with the hunger of a man seeking salvation, and Alexandra savoured his taste, making her dizzy.

And now she held nothing back, expressing everything that stormed through her, grasping the back of his neck, her nails digging into him, wanting to take this man she loved and hold him forever. She whispered and moaned all the words she craved to say, telling him of her love, her need, her passion as she relished the caresses he was showering over her.

Caught up in the avalanche of their love, they were overcome by fierce yearning, carried away in the maelstrom of desire that had been kept pent-up for so many weeks and was now unleashed by the shock of their sudden meeting. This was not a gentle coming together but the desperate relief of two people who had been starved of each other for too long and had finally reached their haven.

It was nearly nightfall now: a clear summer night, so clear the twinkling stars could almost be counted in the velvety sky above. The moon hung like an iridescent pink chalice, watching over the lovers.

The world around them disappeared into oblivion. They touched each other more and more avidly, lips merging in famished exploration, senses communciating without words. Salvador pressed her against him, not gently but in a way that spoke of his violent desire for her. Alexandra arched her body, her arms tightening around his neck, yielding to him and to her own overwhelming need. The tremors pulsing through her limbs obliterated any of his remaining reserve. As her breasts strained against the fabric of her bodice, he shifted his burning mouth to her throat, burying his face in the warmth of her neck, inhaling the sweet scent of her hair as his hands sought the trembling flesh of her silky shoulders. Intensifying his grip, he bent her back so she felt his hardness pushing against that part of her that was begging for release. His lips moved down, finding her cleavage, his tongue exploring hungrily the confines of her dress, lingering sensually between the satiny curves of her taut breasts, breathing in their heady fragrance; and she clung to him, her love for him racing free and unfettered, generous in the surrender of her heart, her body and her soul.

Finally Salvador found his voice, whispering: '*Querida, mi querida*,' against her lips. He lifted his head, his eyes glazed. 'I cannot live with this any longer. *Me vuelves loco*, you drive me crazy!' Alexandra moaned softly while he slowly scattered kisses all over her face.

'Salvador … I can't believe you're here.'

She felt his lips gliding over her skin and returning to her mouth with deep but gentle eroticism. He murmured against her lips: '*Mi querida*, I thought you'd gone for good. We're together now, it doesn't matter, nothing else matters. Oh *mi amor*, how I've missed you, how I've yearned for you.'

His voice moved across her senses; Alexandra couldn't believe he was saying such things to her or how much it was enflaming her body.

Salvador slid the palms of his hands around her back and down her spine until they cupped her silk-covered bottom, bringing her forcefully up against his hips. Alexandra whimpered at the intimate contact, burning to belong to him as his mouth found hers again and she felt him rock against her.

For them time had stopped. They remained thus, in dizzy ecstasy; breath suspended, drunk in a flood of exquisite anticipation, as though remembering a once-forgotten but rediscovered dream. In the uncertain light of a fading dusk, with the moon stealing between the cypress trees, their young bodies were clasped together tenderly, reflecting the total communion of two souls who, after a long quest, had finally found each other.

Lifting his head and looking into Alexandra's eyes, Salvador opened his mouth to say something, but she would never hear the words.

A malevolent voice cut in harshly. 'So this is your pure and innocent Alexandra! She promises herself to one man, while abandoning herself to another.' Tearing themselves apart, they turned towards the intruder. Doña Isabel was standing a few yards away, lantern in hand, smiling triumphantly.

'What do you mean?' Salvador's jaw clenched, as he turned first to the *Marquesa*, then to Alexandra.

Doña Isabel lifted her lantern. It shone on Alexandra's face, which had gone quite white. Alexandra opened her mouth to say something, but quick as lightning, her rival beat her to it.

Eyes flashing daggers of hatred, she made no attempt to spare Salvador. 'Your beloved has been living in Granada for more than a month. And I bet you didn't know that this magnificent reception is being thrown to celebrate her and Felipe's engagement,' she rasped venomously.

Alexandra felt as if she had just been propelled into a nightmare. A shiver of dread rippled up her spine. *Of course, that was why Salvador was there. Don Felipe would like nothing more than to have his rival witness the announcement. Oh, dear God, and Salvador didn't know ...* Dazzled by the brightness of the lantern's light, she lifted an arm to hide her face. She shook her head repeatedly and took a step towards Salvador.

'But it's not true!' she cried, her heart in her mouth, choking as she did her best to hold back the tears. 'It's all a misunderstanding, a terrible misunderstanding! Salvador,' she begged, catching his arm as he was turning away, '*please*, let me explain.' But he wasn't hearing her words.

'I'm sure my brother will thank me for sparing him the most appalling public humiliation,' said Doña Isabel icily, and with that parting shot, she gave Alexandra one final withering glance of victory and swept off back to the house.

She had expected his fury to surface with a stream of angry words and reproaches. Instead Salvador simply looked at Alexandra, his features now rigid. His hard, metallic stare bore down on her, barely hiding the world of hurt behind it. He raised an arm. For a moment, she wondered if he was going to strike her or was simply warding her off, but he lowered it wearily. For a fleeting second, silence vibrated in the air while he contemplated her with the stunned expression of a man stabbed in the back.

'Salvador, please, I can explain everything,' Alexandra whispered, her eyes pleading, staring into that soul-stealing gaze and trembling with fear that she had lost him. Then, as if he could no longer bear the sight of her, he pushed her aside, turned away contemptuously, and disappeared into the night.

'Salvador, please listen to me … please don't do this!' she called out, starting after him. 'Don't be cruel!' Her broken cry cut through the darkness, startling the bats and other night creatures.

Alexandra was dazed; she would have preferred him to reproach her, shout at her … strike her even. At least she would have been given a chance to defend herself. She would have put up with anything, anything except the look of infinite pain he gave her before marching off into the shadows.

Alexandra buried her face in her hands as she sunk slowly to the ground. For some time she lay on the grass, weeping quietly, humiliated, conscious of how powerless she was. When she finally looked up, she realized she was not alone.

She was there, the gypsy from Triana, gazing at Alexandra in silence, her big, piercing eyes both searching and evasive. 'If you'd heeded my call, if you had come to see me, I could have spared you all this trouble,' croaked the old fortune-teller.

In that moment, reason fell away and Alexandra was left with a cold, desperate fear that went straight to her soul. Her rationality crumbled. Finally the power of the gypsies and the enigmatic hand of *maktoub* had caught up with her and claimed her.

'How could you do such a wicked thing, you evil witch!' she cried out, as she struggled to her feet, sobbing.

'Paquita can tell the future,' the *gitana* went on, ignoring the young woman's accusation, 'and the great book says that your destiny is with your lover.' She spoke as if she had pronounced some immutable law.

'What do you mean? Explain yourself!' Alexandra demanded, straightening up and wiping away her tears, suddenly regaining her self-control.

'Beautiful lady from beyond the seas, you have won,' declared the gypsy woman. 'You should rejoice and thank Paquita, instead of crying.'

'What on earth have I won?' Surely she had lost everything now? If this was destiny speaking, she had no idea how to listen to its message or how to find a way through the darkness that now engulfed her. This was a new world to her – perhaps the fortune-teller was her only hope of understanding it.

'Enough of your riddles and tell me what's going on. Please, I beg you!'

The Romany gave her a hooded look. 'First, give me a token of your good faith,' she replied, slyly catching hold of the young woman's arm.

'I don't have any money with me,' Alexandra said, trying to free herself from the clasp of those rough claws.

'Paquita never asks for money,' declared the other disdainfully. Then, pointing a crooked finger to the jewel hanging like a pearly tear from Alexandra's neck, her tone became more threatening. 'Give me that, it should be enough.'

The moon swam timidly between the branches, its milky, pale rays briefly lighting the angular features of the witch. She rolled her gleaming black eyes, which in the semi-darkness resembled two big marbles of shiny glass, and extended a gnarled finger towards Alexandra, who instinctively backed away. Standing among the cypresses, the two figures resembled an illustration from a dark fairytale.

'Here,' breathed Alexandra, as she hastily unclasped the pendant and handed it to the gypsy. Paquita avidly clutched the coveted object, hid it among her rags and then turned away.

'Your fine Count loves you,' she chanted, moving off into the night. She carried on in her characteristic babble, her hoarse, cavernous voice rising in the darkness, as if from the grave. 'By the force of the great and pure love that binds you, the spell that bewitched him and held him prisoner of another's charms is henceforth broken. Go, beautiful lady, go in peace, for it is written in heaven you will share his destiny.' Then, abruptly, she halted and looked round. 'But beware the storm and the horned beast, they will seek you out.'

'For goodness sake, what are you talking about?' Alexandra called out after her. 'What storm? What beast? Whose destiny will I share? Didn't you see what happened? I'll probably never see him again … What shall I do? It's all a terrible misunderstanding!' She stumbled towards the old hag. 'I've given you what you wanted. Now, please, can't you help me? Can't you *do* something?' she implored, tears of despair running down her cheeks. But Paquita was no longer listening; she had disappeared into the shadows beyond the trees, chanting an incantation of strange words.

In the blackness of night, the scarcely visible yet menacing outline of the Sierras towered above the sleeping valley, bare slopes and fissured rocks now sinister, death-like in their silence. It was late but the bullfighter's party was still in full swing. Alexandra slipped through the lighted garden, trying to find a way out without being seen. She could hear the band and the distant clamour of Don Felipe's merry guests but, to her, the night seemed empty and lonely. She hoped that Doña Inés wasn't too alarmed by her absence and wondered whether the *duenna* had gone home or if she had stayed on, waiting for her charge to come back.

Trying to keep out of sight, Alexandra made a detour to avoid passing the crowded terrace, desperate to get back to Doña Inés' hacienda as quickly as possible. She followed a gravel path that led to the rear of the house. From there she'd be able to go through the orchard to reach the road.

It was pitch-dark. The temperature had fallen. An owl hooted somewhere, startling her. A dog barked, and then there was nothing save the night. She was nearly at the north side of the hacienda now. A light breeze started up, enveloping her in its chilly embrace, and she shivered. Her footsteps crunched on the stones, sounding loud to her ears, almost blocking out the ghostly rustling of the leaves in the orchard beyond. The hollow croaking of a toad made her jump again.

Suddenly, a pair of powerful arms grasped her from behind and spun her around, pressing her hard against an unyielding torso. A shaft of moonlight cut across the man's face, illuminating the knife-like planes. It was the *torero*.

'Felipe,' Alexandra gasped, breathing heavily as his hands dug into her upper arms.

'Yes, *Felipe*,' he sneered, his handsome features contorted into a savage mask. 'Were you hoping it was your Count come to claim you? I've heard about your sordid little display earlier. So, you'd rather be with that whoring so-called *hidalgo* than with me.'

Alexandra looked around but the grounds on this side of the house were deserted. She pushed against his chest.

'Please, Felipe, you're hurting me!'

But he ignored her, his breath hot on her face. 'The first time I set eyes on you, I wanted you, *querida*. You could have been the wife of one of the richest, most powerful, most respected men in Spain. I would have given you everything you desired.'

Blood rushed to Alexandra's temples and she stared at him, wide-eyed. 'I would never have had everything I desired, Felipe. I'm sorry.'

'Did you think you could get away with humiliating me?' He delivered the words through clenched teeth. '*Yo, el más grande matador después de Manolete*, the greatest matador after Manolete?'

'No, Felipe, you don't understand. I tried—'

'Tried *what*? Tried to make a fool of me? Did you think I wouldn't hunt you down?' His eyes shone with a mad and savage glitter. 'You've been playing your little games with me but now who has won, *querida*, eh?' The *torero* tightened his grip on Alexandra, oblivious to her distress, and began dragging her towards the terrace at the back of the house. Beyond it, she could see the dimly lit dining room and, inside, the dull gleam of armour and the dark shapes of the instruments on the back wall.

Alexandra's eyes darted to the *torero* in panic. 'What are you doing? Let me go!' She struggled against him but he was too strong.

'I thought you were so innocent, so sweet. You've disappointed me, *querida*. So much …'

Terror rammed into Alexandra. She summoned all her strength and sent her foot kicking against his shin as hard as she could. The *torero* grunted, then lashed out, hitting her hard across the face. She cried out but his hand moved like lightning to cover her mouth; and then his head was at her neck, kissing her hard and biting her skin like a brand, pushing himself against her struggling body. Alexandra heard the tear of fabric as her sleeve was ripped down. She took a breath, preparing to scream, no longer caring that it would bring people running from the terrace.

'Felipe!' Doña Inés stood frozen to the spot a few feet away, her face aghast. 'Let her go, at once.'

The *torero*'s head shot up, like a predator disturbed mid-kill. He staggered back, his chest heaving. '*Madrina* …'

'How could you do this, Felipe? *Es usted un hombre o un animal?* Are you a man or an animal?' Doña Inés whispered. She held her arms out to Alexandra, who ran into them and clung to her, trembling. The *duenna* hugged her close, all the while gazing, horrified, at her godson. 'Why?'

'*Madrina*, I …' The *torero* looked at Alexandra and she could see a dark anguish in his features. It was as if he had quite suddenly fallen out of a trance into the light of shocked realization. 'Please forgive me.' And with no other words, his shoulders hunched, Don Felipe fled into the shadows.

For a second Doña Inés stared after him before searching the young woman's face intently. '*Me querida hija*, my dear child, I'm so sorry. Are you all right?'

'Yes, I'm fine,' Alexandra whispered. 'Please, let's just go.'

The two women made their way back to the Hacienda Hernandez in silence, the *duenna* gripping Alexandra's hand tightly all the way. Back at the house, Doña Inés sat her down at the marble table on the veranda. Picking up a shawl lying on the back of the bench, she wrapped it gently round her quivering shoulders and then sat hugging her.

Unable to hold back her distress any longer, Alexandra dissolved into tears, sobbing wretchedly. She felt sick to the core. How could she ever have let herself be entertained by such a monster? What a fool she had been, how utterly naïve and frivolous.

But Doña Inés stroked her head tenderly. 'I'm so sorry, *querida*. I never thought Felipe was capable of such ...' Her voice caught in her throat. 'I wasn't going to tell you ... it didn't seem right. But now ... you see, there are things I know about my godson. Dishonourable things ...'

Alexandra gulped down the sobs. 'I sometimes sensed a darker streak in him that alarmed me,' she admitted between shuddering breaths.

Doña Inés paused, her usually serene countenance clouded with sadness and more than a little shame. The low buzz of cicadas pulsated in the air, which had become colder now. For a short moment, silence drenched their world. Alexandra waited for the *duenna* to speak but just then a sound struck out in the hushed darkness, a woeful liquid babble of noise. At first she wondered what it was, then realized a pair of nightingales were singing in the tree, pouring their hearts out. She looked up ... The two birds were singing against each other, running up and down a scale in the inky stillness as if their throats would burst. At that moment, it seemed the most melancholy sound she had ever heard.

When Doña Inés finally spoke, her voice was shaky. 'The fears you kept to yourself were well founded. After what has happened tonight, I can see that you now know what, I'm afraid, I've always been aware of ... deep down.' She picked her words carefully, pausing often.

'Don Felipe is blessed with looks, courage and charm but, as the Moorish proverb says, *Beauty is never perfect*. Alas, in his case the flaw is at the very heart of his character. It drove his mother to her grave.' Doña Inés choked on those words as her eyes filled with tears. She let go of Alexandra to take a handkerchief from her pocket and dab at them.

'Forgive me,' she said, clearing her voice. 'Unfortunately, my godson's courage in the arena has not arisen from the desperate need some poor boys have to lift themselves out of poverty: he is already rich. In reality, it's an outlet, you might say, for something ... insalubrious ... in his character.'

She stared into the night. 'Even as a child, though he was often affectionate and craved attention, he was difficult, prone to violent outbursts. I thought he'd grow out of it, but I was wrong. And now that he's an adult, I fear it's taken on a more sadistic bent.' She broke off to wipe her eyes. 'I can hardly say it ... He experiences actual pleasure in watching and causing suffering.' This time it was Alexandra's turn to put her arm around the *duenna*, hushing her as she did so.

'No, I need to say this, Alexandra. I should have said it before.' Doña Inés cleared her throat. 'I realize these episodes were usually brought on by an affront to his pride. He won't accept being thwarted or opposed in any way. I witnessed one of his fits of rage and cruelty one day when he'd lost a bullfight. He mounted his favourite horse and pushed it beyond the limits of its strength ... I saw it die ...' She twisted her handkerchief in her hands. 'He's always assailed by remorse afterwards, of course, but by then it's usually too late ... the harm's been done.'

Alexandra realized now that her grandmother's fears and Salvador's warnings were justified after all. *Why had she been so naïve?* Her mind went back to the dining room and that collection of torture instruments.

'Do his fits of rage stop at animals or does he take it out on people? I mean, before now ...' she asked, gazing down at her hands.

Doña Inés hesitated, as if deliberating what to say. 'There was a girl ... Benita Perez. Her body was discovered not far from Felipe's father's *bodegas*. She'd been raped ... badly mutilated. Several people said they'd seen Felipe in the company of a young woman that afternoon – and there were whispers – but it never went any further, even though the rumours persisted ...'

'Didn't the police question him? Didn't any witnesses come forward?' Alexandra persisted quietly.

Doña Inés' mouth formed into a grim line. 'He was questioned, yes. But Isabel and one of their servants gave him an alibi. Look, Alexandra, I'm not saying it *was* him ... maybe they really were with him when it happened. I just think it's fair you should know everything.

'After that, gossip concerning his private life began to circulate too. It was said that he frequented loose women and places notorious for their debauchery, and that he indulged in peculiar ... practices.' Doña Inés closed her eyes momentarily. 'At the time, a couple of these women were questioned but naturally, their testimony was deemed unreliable because of the immoral way they earned their living. Their testimony weighed little, quite frankly, against that of those so-called honest people who declared under oath that they knew Felipe well and, contrary to rumours, he was a noble-hearted person of irreproachable morality. No firm proof of his guilt was put forward. He was never even arrested. The case was closed and Felipe lay low for a few months until the dust had settled.'

Alexandra gazed directly at Doña Inés. 'And what do *you* think? Could Felipe have …?'

The *duenna* hesitated again. 'This is so hard … you see, I love my godson very much. He's been good to me, so very generous. I don't know if that blinkered me, but in all sincerity, at the time, I doubted he had anything to do with that shocking affair. It seemed he was merely the victim of his brutish reputation … now I'm not so sure.' Once more, her voice trembled. 'He behaved abominably tonight, for which I'm truly sorry. I've been so blind and foolish. I should have guessed something might happen as I knew how much you meant to him. I so hoped you'd be the one to redeem him … Instead, look what he did to you, my poor child.' She gave Alexandra's hand a squeeze and once more wiped away her tears.

'Did you know Salvador was here?' Alexandra felt the tears sting again. 'That's why Felipe came after me. Doña Isabel must have told him she'd discovered us together in the garden.'

Every feature of Doña Inés' face spelled disapproval. 'Isabel has always been *una persona muy desagradable*, a very unpleasant person,' she confessed. 'I've never had any time for her and I'm sure she couldn't wait to deliver that bombshell to Felipe. Yes, I caught a glimpse of Salvador, and had no doubt that his presence here this evening would cause trouble. I tried to find you to warn you. You weren't at dinner, and then I saw Isabel whispering with Felipe. His furious reaction made me suspect something had happened, which is why I came looking for you. I'm guessing you didn't tell Salvador about Felipe's proposal and that Isabel did. Am I right?'

Alexandra nodded mutely, unable to stop the anguish tearing through her.

'You've been the victim of one of Spain's most cruel values ... as if what you've been through hasn't been enough ...' Doña Inés continued. 'Called *la honra*, it condemns a woman who's lost her reputation, even if this is through no fault of her own. In our society, you see, a woman gets her honour from the judgement of others. But perhaps in your case,' she whispered, as though talking to herself, 'all is not lost.' She stood up and took Alexandra's hand. 'Come, my child, you look dreadful! You'd better lie down, even if you cannot sleep. I'll stay with you tonight, I don't want you being on your own.'

It took Alexandra a long time to stop crying. Despite her protests, the *duenna* remained by her side throughout the night. Only as the sky began to lighten and they heard the faraway choir of cockerels hailing dawn, did she feel better.

She was exhausted, devoid of all emotion, all hope. She knew she must go – it was the only way to escape the wreckage of her dreams and her love. Spain had awoken something primitive in her: the fiery soil and burning sun of this land had fed her need to understand herself with an almost visceral intensity. Alexandra had desired passion and she had craved the mystery of love. Now both coursed through her veins, like the blood of her Spanish ancestors, and these feelings now overwhelmed her mind and body, strong as poison.

Escaping the predictability of life in England had been her only thought when she had first arrived in Andalucía. Now, strangely enough, she felt a certain relief, a kind of serenity, at the idea of returning home.

Chapter 15

'Alexandra, darling, how lovely to see you! I didn't know you were back,' exclaimed Gloria Stanley as she detached herself from the little group surrounding her, a glass of Pimm's in hand. She made her way through the hall of her large Belgravia townhouse to the newcomer, in a great rustle of pink shantung and feathers. 'Back just in time for the Season. How clever of you, darling.' She smiled and lightly brushed Alexandra's cheek with her crimson lips.

Lady Stanley was the sort of woman whose ambivalent and complicated character Alexandra had always found intriguing. She had been thirty years old for years but remained young in mind and body – the envy of girls half her age. She oozed charm, had been married a few times and wagging tongues said she'd led a somewhat risqué love life. Nonetheless, or perhaps because of this, she was invited everywhere and her own parties had never gone out of fashion.

'I told you, Ashley, she'd be back for the beginning of our hectic summer social round,' Gloria chuckled, flashing Alexandra's partner one of the seductive smiles for which she was famous. The young man raked a hand through his mop of blond hair and grinned at her shyly.

She ushered the young pair out of the hallway and into the main drawing room. It was grand and typically English in style, the pastel walls adorned with works of well known artists from all over the world, oak floors covered with beautiful carpets from the Orient. Uncluttered, it was light and airy but Alexandra always marvelled at how it still remained cosy in winter when the log fires at each end of the room were lit. That evening, the French doors were open, although only a few guests had ventured out on to the wide terrace, beyond which stretched a meticulously kept lawn; although it was summer, the weather in London was still a little chilly.

When Alexandra made her appearance, there was a brief lull in the conversation while all eyes turned towards her. She was popular and much admired for her talent, with many fans among her friends. The moment of surprise over, cries of recognition broke out from all sides as a crowd gathered around the newcomer.

Ashley Harrington went over to a sideboard where waiters were dispensing cordials and spirits. When he returned, carrying a glass of Pimm's in one hand and a plate of cucumber sandwiches in the other, Alexandra was laughing, trying to respond to her friends' warm welcome. She was wearing a dress of pale-green chiffon that set off the chestnut lights in her abundant hair and gave depth to the colour of her eyes. As he handed her the glass, she smiled fondly at him.

'It's so good to be back,' she was saying. 'Hello, David! Emma, darling, I hear you're now the proud mother of an adorable little girl, congratulations! James, how nice to see you again. When did you get back from India? Charlotte, my dear, you look lovely. That new hairstyle really suits you …'

Alexandra looked radiant and relaxed. Surrounded by her friends, whom she loved and she was confident loved her in return, for the first time she had a sense of fulfilment and peace that had eluded her in Spain.

She glanced at her companion and smiled at him again through the surrounding chatter. Poor Ashley. Ever since she had returned from Spain, Alexandra knew she'd been different with him: distant, in a world of her own. Although the embarrassment of his proposal seemed to be more or less comfortably behind them, somehow things were not the same: *she* was not the same. She wished she could give him what he wanted from her, rather than just sisterly affection. Seeing her back in this familiar setting among all their friends, talking about old times, his relief was palpable. Yet there was an edge to his look this evening that she recognized as discomfort, almost nervousness.

Someone touched Alexandra's arm to get her attention and she turned back to her friends, caught up in the laughter and questions about her travels.

Over the next hour, many guests left but a few remained inside with their lively hostess, who had just ordered more sandwiches and fresh lemonade. Nat King Cole was singing about the mystic smile of Mona Lisa, and Alexandra found herself alone with Ashley on the almost deserted terrace. He looked as if he were about to say something but a couple of hovering guests seemed to interrupt his composure.

'You know, you'll never be totally happy anywhere except here, Lex, in England with your friends, surrounded by people who understand you and appreciate you,' he finally remarked, placing a hand on her slender wrist.

'Isn't it strange?' she replied, turning affectionate eyes on her friend. 'You often say something that echoes my own thoughts. Only a few moments ago I was thinking just that, and yet ...'

'And yet?' he prompted, his pale blue eyes anxiously searching her face for an answer.

'Something seems to be missing, something I can't explain ...' she trailed off wistfully, her eyes clouding, banishing the sunny smile that had shone from her face all evening.

'You haven't taken me into your confidence as you normally do.' He took her slender hand in his and brought it up to his chest, curling the fingers of his other hand round hers affectionately. 'Your letters were so functional, really. Not at all like you. I don't know what happened in Spain,' he went on with a shake of his head, gazing at her intently, 'but it seems to me you didn't find what you were looking for.'

Alexandra smiled ruefully. 'I wish it were so simple ...' She sighed, turning away and brushing a wayward strand of chestnut hair from her face.

'Forgive me if I appear indiscreet,' Ashley valiantly soldiered on, trying to get to the point as gently as possible. 'I don't wish to pry, but may I ask you a question?' Alexandra gently pulled her hand away from his and walked a few steps on the terrace, distancing herself just a little from him.

'Go ahead,' she said quietly. 'But I may not answer it.'

'There's been a sadness in your eyes ever since you got back. I don't think anyone else has noticed it. I wasn't sure but ... that is to say ... is there any connection between your unexpected return and your cousin, Count Salvador Cervantes de Rueda, with whom you were staying?' His question startled her and she turned sharply to face him, making the answer quite plain.

A pink hue crept into Alexandra's cheeks. 'What makes you ask about Salvador?' she muttered, a little unsteadily.

'Listen, old girl, you forget how well I know you.' He smiled ruefully. 'Your letters mentioned him, but far less than anyone else. I suppose I began to read between the lines.'

Ashley paused before removing a sheet of newsprint from his pocket. It appeared to be an article from one of the international society magazines. He slowly unfolded it and held it out to Alexandra, never once taking his eyes off her face.

She drew in her breath sharply as her gaze fell on the headline: 'An old love is reborn,' followed underneath, in smaller print, by: 'Are bells finally going to ring for Count Salvador Cervantes de Rueda and Marchioness Isabel de Aguila?' Alexandra felt faint as the blood drained from her face but just managed to pull herself together.

'Perhaps it's all for the best,' she eventually managed to say in a flat voice. Then, turning her face towards her old friend, she gave him a wan smile. 'I'd like to go home now, if you don't mind.'

Ashley made a valiant attempt to lift her spirits. 'Listen, old girl, I have tickets for *Carousel.* It's opening tonight at Drury Lane. The show's starting late, after the drinks party given for the patrons and actors,' he ventured. 'I remember how much you enjoyed *Oklahoma!* Why don't we go?'

'Thank you, Ashley, you're so sweet and thoughtful,' she told him, trying to spare his feelings, 'but I'm really not up to the theatre this evening.'

'We could make up a party with David and Louise. I know they've got seats too.'

'No, thank you all the same. I really would prefer to go home.'

'I'm sorry if I've spoiled your evening,' he said apologetically. 'I guess I chose to tell you now so that you wouldn't find out later from someone else. I'd hate to see you hurt, you know.'

He looked so wretched she placed a hand on his arm. 'Don't worry about me. I'm quite tough, you know. I'll get over it.' Somehow she managed a smile.

'I'm sure you will, Lex.' He tucked her arm through his. 'Let's say goodnight to our hostess and I'll take you home.'

'No,' she corrected him gently. '*I'll* take myself home.'

Ashley frowned. 'Why on earth would you want to do that? You have no car.'

'It's still light and the walk will do me good.'

'This is quite ridiculous, Alexandra,' he protested. 'You can't walk alone in London at eight o'clock in the evening.'

She tried to contain the exasperation in her voice. 'Come on, Ashley, please don't insist.' She nudged him and gave a little smile. 'You know how it is when I make up my mind,' she continued, raising her eyebrows. 'I'll be quite all right.' After grumbling his disapproval, Ashley helped her on with her coat, gave her a kiss on the cheek and reluctantly let her go.

Once in the street, Alexandra took a deep breath. For a moment she hesitated on the pavement, wondering whether to simply return home by the quickest way or take the more lengthy route back along the Embankment.

She shrugged. It was still light and it was such a beautiful evening. She had always found walking therapeutic, even more so since her stay in Spain, and now she welcomed the time to put some order to the maze of her muddled thoughts.

As it was summer, twilight had not yet fallen. The scent of neighbouring gardens filled the air. It would be a half-hour walk from Belgravia to Cheyne Walk.

Alexandra moved briskly, her head high, taking in the familiar scenes and smells of London in summertime. She had missed the idiosyncrasies of the city: the market traders in Covent Garden shouting out cheerfully; the bustling curiosity of antique hunters in Portobello Road; picking up a bag of roasted chestnuts on Chelsea Embankment in winter; an ice-cream in Hyde Park on warm days; milkmen rattling down the backstreets early in the morning; the silhouette of the city's skyline spiking into an orange-ripple sunset as you walk over Albert Bridge … How different to the things she had seen every day in Andalucía.

Funnily enough, it felt good to be back: a strange bittersweet feeling of warmth and security, tinged with nostalgia, combined with a sense of loss she had never experienced before. Loss of the girl she had been before her Spanish adventure, of a light-heartedness she feared she would never regain.

A chill had found its way into the air, making Alexandra shiver and quicken her step. The rhythmic tapping of her heels on the almost deserted pavement sounded in her ear like the tick-tock of a clock, reminding her of the grandfather clock in the hall at El Pavón. She sighed. A wave of fatigue began to wash over her and, just as closing a door, she instinctively closed her mind to the flood of painful thoughts threatening to break through, and let her legs carry her on down the street.

All at once she seemed scarcely to exist. In a sort of haze, separated from herself, she had the curious feeling that it was rather odd to be her. She was like a person dozing in front of a show – absentmindedly watching the events on stage, not quite grasping what they meant or how they linked together, but merely conscious of the movement of the actors before her eyes.

There was even less traffic now. A bicycle zigzagged its way towards Chelsea Bridge. She passed a muffin man with his bell and then a big, black tomcat strolled from Pimlico Road towards her with a dignified air, signifying he was lord and master of this territory. Looking at Alexandra with half-closed eyes, he mewed, followed her for a few yards and then, for no apparent reason, sniffed the air and went back the way he had come, disappearing round the corner of Royal Hospital Road. Alexandra thought of Marujita's cat. For a moment she tried to imagine the gypsy girl's reaction to the new state of affairs with the man she had so proudly claimed as hers.

She went along Ranelagh Gardens, where young Mozart had once given an organ and harpsichord recital. From Mozart her mind wandered again. She found herself transported back to that far-off afternoon at El Pavón when Salvador had found her playing the piano in the drawing room.

Salvador and Doña Isabel! In the end it was not the sensual young gypsy who had won the Count's heart and defeated Alexandra, but the beautiful *Marquesa*. Life was curious …

How clever Don Felipe's sister had been and how easily Alexandra had let herself be manipulated. The masterstroke had been delivered in Granada, of course. What fools she and Salvador were to have allowed themselves to be so completely duped by the *Marquesa*'s orchestration of the evening. Doña Isabel had known all along that her brother planned to announce his and Alexandra's engagement to a crowd that included an oblivious Salvador. She'd probably been the one who'd persuaded Salvador to come, encouraging him to swallow his pride and put on a courteous front. And, of course, Felipe would have relished the prospect of his rival being present when the news was made public. She knew what she was doing in setting it up, that it would be inevitable that a terrible collision of events would occur.

As it happened, Isabel was able to twist the knife into Salvador herself. Should Alexandra have gone after him? Would it have done any good? Would Salvador have listened to her? Worse still, faced with the Herrera family's false accusations, would he have believed her? No, she would only have succeeded in humiliating herself further.

A fine rain began to fall. Normally, she would have quickened her pace; she had an aversion to getting wet. However, that evening it was mild, and the gentle shower of fine droplets was not unpleasant.

The shrill resonance of a barrel organ grinding out its raucous tune made Alexandra jump then smile. She had never seen one before and would not have encountered it in Seville – but here in London? Alexandra realized there were many things around her she was noticing since she had returned home, and so much she couldn't help comparing to life in Andalucía.

Still lost in thought, she turned right along Chelsea Embankment. Here, the wholesome smell of sea tar mingled with that of wet earth and rain. The traffic was denser: cars, taxis, buses, a few brightly coloured flower wagons and vans making evening deliveries hurtled along the tarmac by the river. Suddenly, and for no reason she could think of, they started to hoot. She smiled to herself. This was a more sophisticated Triana, but nonetheless cacophonic.

The part of Cheyne Walk where Alexandra lived was a row of grand old mansions, some dating back to the time of Charles II. They were set a little back from the Embankment, separated from it by a narrow strip of gardens planted out with shrubs. When Alexandra reached Newton Place, her aunt's townhouse, she stopped in front of it for a moment before mounting the steps to the front door. It was one of the newer Victorian houses with their fine red brickwork, and she took some time to enjoy the curving gables, jutting oriels, terracotta ornaments and white painted balconies. It felt all at once familiar, solid, comforting.

Godfrey, the butler, let her in. Alexandra smiled at the whiskery old man who had known her since she was a child.

'Would you like dinner to be brought up to you, Miss Alexandra, or would you prefer to eat in the dining room this evening?' he enquired, taking her coat and draping it over his arm.

'Thank you, Godfrey, but if Jenny could bring up a cup of broth and some bread later on, that will be fine.' She added that she did not wish to be otherwise disturbed, thanked the old butler and went upstairs. Mrs Jeffrey, the housekeeper, was never there after four o'clock, Aunt Geraldine was away in Kent for the summer and Alexandra welcomed the idea of spending what remained of the evening alone.

After the success of Alexandra's first two novels, Aunt Geraldine had given over the whole of the third floor of Newton Place to her. 'It's only proper,' she had said, 'that you enjoy space and privacy for your hobby.' Aunt Geraldine never referred to Alexandra's writing as anything other than her 'hobby'. Alexandra was convinced that, despite the success of her novels, her aunt was patiently waiting for her niece to grow out of this phase, and one day see sense enough to succumb to the more conventional pastime that was marital life.

Without bothering to turn on the upstairs landing light, she exchanged her shoes for a pair of silk slippers, which were always kept beside the wall at the top of the stairs, a habit ingrained in her from childhood by her aunt.

It was a small suite of rooms, furnished tastefully. They had a meticulous simplicity that reflected Alexandra's personality; at least that part of her nurtured by her life in England. She walked down the narrow corridor panelled in old limed oak to her bedroom, where she put on a silk house gown before collapsing into her favourite armchair in the adjoining boudoir. As she leant her head against the upholstered back, she closed her eyes.

Struggling to bury her feelings in the deep abyss of her soul, Alexandra was sent reeling again as a rebellious wave of anguish washed up on the shores of her consciousness. She fought back, telling herself not to be so ridiculous; she didn't love Salvador and was not unhappy at losing him. Losing him? She had never had him in the first place, that was really the truth of it. A romantic, sentimental fool, all along she had fallen for the Spaniard's charisma, his exotic looks; his charm. That shadow of sadness, which sometimes flashed in his eyes, made him seem vulnerable, appealing to what Aunt Geraldine called her 'Florence Nightingale' side. Perhaps that was why she'd been compelled to rush to his rescue.

What did it matter whether he married Doña Isabel or not? After all, the *Marquesa* was far better suited to him than Alexandra: they came from the same world. She should have known from the beginning that she and Salvador had too much against them – even though their chemistry was compatible, they were wrong for each other in so many ways. Yet, somewhere in the depths of her being, where the small flame of truth and instinct still burned, that small voice was shouting out its dissent and would not be silenced.

Discouraged and weary, she went over to the wide bay window. A pale glow from the bulbous Victorian lamps strung along the Embankment heralded the swift fall of dusk. The misty skyline had deepened to a mournful purple and the dark shapes of working boats and barges on the softly glimmering water of the Thames appeared to take on a more abandoned aspect than usual. How imperial London looked at night along the river, with the bright majestic lines of Albert Bridge overshadowing the colossal four chimneys of Battersea's coal-fired power station beyond. It was almost dark now and the city she loved, normally so familiar and comforting to her, looked at this moment as if it stretched on forever into the night, making Alexandra feel small and alone. *He will never take me in his arms again*, she thought wistfully as tears burnt her eyes. *Stop this immediately*, she admonished herself angrily. *What good is there in thinking about all that? You're just hurting yourself.*

Since her return, Alexandra had woken every morning with a lump in her throat and a heavy heart. She'd tried to drive Salvador from her mind by throwing herself into work, but the Count's handsome face kept returning to haunt her. Like the ebb and flow of the river's tide beyond her window, the events which had taken place during her stay at El Pavón and during the subsequent weeks in Granada surged ceaselessly back and forth in her mind; and although she sometimes thought she had rid herself of her nightmares, they inevitably came thronging back, always more vivid, more poignant, to torture her.

How could she erase the wild ecstasy that had swept over her in Granada when he had overwhelmed her with his love, taking possession of her entire being to the point of making every fibre of her body and every part of her mind vibrate with passion? But, more than anything, how could she forget the look in his eyes, that long, pained look, heavy with disbelief, hurt and contempt burning into her before he left her alone in the garden?

All the same, what was the use of longing now for what might have been? Had he not said that night in Ronda at the Parador de la Luna: '*Once the cork is drawn you have to drink the wine*'? Indeed, the cork had been drawn and, for her, the wine had turned into tears and bitter regret.

Once in London, she had written a long letter to her grandmother but Alexandra's missive hadn't been answered. She couldn't be certain the old lady had received it, as the Spanish postal system wasn't exactly trustworthy. But even if the *Duquesa* had simply chosen to ignore the letter, Alexandra couldn't find it in her heart to blame her for not responding; she had grown deeply fond of Doña María Dolores and felt profoundly guilty that she, like so many other members of the family, had disappointed her grandmother. She could only hope that, with time, the dowager would find it in her heart to forgive her.

She had heard nothing from Esmeralda. Perhaps a letter would find its way to her once her cousin was settled. Alexandra was curious to know what kind of new life the eloper had found with her lover. She dearly hoped she had discovered the happiness for which she had so longed. Her father had not written and, while hurt by his silence, she was no longer all that surprised.

Only Ramón had sent her a letter, in which he briefly announced his imminent departure for the United States. She was pleased he'd found a way to escape the family and follow his own dreams at last. A scribbled afterthought right at the bottom of his card, so characteristic of her scatty cousin, had somewhat disconcerted her, given the recent newspaper revelation. It read: '*Since you left, the sad eyes of our perpetually troubled cousin are sadder and his mood is gloomier by the day.*'

More than once, Alexandra had been on the point of writing to Salvador. At one point, she had even plucked up the courage to finish an entire letter and seal it in an envelope; but when the time had come to post it, she had changed her mind and the letter, like so many other drafts, went to join the pile of scrunched-up scraps in the bottom of the wastepaper basket. And now it was too late.

A knock at the door jolted Alexandra from her thoughts: it was the maid, Jenny, with her supper. 'Thank you, Jenny. Just leave it there,' she instructed her with a faint smile. 'You can go now, I won't need you any more tonight.'

Alexandra left the window and once more sought the refuge of her armchair. She didn't touch her food. Tonight at Gloria's party she had begun to feel relaxed for the first time since returning home and somehow hopeful for the future. Now that feeling was crushed by a dark shadow that overwhelmed her. Burying her head in her arms, she broke down and wept bitterly. Utterly heartbroken, she cried for a long time, with what seemed only brief respites of exhaustion, before despair for the lost love she had never grasped began to beat against her heart again and the tears flowed once more.

Suddenly everything seemed pointless. A wave of bitterness swept over her; she was crushed by a sense of total helplessness. She pushed the electric switch and a crystal chandelier flooded the room with a bright light, dazzling her eyes. Turning it off again, she lit the two candles on her writing desk; their aureoles of subdued golden light were easier on the eye. She had always preferred candlelight to the strong electric glare; it appealed to the romantic in her. The advantages of modern life were undeniable; still, part of Alexandra would have been happy to live in the nineteenth century, with its horse-drawn carriages, oil lamps, bustles and corsets; where ideals of love and beauty were cherished alongside Gothic adventures of drama and mystery.

She glanced at her image in the big mirror hanging majestically above the mantelpiece. Her eyes looked hollow, rimmed with dark circles, and her mouth was a sad little crease. Collapsing back in her chair, she curled up and closed her eyes, trying to calm her mind. She dozed in and out of sleep, her thoughts struggling to find a way out of the quicksand of contradiction and absurdity that gripped her, threatening to suck her down.

Alexandra jolted awake and rubbed her eyes, unsure how long she'd been sitting there. Her head was thumping and she was worn out. She looked up, her mind still numb. The hands on the luminous face of the clock on the mantelpiece pointed to nearly four o'clock. She must have fallen asleep, although she felt in no way refreshed. How long would this torment last? Hours? Days? Years? *I must snap out of this!* she firmly told herself. *After all, Salvador never promised me anything, and if I was naïve enough to indulge in false hopes, I have only myself to blame for being disappointed.*

The next day she would join Aunt Geraldine down in Kent, where her aunt spent most of her time since Uncle Howard's death, a year and a half ago. Alexandra loved the countryside; the air would do her good. What was more, since her return from Spain she had not yet had the opportunity of talking to her aunt and she had no doubt that her common sense would help her take a step back and view things in a fresh light. For all Aunt Geraldine's often strong opinions on how her niece should live her life, Alexandra knew deep down she was fiercely protective and loyal.

Alexandra felt relieved now that she had made up her mind. She went to her bedroom and wrapped herself in the beautiful shawl Salvador had bought her in Seville. '*So you will think of me when you wear it,*' he had told her. If only he knew how much time she spent thinking about him.

She went back to the window; London was deep in slumber. One more night was drawing to an end and nearly four hours of a new day had already passed. Once more her thoughts turned to the Count. Ramón was probably reading something into nothing. No doubt Salvador was sleeping peacefully in his bed, quite oblivious to the distress he was causing her.

The Thames flowed sluggishly in the nocturnal darkness under the lighted bridges. Trees along the river began to tremble as a gentle wind rose out of the east. Alexandra shivered, instinctively gathering the Spanish shawl more tightly about her shoulders.

Soon the sky would flood with a clear pale light as dawn stole slowly and stealthily over the city. The black shadows that had enshrouded the sleeping capital were gradually melting away, one by one.

In the street, the lamps were losing their brilliance; simultaneously, in the now greyish sky above, the stars were slowly quenched. And then the misty veil of shadows slowly lifted and the outlines of the scene framed in Alexandra's window grew gradually firmer, until she saw it clearly and in its entirety. A new day had been born and with it another page of life had been turned.

*   *   *

With dawn, Alexandra had become much calmer and had eventually drifted off to sleep. It was late when she finally awoke. The soft morning light brushed her face and stole quietly to her closed eyes. She gently rubbed her eyelids, still tender and heavy with sleep. The hands of the clock on her bedside table pointed to twenty past nine. Her gaze wandered round the objects that furnished her bedroom. How she loved this room, with its white cotton curtains spotted with blue, and the matching wallpaper. It had remained unchanged since her childhood and she found its familiarity comforting.

The recent events in her life suddenly rushed back to her. 'Salvador,' she sighed. All of a sudden she realized that although she mourned her lost love, she didn't regret her stay at El Pavón.

She had come out of the experience emotionally shattered but so enriched. If nothing else, she viewed life from a different perspective and would now be able to write about it in a new way, with fresh eyes.

She had fallen in love with Salvador from that very first evening at the masked ball ... no, when she came to think about it, from the minute she had laid eyes on him at the harbour in Puerto de Santa María. Had it been love at first sight? She had always wondered what that might feel like, and now she knew what it was to have your world suddenly ignited and turned upside down at the same time. Now she knew what it was to feel alive; to feel every emotion vibrate and rage with an intensity she had never experienced before. Even the de Fallas, and the guilt, shame and anger they inspired in her, had played a part in her growing up, these past few months. It was their bizarre and oppressive ways that had provoked her headstrong rebelliousness to collide with her naïvety, with disastrous results; and yet the thought of the family she had lost and found, and lost again in the blink of an eye, tinged her heart with further sadness.

Alexandra slid out of bed, went to the window and parted the curtains. She was hoping to find a bright clear sky, so she could start her new life serenely on a beautiful summer morning. Instead, it was overcast and grey, and a drizzle of fine rain greeted her. Disappointed, she let the thin marquisette curtain fall back into place. One thing about Spain: it was always sunny, almost too sunny sometimes. Still, it always uplifted the soul.

After ringing for breakfast, Alexandra quickly washed and put on her travelling suit. Leaving for the country without delay seemed the most sensible thing to do. If she remained in London, she would stay at home vegetating, spending one unproductive day after another moping about and thinking of Salvador.

There was a knock at the door and Jenny came in with breakfast. Alexandra thanked the maid and asked her to pack a suitcase so that she could be ready to leave for Grantley Hall after lunch. Jenny nodded obediently; no comments, no questions asked. Alexandra smiled inwardly – how different she was from the fiery, insolent Juanita.

Not feeling hungry after all, Alexandra contented herself with a cup of tea and half a slice of toast with marmalade. She rang Aunt Geraldine from the hall to inform her of her impending arrival.

'Is there anything wrong, Alexandra?' Her aunt's voice sounded concerned.

'No, nothing's wrong, Aunt Geraldine,' Alexandra reassured her. 'I just felt like spending a few days in the country, that's all.'

'Of course, I'd be delighted to see you and hear all your news, my dear, but I wasn't expecting you so soon. You've only been back in London a few days.'

'Well, I've caught up with most people already. Besides, we haven't had a chance to talk yet, as you say. If I take the four o'clock train, I'll reach Grantley Hall by early evening.'

*   *   *

That afternoon, Ashley offered to accompany her by taxi to Charing Cross, where she was to catch the train for Dover. They spoke little on the way. Alexandra saw he was pensive. *He still hasn't really let go of me*, she thought, filled with regret. Over the years, she had taken advantage of the young man's love and good nature but she had too great a respect to keep leading him on. These last months had exposed her to such a range of new emotions and taught her to have a much deeper regard for other people's feelings. Hopefully, they would soon be able to settle into a comfortable brother-sister relationship.

When they reached the station, he accompanied her through the crowds to the train and made sure she was comfortably settled in the compartment before taking his leave of her.

When the moment of parting came, he held her hand tightly in his.

'Alexandra,' he said, looking her solemnly in the eye, 'I feel you're under the influence of some sort of anticlimax in returning to London, which I'm sure won't last. I'm also sure you'll settle back into your old life, with all your friends around you.' He searched her face with a slight smile. 'Yesterday evening, at Gloria's, you were your old self again, the Alexandra I know so well. You seemed relaxed and happy, surrounded by your friends ... back among the people with whom you belong.'

Alexandra parted her lips to say something, but he motioned with his hand for her to stop. 'Please let me finish,' he continued. 'Yesterday, I thought it would be a good idea to show you that gossip article I'd found, though I suspected you'd be upset. I'm not ashamed to admit it, I was hoping the marriage of this count would make you reconsider things ... between us, I mean. But I realize I only succeeded in hurting you and for that I'm deeply sorry. Believe me, I didn't mean to.' He paused for a moment to regain his breath.

'Whatever happens, dear Lex, I'll always be your friend, and if by any chance you do change your mind, don't hesitate ... I mean ... I'll be here.'

She nodded silently, grateful and relieved he would never hold any grudges but also knowing how wrong he was about her now.

'Ashley, dear Ashley ...' She looked into his clear blue eyes, thinking how young he looked right now. 'I know this is hard for you to understand, but that journey to meet my family in Spain has marked my life profoundly in more than one way ... in fact, to a point of no return.'

He tried to protest but, when he saw the expression on her face, he let go of her hand, which he had been holding until now.

'As you guessed,' she said, 'I've fallen in love with Salvador de Rueda.' Alexandra paused, taken aback by the sound of her own confession. She forced back a wave of pain as it resurfaced in her heart. Swallowing hard, she regained her composure. 'Unfortunately, as you might have gathered from the article you showed me yesterday, Salvador doesn't share this love and that ... it makes me deeply sad.'

Once again Ashley made an attempt to interrupt but she stopped him.

'During my stay in Spain, I learned a lot about myself. I grew up. I discovered a new me, the *real* me ... the person hibernating inside me all these years. This experience, painful though it's been, has drawn out who I really am and now I can no longer ignore my true feelings. You see, I must follow them, whether they involve Salvador or not.' She paused and squeezed his arm. 'You mean the world to me, you know that. You're my dearest friend and I always want you to remain so.'

Silently, they shared a smile, as old friends do who understand one another in a way no one else can.

'Ashley,' she called out softly, as he made his way to the door of the compartment. He turned and she went to him, placing a quick peck on his boyish cheek. 'Thank you,' she said with tears in her eyes.

The guard's whistle blew. Ashley gave a sad smile and stepped down from the train.

*   *   *

As the train hurtled through the countryside, carrying her to Dover, Alexandra endeavoured to put her thoughts in order before she reached Grantley Hall, where she would be speaking to Aunt Geraldine about all that had happened. She had not been surprised that Ashley still harboured a small hope that she would change her mind about him but she recognized that she had been right to clear the air between them one last time, to try to make him understand how much she had changed. She knew Aunt Geraldine had been disappointed when she had turned his proposal down; she had always hoped the young couple would marry. Aunt Geraldine was not the only one to cherish such ambitions with regard to Ashley Harrington either. Ever since Alexandra could remember, mothers had been casting covetous eyes on the young man, the ideal suitor from every point of view.

In a way, Alexandra wished she'd never gone to Spain: life would have been much simpler. Yet, she had felt that restless pull even before leaving England. She had been compelled by the threatening tempest of her emotions, warning her that she needed to escape from everything she had known, and that was what had made her turn down Ashley's proposal in the first place.

After all, she had not even met Salvador then, yet still she knew there was something more she could expect from a man. The reasons for her decision were already rooted deep in herself; indeed, in her very character, her true needs and aspirations; she was quite sure of that. It was unfortunate that Salvador, because he had wanted it so, had ended up being no more than the detonator triggering this inner storm, but she supposed she was grateful to him for that, although it brought with it such heartache.

Ashley was predictable as a clock. He promised her a peaceful life of stability, devoid of excitement. Of course, he represented security but Alexandra had learned over the past few months that life had more to offer than safe daily routine, however cosy that might seem. Whereas reason dictated prudence, the blood that ran through her veins urged her to live; to savour life to the full, with no fear of the pain and suffering that went with that. Life was a store of limitless treasures for those who lived it fully. Now that she had made that discovery, Alexandra was resolved to meet the world's challenges undaunted.

It was past six o'clock when she reached Dover Priory. As she walked to the station exit, Alexandra felt light of step and full of renewed vigour. Outside, she was met by Martin, the old driver, in the 1930s Rolls-Royce that Uncle Howard had bought and restored himself as a labour of love. No doubt Aunt Geraldine was waiting for her with a specially prepared dinner at the house. Suddenly she couldn't wait to be back in the cosy and familiar surroundings of her country home.

Alexandra remembered the last time she had been to Grantley Hall with Aunt Geraldine, a few days before her departure for Spain. How long ago it seemed now. They had talked for a long time, drinking lemon tea and sampling the delicious scones baked by Mrs Hull, their Scottish cook. Alexandra had been so excited and full of expectation; what plans, what dreams she had nurtured then. Now she realized how naïve she had been.

Family and roots, she thought; such big words, full of meaning and promise, she had imagined. How empty and futile they sounded now. Alexandra's eyes misted and a lump formed in her throat. Shaking herself, she fought back the tears and tried to concentrate on the view of the rolling green countryside through the car window. It was time to leave these insoluble problems behind her to enjoy Kent.

They drove in silence. The elegant cream car passed the walls of Dover Castle perched at the top of the white cliffs that towered over the town and the harbour below. They went through field after field of barley and hops, with an orchard or two scattered here and there, but the countryside consisted mainly of wide-open spaces of rich pasture, where satin-skinned cows, replete and satisfied, chewed the cud with vacant eyes in the evening sun.

At last they came to two imposing wrought-iron gates, already open, flanked by great pillars of ancient stone. The car turned into the grounds of Grantley Hall and slowly made its way along the long beech avenue leading to the house. Stretching away on either side was an expanse of green lawn, bordered with ancient trees and rare plants, giving the large house in the distance a remarkably handsome and grand setting.

Grantley Hall was an elegant dwelling, dating in parts from the fifteenth century. At one point it had almost fallen into ruin, but had been extensively renovated over the years. In 1830, a new façade was constructed, consisting of a central porch flanked by two gables bearing the family emblem. The turret, on the east elevation of the Hall, and the gallery behind the house constituted the only vestiges of its medieval origins.

As soon as the house came into view, Alexandra was overcome by a sense of serenity. Coming home to Grantley Hall always filled her with a feeling of peace. It was her refuge, a sanctuary to which she had often retreated in the past, when overcome with fatigue or faced with a difficult problem. Her aunt would usually leave her to her own devices, knowing she loved the solitude of writing or walking alone in the grounds. She would go for endless strolls across the fields, accompanied by her three dogs, Caesar, Hannibal and Scipio, exploring the neighbouring villages and basking in every aspect of rural life. The tranquillity of the countryside suited her, and at night she would fall into a deep sleep, undisturbed by the clamorous sounds she had never quite got used to in the city.

As Alexandra watched Grantley Hall loom closer, she smiled to herself, resolving to remain in this haven until her energies were completely replenished and her worries had evaporated. Once rested, she could resume her West End life with a serene mind and a brighter outlook.

CHAPTER 16

A unt Geraldine was waiting for her niece in the drawing room. Alexandra could see her slight figure framed in the window as the car drew close to the house. Lady Grantley was in her late fifties, a woman who dressed with impeccable taste, having spent some time in Paris, where her husband had been posted for a couple of years. Despite her wealth, she always maintained an innate distaste for extravagant habits so her clothes were invariably discreet.

As the old Rolls-Royce came to a halt beside the front door, Aunt Geraldine's face broke into a bright smile, which made her fine, pleasant features look much younger. *Dear Aunt Geraldine*, Alexandra thought, waving at her through the car window, she was such an interesting contradiction in many ways. When Alexandra was a child, her aunt had been somewhat old maidish. Alexandra always sensed that slightly rigid exterior concealed a naturally spirited person but such vitality was suppressed by two things: the first was the need to watch over her wayward and irresponsible sister – Alexandra's mother – the second had been coping with the enormous responsibility of raising Vanessa's equally spirited child. As a result, Aunt Geraldine followed her own code of – at times – repressive rules, which had exercised Alexandra considerably as a child. Nonetheless, she had always known that behind this façade of cool reserve beat a warm and fun-loving heart.

Happily, Alexandra wasn't the only one to notice her aunt's hidden qualities. In a whirlwind romance that had taken even Aunt Geraldine by surprise, the spinster had met Uncle Howard at a hunt ball and married him within months. Alexandra had been overjoyed at her aunt's transformation. The rather starchy attitudes were softened, quite suddenly, and her forceful and somewhat controlling demeanour gave way to a new zest for life. As a result, she allowed her niece a hitherto unsampled freedom that made Alexandra the envy of her schoolfriends. A few in Geraldine's circle criticized her, blaming this volte-face and her new, more relaxed approach on her niece's avant-garde attitude to life.

Aunt Geraldine had been over thirty when she had married Howard. To some men, the presence of her sister's child might have been a burden. Not so Howard, who loved Alexandra as if she were his own. And for the next twenty-three years, Geraldine's liberated joie de vivre had kept the rich and handsome baronet, previously notorious for his colourful romantic life, happy and contented.

Though Geraldine had become less orthodox over the years, adding a moderately eccentric splash of colour to the otherwise conventionally muted pastels of aristocratic country life, vestiges of her conservatism remained. Whether it was as a result of her marriage to Howard, whom she'd adored, or her fear of Alexandra being left alone, her views on the benefits of marriage had always been strongly communicated to her niece. Knowing this, on the journey down to Kent, Alexandra had prepared herself for any turn the conversation at Grantley Hall might take that evening. Her aunt could still be somewhat overpowering in her views when she wanted to be.

Lady Grantley met her niece on the doorstep with effusive hugs and kisses. In a light-blue cashmere twinset and navy skirt, elegant in their simplicity, her only accessory a single row of pearls, she looked understated, yet aristocratic. The only thing that gave away her age was the scattering of silvery threads in her silken, blonde hair, held back in a low chignon The massive crystal chandelier hanging from the ceiling sparkled with myriad lights, which gave the domed hall, tiled in black-and-white marble, a welcoming and hospitable appearance.

'Every time I come back I realize how much I love this place,' Alexandra declared as they walked through the hall. 'It's so peaceful.'

'Yes, it is rather lovely,' sighed her aunt, 'although it gets a bit lonely now that dear Howard has gone. These mullioned windows may look picturesque from the outside, but they don't let in much light. I must confess these old medieval houses, for all their charm, can be depressingly gloomy some days. There's nothing to beat large Victorian windows, if you ask me.' She straightened her shoulders and smiled.

'But I mustn't complain. This way of life suits me much better now than London, with all those parties in the Season. If I still lived there, I'd feel obliged to attend most of them, and I really can't be doing with it any more.' She put a hand on Alexandra's arm. 'Still, let's not dwell on all this. You must have plenty to tell me, darling.'

She surveyed her niece closely with her clear, lively blue eyes, and cupped her cheek. 'You seem a trifle pale and thin for someone who's just spent months in sunny Spain. Have you been ill?' Alexandra shook her head mutely. 'Well, you were right to come home, the country air has always agreed with you. I've had your room prepared. Rose will run you a bath – there's plenty of hot water. Take your time, darling. We can have a drink and a chat before dinner.'

*   *   *

'Shall I pour you a glass of lemonade?' asked Lady Grantley.

Alexandra closed her eyes and nestled deeper into one of the chintz-covered winged armchairs facing the fireplace. 'Umm, I think I'd prefer a small glass of sherry,' she replied languidly. 'I need to wind down, and it's one of the best ways I know these days. Other than a brisk walk in the countryside, and it's too late for that now.'

They were sitting in the small room that had been Sir Howard's study, and which had now been taken over by Aunt Geraldine and transformed into a cosy living room. A jug of lemonade, a decanter of sherry and a plate of canapés stood on a side table next to the door. The habit of nibbles with a drink before dinner dated from the days when the Grantleys had lived in France. Geraldine's English friends viewed this continental ritual as a minor eccentricity, which they found charming but never tried to emulate.

Lady Grantley poured a little of the amber-coloured liquid into a glass. 'There you are,' she said, handing it to Alexandra. 'I haven't had sherry for a while. I think I'll join you.' For a while, they sat in silence, sipping their drinks and watching the blaze in the hearth.

'Now, my darling, tell me all about that wonderful trip to Spain,' said Lady Grantley, casting a sideways glance at her niece and reaching for a canapé. 'I must say, I can't get over how pale you look. Not a very good recommendation for Andalucía.'

'No, not really,' Alexandra agreed with a hollow laugh. She stared blankly into the contents of her glass before replying. 'I'm afraid I made a fool of myself and fell in love,' she blurted out.

Lady Grantley studied her niece as she sipped her sherry. 'Darling, you're such an incurable romantic. Which is perfectly lovely, but you do feel things so deeply that it's always worried me.' She paused, detecting that underneath her calm exterior, Alexandra was brimming with emotion that needed to spill out. 'Do you want to talk about it?' she added quietly, putting down her glass.

'Oh, Aunt Geraldine, I feel so wretched.' Alexandra shifted restlessly in her armchair. 'No, "wretched" is the wrong word. Anger describes my feelings a lot better. Anger against him, against circumstances ... and not least, against the stupidity that made me behave like a naïve schoolgirl in the throes of her first love.' Alexandra spoke as though her veins were charged with electric currents, her speech hurried and staccato, alive with a passion repressed for too long. The dark rings encircling her eyes made them seem unnaturally wide and bright. She looked feverish, and her flushed cheekbones appeared unusually prominent in the slender oval of her face.

'Darling, don't be so dramatic!' Geraldine picked up her glass again. 'Surely it can't be as bad as you make out?'

At this they were interrupted by a new butler whom Alexandra didn't recognize, who came to announce dinner was served. Well beyond the first flush of youth, he was dressed in black trousers and tailcoat. 'Thank you, Miles,' Lady Grantley said, rising to her feet. She turned to her niece. 'Let's discuss this matter further over dinner,' she suggested.

Alexandra followed her to the door. 'Where's Wilson? Is he ill?'

'Yes, poor man. He's injured his back so Miles is with us for the summer.' Her aunt lowered her voice. 'He's a good man, though I think he's a lot harder on Rose than she's used to.'

They entered the long, panelled dining room, hung with family portraits. Previously, it had been used as the refectory and was one of the few surviving parts of the old building, forming a large part of the gallery at the back of the house. The fifteenth-century dark oak table, which came from an abbey in Berkshire burnt to the ground in Henry VIII's scourge, was beautifully laid with silver and crystal. As a child, on a grey day, when the weather was particularly gloomy, Alexandra's fanciful mind had sometimes conjured up all sorts of monks' stories to fit her imagined history of this formidable-looking piece of furniture

They went on talking as they tucked into the meal Mrs Hull had carefully prepared. Alexandra always loved the old cook's velvety fish soup and the Beef Wellington that followed was one of her specialities and a real treat. Cheese and fruit were offered, but declined, and they ended supper with one of Alexandra's all-time favourites: apple pie and clotted cream, made in the manor's own dairy.

A pot of steaming coffee awaited them when they returned to Aunt Geraldine's snug retreat. By this time, Alexandra had unburdened herself completely to her aunt, ending with her final humiliation at the hands of Doña Isabel on the evening of the *corrida* party, when Salvador had looked at Alexandra with such pain and contempt in his eyes; and then the shock of the newspaper article announcing their engagement.

'That's the whole pitiful story,' Alexandra declared as she curled up in the big armchair. The effects of the wine and the delightful meal, as well as the relief at having discussed her troubles and confided in Aunt Geraldine, made her feel more relaxed now. Suddenly El Pavón, Marujita, Don Felipe and the gypsies seemed rather remote.

'These Latin Romeos are all the same,' declared Lady Grantley, shaking her head disapprovingly. 'After what happened to your mother …' She broke off, looking frustrated. 'They love with the bold passion of young stallions, the stubborn recklessness of bulls, and believe themselves heroes out of some swashbuckling tale from the Middle Ages. For love and honour, they will even duel to the death. Such men are ready to sacrifice their young and beautiful lives for an ideal that's no more than the product of their fanciful and fertile imaginations. Don Quixotes, the lot of them!'

Alexandra could barely suppress her laughter at this portrayal of Salvador and his compatriots. 'Is that what you really think?' she smiled. 'Your description sounds rather harsh.'

'Harsh but true, my dear. That's why I wanted you to be brought up here in England, away from all that melodrama.' Lady Grantley smoothed her hair, as if by tidying it she would restore in herself a feeling of composure.

'I can't imagine *Papá* was ever like that,' Alexandra murmured, almost to herself.

'Darling, believe me, Alonso was every bit the intense young Spaniard and when your mother met him she was swept off her feet. Then he changed. No doubt your grandmother had something to do with it. She always did like her sons to be under her thumb. After Vanessa left …' Geraldine took a sip of coffee, '… Alonso rapidly became a shadow of the man he had once been. I must say I hardly recognized him when he made his visits to London. I think he hoped she would one day come back to him … Who knows?' She waved her hand. 'But the damage was already done and your mother learned a hard lesson. Her heart was broken, which is why she flew into the arms of another man.'

Alexandra stared pensively into the fire for a moment before glancing up at her aunt. 'So what is your advice?'

Geraldine sighed and put down her cup. 'For once, I have none,' she said plainly. 'You must make up your own mind. All I can say is that with the Salvadors of this world, life is wonderfully exciting and full of the unexpected. Today, you may be floating on clouds and then tomorrow, without really knowing why, you may find yourself in the bottom-most pit of hell. If that's what you're looking for, then he's the man for you. If, on the other hand, you prefer a normal life, something steadier and more natural, then you should thank your lucky stars this romantic idyll didn't go any further.'

They were silent for a moment. A trace of wistfulness flickered in the depths of Alexandra's green eyes and a sigh shuddered through her. For all her resolve to accept she had lost Salvador, deep inside her that little voice of instinct rose again and fanned the tiny flames of hope that were refusing to die. 'Do you think he loves me?' she whispered the question bleakly.

'I really can't say, my darling. His behaviour certainly seems odd. Can you ever tell with that sort of man? Anyhow, you said he's engaged to the Marchioness, so the matter is settled, I suppose.' Geraldine paused, giving her niece a sidelong glance. 'If I were you, I'd reconsider Ashley.' She held up her hand. 'I know what you're going to say …' She got up to pour herself another cup of coffee. 'But do hear me out, just this once. Everyone knows he's mad about you. His cousin Edwina was only talking to me about it the other day. Poor boy, he missed you terribly while you were away. You know he'd devote his whole life to loving you, don't you?'

'That's just it – a life that would be one long, dull journey!' Alexandra met her aunt's reproving gaze. 'Sorry, that came out a little harshly. Ashley is a dear, dear friend but nothing more: it could never work.'

Lady Grantley sighed. 'My dear, you must do what you think best. You asked my advice and I've given it to you. I know nothing of Salvador – other than what you've told me – but you must see, if he's already spoken for, what use is there in pursuing a dream?' She shook her head disapprovingly. 'Nothing good ever came out of your mother's association with such people. Vanessa was always the more passionate and foolhardy of the two of us. I tried to caution her too, all those years ago, and now I find myself pointing out the same pitfalls to you.'

Her expression softened and she leant forward a little in her chair. 'Darling, it's just that I don't want you to ruin your life the way your mother did. I realize you feel that I've nagged you far too much about settling down, but I want to know you're happy and secure.'

She smiled and continued. 'I know Ashley well. He belongs to our world and, what is more, he's a fine-looking and dependable young man. He has all the qualities to make him a good husband, the very best, and he'll undoubtedly have a brilliant career at the bar.'

There was a stiff moment of silence when Alexandra appeared to be mulling over her aunt's words before she spoke, evenly. 'Not once did I think of Ashley while I was in Spain. I admit he'll make some woman an excellent husband, but I have no yearning for him, don't you see? My feelings for him are quite different to those I have for Salvador. Between Ashley and me, there are none of the things that seem so important in a couple. It didn't used to bother me because I was ignorant of them, but they're evident to me now. As I said, Ashley is like a brother, no more than a friend. I love Salvador.'

'Aren't you confusing pity for love?' Lady Grantley ventured.

Alexandra was vehement. 'No,' she declared, feeling the colour rise in her cheeks. 'No, of that I'm absolutely certain.' How could she tell Aunt Geraldine that each night she went to bed yearning for Salvador's touch? How could she explain the fire and the passion that took over her whole being whenever she thought of his kisses? How else could she account for the sense of loss she felt on learning of his engagement to Doña Isabel? Her love for him was an ineluctable truth that she could not deny any more and that was her whole predicament. 'You married Uncle Howard for love.' she persisted. 'Can't you understand what I'm feeling?'

'Yes, I loved Howard, more than I can describe …' Geraldine paused, gazing intently at her niece. 'And your mother loved Alonso. But it's not always the existence of love that guarantees happiness, my dear. I was lucky to have had so much on my side. Your mother was not. And it pains me to see the same happening with you.'

'Mother was unlucky,' Alexandra's green eyes sparkled with emotion. 'But I disagree with you. Love, if absolute, should always be the most important thing. I cannot live a lie.'

'In that case, what can I say? You never know. Maybe all is not lost.' Geraldine eyed her niece over the rim of her coffee cup. 'You know, don't you, that I do realize how much this trip has meant to you.'

'You *do*? You always seemed to hate the idea of me going at all.'

'Yes, I did. I thought I had lost you when you left. It looked like everything I ever feared was coming true. I was so relieved when you came back. And then, earlier, when you spoke of this Salvador … well, at first it seemed I was right but from the way you describe your experiences, it now occurs to me how deep your affinity with Spain has become. Your mother never had that.' She gave an elegant shrug of her shoulders. 'Perhaps that gives you a greater chance of finding happiness there.'

At this they exchanged a slow, warm smile of understanding that spoke volumes. Alexandra gazed down at her hands as another thought struck her. 'Supposing the article wasn't just a rumour, the sort of gossip one finds in society journals, and he is actually engaged to Doña Isabel?'

'He will have simply made life that much easier for you,' Lady Grantley said as she raised herself from her chair. 'Come now, it's getting late and, judging by those circles under your eyes, you don't seem to have had much sleep lately.'

'You're right,' Alexandra confessed, yawning. 'But I'll sleep well tonight. The air down here always makes me drowsy.' She gave her aunt an affectionate kiss. 'Thank you, Aunt Geraldine,' she said gratefully. 'I don't know what I would have done without you all these years.'

At this Lady Grantley's eyes misted over. 'Go up to bed now. I'll stay here and read for a while. Sleep seems to escape me these days.'

'Goodnight, then.'

'Goodnight, my dear.'

*   *   *

Nearly nine months had gone by since Alexandra's conversation with her aunt. There had been a few conversations on the subject since then, but to no great effect. With the acceptance of her love for Salvador had come a raging grief at her loss that consumed Alexandra entirely. Aunt Geraldine watched helplessly as her niece retreated into a mournful silence.

Again and again Alexandra had put off her return to London. She had no desire to resume her busy, sophisticated city life, no wish to see her friends, go to concerts or the theatre. All she wanted was the space and solitude to cope with the pain and persistent misery into which she felt herself sinking little by little, day after day, until she believed it would engulf her whole being like quicksand.

She had spent many weeks after her return to Grantley Hall in the darkness of her room. Curled up in bed, she refused to see anybody, her trays of food turned away, untouched. Sick with self-deprecation, she was full of regrets, asking herself over and over how could she have been so reckless as to get embroiled in such a hopeless situation? Her foolish behaviour, as well as her misplaced pride, had played a large part in this mess; now Alexandra's hope of being forgiven was forever dashed and the love she couldn't deny burned within her like an agonizing fever. As hard as she forced it away from her conscious mind, she could not deflect the corroding stabs of raw jealousy that knifed through her whenever she thought of Salvador and Doña Isabel's photograph in the society magazine. Still, what use were regrets? Where Salvador was concerned, her fate was sealed, and she had to figure out what she was going to do with the rest of her life. She must stop torturing herself and get on with living. By now, they were probably married and that was the end of it.

Gradually, she picked herself up. Winter had come and gone at Grantley Hall and, although the whipping wind and the frost covering the grounds reflected the bleakness inside her, Alexandra had begun to push herself towards recovery, taking back control of her life. She remembered the quote from Thomas Hardy's *Tess of the d'Urbervilles*: '*A strong woman who recklessly throws away her strength, she is worse than a weak woman who has never had any strength to throw away.*' She was determined not to throw away her own strength and, in a bid to focus her mind and channel her emotional restoration, she began pencilling notes for a new book, a tragic romance.

There had been a letter during that time, one that had spurred Alexandra's resolve to reclaim her life. Ramón had written from America. After arriving there at the beginning of the year, he had already bought a ranch. Writing with his usual charm and impish humour, interspersed with anecdotes about the country and its people, he seemed happy and liberated in his new life, and it occurred to her that if he had the courage to begin again, so too could she.

Much like someone recuperating from a long and debilitating illness, Alexandra slid into a day-to-day routine of reading, writing, and endless long walks in the countryside or on the beach, slowly allowing her wounds to heal. The time spent at El Pavón and in Granada seemed an age away but the sense of desolation and loneliness that had emanated from that experience was still never too far away.

*   *   *

It had been raining since the morning; a fine, persistent spring rain. By the time Alexandra came down for her daily walk before supper, the drizzle had stopped, leaving the countryside fresh and green. A rainbow appeared in the west as the sun made a shy appearance, moving suddenly out of the clouds. Alexandra breathed in the air, pure and crisp after these vernal showers, and the fresh smell that rose from the wet earth. Nature had taken on a new brilliance, a dewy lustre full of anticipation. Everywhere, the rain had formed droplets, sparkling little jewels that slid down the leaves like specks of quicksilver. Birds twittered joyfully, welcoming this unexpected sunny spell and the promise of new growth.

So why was she not similarly hopeful, light-hearted and confident of the future? It had been spring last year when she arrived in Andalucía, so full of dreams and plans. Now, the sight of everything on the edge of bursting into bloom gave her a strange sense of unease. Feelings she had fought to smother these last few months quietly reignited with this relentless budding of life around her.

At this hour, the place was deserted. Gideon, the head gardener, had gone home, along with the other retainers who worked in the grounds of Grantley Hall. Alexandra took the path that wound down to the part of the garden that bordered the lake; a special spot she had run to over the years whenever she'd wanted to think, or to escape. That evening she needed solitude, and it was only natural that she should seek out this little patch of paradise. Here, somehow, she would shake off the burden of undesirable feelings that, since sunrise, had come back to assail her.

In the small hours she had dreamed of Salvador; a clear, vivid dream that left her shaking, panting, her body still throbbing to the frenzied rhythm of his passion, lips burning with his fierce and punishing kiss. All day long she had been restless, finding it impossible to settle to anything. She could feel the tension building as the volcano she had thought dormant once again started to grumble away inside her.

The landscaping of the hills and dips in this part of the vast garden had been designed to captivate the imagination with its subtle intrigue, creating changes in elevation and making natural divisions. Interesting little outdoor spaces and arbours had emerged from this cultivation, filled with flowers, especially rose bushes. Nearest the house stretched the kitchen garden, with its colourful splashes of red vine tomatoes, yellow and orange nasturtiums, and bright-green dangling runner beans. A level below this lay a secret garden of smooth grass bordered with great vibrant bushes of rhododendron and white roses. Alexandra had written much of her first novel on the bench here, atop a small hillock, on a carpet of bluebells under the beech trees. From there, she could see straight down the mossy verge, now sprinkled with daffodils, to the lake below.

That evening the lake was dark and smooth, not a ripple disturbing its silent waters. Alexandra sat on a massive stone slab at its edge, close to an arc of trees. Surrounded by a tangle of creeping bunchberry and ivy, she almost resembled a piece of sculpture. Her arrival had scattered a family of ducklings: the mother duck, having spotted the young woman, waddled up the bank and took refuge under a large leaf. She called her young to her, who came and buried their heads in her feathers. Alexandra watched silently as a sole lizard basked in the waning rays of the evening sun. It looked back at her, sniffed the air disdainfully, then strolled off and disappeared into the undergrowth.

She sat there a long time, totally still, as though her excessive anguish, in the way a wound might, demanded complete immobility. In the distance, on the other side of the lake, the tall, thick figures of conifer trees formed a screen barely darker than the ambient soft-hued light of dusk. It was getting late: soon it would be dinner-time and she had best be starting back if she wanted to change.

She roused herself from her misty torpor, taking care not to make any noise lest she disturb the little feathered family that had now abandoned their refuge and were pecking away cheerfully at some grain in the grass, just a few feet away. It was no good, though: as soon as she stood up, they took fright, scattering in all directions, quacking furiously.

She started back, heaviness, like lead, pressing on her soul. More than nine months had gone by and still she could not escape Salvador's memory. She thought that the pain had subsided but judging from the way she felt this evening, she would never be free of him. The past would always be there, plaguing the future.

'Miss Alexandra!'

She looked up to see the ageing butler hurrying as fast as he could across the lawn. Alexandra went to meet him by the bank of rhododendrons.

'Goodness, Miles, you're out of breath. What is it?'

'Miss Alexandra … a letter … I'm terribly sorry. Rose took delivery of it this afternoon and then … well, it appears she "forgot" about it.' He raised an eyebrow. 'I've had words with her, of course.' He handed over a slightly battered-looking cream envelope. 'The postmark is from Spain, Miss.'

Alexandra's eyes widened as she took the letter. 'Thank you … Thank you, Miles.'

As the butler hastened back to the house, she turned the envelope round in her hands, hesitating. Without being familiar with any of her cousins' handwriting, she couldn't be sure if it was from Esmeralda or Salvador, or perhaps Doña Inés, as the *duenna* had been such a good friend to her, but then she noticed the Madrid postmark.

She started back the way she had come, towards the lake. It seemed the best place to open it. Back at the stone seat, she tore open the letter. It was from Esmeralda.

My dear cousin Alexandra,

I hope this letter finds you well. My aunt gave me your address in England. I know she's written to you too but it may be many months before you receive our letters, if at all. You must be wondering what happened to me, though I'm sure you always guessed that I'd take the first opportunity to leave El Pavón.

I have so much to tell you, and it's a shame that you are not still in Spain so that we could meet.

The first thing you should know is that there has been an accident and Salvador is in hospital. He has been in a coma for a month now. To begin with, the doctors didn't know if he would live or die and still can't tell us when he will come out of it …

Alexandra turned the envelope over in her hand to look at the postmark again. Last July! Who knows what had happened since then? She read on, hands trembling, desperate for more news of Salvador.

I cannot tell you any more at the moment, as the details are too complicated for a letter, but we will just have to wait and pray for him. My aunt is, of course, more worried than she will admit. But you know how Tía is. She keeps saying: 'Where there is love, there is pain.' She talks about you often.

Heart racing, Alexandra turned the page and quickly read the rest.

We have had a reconciliation, Tía and me. As soon as I found out about this dreadful accident with Salvador, I went back to El Pavón. Perhaps that helped bring us together. Also, Enrique and I are now married and we're expecting a child next spring.

Apparently, the *Duquesa* had finally given them her blessing. At least that was one piece of happy news. Alexandra went on to read, with some surprise, that Mercedes had been married off last year, shortly after Alexandra's departure, to a young man from one of Andalucía's oldest aristocratic families. It seemed he had admired her from afar for quite some time. Alexandra reflected wryly that her father would probably be relieved, although she couldn't help but smile when she read Esmeralda's somewhat gleeful description of Doña Eugenia. Despite the fact that the marriage suited her stepmother's snobbish standards, the reality that her precious daughter would no longer be the grand lady of El Pavón had definitely put her nose out of joint.

As for Fernando Lopez, it turned out that he had completely disappeared after the gypsy horse fair and had not been seen since. Even though she was no longer at El Pavón, and was now respectably married, Esmeralda wrote that she was nonetheless highly relieved that the steward had gone.

Alexandra finished the letter and sat gazing across the lake. Part of her wanted to leave for Spain right then, that night, no matter what the consequences. There was no mention of Doña Isabel in Esmeralda's letter, or of Salvador's engagement, and Alexandra wasn't sure she could bear the hurt and humiliation she would feel if the *Marquesa* were there, as his wife, nursing him ... But, if the man she loved was fighting for his life, then where else could she possibly be? She closed her eyes tightly as her heart gave a dreadful shudder ... so many months had gone by and who knows what might have happened by now? Salvador could be no better or, worse still, fate may have dictated a more tragic path.

Alexandra looked up at the darkening sky. Rising up from the stone seat, she pushed the envelope into the pocket of her dress. She had been out for such a long time now that Aunt Geraldine would be fretting.

Night was falling – a clear, crisp, near-summer night with no moon, although myriad stars twinkled in the navy-blue sky above. The cool air was bracing. Alexandra pulled her Spanish shawl more tightly around her and quickened her pace.

But then she froze. The figure of a man was silhouetted against the sky, at the top of the hill ahead. He was coming towards her. At first she couldn't make him out but all of a sudden she felt a pang of shock. *It can't be!* She drew in a startled breath and a lump formed in her throat, tears rushing to her eyes. She would recognize that figure instantly, wherever she was, until the end of time. Rooted to the spot, transfixed, like a statue, her heart raced furiously as she watched the tall, elegant, magnificent form of the man she loved draw closer.

'Salvador,' she whispered. *Salvador is here? How is that possible?* A hundred questions rushed through her mind, causing every nerve ending to pulsate with heightened awareness.

It seemed a lifetime before he finally reached her, stopping a few paces away. Gazing at each other, a silence hung between them.

'What are you doing here?' she managed to croak eventually, the sound choking in her throat.

Seconds passed and then Salvador reached out to take her hand but she shied away nervously, her eyes wide with alarm.

His eyes bored into hers. 'I had to see you.'

Alexandra's hand moved, trembling, to her side, where the letter lay in her pocket. 'Esmeralda … I've just received a letter from her … she told me that you've been in hospital … that you nearly died, but not why or how.' She tried her hardest to keep her voice steady. 'Are you all right? How could you have kept that from me?' she whispered. They stared at each other again. Alexandra didn't dare to reach out and touch him; she was too afraid of him standing there, so alive, in front of her.

'I'm completely recovered, as you can see.'

'But what happened? Esmeralda said you were in a coma …'

'Let's not talk about that now, *niña.*'

'But—'

'I've come to bring you home to El Pavón.' His voice shook a little.

She willed her hands to steady themselves. Salvador was alive and well. Astonishment and relief warred with that part of her still bruised and bleeding inside. He refused to explain, and now such a declaration? Alexandra's head was reeling. *What was happening? What was he playing at?*

'If this is a new game, Salvador, I don't have the stomach for it any more …'

But he silenced her by placing two fingers on her lips, and she flinched as though the mere contact of his touch burned her.

He looked disconcerted. '*Niña*,' he whispered, 'I'm not here to cause you pain but to beg your forgiveness.'

Alexandra tensed, still on her guard, trying to regain her composure. Her mind scrabbled numbly for an explanation for his sudden presence here. Surely her grandmother, the *Duquesa*, had sent him on this mission? She would not have approved the union between her nephew and Doña Isabel; she needed an ally at El Pavón, someone she could trust to help her with the administration of the hacienda. Perhaps Salvador's accident had made the dowager renew her matchmaking hopes.

'How did you know I was down here?' she demanded, ignoring his humble words.

'Your aunt told me you were probably by the lake and gave me directions. She was worried, and said you'd been on edge all day.'

'I see.' Alexandra nodded. If ever she was to protect herself against the pain this man represented, she needed to hold all her strength together now. 'To return to the main reason for your visit,' she added abruptly, forcing herself to be blunt as she ignored the frantic pounding of her heart. 'El Pavón isn't my home. Grantley Hall is where I belong and I never want to leave the house where I grew up.'

At this he moved closer to her, his dark blue eyes dwelling on her face anxiously. He drew a deep breath. 'Alexandra, will you let me explain? There's no need for you to be alarmed, really,' he said soothingly.

In the pale glimmerings of dusk, she could make out his familiar features. Salvador looked tired, a bit haggard. He was thinner, hollow-eyed, his cheekbones more prominent, and the furrow across his brow seemed to Alexandra deeper than she remembered. He had aged a little too, making him somehow even more attractive. During these last months, he must have had a terrible ordeal. Suddenly her heart swelled with love and she wanted to reach out to comfort him. Only pride and a new sense of self-preservation kept her from throwing herself into his arms and forgetting all the pain, the anxiety and the hurt that had been her life since that night in Granada. Yet, he had made his decision, which involved a future with Doña Isabel, his first love. Did he now want to pull Alexandra back into his world to flaunt his new union in front of her? No matter how much she yearned to take away his suffering, or how desperately she wanted to know the truth about him and Doña Isabel, something inside her was too afraid to let him speak.

She braced herself, her chin now defiantly tilted, though the effort was almost undermined by her shaking. 'The time for explanations has passed,' she noted, hearing the sharpness in her voice. Inside, she hated herself for letting her pride interfere and make her turn away from him so cruelly after all he'd been through, but the sickening fear that crushed her was too strong to fight.

'I'm glad you're recovered, even though your justifications don't seem to extend to telling me what happened. However, you're a married man now. I wish you and Doña Isabel a very happy life together. I know my grandmother sent you, and you can tell her I'm not leaving,' she continued, moving past him and starting to make her way back to the house. 'This is my decision and—'

Quick as a flash, halting her tirade, Salvador caught hold of her wrist, and whisked her round, forcing her to face him. His glare collided with hers. 'I'm not married, *niña*. I could never marry anybody but you. I love you, *querida*, I love you more than life itself.'

Salvador's eyes burned into Alexandra's. Caught by their fire, she gave a soundless cry as, in the next second, he pulled her against him, crushing her feverishly in his arms. As his head slanted down hungrily towards her mouth, never, for an instant, did she sway or resist. The all-consuming, powerful longing was rekindled, as the thrilling surge of incandescent passion exploded between them. Closing her eyes, she wound her arms tightly about his neck.

'*Mi tierno amor, mi dulce amor,*' he kept whispering as his lips went to her eyelids, her cheeks, her neck, her chest, in softness. His trembling hands were now unfastening the buttons of her top. She didn't resist, instead letting them delve inside her shirt, cupping her breasts, his fingers caressing her, tugging and rolling at the tips until they became hard little peaks. His mouth slid to her throat. The world swirled around Alexandra and she gave a thrilled sigh when his tongue flicked out and eagerly explored the inside of her open blouse. Sensually it probed, lapping the small hollow between her breasts, until they swelled against his hard and ravenous mouth. Wild warmth flooded her whole body, pulsating almost unbearably between her thighs.

And now, sensing the overwhelming power of Alexandra's need, Salvador wrapped his arms around her body and with a firmer grip drew her tightly to him, whispering her name again and again. '*Hemos perdido tanto tiempo mi amor, mi querido amor,* we have wasted so much time, my love, my dear love.' Alexandra's head fell back and his mouth found hers once more; hot, hungry and demanding, he was savagely devouring her lips. '*Sólo tú serás mi esposa y mi hijos tienen*, only you will be my wife and bear my children,' he murmured passionately between feverish kisses.

Now, he drew his hand down the column of her spine. The darker side of his desire seemed to hold sway and then, bending her over his arm, Salvador lowered Alexandra to the ground. The extent of his love and how much he wanted her was evident in the power of his virility pressing urgently against her and she arched, seeking the heat of his arousal. Now her whole body ached and burned for him. Her breasts were in full view, beautifully tightened under the cool air of night, the pink soft aureoles puckering into excited peaks.

His palms ran over her expertly, and she was lost to everything but his kisses and caresses. Moisture flooded her most secret part as his hand slid beneath her skirt. Then, murmuring erotic words of desire, Salvador's fingers snaked up the inside of Alexandra's silken thighs. He found her damp and swollen need and her breath sucked in with delight as he delved deep into her scalding heat. She parted her thighs against his sensuous touch, moaning helplessly as his fingers stroked and encircled the core of her desire. He kept up that rhythmic caress, gradually increasing the pressure, encouraged by her gasping sighs which rose in strength as craving seared through her. Alexandra wanted this moment never to end. Fine tremors raked her body as she cried out her love for him and all the while he stroked her with a single-minded purpose, building up her arousal until she exploded in an agony of pleasure.

Shifting gently away from her, he tilted her chin up, his gaze boring intently into the green pools of her eyes, still dazed by the overwhelming ecstasy her body had never experienced before. Salvador smiled and reached out tenderly to brush a few wisps of hair that had come away from her chignon.

'*Ti amo mi dulce e inocente paloma*, I love you my sweet, innocent dove. I think I have since the first time I glimpsed you in Puerto de Santa María,' he said softly. 'I know there's an awful lot of explaining to do and I promise that I will answer all your questions. Be patient with me, *niña*,' his voice pleaded openly, astonishing her. His hands tightened on her face in a gently demanding spasm, those blue-grey eyes possessive. 'These past few months I've been to hell and back at the thought of losing you. I felt guilty about all you'd been through because of me,' he added earnestly. 'I can't tell you how much I regretted Isabel's interference that night in Granada. I've wasted so much time, but it's all come right now, believe me, *mi amor*, and I've made this trip to clear everything up between us. Come home to El Pavón. I want you to be my wife.' He was talking in a rush, his eyes never leaving hers as they darkened to blue.

He raised her hand and kissed it. '*Decir que usted me perdonará*, please tell me that you'll forgive me, and that you will share your life with a humble man who'll spend his trying to make you happy?'

A few seconds elapsed before his words infiltrated the haze that clouded Alexandra's mind. Though still trembling, she smiled softly, unable to speak as she felt her heart soar with happiness. The expression on her face was more eloquent than words. He had come for her finally, as she had always hoped. This time it was real; her dream had come true. The impulsive little voice inside that had never left her but had been muted for so long was now shouting out loudly with delight. Her eyes welled up with tears of relief and love for this man she knew no other could replace, and she nodded her consent.

Salvador pulled her tightly against him and kissed her hair. She could feel his chest rising and falling rapidly. '*Es usted muy seguro, mi corazón?* Are you very sure, my heart? Spain is a long way from England and there will be times when you'll miss your family and friends.'

Alexandra clung to him. 'You are everything I ever want now,' she insisted.

He took her face between his hands and looked deep into her eyes, the emotion clear in his. 'And you are everything a man could ever dream of, *me querido amor*. But it's late, your aunt must be worried,' he added, frowning.

'Yes, we've been away a long time,' she whispered, gazing up at him in utter adoration. He helped her up; she gently gave him her hand and together they walked back to the house.

*   *   *

The next day drifted along and there was a sort of hazy magic to it. The past hadn't been mentioned or, more to the point, it had been conveniently ignored. Aunt Geraldine had tactfully left the lovers to themselves, making some excuse about visiting friends for a few days, though she had seemed quietly pleased at Salvador's arrival. Alexandra and Salvador were free to make their reacquaintance, savouring the enchantment of new discoveries and making the most of each other after so much wasted time. Caught up in her feelings of overflowing love, Alexandra was nevertheless aware of that subdued curiosity inside her, quietly floating in expectation.

Now the moment had come. Down at the lake, they sat against the trunk of a massive oak beneath its dappled purple shadows. It was an unusually misty, warm day for spring, with no cloud in the azure-blue sky. The air was fresh and rich with the scent of new grass, still sparkling with dew. Everywhere, the trees had donned their brilliant new green coats, and the garden bloomed with a profusion of daffodils, azaleas, bluebells and other colourful flowers carefully selected by Aunt Geraldine, who was a keen gardener. Nature was out in full glory. The sun-drenched garden was alive, vibrating with an abundance of living things of which Salvador and Alexandra were evidently only a minute part. Bees, butterflies, wasps and all sorts of other unknown insects buzzed, hovered and flew above the scented bushes and the carpet of wildflowers spread over the meadow that stretched around them.

'I missed you every minute this past year,' Salvador whispered, his voice hoarse with emotion. 'I wanted you, longed for you, every waking moment of the day and night.' He closed his eyes as though the mere recollection of those not-so-far-off days was still too painful. 'Worse yet, I knew deep down that you felt the same and that my stubbornness, my jealousy, and my irrational conduct had driven you away.'

Alexandra gave him a long, considered look. 'So when did you end up in hospital?' she asked, trying not to sound too blunt.

Salvador went on huskily. 'It happened only a few days after you left. I would have come here almost immediately if not for that. As you know, I was in a coma for several months.'

'Oh, Salvador, if I'd known earlier ...' Alexandra turned to him, her brow furrowed with concern as well as helpless frustration.

'As you've seen, censorship and the postal system in Spain make letters out of the country so unreliable. There's no way you could have known any sooner. It's fine, *querida*, I'm recovered now.' Salvador touched her face with a soothing finger.

'Luckily, Doña Inés heard through the grapevine that I was in hospital and came to visit once I was conscious. She told me all about the misunderstanding that night in Granada and how devastated you'd been afterwards. She said you were innocent of all you'd been accused, that you loved me deeply and that you'd been the victim of Isabel's malicious set-up. At the time,

I was too sick to take any action, though both your grandmother and Esmeralda wrote to you. The doctors couldn't say how long it would take me to recover, they were afraid I'd be crippled for life. What would I have had to offer you then, *mi amor*? Half a man ...' He glanced at her, uneasily. 'I've never wanted your pity, *querida*, only your love, always ...'

Tears welled as Alexandra met those haunting dark-blue eyes. She put her fingers to his lips to stem the flow of words, unable to bear the sad expression on his face. 'Oh, Salvador ...'

He smiled ruefully. 'I had a lot of time to think things through, about the way I'd behaved, and how it must have been for you. I had to wait and pray that I would soon be well enough to come to England and beg your forgiveness, hoping you still loved me enough, and would still have me.'

Alexandra paled. 'What kind of accident could have left you so sick?'

Salvador stiffened. 'It was a bad one,' he said slowly.

His words sent a quiver of alarm through Alexandra. 'Yes, but what happened exactly?'

A long silence followed. His eyes looked glazed, as though remembering was deeply painful. 'Can I tell you about it later?'

Alexandra nodded, though deeply curious. It had never occurred to her that he could have come to any harm or might be in danger. Her heart turned over sickly, her emotions a mixture of dread and shame as reality dawned. She had badly misjudged him: he had been fighting for his life while she was busy nursing her pride and feeling sorry for herself, instead of being at his side, nursing him back to recovery. She could have lost him and never known the truth until it was too late, all because of an unlucky combination of coincidence and crossed wires. Tears began to roll down her cheeks.

'Oh, Salvador, I'm so sorry,' she whispered, her lips trembling. 'I should never have gone off on my own with Don Felipe. I was angry and wanted to hurt you but I was foolish, arrogant and naïve. How can you ever forgive me?'

'Hush, *niña*,' he said, taking a handkerchief from his pocket and wiping her tears. 'Doesn't the fact that I've made this journey tell you anything? There's nothing to forgive, *mi paloma blanca*.' He stroked her face tenderly. 'You're not the only one to blame. I loved you from the first moment I set eyes on you but, because I had many unresolved problems and no immediate answers, I did not dare begin something with you without knowing how it would end.'

He lit a cigarette and drew on it for a while in silence, arms resting on his bent knees. Then, leaning back against the tree trunk, he gazed ahead. 'When the baby died, my ties to Marujita were broken. I grieved for the child but, after a while, I realized there was a glimmer of hope for us, for you and me. For the first time, I could see some light at the end of the dark tunnel.'

He turned his head to look at her. 'Truly, all the while, I was protecting you, though I can see how it probably seemed. I didn't want you to become entangled in my troubles with the *gitanos*. I know I was weak and irresponsible at times. *Usted es una joven muy bella y deseable*, you are a very beautiful and desirable young woman. But afterwards, I always felt ashamed that I'd taken advantage of your vulnerability. My automatic reaction then was to go about setting lines we couldn't cross, even if that meant misleading you about how I truly felt and driving you away.' He smiled awkwardly. 'It is unfortunately my way, *querida* ... putting up barriers when what I feel is too intense for me to deal with.' There was agitation in his voice.

'Then came the *corrida* at Ronda, and the introduction of Don Felipe into the frame.' He took a deep breath before sighing. 'From then on, the most fierce, corroding feeling took over my life. Subsequently, all my attitudes, arguments and reactions were skewed by it. Jealousy, *niña*, is a very destructive fault.'

'But Salvador, you had no cause to be jealous,' Alexandra pleaded in frustration. 'I was just trying to attract your attention. You kept blowing hot and cold, and I couldn't understand what you expected from me. I guess I wanted to make you jealous, the way I was jealous of Marujita and Doña Isabel. Believe me, I know exactly how destructive jealousy is. There appeared to be two women in your life to whom you gave attention, rather than me. I was completely confused all the time – you kept pushing me away. My pride was hurt, and I needed to get even,' she added, trying to keep the defensive tone from her voice. 'I admit that I was attracted to Don Felipe at first. I found him good-looking, smooth and gallant. He made me feel special while you were busy rebuffing me but, I swear to you, nothing ever happened between us.'

Salvador raised his eyebrows. She heard the breath catch in his throat as she spoke. He stiffened, his mouth tightening to a thin line. Steel-grey eyes fastened on her face and ice fleetingly replaced the warmth that had filled them since his arrival. Beneath his gaze she couldn't help but quail; the old jealousy had not yet turned to cinders and was still smouldering inside him.

'That evening in Jerez, I saw you both. You were kissing.' She winced at his tone. The nightmare was starting up again.

'No, no, Salvador, you're wrong,' she cried out, tears stinging her eyes. 'Felipe *forced* his kiss on me. I struggled and was pushing him away when you arrived. I did try to explain but you wouldn't listen. I swear it's the truth. After that incident, I never once let him touch me again.' She was thankful that Doña Inés had agreed to keep the terrifying ordeal she'd suffered at the hands of Felipe to herself – the consequences of Salvador ever finding out were unthinkable. 'You must believe me, I've never wanted another man but you. I could never belong to another man but you.' Her eyes blurred with unshed tears.

Salvador sighed before his mouth curved softly into a smile. 'I know, I know, *niña*, of course I believe you,' he reassured her quietly. 'It's just that I still can't bear to hold that image in my head, even though now I know it wasn't what it seemed. During the long months I spent in that hospital room convalescing, I had plenty of time to mull over every detail. I realized neither of us had behaved normally. There were too many adverse winds clouding reality.'

Reaching out for her hand, he turned it over and gently kissed her palm before placing it against his cheek. 'But you see, *querida*, I'm weak,' his grey eyes skimmed her face wretchedly, 'every now and then the old pain bubbles to the surface. Jealousy, that angry beast, claws mercilessly at my insides and my misery is unbearable.' Salvador broke off. The frost in his eyes had melted. Alexandra gazed into them and saw the appeal for forgiveness, the mixture of strength and vulnerability, the passion, the desire and the genuine love that had replaced it.

How she loved him in this moment. She felt her fears and her heart dissolve into waves of tenderness. Raising herself on to her knees and leaning towards him, she kissed him again and again, slowly, so slowly ... On the eyelids, the cheeks, the throat, her fingertips stroking his shock of black hair adoringly, sensuously exploring every inch of his face, willing her touch to erase the pain, aching to convey to him her own passion, and her deep love.

With a groan, Salvador gripped her shoulders, drawing her into his powerful embrace and they entwined themselves beneath the tree. His mouth sought hers with a searing, devastating possessiveness that was a new thing, and it shook her to the core. 'I will never let you go again,' he breathed, his face buried in her neck. '*Usted es el mio, mio, mio*, you're mine, mine, mine.' He crushed her against him, his hands roaming over her body, sending shockwaves and surges of pleasure through her secret places.

The sound of barking startled them. Caesar, Hannibal and Scipio hurtled down the hill, harbingers of Miles' arrival with a picnic lunch. The dogs launched themselves at the couple, in their excitement, ecstatic yapping, leaping and tail wagging decisively interrupting their moment of intimacy. Salvador and Alexandra sprang to their feet, laughing.

'Saved by the dogs,' said Alexandra as she brushed the grass off her skirt and tried to instill some order to her hair. What would Miles have thought if he'd caught them in that fiery embrace? She smiled mischievously to herself.

The butler soon appeared, moving gingerly down the hill, carrying a tray laden with china and silverware, a jug of lemonade and a bottle of champagne, closely followed by Rose with the picnic baskets. A copious lunch of cold chicken, veal-and-ham pie, pickles, potato salad, cheese, butter and a large loaf of freshly baked bread was spread before them on an Irish linen tablecloth.

'The glory of English picnics!' Alexandra whispered to Salvador, smiling. 'Thank you, that will be all,' she told Miles and Rose once they had finished laying out the contents of the first basket.

'Will you not need us to unpack the other basket, Miss? It contains stewed plums from the garden, frozen after the autumn, a bowl of creamy rice pudding and the first cherries of the season, early this year and freshly picked this morning,' said Miles. 'Mrs Hull has also included a thermos of tea, sugar, milk, a pound cake and a tin of biscuits, for later in the day.'

Alexandra laughed. 'No, thank you, Miles. I think we'll have enough trouble getting through the first one. Will you please thank Cook on our behalf for this wonderful spread? Would you also tell her that as my aunt is out to dinner tonight, we would just like a light supper this evening.'

'Yes, Miss. Shall I uncork the champagne?'

'No, thank you, Miles. That will be all.'

Salvador beamed. 'Surely a feast fit for a king,' he declared when they were sitting alone again and had toasted each other with a glass of champagne. 'And sugar too? What luxury! I thought even the English upper classes were subject to rationing ...'

Alexandra laughed. 'And so we are. But we're lucky enough to have our own dairy farm and chickens, and we grow our own fruit and vegetables. Mrs Hull had always been rather extravagant. Dear Uncle Howard loved his food and Cook always made it her business to indulge him, taking pride in conjuring up new and interesting dishes for him. But since the war she's become resourceful with it, a happy combination. She's been in the Grantley family for forty years and her mother before her was cook to my uncle's parents.'

'It's good when the staff stay for generations in a household,' Salvador noted, handing Alexandra some cutlery. 'They become part of the family, don't they? Agustina is more a friend to my great aunt than an *ama de llaves*, a mere housekeeper. Both her mother and grandmother worked at El Pavón before her. It's the same for Sarita, she's been with us a long time. When she's old and cannot work any more, her daughter María will take her place.'

'And what about Marujita?' The question was out before she knew it. Alexandra had been burning to ask what had happened to the gypsy girl and hadn't known how to go about it without sounding foolish and jealous; this was her chance. Her voice was just a little nervous as she concentrated on her plate, fumbling with her knife and fork.

There was a pause while Salvador took another sip from his glass, savouring the champagne. He hadn't missed the faint tremor in her voice and glanced sideways at her. Without a word, he put down his glass and, reaching out, turned her face slowly towards him, lifting her chin upwards. The grey eyes, which had deepened to cobalt blue, dwelled sombrely on hers.

'*Cariño*, Marujita has gone. I'm afraid things didn't turn out well for her. When she saw I couldn't be manipulated by her or her family, she became reckless.' Salvador looked off into the distance, his arms resting on bent knees.

'One day I caught her in your grandmother's room trying to steal some jewellery from the cupboard. She'd obviously made a copy of the key. Had she been on her own, I might have let her off with a flea in her ear but she was with one of her brothers, who attacked me when I discovered them. Like most gypsies, he carried a sharp *navaja*. The blade caught me between the ribs and punctured my lung. An ambulance was called and my aunt had no alternative but to hand them over to the *policia*. That was the accident … now you know it all.'

He let out a long sigh. Though his dark blue eyes were fixed on hers steadily, his hand trembled slightly as he smoothed it over his head. 'I know I hurt you, my love, and I deeply regret that. Maybe I should have been more brutal but I owed my recovery to her, you see, after my previous accident … and she did bear my child. Ruthlessness is not in my nature and back then it seemed the right way to deal with such a delicate situation.' He gazed out into the distance again.

'She will spend some time in prison now. I'd never have wished that on her. After all, she once gave me back my life. As for her brother, he'll be in there much longer. As we say, *así es la vida*, such is life. I just wish I hadn't been such a fool all along.' Pain was etched on his face as he gazed ahead and Alexandra felt it keenly.

Salvador paused and she stared at him, horrified at the turn his story had taken. Her heart went out to him. 'Are you completely recovered from your injuries?' she asked.

He smiled ruefully. 'Yes, only a small scar is left to remind me of my recklessness.'

Disturbing emotions swamped Alexandra, thinking about the woman who had shared his nights and given him a son. 'Did you love Marujita?' She had to ask the question; she must know, even though the answer would have made no difference.

'No, I never loved her … not in the way I love you. It was more of an earthy attraction, later tinted with gratitude and remorse because of the child. I never promised her anything. And this was all before I met you. There has been nothing between us since you – though that didn't stop her from trying, I admit. Still, I don't blame you for doubting me or being jealous.'

Alexandra swallowed back the lump constricting her throat, more shocked than she wanted to admit to herself after these new revelations. 'I wasn't jealous of Marujita,' she retaliated, her green eyes sparkling with indignation that he should say such a thing, and now embarrassed at her previous confession, 'not really, anyway. I never thought of her as a serious rival, not compared to Doña Isabel, but she always implied there was more between you. I just couldn't understand what was going on. She was insolent and cocky, taunting everybody as though no one and nothing could touch her. Besides, you never really explained the relationship between you, or told me openly that you loved me. You seemed protective towards her, even defying members of your family to keep her by your side. And then you fathered her child. What was I supposed to think?' She was quivering and spoke fast, almost breathless in her agitation.

But Salvador's eyes caressed her face. 'Alexandra, *cariño*,' he said gravely, in a tone that made her anger melt almost instantaneously. 'That's now all in the past. I love you, I want you to be my wife so I can spend the rest of my life with you. There'll be no more separations, no more misunderstandings.' He smiled and dropped a little kiss on the tip of her nose.

'We Spanish men don't like to let our wives out of our sight. We suffer an innate feeling of insecurity which makes us possessive and jealous, and I, *mi amor*, am no exception to the rule, as you've experienced.' They both laughed and he drew her into his arms tenderly.

Alexandra turned her head and pulled away slightly. She looked up at him with anxious wide eyes. 'Salvador, can I ask you another question?' she said sheepishly.

'Of course, *niña*, go ahead. I want to set the record straight so there'll be no more misunderstandings between us.'

'Were you engaged to Doña Isabel?'

His strong hand tilted her face towards him. 'It was a long time ago but I think you already know about that,' he said.

'No, I don't mean that engagement. I saw a cutting in a magazine, it said that you were to be married.'

Salvador laughed, his finger stroking her cheek lovingly. 'Ah, Alexandra, Alexandra, mi *dulce inocente amor*, you mustn't believe all you read in these society journals. I know well the photograph you're referring to. It was taken that night in Granada at Don Felipe's reception, just before you and I met in the garden. After that, I went straight back to El Pavón and I haven't seen her since.'

He looked at her earnestly. 'You must believe me when I tell you that Doña Isabel ceased to mean anything to me a long time ago. I did love her once and it took me months to come to terms with our broken engagement. I didn't intend to fall in love again but then you came along and it seemed I'd been waiting for you all my life. I knew it practically from the time I first laid eyes on you that afternoon in the church, but especially after the masked ball. However, I needed time to sort myself out. I tried to explain this to you but I don't think I did it very well. You were so rebellious, *niña*, so stubborn.' For a few seconds his eyes were intense with emotion as he gazed down at her.

'Oh Salvador, I love you so much,' Alexandra said, throwing herself back into his arms. 'My pride got in the way … I thought that you didn't love me … you never said it openly. To me you seemed to be doing your duty. I'm so sorry, please forgive me.'

'My only hope is that you understand now why I acted in this way.'

'I do, I do,' she whispered. 'Don't ever let me go.'

'I won't.' He held her tightly as she curled up in his lap. They clung passionately to each other in silence.

After a while, staring down gravely into her eyes, Salvador asked: 'Do you think that you'll be able to live in Spain for the rest of your life and be happy? How will you deal with our traditions and rules? Your world is different in so many ways.' Concern shadowed his features. 'You're used to an English way of life, the bright lights of the city, to a much freer code of conduct.'

Alexandra gazed up at him tenderly. 'I'll be happy if you're with me. I love you more than I can say. The last year taught me in life, one needs to compromise. I thought I'd lost your love forever. Day after day I hoped and prayed you would come for me, and my dream has come true. How could I ever jeopardize that again?'

'Then there are no misgivings, no doubts?' Salvador ran a finger down her cheek, his eyes darkening with apprehension. 'You won't pine away as your mother did, thinking of family and friends? You won't long for the snow and the changing of the seasons of England, or see yourself chained to what you've regarded in the past as a "backward and bigoted country"?'

She glanced at him. 'I won't … at least, I don't think so,' she added in earnest. 'Still, you will let me travel to England from time to time, won't you?' she smiled. 'You won't keep me prisoner at El Pavón?'

'Oh yes, *cariño*, we have big tall dungeons at El Pavón, where we like to incarcerate rebellious young ladies.' Salvador chuckled and then kissed her softly with an intoxicating sweetness, barely touching her lips. 'We will travel together,' he promised. 'We'll visit your family and teach our children they have two homes, that they are part of two countries and must adapt to the ways of two societies.'

But Alexandra looked doubtful. 'What about everybody at El Pavón? Do you think they'll forgive my recklessness, my stay in Granada? Even for England, that little jaunt was risqué. I failed my grandmother dismally, I know, and I'm sure *Papá* was disappointed in me too. My stepmother already hated me, though I can't say I care what she thinks about me now. I think she hoped you would marry Mercedes. But let's face it, all things considered, I don't seem to fit their idea of a respectable Spanish wife.'

'Hush, *mi amor*, you worry too much,' he remonstrated gently, stroking her face with the back of his fingers. 'For your grandmother, this union is a dream come true. She was devastated when you left, and is waiting impatiently for me to bring you home ... as my bride.' His mouth twitched as he tried to hide his amusement. 'True, your unruly temperament may sometimes interfere with our austere conventions, but Doña María Dolores can see beyond that,' he reassured her. 'On the contrary, your intelligence, energy, intransigence and, most of all, your loyalty, make you the ideal person to manage the difficult task of running the hacienda by my side,' Salvador explained. 'You're a most amazing woman, *mi amor*, didn't you know that?' He hugged her lovingly against his lean frame. Feeling herself relax, Alexandra smiled up at him.

'As for your father, *niña*, he's a happy man. Did Esmeralda mention that he married off Mercedes last year, shortly after your departure?'

Alexandra raised an eyebrow. 'Yes, that was unexpected.'

'She's already pregnant. So I think that Doña Eugenia will have enough to occupy her, at least for a while. I'm sure she'll leave you in peace. Anyhow, as my wife, you'll be head of the household. That alone will command respect from everyone, even if they don't like it.' Salvador shrugged as though, now sorted, it wasn't worth thinking about.

'I received a letter from Ramón. I'm glad he's happy in America. I do hope he settles down too and finds as much happiness as Esmeralda.'

Salvador shifted her gently off his lap and poured them both another glass of champagne. 'That reminds me,' he said, 'I have quite a few letters for you back at the house that I brought over from the family, as well as one from Doña Inés. They took the opportunity of using me as their postman to make sure you heard from them.' He handed her a glass of champagne.

'And I heard from Ramón just before I left. He hasn't married yet, and knowing Ramón, he'll take his time finding the right girl. As for dear Esmeralda, she's living a quiet and happy life with her husband in Madrid, though she came back to stay at El Pavón a few times when I was ill. Enrique is a good man. They're due to have their child any day now too. The *Duquesa* is delighted.'

He paused and sipped his champagne, surveying her with amused indulgence. 'Have I forgotten anybody, my love?'

'Yes, how is Agustina?' she asked, remembering the old retainer and the kindness she'd shown her.

'Oh, she's as sprightly as ever. Good old Agustina, I don't know what we'd do without her. She's always been a tower of strength. We all lean on her and she never falters. She's very fond of you, you know that? She was truly happy when I told her of my intention to ask you to be my wife.' He sipped his champagne and grinned at her over his glass.

'And are the gypsies still there?'

Salvador laughed. 'Oh yes, they're still there. They'll always be there. As the gypsies say: "*We are all wanderers on this earth and our souls are fused with the countryside.*"'

Alexandra felt herself inwardly shudder. Still, she pushed any dark thoughts determinedly aside and laid her head on Salvador's shoulder. She wasn't going to let anything mar this blissful day.

'Any more questions, *mi paloma blanca*?' he asked cheerfully.

'No,' she said, smiling up at him tenderly. 'No, I think you've answered them all … at least for today.'

'I should think so too,' he said, warmth and laughter dancing in his eyes.

Alexandra snuggled back into the security of his arms and he held her close for a long time. Hours passed as they sat there, quiet and contented, savouring the sweetness of their newfound happiness.

EPILOGUE

Two months later

Alexandra stood on the terrace of her luxurious *parador* room, overlooking Cádiz. Even as night was falling, the city shone with a subdued, translucent radiance and the breath of the sea filled the air. This was the last night of a one-month honeymoon, during which she and Salvador had stayed most of the time on the French Riviera and which ended here in Spain.

There had been a magical wedding at Grantley Hall and Alexandra had been relieved that her aunt had accepted their union with a sort of philosophical enthusiasm. Geraldine had finally got her wish, to see her niece married, and it appeared that Salvador had succeeded in charming her. 'There certainly seems to be something about him,' she conceded. 'I'm truly happy for you, darling,' she had whispered in Alexandra's ear. And although they beamed at each other, the eyes of both women were filled with tears as Alexandra and Salvador climbed into the vintage Rolls-Royce and waved goodbye to the cheering guests amidst a flurry of more confetti and champagne corks.

After the wedding, the happy couple had flown to Nice. From there, they had taken a car and toured the length of the coast from the French-Italian border to St Tropez, currently the Côte d'Azur's most fashionable resort, which Brigitte Bardot, France's number-one star, had helped to put on the map.

'I must take my bride to Cádiz – the Bride of the Sea, as we sometimes call it in Spain,' Salvador told her the night before they left France. They were curled up next to each other on the sofa in their hotel suite, his arm lying across her shoulders, her head resting on the strong expanse of his chest.

'That's a surprise! I've never been to Cádiz,' she said, her green eyes gazing up at him adoringly. 'I thought we were going straight back to El Pavón.'

Salvador smiled at her, kissed the tip of her nose and then chuckled. 'Didn't you know, *querida mio*, that your husband is full of surprises?'

Indeed, Cádiz was the most fabulous surprise and what a bride it turned out to be. Not quite an island, it was a city of dazzling white houses set on a rocky peninsula, jutting out to sea with the sapphire-blue waters wrapped around it. A jewel that towered over the Atlantic, she well deserved her name. Brilliant and sparkling like a diamond in the sunshine, Alexandra found her beauty just as arresting at night, under a velvet sky studded with stars, when the city was reflected in the almost unearthly phosphorescence of the ocean. If she and Salvador were ever lucky enough to conceive a daughter, she reflected, she would like to call her Luz – 'light' in Spanish – their beautiful tribute to this dazzling city.

The air vibrated with silence. Alexandra was happy, though maybe a little apprehensive as to the future at El Pavón: she would have to get used to an entirely new life with different responsibilities and a whole new set of rules, many of which she was still ignorant, despite the few months she had spent with her family at the hacienda. But she was happy for her prayers had been answered – in the end Salvador had come for her. He loved her deeply, she had no more doubts about that. There may be tribulations in the future but nothing they couldn't overcome together.

She didn't move when he walked on to the terrace and she felt the caress of his hands moving over her back. She guessed he was naked and helpless longing flooded her. Closing her eyes, she let herself float on a lazy sea of desire. Through the fine silk of her dress, her oversensitive skin could feel the heat radiated by her husband's body.

His hands slowly unbuttoned and drew the garment from her shoulders. She could feel his satiny mat of chest hair just touching her back. Instinctively, she leaned into him, enjoying the sensation of his flesh against hers and the hardness of his arousal that told her how much he wanted her. She moaned softly and, in answer, his palms swept upwards to cup her swollen breasts. He lifted them and pressed them together, toying with their rosy peaks until they were hard and taut, and every inch of her was quivering and aching to be quenched.

His head came down to kiss the small vein throbbing beneath the almost translucent skin of her throat and deliberately, slowly, his lips travelled to her sensitive nipples. His mouth was warm, his tongue hard as it flipped over one peak, then the other. The ache in her loins was reaching its peak. She was trembling, whimpering with ecstasy, parting and licking her lips, murmuring his name passionately and twisting her neck round to seek his kiss.

He spun her around in his arms and, with one movement of his hands, peeled off the last piece of clothing that covered the private lower part of her body, his palms lingering caressingly on the firm curves of her bottom. They were both naked now. Lifting her up, he carried her to the oversized cushions that were arranged, Moorish fashion, a few paces away on the marble tiled floor of the terrace, under the starry sky.

Salvador's eyes darkened to deep blue as they slid up and down Alexandra's beautiful body. 'Such beauty, such perfection, *querida*,' he whispered, his voice thick with desire.

'And yours,' she murmured, moving her hands forward to touch him, his potent masculinity coaxing a feverish response that coursed through her. She wanted him with an intensity she had no idea she could feel until she had discovered it in his arms. He was beautiful, a body of steel under a bronze skin of velvet and, during the past weeks, she had become addicted to his expert lovemaking.

He drew back. 'Wait … not yet, *querida*, the night is long,' he said huskily as he lowered himself on to the cushions and slid behind her. A deep shudder of anticipation reverberated through her and she sucked in her breath as he slipped his strong, warm palms under her, this time cupping her bottom, lifting it and gently pulling it backwards against his groin. Then slowly he placed her top leg over his hip, drawing it slightly back as he did so.

'Close your eyes and let yourself go' he whispered, his voice hoarse, warm lips brushing her ear. 'I'm going to please you, *querida*, like never before.'

Alexandra's senses were spinning, excitement running through her whole body; she was tingling almost unbearably, longing for his touch. The extent of his need was pressing hard against her. Her senses leapt in response to his ardent words as he breathed them feverishly against her temple, telling her how beautiful she was and how he hungered after each and every part of her; how he loved the scent and the taste of her. His breath was on her cheek, and then his mouth, tongue and teeth went to work on her earlobe, down to her neck, then her shoulder. While one hand had found her breasts, the fingers of the other delved, erotically and possessively, into the secret part of her that she had jealously kept private before Salvador.

He parted her swollen lips, massaging them gently but not going any further.

'I am pleasing you, *querida*, yes? It feels good, so good … but you want more … you're aching for me to touch you there, in the middle … yes, I can feel you trembling, wanting me to stroke you there … you are so swollen you cannot bear the torture any more. But for the moment I'm making you wait … the reward, you'll see, will be so much greater.'

Her pupils dilated, Alexandra was breathing heavily and moaning her need and her pleasure while Salvador continued to whisper to her, his sensual fingers stroking her delicately and, from time to time, applying the firm touch he knew she craved, responding intuitively to each of her moans but always avoiding that place where she wanted him most.

'Salvador, please, please …' she cried out.

'Yes, yes, just a little longer, *querida*.' He sighed softly against her ear. 'Yes, I can see you're ready for me now,' he murmured as he found the core of her and she cried out his name again and again, pleading with him, urging him on, every cell charged up by the high voltage of heat he was feeding her.

'Yes, *querida*, you want it harder and faster,' his caressing voice continued to whisper intently in her ear. 'Yes, spread your legs a little wider like that … you're so warm and moist now, I can feel how much you want me. I'm hard, very hard, and soon I will fill you and you will know and feel inside you my desire.'

His palms slid underneath her and moulded themselves to the feminine curves of her hips, drawing her closer still, hugging her tightly in his strong arms and then, with one deep, intimate thrust, he joined her only too willing body.

She let out a cry at his plunging penetration. His thrusts were agonizingly slow and deep and she gasped with pleasure at every invasive shift of his hard masculinity, causing him to groan loudly and only intensifying his desire to please her. Now they were both on fire, devoured by the flames of their passion that had snapped out of control, raging through them, wild and mindless, into an ecstatic inferno. She forced her spine against him, wanting to be even closer, curving herself against his strong body to feel him even deeper inside her. He relished his exploration of her warm, moist centre, her blind surrender fuelling the blaze erupting fiercely between them.

They were now hovering on the edge of a deep precipice, a sea of liquid heat cascading through them, utterly possessed by a drug they both craved. Their synchronized movements grew faster and wilder. Soon they were waltzing on the crest of a wave of love, revelling in an ocean of tortuous pleasure they never wanted to end. He made her climax again and again, taking her every time to greater heights, while he held on, controlling the rush of his own need, wanting to satiate her before he gave in to his own impulse.

And then there was no more thought. As she cried out her pleasure for the umpteenth time that evening, he tensed, blood drumming in his veins, a fierce tremor seizing him, and he went to meet her, finally allowing himself to feel the rapture he had been holding in check. Their flesh pulsed and shivered wildly as though they were totally possessed in a world of their own. Time and space had changed out of all recognition as surge upon surge of voluptuous pleasure washed through their bodies, and they clung desperately to the final sweet note of their lovemaking until, finally spent, they lay back happy with the feeling of completeness that they had never known existed.

Propped up on his elbow, Salvador stared down at his wife. Alexandra's face rioted with colour as she recognized the desire reflected in those dark blue irises and felt the same desire within. His eyes gleamed with sensual promise and she felt her wanton flesh pulse again in response, yearning for his possession.

'Salvador,' she murmured against his mouth as his head came down to claim her lips, 'Salvador, we've just ... we can't!'

'Of course we can, my passionate love ... my wife, my wild, insatiable lover, *mi amor apasionado ... mi esposa, mi amante salvaje*,' he whispered, his words disintegrating to a stifled chuckle as Alexandra's hungry and impatient mouth silenced him with a kiss.

The starlit skies shone upon their intertwined bodies. The moon beamed as it glided majestically across the horizon, filled with a promise of wonderful tomorrows borne of their love for each other; a love that had surmounted so many obstacles to emerge as solid and steadfast as the Sierras and, like those stoical giants, it would last forever.

About the author:
Q AND A
WITH HANNAH FIELDING

Viva España

What made you decide to set a love story in Andalucía?
While in my early teens, I saw a film called *The Pleasure Seekers*. It was set in Spain and I thought it the most romantic film ever. The two leading actors were Gardner McKay and André Lawrence – typical alpha-male heroes who, with the wonderful setting and atmospheric music, triggered my imagination. I wrote my own short story and from that, years later, stemmed the plot for *Indiscretion*.

What is it about Spanish culture that attracts you?
In one word, everything! I grew up in a house overlooking the ever-changing blues of the Mediterranean. My fondest memories are of azure skies, dazzling sunshine and sweet-fragranced gardens. Spain is all that and more … Spain is a land of flamboyance and drama. Where else would men flirt with death every afternoon for entertainment? The people are emotional, intense; their culture, their music, their traditions personify passion and fire. Even their national dish, paella, is a rainbow of vivid colours, with a taste to match. Life is lived to the full. The Spanish seem to be totally in tune with James Dean's immortal words, 'Live as if you'll die today.'

Have you ever met a real gypsy?
I have always been fascinated by fortune-telling, something that is reflected in all my books where, one way or another, either my heroine or hero encounters a fortune-teller: some good, others downright bad.

And yes, I have met a real gypsy, twice in my life. Once in Paris, in 1974, as I was hurrying through the Place de La Madeleine: she was the one who approached me, very much in the same way as Paquita approaches Alexandra in *Indiscretion*. It was a daunting experience: not only did she try to extract money from me but her sinister prediction about someone I knew came true. The second time was at a fair in London's Berkeley Square in 1977, where, this time, I deliberately entered a well-known gypsy fortune-teller's tent because I was at a crossroads in my life. I was told I would be married within a year and that's exactly what happened!

What is one word you would use to describe *Indiscretion*?
Passion! Everything about Spain breathes passion: the fiery colours of the Spanish countryside with its wonderful vistas, the amazing dawns and sunsets, the rugged but vibrant earth – all so breathtaking they put a spell on you. And then the ardent personality and charm of the Spanish people themselves, their heart-rending music and the intensity with which they live and love.

Passion lies at the heart of this story: the fervent romance that evolves between Salvador and Alexandra, and the trials and tribulations they must endure to win their happy-ever-after – a story that grips your heart as you follow them through a tortuous path wrought with jealousy, lies and revenge.

A Writer's Life

Do you base your characters on real people?

I probably do subconsciously. On my travels and during the periods I have spent living in various countries, I have met so many interesting characters so some of this is bound to come out in my writing. But there is no specific character or situation in my novels that is connected with people or events I've encountered.

Are you like any of your heroines?

All of the main female characters I write about have a little of me in them. I think you write best when you write about what you know. My heroines are, to a certain extent, naïve where emotional experience is concerned, and that is definitely an element that reflects my own naïvety when I was young. I was very protected as a child growing up in Egypt and the big, wide world came as something of a surprise to me when, in my early twenties, I began to travel. Coral, the heroine in *Burning Embers*, possesses this quality most strongly and her story is a rite of passage. In *Indiscretion*, Alexandra also has an emotional freshness that comes through immediately, a quality that Salvador, being a conservative Spanish male, finds highly attractive. Her unworldiness might land her in trouble (as mine did on occasion!) but, nevertheless, her innocence is not without charm. Many of the heroines in my earlier books also have an artistic quality that I share.

What made you decide to set your novels in the second half of the twentieth century, rather than in a completely modern setting?

Because it's a period I know well and I think I write best when I'm able to tap into my own experiences. Also, those fifty or so years have seen such major changes in society and there is much to explore in terms of romance in that era.

My first novel, *Burning Embers*, for example, is set in 1970 because I wanted to write a traditional love story with a naïve heroine but one who is very much a product of the sixties social revolution, from her fashion sense and independent nature through to her career as a successful freelance photographer. Also, I wanted to capture the beauty of Kenya at a time when independence was brand new.

Venetia, the heroine of *The Echoes of Love*, is a professional woman working abroad at the turn of the new millennium; she has some sexual experience before she meets the hero, Paolo, and the modern nature of the times means their passion is free to express itself far more physically than in previous decades.

In *Indiscretion*, it is 1950 and the heroine, Alexandra, represents the new 'liberated and free' woman of the post-war years. Her journey to Spain, though made in order to meet her estranged family, is just as much a journey to discover her real self and escape the straitjacket in which she'd lived all her life up until then, one largely imposed by the social expectations of her time.

Do you have a favourite 'romantic decade'?
I struggle to choose! I think perhaps the 1960s because it was a time of such social and cultural revolution, with sexy new fashions, daring new musical styles and artists, and sublimely romantic and colourful big-screen premieres such as West Side Story. It was a time characterized by new freedoms, and with freedom comes heightened romance.

And your all-time favourite quote?
It is by Toni Morrison: 'If there's a book that you want to read, but it hasn't been written yet, then you must write it.' What better incentive is there to write?

Packing Up My Suitcase

What was your first great travel experience?
I was fifteen and my parents, my sister and I took a cruise on the Nile in Egypt between Luxor and Abu Simbel, Nubia, before that great temple's relocation. In those days, Lake Nasser had not yet been created and Abu Simbel stood on the banks of the Nile, all but intact since the thirteenth century BC. While the boat glided dreamily on the Nile, I was drawn by the utter tranquility and sense of history there, surrounded as I was by an ancient world of ruins and the age-old scenery of fields and villages, where people were living as they had a thousand years ago.

What was your favourite journey?
I think visiting Seville, during the Semana Santa, the Holy Week. It is a truly emotional experience that no one should miss.

And your top five places worldwide?
Aswan, Egypt: a felucca trip on the Nile at sunset is a most romantic and soothing experience.

Le Mont Saint-Michel, Brittany, France: a place of wild beauty, full of ghosts from thousands of years of history.

Cádiz la Joyosa, Spain: a white-and-blue town of pale domes and spires that sing of the sea.

Kenya: for its unequalled safari parks and its fabulous sunsets.

Portofino, Genoa, Italy: because it is quintessentially Italian and embodies all I love about Italian music, fashion, food and the beautiful language.

Inspirations

What inspires you as a writer – romantic or otherwise?

Even more than people, countries have been my main source of inspiration. For me, each place I visit is a new and exciting setting for the plot of a novel. I draw on the richness of its people, its history and all it has to offer in the way of cuisine, language and customs to create fabulous places where my characters can meet and fall in love. I can say that my books are born of my travels.

You divide your time between the south of France and the south of England – what inspiration do you find from such different locations?

My nineteenth-century Georgian house in Kent is a couple of miles away from the sea and the rolling countryside around Dover Castle. I love the house because it's my home: the place I always return to, where my children grew up and where I have spent my happiest years. In summer, the weather is temperate and balmy, just as I like it; and the garden, with its orchard and its giant beech trees, is a picture postcard. The autumn and winter months bring their own charm. In autumn, when the leaves of our trees turn vibrant yellow, orange, amber and even crimson, I sit under one of those trees, breathe in the pure air and gaze in peaceful silence at the amazing view or go for long walks in the countryside, conjuring up my romantic plots. When it snows, once more the landscape changes and the views of my village are breathtaking. At that time, there is no better feeling than snuggling up in an armchair in front of a log fire with a good book.

For the other half of the year I live in France, on the southern coast of Provence in the county of Var. My house there is a *mas* and has a totally different feel to that of my home in England, being modern with stone floors and delicate voile curtains. I love that part of France because of the wonderfully warm weather, the brilliant colours of the vegetation, the Mediterranean sea with its ever-changing blues and golden sandy beaches, the array of local fish and fruit and vegetables you find at the open-air stalls in the marketplace and the happy-go-lucky, friendly people. For me, my home in France spells sunshine, blue skies, a swim in the sea and writing in a room with a wide picture window overlooking the amazing ocean.

Find out more at **www.hannahfielding.net**